THE
WOMAN
INSIDE

THE WOMAN INSIDE

E. G. Scott

First published in Great Britain in 2019 by Trapeze,
an imprint of The Orion Publishing Group Ltd
Carmelite House, 50 Victoria Embankment,
London EC4Y 0DZ

An Hachette UK company

1 3 5 7 9 10 8 6 4 2

A CIP catalogue record for this book is
available from the British Library.

ISBN (Paperback) 9781 4091 8534 5

Printed and bound in Great Britain by Clays Ltd, Elcograf S.p.A.

www.orionbooks.co.uk

To Our Parents

prologue

HE FLASHES A million-dollar smile before getting into his bloodred BMW. It purrs to life and the sound of pebbles crunching under tires reminds me of the first time I was brought here. The circumstances were very different. I was never meant to leave.

That night, I relied on my remaining senses since I couldn't see where he was taking me. The tidal wind through the trees could have as easily been the ocean in the darkness, the pungent notes of pine and salt mixed together. My heart was at a standstill as I felt the car slowing and heard the rocks beneath the treads. I had no idea how my life would change once we stopped.

The friendly honk of the horn brings me back to where I'm standing, in front of the house. I wave goodbye, the three canary-yellow carats on my finger sparkling in the afternoon sun. The car accelerates, kicking up a wave of smooth rocks. He looks back once more and winks, his handsome profile in the driver's side becoming obscured the farther away he moves until he is no more. I expect it isn't the last I'll see of him.

I step over the threshold and smile as I close the world out. So much has happened to get me to this one step in my new life. I live here now.

I absorb the grandness before me. What has been built around the cold slab I lay on, barely alive that night, is a dramatic contrast to my surroundings now. The double-sided stone fireplace ascends breathtakingly to the top of the cathedral ceiling and beyond. The many surrounding windows create a lovely prism effect on the hardwood floors. I stand in the apex of the foyer for a few minutes, breathing it all in. The open second level looks like a choir loft, and the foyer like a pulpit.

I walk through each room, slowly taking in every detail. I flash back to the last time I was here, in the dark, severely in pain, unsure of my survival. Every inch takes on new meaning now. I run my hands over carefully selected wood, stone, and granite and take my shoes off to feel the various wonderful textures under my feet.

I pass by the basement door, knowing it may be a long time until I can traverse those steps without thinking of that first climb in the darkness. But I'm thankful I'm back now, and on my terms. I've resolved to leave the dark pieces below, locked away. Now is the time for new beginnings.

The smell of industrial-grade cleanser hangs in the air, any evidence of what happened here otherwise erased. I don't care. It is a reminder of how hard I've fought. The house around me is silent. Peaceful. I feel a hard-fought new emotion, calm happiness, hovering somewhere between my heart and throat.

Paul is everywhere. He is in the cherry floors below and the pine beams above. He is in the sweeping picture window that dominates the entire back of the house, looking out onto a stage of dense trees and sky. It cuts deeply that this house was not constructed for me. But it was built with love. And desperation.

I close my eyes and picture my first night here. The sound of his car idling. The darkness. Being cast aside, then found again. Another chance for everything I've ever wanted.

The darkest roads lead us to the light eventually.

part one

one

REBECCA

After

DUFF ALERTS US to their presence before the doorbell rings.

Paul bolts from our naked tangle into gym shorts and a T-shirt. I stay unmoving under the cool sheets, my back to him. In spite of the collective disappointment and frustration, he kisses me quickly before descending the stairs to greet the unwelcome interlopers into our morning of unsuccessful lovemaking.

Heart pounding, I pull a nightgown over my raw skin. I wait until they move into the kitchen with our excited Newfoundland, Duff, in tow, his nails clicking on the wood and then tile floor behind the men, before I move to the top of the stairs. I am out of sight but can hear their questions and Paul's calm responses.

I wait for my cue to join him, then quietly repeat a mantra with each step. *We will not be caught. We will not be caught. We will not be caught. We will get away with it.*

Little do I know that two detectives showing up at our door will be the easiest part of today.

♦

I PUSH PILLS for a living.

I'm paid ridiculously well for it. I've spent the last twenty years getting to know doctors and what they need to help their patients feel better. I know how to talk to them in a way that allows them a feeling of superiority, but they also trust what I have to say and want what I sell. I can make side effects and drug names sound poetic. I can also tell in a matter of minutes which perfect pill will work the best for each person I encounter. I especially know the chemical alchemy that works the best for me. Self-awareness is important.

By the time I reach my desk, it is well past nine A.M. and the morning's events so far have me rattled. I feel like we composed ourselves as well as we could, but doubt and worry linger. I've treated myself to an extra chill pill on the commute to regain some measure of calm.

The red light on my phone blinks ominously. Mark has already sent me an email to come to his office and a nearly simultaneous text reiterating the request. I look up and see him standing in the doorway of his office with his usual Starbucks order in hand. "Marv" is written on the cup in sloppy cursive and I laugh in spite of the day's tone so far. In his other hand is his usual prop, an unlit Cuban, which he'll chew and slobber over on and off all day until he can smoke it in the comfort of his home. His face looks more serious than smug, which is unusual. He summons me with a gesture and turns on the heels of his Gucci shoes. Someone could use a Xanax. I guess I can't blame him. I've just learned that he's also having some trouble at home.

I raise my eyebrows in his direction and deposit my stuff on my chair. I try not to pay too much attention to the conspicuous glances of my coworkers. Most of them are medicated from alprazolam to Zoloft, but there are more than a few whose dosage I could recommend upping. It is a remarkably unhappy group of people given the mood enhancers we have access to.

I swallow back the growing feeling of dread that started brewing with my unexpected visitors this morning, steel myself with a flick of half an Oxy into my mouth, and wash it down with my coffee. Always black. The dairy and sugar will kill you. I head toward Mark's office.

"Rebecca, take a seat."

It is immediately apparent that he is not closing the door in the same way he has been in previous weeks, when cubicles emptied and he's tried to convince me of the virtues of the "magic" bottle of vodka in his desk, known to transform bad decisions into "irresistible ones" (like frantic clothing removal). Unluckily for him, I don't believe in magic, and both vodka and Mark make me nauseous. But he has been more persistent with Sasha gone, and the alarming rate of my increasing cravings and depleting supply is making it harder to say no to him.

"Mark." I give him my best coy smile and coil a lock of hair around my finger. "Why so serious?"

He's unamused. Angry even. And I know why.

His wife, whom he thought had up and left him three weeks ago, turns out, is missing. Whether he knows that I've been informed of this by the police yet is undetermined. If Sasha and I were actually friends and not just pretending, I might actually have some clue as to her whereabouts. Whether or not I would have shared this privileged information with the detectives this morning, I can't say for sure. And I certainly would not have confessed to Paul or to the police that her absence does not bother me one bit.

His face registers something resembling concern, but he unfurrows his brow quickly. This isn't what he wants to discuss with me. I'm a little surprised that he's continued coming into the office in the midst of the investigation, but I suppose the routine is comforting for him. I appreciate the need for the predictable during crisis. Paul and I have been doing exactly the same.

I want to feel bad for him, but I know what a terrible husband he is. I've heard about his apathy frequently in the locker room at the spin studio from Sasha and heard many whispers down Cubicle Lane of his infidelities.

And have been hearing the best of his worst pickup lines firsthand, regularly, for years.

I consider telling him about my early morning visitors but think better of it. He's pensive while he sips his coffee. His face darkens.

"Rebecca, I can't protect you any longer. People are asking questions. Someone made an anonymous tip to corporate that our relationship was 'questionable.' I've got all kinds of heat on me now from the morons in HR. I don't know who you've been talking to, but it was monumentally stupid. With the world as it is now, I'll end up losing my job, not you, over some dumb jokes. And there's been some speculation about your access to the drug samples."

It takes a moment for my panic-stricken synapses to connect. The residue of this morning's painkiller has rendered me a tad paranoid and disoriented. I'm not sure how to respond, so I nod and mirror his seriousness.

"You are a great rep, or you were a great rep. But you've gotten sloppy and frankly embarrassing for the company. I get that you like to get fucked up, I like to get fucked up too, but you've been taking too much of the samples and people have started to notice."

Fuck. It is dawning on me where this is headed. Absurdly, I picture his wife, Sasha, pedaling for her life next to me in spin class, where she'd been rain or shine every morning, until she wasn't.

"I'm not taking anything beyond what you've been giving me. Honest." This is of course a lie.

"Your work has slipped. You've been acting strange for months now. Come on, Rebecca, you know better than anyone that all this shit has bad side effects. You've been taking too much. This is rookie behavior. And let's face it, you are getting a little too old to still be a rep."

Just like Mark to twist the knife. He can't help himself. My back tenses.

"Mark, you know how much money I've made for this company, and how much money I've saved for them—"

"Rebecca, please. I have bigger problems than you right now. I'll make this simple. You're out. You can do this the dignified way and resign, leave immediately, and not attract any more attention. Or I can make an official complaint about your deep dipping into the samples that will bring a lot of unwanted attention your way. I can keep HR off your back if you don't make a thing out of this. I think it's in your best interest to keep your dignity intact, don't you?"

It's in *his* best interest if I quit. If he fires me, he knows I could flip things on him and tell HR about his "stupid jokes." Even worse, I can tell them what I know about his questionable relationship with the truth as it pertains to a certain catastrophic drug trial. But somehow I know this information will be more useful to me in other ways. I decide to save it for a rainy day. Still, I need Mark more than he needs me.

"Rebecca?"

I open my mouth to unleash.

"Don't make a scene. Unless you want to be cut off completely from our arrangement outside of work. We're done here."

His tone is so admonishing it takes the wind out of me. But I'm relieved that he isn't cutting me off outright. And I know bringing any more attention on me, and Paul by association, would be monumentally stupid right now.

I feel woozy and need fresh air more than anything. I nod, move from the chair to my workspace, and pause to grab my purse. When I reach for my laptop, Mark's assistant, Christina, a trout-lipped twenty-five-year-old in a dress better suited for a casino, pounces and yanks it from my hands.

"That belongs to the company." Her shit-eating smile reveals unnaturally white teeth. She never liked me.

I don't look back. I can feel them all staring. I keep my composure long enough to make it to the elevator. When the doors close I allow myself one solitary sob and suck it up so hard I feel like my rib cage might break open from the pressure.

By the time I get to the ground floor, I know what I need to do. I may have to deceive Paul slightly in order to get him to the airport. The real question is, do I want him to be part of the new life I'm imagining?

I move to my car and get myself seated and locked and start the engine before I exhale. I pop the glove box open and am relieved to see my passport is still where I left it from last week's trip to the DMV. I retrieve it and put it in my purse. I debate driving home to pack but decide we can get whatever we need when we are comfortably out of the country. New start, new wardrobe. I calm at the thought of warm sun on my face and shoulders, washing down easily procured painkillers with margarita chasers. We can be free of all this in under five hours if I move quickly. I'll buy the tickets online on the way to the airport. I'll even treat us to first-class tickets. God knows, I've earned it today.

I fire up my iPad, grateful for the 50 percent battery power, which should be enough for me to get everything I need in place before it needs to be charged again. I haven't looked at the balance recently enough to know how much exactly is in our joint savings account, but it's somewhere north of a million at this point. I open the Citibank app and log in with our shared credentials.

I practically choke when I see the puny number on the screen. I'm confused. I refresh a few times and the same much smaller amount remains. It is nowhere near enough money. This can't be right. I'll have to go to the bank. I quell the beginnings of a brewing panic attack.

As I pull the car out of the lot, I see their gray Crown Victoria pulling in. The shorter one glances in my direction and I think I see him do a double take, but I look away quickly and pull onto the main road. In the rearview, I watch the car edge into the spot next to where I was. I slow my pace and see their familiar frames stepping out of the car and moving toward the office building.

Things are getting worse quickly.

◆

I CAN'T REMEMBER the last time I've walked past the vestibule of cash machines into the desert of the bank. But when the screen on the

ATM displays the same paltry amount of money in our account, I have no choice.

The perspiring bank manager sitting opposite me looks extremely jarred by the fact that I've requested human intervention. I can tell that interacting with an irate woman before noon is the last thing he wants to be doing right now. He would greatly benefit from about ten milligrams of Klonopin every three hours for the rest of his sweaty days.

Sorry, Jason, no more access to a case full of pills that I can dip into and slide across the desk to make this encounter easier. Even though the news of my firing has barely permeated, I realize that I no longer know who I am without my job. The next time someone asks me, "What do you do?" I'm not sure how I should respond. Or what I am going to tell Paul.

While Jason struggles to find my money and avoid eye contact, I take inventory of the day so far. A pretty bank employee saunters by and chirps "good morning" so perkily that I want to trip her. Good morning, indeed. Police at our door. Fired from my job. Life savings apparently gone. Pill supply dangerously low. I'm swinging back and forth between disbelief and blinding rage.

He clears his throat a few times before nervously confirming what I already know. His voice squeaks with each word. "Ma'am, the account balance is five thousand dollars. I'm not sure what else I can tell you."

Our joint account is roughly nine hundred ninety-five thousand dollars less than it should be. This news—and being referred to as "ma'am"—enrage me equally. Panic knocks hard.

"Jason, can you explain to me how twenty years' worth of savings has suddenly evaporated?" He flinches from the volume of my voice.

"It looks like the cosigner has made a number of large withdrawals and transfers in the last few weeks." He pulls anxiously at the knot in his tie.

Paul. Whose idea it had been to open the account the day we were married. So we could one day build the house we'd been talking about since our first date. My blood pressure plummets. It doesn't look as if Paul deserves an invite to my permanent vacation after all.

I fight the urge to take Jason's pathetic name placard off his desk and shove it down his fleshy throat. I don't explain that I intended to withdraw all of said nest egg and fly away somewhere far and that he's significantly clipped my wings.

"I don't accept this, Jason. How in God's name could my husband have taken all of the money without my approving or cosigning something?!" I'm jarred by the snarl that comes out of me.

My agitation draws some glances from Jason's coworkers, who look relieved I didn't end up in their care. New beads of sweat appear on his forehead and upper lip. As he clicks away on the keyboard and squints at the monitor in front of him, the meds have started to kick in. The chemicals flood my receptors and quiet the nausea and panic slightly. The key is not to flip out. I can do this.

I edge another perfectly oblong pill from my blazer pocket and casually place it in my mouth. The saccharine chemical taste dissolving on my tongue is instantly comforting. I normally don't take this many pills in the middle of the day. But today's events have justified some decisions to the left of normal.

My mind wanders and I wonder who the "anonymous tip" to HR could have come from. I'm not surprised that I have enemies at work; the question is which one of them did it. My attention transitions back to the present before I get too tangled up in that. That mystery will have to wait.

I glance around at the wasteland that is the cubicle section of the bank. A few youngish people in starter suits sit in nearby workstations uplit by their phones. I can tell by their hand movements they are swiping away their boredom. I am trying not to scream while Jason stammers that, yes, Paul, my responsible, predictable, reliable husband has been steadily bilking our joint account. As recently as yesterday, as a matter of fact.

As though he had an escape plan of his own.

Jason apologizes again and offers to email me a copy of the withdrawal dates and amounts, and I nod and murmur something resembling a yes as

I regain enough composure to stand. When I start to walk, I feel my legs wildly trembling with rage.

In my car, I hear myself singing along to the radio, even though I know that can't possibly be the appropriate response to today so far. The spring sky is as clear and expansive as I feel, and I realize it is April Fools' Day. This would be the ultimate prank. I blink and see that I've pulled into our driveway with no recollection of the time in between leaving the bank and arriving home. Time is doing funny things today.

His car isn't in the driveway. Given the time, this is to be expected. Luckily there aren't any other cars lying in wait either. I change my mind and back out, deciding it would be best if no one knows I'm home, round the corner, and park behind the house on a service road that stands deserted save for a few daily ride-throughs of the kids in the neighborhood.

I walk through our back gate and close it behind me, hearing the lock catch.

I float from the yard, unlock the back door, and beeline through the kitchen to the couch, knowing that's where I'll find his laptop. Duff bolts upright, happy to see me. He nuzzles my hands in the direction of the kitchen where his leash is hanging, but all I can muster is a pat on his enormous head.

He turns his broad black-and-white back to me and collapses into a 150-pound heap at my feet, content in his uncomplicated bliss. I love him, but he has always been Paul's dog first, and the thought of my thieving, lying husband flames up in me. I pull Duff by his collar to the back door and outside. I need to be alone while I investigate. He whimpers for a moment before a squirrel catches his next flash of attention and he's run to the far end of the enclosure.

Our house is simple and straightforward. The modest two-story cottage is set back from the main road on a corner plot with a white picket fence enclosing a small backyard. The fifteen-hundred-square-foot two-bedroom (one of which Paul turned into a home office), two-bath felt like a palace when we moved in ten years ago from Manhattan, leaving behind a significantly more expensive six hundred square feet.

The days of being perpetually entangled in each other's bodies cooled quickly after the first few years with the lack of a door and general personal space. And then came Duff, who weighed one hundred pounds by the time he turned six months, so we'd literally run out of space in our own bed.

Duff may have been a bit of a Band-Aid puppy when we couldn't quite decide about kids. I'd always wanted children of my own, in spite of the deep fear I had of exposing kids to any of the damage that had been done to me. My desire to have a happy family as seen on TV and in movies grew exponentially when I met Paul, and the small voice of doubt was drowned out by the one of hope.

But, in the end, his voice became the loudest on the subject. His well-rehearsed diatribe about how children ruined perfectly good marriages and that most people just had children out of a need to fulfill their own sense of self-importance won out in the end. For better or worse, I let him take the lead on our major life decisions. But there were definitely moments when I wondered if I'd really come around to sharing his view, or if I was just afraid I'd lose him if I challenged it.

A boozy post-brunch stroll past the neighborhood pet store and our collective love at first sight with the deceptively pint-size pup was impulsive but genuine. And co-parenting a puppy seemed like a happy compromise. Neither of us had any pets growing up, and we'd always wanted a dog. He was anointed "Duff" by Paul and would grow to nearly outweigh both of us and eat a quarter of our rent in dog food, becoming the final furry straw for leaving the city.

Seventeen years earlier, we filled one small moving truck with the contents of our apartment, bound for Paul's hometown of Stony Brook, Long Island, where a family friend offered us a good deal on a newly built starter house. A five-minute walk from the water and a backyard twice the size of our apartment quickly eased the shock of being outside the city looking in. Things were great and seemed like they could only get better. How wrong we'd been about that.

I survey the kitchen, which opens into the living room, and catch my reflection in the large gilded mirror from an estate sale years ago hanging above the fireplace. I look strung out from the day's events, my eyes wild and puffy like I've been up all night crying. My brown hair looks duller than usual and my skin tone is sallow. I've been called beautiful, but certainly not today. I have yet to shed a tear, but I've never been a big crier.

I decide that noon is a perfectly respectable time to pour myself a large glass of something alcoholic. The blurring effects of the meds are starting to wane, giving way to a lot of feelings that I have no use for at the moment. I know enough not to take any more pills for at least two hours. I refuse to accidentally overdose and give them all the satisfaction.

We aren't big drinkers, so the only alcohol on hand is a bottle of champagne from our last wedding anniversary. It's a good bottle. The kind that costs upward of two hundred dollars and is reserved for extra-special occasions. Paul brought it home for our nineteenth anniversary with an armful of long-stemmed red roses and a Tiffany's gold bangle bracelet. I hadn't done anything for him beyond getting him a lame anniversary card at the drugstore in a dash on my way home from spin class. Embarrassed and a little ashamed, I got defensive and shut down. It was the first anniversary in at least four years that hadn't been skipped over and unacknowledged by both of us.

He had gone off script and it shamed me.

He'd been affectionate and nostalgic, and I couldn't muster any of that in myself, even to be kind to him. We'd been so hot and cold with each other since he'd lost his company, and had all but stopped having sex. I'd been taking probably more pills than I should have and my sex drive was nonexistent at that point. Where I used to feel desire and sweetness for him, I only seemed to harbor irritation. I told him I didn't feel like having a champagne hangover and wanted to do nothing more than go to bed. He'd been aloof and said if I was going to call it a night, he might go for a drive. I didn't think to ask him where to.

Suddenly the changes in my dear husband in the last weeks are taking on a much more complicated bent. A thick sense of déjà vu sets in. Clues that I placed out of view in favor of my own interests are coming into focus with alarming clarity. It is remarkable how much we can obscure the glaring things into near invisibility if our will is strong enough.

I pour the first glass and immediately gulp it down. It didn't even occur to me to call Paul after I left the office. He's supposed to be the person I call in times of crisis. Especially after everything that's happened before today. The phone is right next to me, but it feels out of reach. I can't tell him about getting fired. If I do that, the questions will start, and I know he'll assume it is the pills. And he'd be right, but I can't let him know that.

I shouldn't have ever indulged Mark's bad behavior, but after things got so out of control that night in our bedroom, I started to allow it, and even expected him to be out of line with me. Perversely, I came to depend on his attention to keep me motivated at work and distracted from home. And there were practical, chemical motivations he had access to and provided.

Part of me had been expecting that the whole aging-pharma-girl thing was careening toward an end. No amount of injectables could change that. But this is the worst possible time for this to happen. This isn't just about the pocketed samples; this is about my age and competition. And my declining performance. And what I know about Mark.

The new crop of reps was being requested by the new doctors, and my hard-earned relationships with loyal, if not sometimes inappropriate, MDs were coming to a natural end as they were retiring and being replaced by ambitious thirtysomethings out of med school. They flooded the city and surrounding suburbs with thriving practices teeming with the anxious, the apathetic, and the impotent. The younger doctors with their idealism and newly minted practices were the ones who were still green enough to take an hour out of their impossibly full days to give the young, beautiful pharma reps a piece of their time and an order of new meds to ensure return visits. My dance card has become less and less full lately.

The champagne has brought on quite a nice buzz and I assume the position. With Paul's laptop on mine, I take an exaggeratedly dainty swig of Veuve Clicquot, pull my hair up, and sigh, as though I'm being watched. Quite the portrait of a lady. Given our history, you would think this wouldn't be the first time I'd spied on Paul. And technically it isn't. Stupidly, I thought we'd moved past this, though. Amazing how quickly the trust has been replaced by something far more smoldering.

I'm in easily. I know all of Paul's passwords. They are always the same, my nickname or our anniversary date. I examine the photo on his desktop. It is an old one, taken in the early years of our marriage. The summer we moved to the East Village and started working in earnest to save for the life we both wanted so much, unhampered by fear or doubt. Two dumb kids with optimism about our life ahead, mad about each other. I'm mildly surprised that Paul's chosen a picture of us. My generic ocean-backdrop wallpaper feels so hollow in comparison. I barely recognize myself. My eyes are brighter, my face smoother. I'm smiling and staring at Paul instead of the camera. He's facing forward. He's got a smile so big it seems to expand in real time. He hasn't aged as much as he should have since this was taken. In this version of him, his body is more lithe and his hairline more prominent, without the smattering of gray it now has. I examine the handsome face that I've looked at more times than my own and recognize nothing.

I click on his email, inhale slowly, and get ready to meet my husband again for the first time.

two

PAUL

Before

MY WIFE AND I are different types of liars. It's one of the interesting things you learn after nearly two decades of marriage. I tend to get creative with the details. She, on the other hand, selectively omits.

Rebecca and I came to each other with roughly the same amount of damage. I suppose that for both of us, the lying comes down to control, an attempt to manage our past by reconfiguring our present. This was explained to me as a child by the psychiatrist who was assigned to my case. I think I remember so clearly because I was desperate to make a good impression.

"Paul, you can call me Dr. A, okay?" Her smile warms me from the inside.
"Okay."
"Paul, do you understand what happened to your parents?"
"Yes, Dr. A."
"You understand that it was an accident? That it wasn't your fault?"
"Yes, Dr. A."

"Paul, look at me. It was nothing you did."

"Okay."

"Okay, sweetie."

She wore a fine silver necklace with a small sapphire pendant that looked like an heirloom and matched her eyes. I remember the way it rested against her skin, accentuating the delicate lines of her cleavage. She was kind and put me at ease.

◆

WE TELL OURSELVES lots of things. Lots of pleasant, hopeful lies.

When Rebecca and I were first married, man, were we crazy about each other. Just over the moon, two wild, wide-eyed kids. And what eyes she has. Sultry, smoky, sleepy yet savvy. I was defenseless against them. And we were hopelessly in love. It was beautiful. And stupid. And I believed then—I really believed—that we could see each other through anything. And in a way, I suppose we have.

Rebecca and I used to make love for what seemed like days on end. I'd get swallowed up by those eyes of hers as my mouth melted into her full lips and her dark, flowing hair swept across both of our faces.

"You love me?"

"Desperately, Madoo."

"I need you so badly."

"You've got me. You've got all of me."

"Baby, I need you to fuck me."

Time had a way of evaporating when we were tangled up in the sheets, or standing up in the shower, or finding creative uses for the secondhand furniture we'd accumulated. We even managed to find some kinky ways to utilize my small collection of neckties. Only when we'd pry ourselves apart in sated exhaustion did the world around us return to any semblance of order.

◆

WHEN YOU'RE YOUNG and dangerous, everything is available to you. The world seems utterly gift wrapped. You have a beautiful young wife with a hot ass and a way with words that makes you feel a little weak, in a way that you can allow yourself to be. In a way that feels vulnerable, but you welcome that vulnerability. You let it in, because your relationship is solid. The bonds of marriage are impenetrable and protect you from the outside world.

Not that you really need any protection. Everything else is going beautifully. You have a thriving contracting business. People are racing to build new houses. You can barely keep up with the number of projects you're juggling, but when you get thrown yet another, who are you to say no? You can do it. You're the king. You can keep all of those plates spinning. You're even able to make the time to dig, pour, and build the basement foundation and lay in the utilities for the dream home you're designing for that gorgeous wife of yours. The one who's killing it at work herself. And when you lay her down, and you're on top of her, she looks at you like she's on top of the world. And that makes you feel as if you are. And, after all, you are. You're it. You're the fucking man.

Then reality wallops you, and it feels like getting hit in the face with a sackful of nickels. The market crashes, construction halts, and you're sitting there with your dick in your hand. The money dries up immediately, and suddenly you've got a dozen half-finished projects and no prospect of completion in sight. You're no longer holding the sticks on which you were spinning all those plates. Through nothing other than bad luck and bad timing, you're completely screwed. You've got a ton of money out and nothing coming in. Your ambition has come back to haunt you.

And there's your ego, needling you. Your wife is understanding. She really is. She's supportive, she's compassionate, and she listens. But she can only listen to what you tell her, and you're not telling her everything, are you? You're not telling her what's really eating at your guts, the stuff that's keeping you up at night even as you lie as still as possible next to her so she thinks you're sleeping soundly. You don't want to burden her with all of that. Why would you need to? After all, you're the fucking man. At least, you were.

You've been slammed into a different reality, and it stings like hell. Your beautiful, charismatic wife, who could sell wool to a sheep, is absolutely cleaning up at her job—not to mention taking full advantage of the pharmaceutical perks. At some point it strikes you, in a morbidly funny sort of way, that there might just be a connection. The economy is in the tank, and people can't get medicated fast enough. Maybe fate does have a sense of humor.

You sit around the house, trying to figure out some way to revitalize your career. You scramble, you scratch, you reach out to whoever might take your call. You try to think of something. Anything. But you're looking at nothing. And all of those gaudy, glistening trophies on the mantelpiece? They're looking at you. Those testaments to your wife's sales numbers and general dominance in her field? They're looking down at you, judging you, pitying you. Asking themselves what kind of man you really are.

It takes a while to sink in, but the blow is no less harsh. Your wife is now handling shit. Because you no longer can. The woman you affectionately refer to as Madoo—your dove—has been left to take care of you, because you can't be a man anymore. You've never been one to wallow, but you're feeling pretty sorry for yourself now, aren't you? And it's grinding away at her, that's for sure. You find yourself feeling relieved that you decided against bringing kids into the equation.

She would never let on, but you can see it in her eyes. She's a little more tentative with you, as if she's addressing your pride first. She lets you take the initiative more, and it feels like a concession. Whereas you two used to dance the dance fluidly, seamlessly, you can now feel her making a point of letting you lead. And when you do make love, she doesn't look you in the eyes the same way anymore, and you can barely bring yourself to look into

21

hers. There's a rigidity that creeps into her body. She doesn't open up for you the way she used to, doesn't take you inside with the same abandon. It's as if you're drifting by each other.

You start to wonder what she's still doing with you, why she hasn't left yet. Her head is elsewhere, and you figure her eyes can't be far behind. It gets to the point where you're surprised at her having stayed, then disappointed in her weakness for doing so. Why wouldn't she just go? You would have. What's she waiting for?

You try to project the outward signs of a healthy, functional marriage: mutual respect, support, caring. And those things are still there. But something else has crept in, eroding the edges and eating away at the heart of your relationship. You feel it in your daily lives, and yet neither of you is able—or willing—to address it. And it certainly has put its stamp on your sex life. You're now at the point where you're not interested in making love with her anymore. You need something raw, more animalistic, to fill the need.

◆

SHEILA WAS A MISTAKE. But I suppose things are only ever mistakes in hindsight. I never meant for it to happen, but it happened all the same. When we met, I was two years into my run of unemployment, still plotting my path back to success. My daily ritual of taking walks down to the bay with Duff both got me out of that prison of a house and helped focus my brain, bringing me closer to my next great idea, which was always just out of reach.

Sheila lived a few blocks away and would often be out walking her dog around the same time that Duff and I were stretching our legs. She wore her ash-blond hair in a loose bun and always looked effortlessly, casually put together. She was a few years younger and exuded an energy I found myself drawn to. I figured out her schedule, and after a few days of polite waves, I stopped to speak with her.

"Good morning."

"Hi there. And who's this big fella?"

"This is Duff."

She leaned over to pet him, revealing a glimpse of lace trim where her bra crept out from the neckline of her shirt. "Hi, Duff! You're a sweetheart, aren't you? And who's *this* big fella?" As she looked up at me, her liquid blue eyes cast a mischievous radiance.

"Paul. Duff here's the smart one. I'm the big dumb animal of the pair." I did my best to return her look.

She smirked, her lip gloss catching the sunlight. "Well, at least you're not slobbering, Paul. Give yourself a little credit." She held my eye for a long moment, then extended her hand. "Sheila. This is Molly."

She had a warm, firm handshake. The dogs had finished sniffing each other, and as I bent down to pet her black Lab, I noticed Sheila cover her wedding ring with her right hand. At that moment, something shifted in me.

We'd do it at her place, while her husband was out of town and the dogs were running around in the yard. We did things that Rebecca and I hadn't done in ages, and with a heat and intimacy I hadn't felt in years. Sheila looked at me, touched me, made me feel about myself the way my wife used to. And so I let myself believe that Sheila meant more to me than she did. And for a while, I really was convinced.

three

REBECCA

Before

I NEVER SET out to sleep with a married man.

I met Paul at an open house in Woodstock barely a year after I graduated from college. I wasn't in any financial position to buy a house, but I would spend my weekends poring over the real estate sections of towns close enough to get to by train but far enough that I could step into a different life for a while. When I'd walk down a tree-lined country road or watch the ocean lap at the shoreline, I saw what my life could be: calm, secure, and happy. Days filled with family picnics and bike rides, building sand castles at the beach, a house covered in snow and Christmas lights. All the collected mental snapshots of the life I hadn't had but wanted to. I was tired of waiting for it to begin.

I'd been walking the perimeter of one of his first major projects, listening to the broker list the amenities of the gorgeous alpine Craftsman, when he emerged from the trees in the back of the property. He glided across the grass with such swagger, I got a little dizzy. He was the most handsome man I'd ever seen in real life. His head of thick brown hair showed no sign of quitting, and his warm smile revealed a slight gap between his front teeth, a feature that I found as sexy as a good body. Another thing he had going for him.

He swooped in and took me by the arm, leaving the irritated broker midsentence. My body began to crackle when he took my hand and threaded it through the crook of his right elbow.

"You looked like you needed rescuing."

"More than you know."

"Glad I can be of service."

I waited for him to let go, and when he didn't, I held on tighter, staking my claim. Never before had being touched by a complete stranger felt so electrifying. My heart was beating so hard I was sure he could feel it through my muscles and skin and the fabric of our clothes. I waited for him to talk again. I was too nervous I'd say the wrong thing, and surprised at this stranger's ability to bring out an unknown shyness in me.

"So, what do you think? Are you in love?"

I blanched and started laugh-coughing. He nodded to the house. I composed myself. "Yes! I am in love. I do, I love it."

"So, is your husband inside?"

"I haven't been inside yet. Maybe today is my lucky day."

"It seems to be that kind of day, doesn't it?" His ease and confidence were catnip.

"I love the house. But . . ."

He exaggerated clutching his heart with his hand. I was glad he was still holding on to me with the other one. "But?"

"It is way too big for just one person."

"You don't strike me as *just* anything. But I'm glad to hear that you're one person."

I don't know if he saw me watch him slide his left hand into his coat pocket. I'd already seen his ring. But with the way things were going, I didn't feel like it was going to be much of a problem.

"So, what about you? Are you in love?"

"At first sight."

He'd pulled my arm, and I winced.

"I'm sorry! Are you okay?" He was genuinely concerned, which only added to his attractiveness.

"Oh, it isn't you. It's a childhood injury that flares up now and then." I held out my other hand, inviting him to pull that one in whatever direction he wanted to lead me in.

"I'm glad I didn't hurt you. I would never forgive myself. I'll need to spend the rest of the afternoon protecting you."

When he kissed me, I felt my knees give out. He steadied me expertly, as if women swooning in his arms was something that happened to him regularly. He took my hand and pushed the stray hair out of my face. We walked toward the woods and away from the rest of the world. Without the smallest hesitation I let him guide me. He squeezed my hand every few feet like Morse code. I squeezed back.

◆

LATER, AFTER EVERYONE had left and we made love in the house, he told me he'd come to hang the final touch, a small wrought-iron heart he'd forged. It was the signature to his projects. He'd make a metal piece significant to the people moving in. Yet, that morning he found out that the original owners' marriage hadn't lasted long enough for them to live in the house he'd built for them. Instead, he gave me the heart and said we could have their love since it was ours to take.

After

Paul's desktop is so streamlined I know something is off. This is the computer of someone who is focused and organized. Paul might have gotten his mojo back for sales, but not for organization. Or so I thought. Part of me wonders if he's had some help with this overhaul. Someone young and earnest perhaps. I push the thought away with a quarter of a Xanax, knowing well that I've lapped my maximum intake for the day at least twice. I never take this much in one day. Paul would definitely notice and disapprove. Although, today I don't especially give a shit about what he would or wouldn't approve of.

His desktop files are split into two columns: the left for his various contracting properties dating back from the beginning, organized by address; the right for his current properties. And one outlier folder with the Cold Spring Harbor address.

I do a perfunctory search of the files on the left, but I know there's no money in them, ours or otherwise. I gulp back the champagne and disappointment, looking at the symmetrical icons, each with someone's dream-home-never-to-be. I click on the folder for our three acres in Cold Spring Harbor. It is completely empty except for the property deed. I'm surprised by how much this absence of content stings.

Paul bought the land as a wedding present. The night we married, we pitched a tent on the property and giddily mapped out the floor plan on the pizza box that our dinner had come in. We vowed that any bit of cash we could scrounge would go into the joint account that Paul opened under both of our names. Forgoing the honeymoon was the first of many sacrifices for that dream.

Competition was the major motivating force for both our savings and our sex life. If Paul contributed two hundred dollars one month, I would go without a new pair of shoes or get a chain-salon haircut to be able to kick in two-fifty. Often, he would up the ante the following month. The growing account was the tie that kept us tethered. Neither of us had grown up with money, so being able to earn it and squirrel it away was a new feeling of power and control.

We shared the desire to do better, earn more, have measurable progress. The first years of the joint account were celebratory at every milestone. The bigger the number got, the stronger our marriage became. At least, it felt that way at the time.

I click into our bank account for the third time in as many hours. The diminished balance confirms that the nightmare of today is real. Had we really gotten so far away from each other that I'd stopped looking, and Paul knew I had? Time had passed in the intangible way that it does when you aren't paying attention. I didn't see the tether fraying to such a precarious degree.

There was a point when Paul was busy with work all the time. The money was coming in more rapidly and going into the account in larger amounts. I'd never seen him so driven, so motivated and successful. In moments, his confidence bordered on hubris, but it was a turn-on. If he said out loud that something was going to work, it always did.

I look at my phone to see if he's called. He hasn't. I should call him and confront him, but I need more information.

I open the back door and Duff bolts inside, running around in circles for a treat, which I give him with shaky hands. His ears perk up and he lets out a bark before darting upstairs to the bedroom.

Suddenly alert, I pull the fireplace poker from its stand and follow. I've left my phone on the couch with the laptop and immediately regret my decision to investigate the noise over leaving the house and calling the police or Paul. But neither course of action would be wise. The last thing we'd want is for cops to be nosing around our bedroom. Less risky, but still not ideal, is calling Paul. But I haven't figured out how I want to deal with him or how I'm going to tell him about my job. So calling him is off the table.

Duff has pushed open the slightly ajar door. I can't remember leaving it open; it's something we don't do during the day, to keep him contained to the main part of the house. The Xanax is doing its job, because I'm able to step over the threshold of the bedroom, weapon in hand, with some degree of calm.

The bedroom is empty and as we left it this morning. The only out-of-place thing I can see is that one of the bedroom windows has been left open, and the sash from the curtain has come loose and is being tossed against the windowsill by the breeze. Perfectly rational explanation. I relax.

I move to close the window and return the sash to its hook, when I see a MAC lipstick tube on the newly laid carpet, sticking out from under the chair. I pick up the tube and see that it isn't one of mine. I remove the cap and think I recognize the bright red shade as hers. I cap it and look at the name on the bottom. Lady Danger. I tell myself it has been there all along and I missed it when we replaced the rug. I put the tube in my pocket, call Duff out of the room, and shut the door behind us. I'll leave that particular worry behind closed doors for the time being.

Back on the couch, I root around on his laptop and the knot in my stomach grows tighter with each click. I know that I'm looking for evidence of another woman as much as I am for the money. My insecurity disgusts me. All along, quietly, I felt like the lesser catch in our marriage. Now that old anxiety reverberates. I initially doubted my ability to become the woman he wanted me to be, the girl he thought I was when we met. I pushed the fear down as deep as it would go and locked the bulkhead tight.

My phone vibrates. Paul's calling.

"Hey, you." My voice sounds ten times steadier than I feel.

"Hi, honey. How's work?" In Paul's universe, his wife still has a job. I straighten up when I realize that I haven't spent much time thinking about how I am going to conceal my new unemployment status. Since my plan of leaving the country is a nonstarter, I need to come up with a new one. Better that Paul thinks everything is status quo in the interim.

"It's fine. Not too busy. Mark's being a bit of an asshole, but that isn't anything new."

"Yeah, that guy is more than a bit of an asshole. I'm sure even more so now that Sasha's MIA. Sorry you have to deal with him."

"I wonder where she's gone. I hope she's okay." I couldn't care less, but I am curious how much thought Paul's given to her whereabouts today.

"I'm sure she's fine. More than fine. She's probably off spending Mark's money and getting off on the idea of people looking for her. She's *always* been about the attention." The affectionate amusement about how Sasha "had always been" stings.

"You would know better than me." The bitterness in my voice is subtle, and I feel myself edging toward a fight we don't need to have today. Luckily, he doesn't take the bait and changes the subject.

"Listen, the detectives showed up at the open house. I wanted to call sooner, but they were hanging around until people started arriving."

My blood runs cold. "After coming by this morning? What did they want?"

"They wanted me to come to the station and answer some follow-up questions."

I'm careful about anything I say on the phone. I know Paul is as well. We've seen enough *Dateline NBC* episodes to know better.

"Did you tell them that you would?"

"Of course. But I told them not until I get back from my trip with Wes."

In the chaos of today, I'd completely forgotten that Paul was due to be out of town for two days for a brokers' convention in Florida, leaving tomorrow morning. A well-timed excuse for some beach time as a write-off. I'd opted not to join him for a number of reasons, the main one being that I hadn't been invited.

"Did they bring up anything other than what they asked this morning?"

"No. Just more of the same." He's got an edge.

"I just meant . . . never mind. Did they say anything about a lawyer?"

I can tell by the cadence of his exhale he's frustrated with me, but I'm not sure about what exactly. I want to give him a good lashing about the bank account to show him who should really be pissed in this conversation.

"They're probably going to come to talk to you again. They wanted to speak with me alone, and I'm sure they'll want the same from you."

My tongue is practically bleeding from biting it about the money. If I do it now, I won't have enough information on the back end to know if he's lying. If I can't pick apart the thread of lies right away, it will all get too tangled. Better to wait. But the prospect of Paul getting on an airplane tomorrow unleashes a surge of fear in me.

"What time are you home tonight?"

"Late. Remember? Wes and I are taking out the Murray Hill assholes. They are looking to get a bit of the local flavor before they drop a few million on weekend house number three. And I brought my bag for the trip just in case I decide to crash at Wes's. We have an early flight."

"Oh. I thought I would see you before you left."

"Sorry, love. You'll be asleep if I do make it home tonight anyway." He softens.

He's mistaking my lament for wanting to see him out of love. I'm careful to keep the meter of my voice even and not sound too forced.

"Right. Well, I'll miss you."

"I'll be back before you know it."

"Love you, honey."

"Mean it?"

"More than anything." I don't miss a beat.

The grandfather clock in the hallway chimes four times. The sound is equally familiar and disorienting. I stretch my legs before I get back to sleuthing and click around in the more obvious secret-keepers like email and Facebook. He hasn't posted anything for more than a year, and there isn't as much as an exchanged emoji or vaguely flirtatious comment with an old high school girlfriend. I pull up his activity log and see that the only lurking he's been doing is on competing real estate companies' pages in the area. I leave FB and start clicking around in his folders. Frustratingly, he's logged out of his email, and the usual passwords aren't working. I pull up recently opened Word documents and see that our insurance policies have been opened by Paul in the last month. I skim through the fine print on his policy and mine, but nothing looks out of place.

The complete lack of porn tucked away in some innocuously named folder is the most suspicious thing so far. Whatever it is I think I'm going to find is well hidden or nonexistent. I try to come up with explanations about why he would have taken the money and not told me that would make sense. I come up empty in that effort as well.

I take a moment to look away from the screen and around our home. For all of the dream planning we did for the house in Cold Spring Harbor, the cottage suffered. If a home is a reflection of the people who live in it, we are utterly beige. This was supposed to be our transition home before the real one. The knickknacks and mass-produced wall art is stuff we picked up in the checkout line at Bed Bath & Beyond as an afterthought. Our house could be a page out of a catalog for the domestically unimaginative. Even as the years passed and we remained here, we didn't put any money into making it ours. Looking around at it now, I'm realizing how boring it all is.

The widowed ceramic bookend on the mantel, a turquoise Chinese guardian lion, is the most ornate thing in the room. Paul hasn't even noticed its mate missing. There seems to be a lot of that going around.

The bookend met its demise when Paul came home one night, a couple of years earlier, drunk. This in and of itself was disturbing since he wasn't one to lose control and generally didn't drink more than one or two light beers. This night he appeared to have had nine or ten. He'd sat on the couch next to me, our arms almost touching, physically closer than we'd been in a long time. I'd been itching to take a pill, feeling the weight of whatever he had to tell me engulf us and wondering if he'd even notice in his impaired state. I controlled myself. At that point I had stricter rules about my daily limit.

"My business is done. There's no money coming in. Absolutely none," he told the floor. "I fired the last of the guys today. Some of them refused to leave, said they'd stay on and help finish the jobs. They didn't understand that no one was going to pay to finish any of those houses." Duff came over to him, sensing his despair, and rested his giant head in Paul's lap and whined. Paul cried quietly into his fur. "It was awful. One of the worst fucking days of my life."

I hated seeing him this way. I'd never seen him get completely vulnerable, even when he was talking about things that had happened when he was growing up. Terrible, traumatic things didn't break him like this. I also had no idea how to comfort him. I'd never learned how to do that when I was a kid. Nobody had ever done it for me.

I wish I could say that I meant everything I told him, or that I didn't just say the same rote platitudes in three different ways. But I was processing the newfound distaste of this weak side of him.

"It will be okay, honey. It will get better. Things will start turning around. And we don't have to worry about money too much. We always have my salary and the Cold Spring Harbor money, worst-case scenario."

I didn't mean it. I would be furious if we had to start living off that money. He tensed up.

"Absolutely not. We are not touching the money for the house. I'll figure something out." He was wobbly when he stood but steeled himself and walked upstairs and fell face-first into bed. He was snoring loudly by the time I reached the top of the stairs.

After I turned his head to the side so he wouldn't asphyxiate, I stomped downstairs, grabbed one of the bookends, and threw it against the back of the fireplace, where it spectacularly exploded into hundreds of ceramic shards and dust. My fury was so much bigger than my control or awareness of it. I didn't realize what I'd done until many minutes later. Sometimes my anger is like that. The rage has been within me for so long, I wonder if I came out of my mother that way. I've worked hard to keep it under wraps, especially from my husband.

The streetlights come on and the last tendrils of sunlight cast eerie shadows on the wood floor. Hours have passed as I've clicked through dead-end folders and documents. I move to his real estate folders. All of this snooping is making it clear how removed I've been.

I open a to-do list dated around the time he was first out of work. "1. Find a new job, 2. Train for a half marathon, 3. Start cooking, 4. Work on house blueprints." He'd abandoned the list shortly after he created it, clearly. Best-laid plans. He started to wilt after his business was gone. The couch became his "office" and his pajamas his "work clothes." We joked about his early retirement and made light of his facial hair cultivation, but resentment and anger metastasized in me.

Paul being home all the time put me on high alert about finding better hiding places for the additional pills I'd started to need. I wasn't going over the line, but the line had moved a few paces forward to cope with our new arrangement. I had my acceptable, legitimate prescription pills in the medicine cabinet as usual, which were "as needed," and my supplementary supply in places I knew he wouldn't stumble upon in his newfound time in our house all day long.

My obsessiveness wasn't limited to my chemical self-medication. I hid in my job. I began to exercise twice a day to have excuses to be away from the house and to reassure myself that I wasn't overdoing it with the pills. If I could run three miles and then spin, I was healthier than most of America.

It seemed like the more active and extreme I became with work and working out, the less motivated he became. We had always been a seesaw of ambition, but now he was deadweight. I couldn't stand the sight of him licking his wounds. I knew it wasn't his fault that people could barely afford their current mortgages, let alone build new homes, but my anger, unchecked, just kept growing. Defeated was a terrible look on him. I didn't marry a man who would grow a beard and stay in his pajamas all day. That wasn't him. Until it was. He was giving up and I had to look away. I now push back against the crushing feeling of how different things could have been if I hadn't.

I offered up antidepressant samples from work to try, in the hopes they would make up for my absence of empathy and understanding. He refused, never a fan of pharmaceuticals as a solution. He found them to be "the easy way out." For me, things at work had gotten especially bad with the Euphellis trials. I'd started taking an Ativan to get through the evenings. I found that with a glass of wine, mixing pills and alcohol—

something I'd never imagined myself doing—made the distance between us feel vaguely cozy instead of strained. Though whether I felt the reality, we continued to move apart until we were barely speaking. He would retreat to one end of the couch and stare at his phone for hours, allegedly reading the news, while I'd lose myself on the opposite end in hour upon hour of whatever show we could agree to binge.

It was Wes, one of his oldest friends, who finally snapped him out of it. Wes had made millions convincing the greedy adult children of Eastern Long Island to sell their parents' modest homes and property for seven and eight figures to the rich and striving. Wes, who knew the potential sales savant my husband was, saw an opportunity.

The morning after the call from Wes, Paul had already gotten out of bed, gone for a run with Duff, and made me breakfast before my alarm went off. He was shaved, dressed in a suit, smiling hugely over a cup of coffee. He was the spitting image of the man I'd given up hoping would return. I felt an old stirring for his hands on my body. He could tell. He put his arms around me and whispered my nickname into my ear before gently pushing me to the floor. Then he passionately told me all of his plans for getting back on top.

I poke around the official-looking sell sheets for Hamptons houses, one larger than the next, some with Wes's well-chiseled headshot featured, others with Paul's smiling face and contact info. I click on a "Sold" folder, and then a sell sheet for a modestly sized bungalow in Southampton overlooking the ocean, surrounded by a spread of land three times the size of the actual house. The asking price was seventeen million dollars, an amount carrying a commission of at least a million. The sale was nearly a year ago. Why Paul would leech our life savings with a commission like that is baffling.

The old stir of pain becoming rage thunders deep in me. Paul has greatly underestimated my capacity to make plans of my own.

four

PAUL

Before

IT'S AMAZING HOW GOOD you can be at something precisely because you don't give a shit about it.

My plans to get my business going were still stalled, and I was really itching to bring money into the equation. Rebecca being the sole breadwinner had worn our marriage just about as thin as it could stand, and what had begun as a quiet whisper of resentment had slowly grown into a steady drone.

"How was your day, babe? Anything exciting?"

"Whole lot of the same. How was work?"

"Same old. Mark's being Mark, so that's a ton of fun. Did you and Duff get down to the beach?"

"Yup. Just like every other day." There's so much edge to my response that I'm surprised it doesn't slice my mouth on the way out. As the words hit her ears, I watch her eyes narrow. *In three, two, one . . .*

"Um, okay. Just touching base. You want to talk later?"

I do not. "Sure thing, kid. Oh, and I noticed your stash in the kitchen cabinet is getting a little low. Might be time for a refill." I excuse myself and step into the office, as if I have things to do.

My wife certainly seemed comfortable wearing the tailor-made pants in our relationship. I'm not sure if she still even monitored the balance in our joint account—I hadn't been able to contribute anything for a long time, after all—but I'm quite positive that she was still dumping her share in there like clockwork. I could just picture the smirk on her face as she deposited the money. The smirk that would only soften to become something more gently malevolent.

God bless Wes. I got the call early in the morning as I was sitting on the back porch.

There was still dew on the grass.

"Wes."

"Hey, limpdick."

"What's up, fuckface?"

"That wildebeest still eating you out of house and home?"

"You still getting fat off of swindling morons into overpriced prefabs?"

"Funny you should ask."

He ran me through the ins and outs of the real estate game, got me licensed, and set me up with some decent properties, considering my rookie status. Nepotism really does make the world go round.

I found, quite by accident, that the key was not caring. And I couldn't have cared less. If I couldn't build houses, I thought, I wanted nothing to do with the real estate business. The amazing thing was, my shitty attitude began to pay dividends almost immediately. My lackadaisical approach to the whole enterprise had the effect of luring the client in. I pulled off an unprecedented percentage of sales in my first year on the job. Even Wes was astonished.

I realized quickly that the oversell was where most agents went wrong. Push this address too hard, that amenity too much, and you lose the client before you have a chance to get the hook through their lip. They sense the desperation coming off you and they shut down before they've had the opportunity to get turned on. The trick with these marks—and they are marks, after all; we're just the confidence men running the hustle—is to get them all worked up through the power of suggestion. Give them just enough to whet their appetite, but not enough to slake their thirst. Size them up, figure out what they're looking for, and proceed accordingly. Mention this feature, underplay that one. Start with something inessential, then bury the thing that's going to ultimately get them on the line. Let them suss it out, feel like they've dug it up themselves. In the end, it's really all seduction. And I'd like to think that's an area I'm well versed in.

◆

"YOUR HUSBAND DOESN'T do it like this, does he?"

"No one does it to me like you do, Paul."

"Whose is this?"

"It's yours, baby. It's all yours."

"That's right."

"You can handle it, can't you?"

"Keep getting cute with me and we'll see if *you* can handle it."

"I want it. I want it so bad."

Thank God for Sheila. Before Wes came through with the real estate gig, she really helped me keep it together. I was beginning to flounder. Doubt was sinking in. And I'm not talking about your everyday, occasional, on-the-surface type of doubt. I'm talking about the kind that gets its fangs into you and begins to gradually, mercilessly sap the fucking life out of you.

Looking back, I was a pretty sad sack. Actually, I was a complete wreck. I was wandering around the house, unshaven, in a bathrobe, barely communicating with my wife, much less the larger world outside my door. The only thing I had going for me then—the only thing that kept me at all together—was those days with Sheila.

When she and I first met, I was in a better headspace. I was still optimistic that I was on my way back up the ladder. To my mind, it was simply bad luck that had kept me out of work for as long as I'd been. Duff and I would meet up with Sheila and Molly for our morning walks to the bay. We'd let the dogs off leash to run around while we caught up on each other's day. We'd take the dogs back to her place, where they'd scamper around in the yard while we defiled each other. It was a very enjoyable diversion.

Things changed. Over the course of the next year, we began to gradually sink deeper into a shared hole. Not because of each other, but because of the chaos that was swirling through each of our lives. I had become increasingly dejected by what was seeming more and more like a hopeless dream of returning to my former professional glory, and she was finding herself trudging through the quagmire of a steadily fracturing relationship with her husband. His job took him out on the road most of the time, and it had become clear to her that he was carrying on an affair with one of the coworkers he traveled with. The sting from that revelation, along with what I'd come to understand as long-running emotional abuse on his part, was really fucking with her.

These parallel circumstances had the effect of pulling us closer together as they pushed us farther apart. We were each isolated in our own frustration and quiet rage, and desperately clung to each other to keep from getting sucked down. It was all we could do to not completely give up and give over to the darkness.

We abandoned all pretense. We stopped meeting with the dogs for walks to the bay. As soon as Rebecca would leave for work, I'd let Duff out to run around in the backyard and head to Sheila's. We began to speak less and less. There was little need for it, as neither of us had much worth saying. All the talking we needed to do we did with our bodies. She began to leave the front door open, with only the screen door between her and the animal that was now making visits to her home. I'd walk through that door and find out what I was in for. Sometimes she'd grab me as I came in, push me up against the wall, and begin to ravage me. Other times, she'd be sitting, naked, on the sofa, waiting for me to manhandle her.

We figured out a rhythm, silently. We'd size each other up and figure out who needed what. It became the way in which we communicated the frustrations and resentments in the other parts of our lives. I'd walk through that door, and we'd take one look at each other and figure out instantly who needed to get fucked and who needed to do the fucking.

It emboldened us. After a stretch of confining ourselves to the living room, she slowly began to coax me upstairs. We'd do it on the steps, up against the wall in the hallway, and, finally, in their bed. The idea of me sticking it to her to stick it to him in the place where they slept became a huge turn-on for her, and then for me. It made me feel more virile, like I was the man of the house again. Not my house, mind you, but that was hardly the point. She'd run her fingers over my stubble as I worked away inside of her, and I felt for the first time in a long time like my old self. I felt wild. And rash. Which is what led me to do the thing I did next.

"Hmm." She looks around the bedroom, taking it in.

"What's that?" I watch as she studies the details of the space.

"Didn't think this is what your place would look like."

"You here for the *Architectural Digest* tour, are you?"

She turns to me, bites her lip, and slides a hand between my legs. "You know what I'm here for." She begins working the buttons loose on my shirt with the other hand. "And you're sure your wife's not going to be coming home anytime soon?"

"Maybe don't talk about my wife." I hear the edge in my voice.

She bites my earlobe a little too hard as she whispers, "Maybe make me."

I wouldn't say that marriages are built on secrets, but they certainly help to sustain them. Especially twenty years in. After bringing Sheila into our home, I began to feel something like relief between Rebecca and me. With my needs being taken care of, my resentment and frustration ebbed. I discovered a newfound warmth toward my wife that I realized had been as dormant as our sex life. Fucking my mistress became the pressure release valve between my wife and me.

In a way, I guess you could say that I did it for her. For us. For the marriage.

five

After

EVERY SECRET HAS been for him. The ones I've kept and the ones I've shared. They were all necessary for the sake of our marriage.

Yes, I've colored outside the lines of the basic marital rules more than a few times. I've held back. I've omitted. I've said one thing when I've really meant another. I've used my body when my words weren't enough.

I believe these things have made me a good wife. Most people would say that complete openness is the most important thing in a healthy relationship. Most people would say that if their spouses were standing nearby, at least.

This year will mark the half of my life that we've been together. Fifty percent of my time on earth has been making decisions with "us" in mind. It has been as much time letting go of the dreams as I spent creating them. After that long, you start to lose all concept of who you were alone versus who you are as half of a couple. My secrets have kept me from ceasing to exist completely. In the beginning it was the things we told each other and no one else that kept us focused on each other. Then it became the things

41

we didn't tell each other that seemed to be holding us together. But that fell apart, of course.

If you asked Paul if he's ever seen the real me, there would be no question in his mind. As far as he knows, he's seen me at my weakest, most emotional and unhinged. Until the night in our bedroom, he really had no idea how violent my unhinging could become.

I love my husband. Even if he is a lying, thieving prick of a man. I've done plenty of things that most people wouldn't ever understand and would qualify as more of a betrayal than his spiriting away our money. I wouldn't change any of it, even now. Except while Paul might not know the real me, he knows the worst thing that has ever happened to me and believes that he knows the worst thing I've ever done. And that is far more dangerous to me than anything else.

All the same, I know his worst too.

◆

I WAKE UP IN THE DARK, confused. I see that it is nearly ten P.M. I've passed out on my right side and my shoulder is screaming. I reach into my purse for one of the pain pills and swallow it dry. I realize I only have one pill left and a flicker of panic shakes me. I try to remember where I've hidden my emergency supply. Lately I haven't seemed to be able to keep track of how many I have, or where I've hidden them. I kept a list for a while of my hiding places but managed to hide that so well, now I can't even find that.

I hear the sound of water running upstairs and a bolt of energy snaps me to attention. Has Paul come home? Duff is nowhere to be seen, so he must be in our bedroom with his master. He is always the most loyal to him, when given the choice.

"Paul?" The continued sound of water above me is the only sound in response.

I scramble around the couch cushions for my phone, which isn't visible on any of the usual surfaces, and check my purse, coming up empty.

"Duff? Come here, boy." The sound of water seems to be getting louder and I try to remember if I started the shower before coming back downstairs and falling asleep. I definitely did not.

Without Duff or my phone, I feel defenseless climbing the stairs in the direction of the bathroom. I decide against a weapon of any kind, which will undoubtedly look a little crazy to Paul. I consider what I'm possibly going to say to confront him and decide halfway up that I won't say anything tonight. I'm too tired for a fight and honestly relieved that he's home and I'm no longer alone in our house.

When I reach the top of the stairs, the bedroom is dark, but I can see the light from under the closed bathroom door as I move through our room. I knock on the door lightly, realizing the sound is the bath, not the shower.

"Paul? Honey?" There's no response, and I conclude that he must not be able to hear me over the water. "I'm coming in, okay?"

When I push open the door, I see that the shower curtain is half closed and that the tub is inches away from spilling over. The windows and mirrors are fogged up, and the steam clears enough with the door open for me to see that the bathroom is empty. I move quickly to the spout and stanch the flow.

I survey the empty room. On the counter I see a neatly folded towel, a single straight-edge razor sitting on top of it, and off to the side, my phone. I sit on the edge of the tub to get my bearings and retrace my steps from earlier today until now. I have absolutely no recollection of coming upstairs, starting the bath, or leaving my phone out, let alone a razor blade or the towel. The scene is out of a scary movie.

Knowing that a side effect of the pills can be paranoia, I remind myself that the simplest explanation is usually the correct one. I am not losing my grip. Paul must have come home and been careful not to wake me, started the bath, and left to walk Duff, forgetting about the running water. Although this seems completely uncharacteristic of him, given his general OCD about faucets, lights, and locks.

The house has taken on an eerie silence aside from occasional water dripping. A shudder moves through me when my hand comes into contact with the plastic curtain. I stand and pull it open, revealing the half of the tub that was concealed. Bobbing up and down like a bright orange buoy is my emergency OxyContin bottle.

Paul is getting very creative in his passive aggression about my self-medication. I grab the bottle angrily, flinching from the still-hot water. I barely register the pain before the vibrating phone on the counter diverts my attention. I see a text from Paul.

Hey Babe. Did you get my message?

Yes, babe. I've seen it. It is a little dramatic, if you ask me. I'm suddenly reinvigorated by the earlier rage returning.

Yes I got your message. What the hell? Where are you Paul?

As the message bubbles percolate, I realize my mistake. I see the missed call from Paul and a new voicemail notification on my screen. Dread reverberates through me.

?????? What do you mean? Are you okay? I'm at Wes's. Did you listen to my voicemail?

I type quickly.

Sorry. I just woke up. Was confused. Listening to the message now.

I move out of the bedroom and downstairs as I click into my voicemails.

"Hi, honey. They made us do shots. Wes is wrecked and threw up out of the Uber window. I am pretty fucked-up too. But I think they're going to offer in the morning, so mission accomplished." His voice is calm and collected, though a little louder than usual. He doesn't sound wasted, but I'm hardly a good judge of sobriety at the moment. "We're at Wes's house now, and I had to pay the driver extra to stop yelling at us and to cover the car wash. I'm gonna do the responsible thing and sleep here tonight and go directly to the airport tomorrow." He laughs when he says "responsible," his tenor faintly apologetic. Hard to believe that accountability is on his mind at the moment. "I'm seeing double. Love you." My stomach somersaults. He's definitely lying.

When I reach the kitchen, Duff is outside the kitchen door fogging up the glass in giant wet-snout intervals. His tail wags impatiently. It is hours after his dinnertime. I wince at my neglect and flick the lights, letting him know I'm on my way. He jumps on the glass in a frenzy as I grab his food dish and let him in. I make it halfway to the floor before he knocks into me. Dog food cascades on the floor. And he is off, attempting to chase in four different directions. The plastic on the tile activates my jangled nerves. I sit on one of the chairs and breathe deeply, convincing myself that I've just experienced a minor fugue state and everything is fine. I push the panic down and focus. Me. Here. Now. Awake and aware. Duff happily crunching on his food. The full bottle of painkillers in my hand.

I move my shoulder around in small circles to get the blood flowing. The site of the most recent injury has all but healed on the outside, but the old ache from the first trauma has been seemingly reignited by the new. I've got to remind myself to keep it mobile, since the painkillers do their job so well. It's funny that I was taking them long before I had real pain; now I can barely remember what it was like before the most recent wound. I can't actually recall if the ache in my shoulder was real or some unshakable phantom sensation I'd been unable to let go of from my childhood. I only remember the paramedic moving my face to the side and showing me a picture book that was meant for someone much younger while another popped my shoulder back into place. The explosion of pain was the worst thing I'd experienced so far in my relatively young life. Well, second to having it ripped out of the socket hours earlier.

Now I have to take more beyond the actually prescribed amount, which puts me at always nearly out of pills. Even funnier: It wasn't because I worked in pharma that I got hooked on them; it was because of Sasha. She was so deceptively together and perfect I never considered that she had a problem. My association with her and our secret together never felt like anything dangerous, only ripe with the possibility of improvement and inclusion for me. If I did more of the things she did, I would be more like her. And Paul had once described her as "unworldly" and I wanted to capture that in myself.

I chug two glasses of water and consider eating something to steady myself before I set out on further investigations. I stare into the well-stocked fridge out of ceremony, scanning over the depressing spread: green juice, yogurt, kale, and myriad other virtuous foods. Even if I was hungry, there is nothing appetizing here. I linger in the cool for just a little longer. The burn running north of my throat to my cheeks abates for a few precious moments.

In the living room, Duff's already curled up in his dog bed. I'm itchy in my work clothes so I move quickly upstairs to our bedroom and strip down in the dark. I ball up my silk Tahari sheath before chucking it into the walk-in. I peel off my bra and panties in the direction of the hamper. I flinch hard when I see someone watching me from the chair in the corner of our room and jump back, slamming hard into the door handle. The impact knocks the wind out of me, and I sit naked on the floor for a few seconds before I turn the light on and realize that my watcher is a pile of pillows that Paul has taken off the bed. Everything feels dangerous now.

I pull on a tank top and yoga pants. When I flip the light off, everything is so utterly dark that I can't see anything. As my eyes adjust I catch a flash of movement near the trees. I let out a yelp and duck down fast. As I edge closer to the window on my knees, I hear Duff bound up behind me and pant happily in the direction of my phantom. Of course there isn't anybody there. If there had been, one of the three newly installed motion detectors would have illuminated the yard and Duff would be barking like crazy.

I shake off the feeling of being watched as I enter the bathroom to pull the stopper from the bathtub drain now that the water has cooled a few degrees. I grab some toilet paper from the roll and carefully wrap the blade a few times before dropping it into the wastebasket under the sink.

As I head to Paul's office, I respond to his voicemail with a text:

Going to bed.

Had a long day.

Drink water.

Call me before your flight.

Hopefully this will deter any follow-up calls tonight. I don't know if I have the self-control to keep avoiding him.

Absurdly, I knock on the door first. I turn the knob and am surprised to find that it doesn't budge. This stumps me momentarily, since it is the first locked door in the house that I can remember. I try to recall a time when we ever used the locks inside the house and can't think of one. I twist the handle again and accept that certain measures are required.

I kneel down, eye level to the knob, to estimate what I'm up against. It's a pretty run-of-the-mill warded lock. Easy enough. I go to the kitchen and grab two paper clips from a listing packet that Paul's left on the counter. I've blocked out most memories of my youth, but the choreography of pin-to-pin cracking is as natural as breathing. While most kids were learning how to ride bikes, I was watching my father pick the locks on doors separating my mother from him. Kids are like sponges, and I absorbed. I'm in easily.

It takes a minute to find the light switch when I step in. This has always been Paul's space. I'm overly careful not to trip on any of the towers of detritus I know are there. When I find the smooth switch and illuminate my surroundings, disorientation sets in. Paul's office is pristine, as suspiciously tidy and clean as his laptop was. His piles of boxes, blueprints, and contracts are gone without a trace. It appears that while I was throwing myself into work and spin class, Paul was cleaning up old messes and making new, bigger, invisible ones. The surface of his desk is completely clear except for a copper letter opener with Celtic knots winding around the handle.

A chair that's been in Paul's life longer than I have sits neatly behind his desk. I sink into his imprint, momentarily worried he might notice the change in the worn leather. This is the desk of a confident man: big, sleek, and leather. The two medium-size drawers on the right are as they always have been. I pull the brass knob of the top one and find it unlocked.

It's empty save for the usual desk fare: a calculator, a stapler, and some pens. These items don't hide the glaring absence of his handgun. It wasn't exactly the most secure way to store a potentially lethal firearm, but without kids in the house, the easy access had never posed a threat. I shudder at this thought now. I know he's moved it out of the house and away from us.

I've gone back and forth about being relieved it is out of the house and

47

wishing it were within arm's length, especially at night. Today I feel equally ambivalent and conclude it is probably best for Paul that I don't have access to a gun.

I attempt to open the second drawer but it doesn't budge. Interesting. I jimmy the keyhole easily using a bobby pin from my unwashed and haphazardly updone hair. They work better on a pin-tumbler lock than a mangled paper clip because the shape of the ends when the plastic bits are removed is a perfect fit. As expected. Inside the drawer sits a medium-size lockbox I've never seen. The irony of my husband putting this many locks between me and whatever he's hiding is rich. He has no idea of my childhood talent, and I wonder how he'd feel if he'd seen how far I'd managed to get through his obstacles. Most wives would have stopped at the locked door.

I lift the lever-locked metal box and place it in front of me. I'll need both hands to get into this one. I decide the letter opener will do just fine and thank Paul for leaving it out. The slender tip slips in easily and I pull up and left with one smooth flick of my wrist. An image of my father flashes in my head as I hear the click. Once he caught on that I was watching him pick locks, he amused himself by showing me how to tackle different kinds of catches and clasps. For a short time it bonded us and kept him away from my mother, who continued to lock herself behind the bedroom door, even after he picked it over and over until he finally just removed the knob altogether. Inside the box is a blue velvet jewelry bag that looks like a movie prop. I pull the ribbon closure, spread the mouth of the bag, and tip it into my hand. I half expect gemstones to cascade into my palm like at the end of the movie *The Goonies,* a favorite of mine from childhood from one of my early foster homes. It was the only VHS they had, and nobody cared if I watched it five times a day. It made me happy in an otherwise miserable arrangement.

Instead of jewels, though, a ring box slides into my hand. Inside is an engagement ring I've never seen. It is a stunning canary-yellow diamond, and much bigger than the one currently on my finger, a modest solitaire that he got me while he was still married. This new one looks to be about three carats. Not a million-dollar ring, but definitely worth a big chunk of life savings. Could this be Paul's plan? To give me an upgraded ring? It seems unlike him to use our house money for a single piece of jewelry, especially given how things have been between us. This can't be the only thing he's hiding.

There is an envelope sitting at the bottom of the box. It is unsealed, and from it I extract a small stack of Polaroids. Before I flip through the synthetic plastic squares, my eye catches a familiar translucent orange bottle pushed to the back of the drawer, behind the lockbox. My stomach drops with the thought that Paul has discovered one of my hiding places and confiscated my stash, but this fear dissipates quickly after I snatch the bottle. These are definitely not mine. I don't need to read the medicine name to know what I'm holding; the blue rounded-edge diamond pills are unmistakable. Viagra. Another secret. And one I'm definitely not reaping the benefits of these days. Who is? I feel sick.

The top picture is a redheaded bombshell whom I've never seen before, but judging by her hairstyle on top and below had been photographed in the late seventies and predated me. The photo below is of his first wife. I've only seen her a handful of times, and only in photos mistakenly mixed in with the belongings of his that were carried over from their life into ours. She and I couldn't be more different physically; her icy blond bob was an echo of Debbie Harry, and her zaftig body curvy and luscious against my small breasts and narrow hips. The next nude is someone I know immediately, even though this version of her existed twenty-five years before I met her: Sasha. This one cuts me the deepest, and I wonder how recently and how often he's looked at this one. She was as stunning then as she is now, something Paul has said out loud more than once. I flip the picture over, the sight of it bringing on a wave of nausea. There is no picture of Sheila, but I know that is only because of advancements in technology. I've seen those pictures on his phone. The last one is of me. I guess I'm glad I made the cut, but still disturbed by the collection.

I flash back to the night Paul plied me with a joint and Miles Davis. I was bashful and self-conscious, but he was convincing. He wanted something to look at when we couldn't be together. He told me that it was a first for him to take a picture like that as much as it was my first time to be photographed. Clearly, that was not the case. I pause on the picture of my twentysomething-year-old self momentarily to marvel at the beauty of my own young body, and regret not appreciating it while I had it.

I'm almost too distracted by the photos and pills to notice the black notebook camouflaged by the black felt lining the box. I lay the Polaroids in a line across the surface of the desk and place the bottle of Viagra right side up next to the pictures. With trembling hands, I extract the Moleskine and see that there is a thick envelope tucked inside, its edges sticking out just slightly. I open that first, my heart racing with anticipation of its contents. I lift the flap and liberate the folded paper inside. It is a multiple-page letter with *Dear A* written at the top of the page in Paul's hand. My phone convulses loudly on the desk and a text with Paul's name floats to the surface. I refold the pages and tuck them back into the journal.

Love you. Miss you.

Hate sleeping without you.

Sweet dreams.

Out of all the possible alibis, Wes is perfect. But of course my husband is not at Wes's house. And he may be sleeping without me, but I'm doubtful that he is alone.

I return the Polaroids into their envelope and into the drawer. Before I return the ring to its hiding place in the drawer, I take a picture. I keep the letter and the journal. I have all night to read uninterrupted.

In the kitchen I pull the kettle from the back burner to the front and listen for the flame to catch. As the slow build of the kettle goes from a slow whistle to shrieking, I lay the journal to the side, unfold the letter, and start to read.

six

Before

IT ONLY TAKES that one slip.

Any relationship is a high-wire act. Maintaining an affair is like walking a greased tightrope with a gorilla hanging off your back. If things go wrong, the destruction can reverberate catastrophically. Which is why I had to cut things off with Sheila when she did what she did.

◆

BY THE TIME I'd had my mistress in the bed I shared with my wife, the cracks in my affair were starting to show. I had sensed from the get-go that Sheila was a little nuts, but that had been part of the turn-on. In hindsight, I think the desperation we were each wrestling with had the effect of bringing us together in this insane whirlwind of raw, unbridled chemistry.

Every relationship is governed by its own particular rhythm. The rhythm of my relationship with Sheila was an uneven one and proved to be our undoing. Things had been humming along steadily for about a year, with Rebecca and me becoming increasingly estranged as Sheila and I continued to hold on to each other for oxygen. I can venture to imagine how things would have shaken out if we had continued along that same trajectory. But then the phone call came.

Wes reached out just in time. It has since occurred to me that Rebecca might have contacted him on my behalf, though I'd never give either of them the satisfaction of acknowledging this. Deep down, I think I only took him up on it because I could sense what awaited me if I stayed on the path I'd been careening along, and the thought of one more pitying glance from my wife decided it.

The ascension began quickly, and with it came a big adjustment in perspective. I began to feel my former confidence seep in. I had purpose again, and I could feel the dynamic with Rebecca shift back into place. In fact, I think I only grasped the full measure of how far things had slipped when I was able to look at us anew. Two people can only truly challenge each other when they stand on equal footing, and we had been steadily slipping away from each other for quite some time. But now we were back, and I'll tell you that I've never had a partner who measures up to my wife.

I stand in the kitchen, drinking a cup of coffee, soaking in the morning sunlight through the sliding door. I hear Rebecca's footsteps approaching from behind. I can smell a faint trace of her perfume.

"How's the ol' Wes-and-Paul smile-and-sell game looking for today?" She wraps her arms around my stomach, lacing her fingers together, and rests her head on my back.

"Promising, Madoo. Showing a plum spot on the ocean out in Amagansett, then a rental a little farther up the island. Wes likes the two guys looking at the ocean house."

"As in, Wes thinks he can get them to cough up some serious dough?"

"Something like that."

"Wait, two guys?"

"Yup."

"A couple?"

"That's right."

She unclasps her hands and starts working them up toward my chest. "Well, well. I think you two dreamboats got this one in the bag. Just flash those pearly whites. And, um, maybe get a little closer . . ."

I turn around in time to catch her winking at me. The old spark of trouble is back in her eye. I only now realize how much I've missed it. I put my mug down on the counter and wrap my arms around her waist. "Oh, I didn't realize that sort of thing turned you on."

"You know what turns me on."

I hike her up onto the counter. I move close to kiss her but hesitate an inch from her lips. "But, babe, you're going to be late."

"Not if you're quick."

All of this came with consequences, of course. As the passion was being rekindled with my wife, it began to take a back seat with my mistress. Funny that my marriage should start to take cues from my affair. And the steadily widening gulf between Sheila and me magnified the physical cooling off. Whereas my relationship with Rebecca was built on climbing the ladder together, my relationship with Sheila had become all about the dynamic of decline. And here we were: she continuing her slide, and I was on the climb. So I understand what pushed her to such a rash move, but I certainly could never condone it.

◆

WHEN REBECCA AND I FIRST got together, we were both traveling light. Part of the allure was the chance to build a life together, and neither of us came into the marriage with much in the way of material possessions. I was more than happy to leave most of the furniture with my first wife, and my second wife seemed practically nomadic in her lack of attachments. One of the few things that she brought into our life together was a pair of ceramic Chinese lion bookends.

"You like these up here, babe?"

I turn toward the cockeyed bookshelf to see the ornate matching blue-green lions staring at me. They lend an exotic air to our modest space. "Where'd you turn those up?"

"Trip to China . . . town." She winks as she says it.

"Oh, let me guess. 'Finding ourselves,' were we?"

She offers me an overly earnest look. "I wasn't found until I found you, Paul." Then she sticks her tongue out at me.

I try to hold a straight face but can't keep it together. I break into a grin. "I love you, babe."

"Yeah, yeah. You just don't love my decorative sense."

"Well, maybe I'll learn to."

The bookends accompanied us from our apartment to our home on Long Island, where they took up watch on either end of the mantel above the fireplace. It was after Sheila's last visit that I noticed one was gone.

Physically, she and I had cooled off noticeably. The seams were showing in our relationship. She was becoming much more clingy and much less attractive. And I couldn't quite pinpoint it, but something suspicious had taken shape with the story of her husband. It was nagging at me. The details didn't quite jibe.

Things were going in a different direction for me, and the truth of the matter—as I was finally recognizing it—was that I could only be in the proper headspace at any given time to maintain one of my relationships. There was no way to juggle both without the bottom dropping out.

One morning, as I was heading downstairs from a shower, I heard noise coming from my office. Startled, I grabbed the poker from next to the fireplace and approached the office door with a light step. I suddenly remembered that the pistol I keep in the house for protection lived in the desk drawer in my office, and I prayed that whoever was rifling around in there hadn't yet found it. I took a deep breath, flung the door open, and found Sheila sitting in the leather chair behind my desk, wearing nothing but one of my neckties and a smile. She had one leg flung over the armrest and was biting her lower lip. She slid the desk drawer shut as she stood up and circled around to the front of the desk.

"What the fuck are you doing rooting around in my—"

"Trying to get your attention," she purred. "It's been hard to get your attention lately."

"Yeah, I, umm . . . ," I stammered.

She eyed the poker in my hand. "What are you going to do with that?"

I dropped the poker to the ground as she slid herself onto the desk and reclined, one hand gripping the edge of the mahogany.

"So, do I have your attention now?"

◆

WHEN WE FINISHED, I went to the bathroom to give her a chance to dress quickly and let herself out. When I came downstairs a few minutes later, she was still sitting in the living room, staring out the window in silence. Annoyed, I made my wishes very clear with some terse words. She stood up, hugged me for a very long moment, and kissed me hard. She grabbed her handbag off the sofa and walked out without a word, tears welling in her eyes.

It wasn't until later that day, when I went to replace the poker next to the fireplace, that I noticed one of the bookends missing. Honestly, I couldn't even remember the last time I paid those things any attention, between their being permanent fixtures in the background of our daily lives and me having been largely distracted for the past year. But suddenly, there it was. Or, rather, there it wasn't.

The absence was glaring and sent my mind in all sorts of directions. Though the theft could almost be seen as sweet on the surface, a way for Sheila to hold on to a piece of what we had, I couldn't ignore the diabolical underpinnings of her actions. *Did she take the bookend in a moment of pure emotion, or had it been more calculated than that? Was it completely impetuous, or had she sensed this moment coming and figured out a way to stick it to me?*

I thought back to the moment when she left. I imagined her walking away, a sly grin spreading across that tear-soaked face of hers. Clever, really. She must have sensed that the bookends belonged to Rebecca and that the absence of one would therefore be noticed. She had of course reasoned that *I* might not notice the theft and would be stumped when Rebecca brought it up. Just think of her now, amused at the thought of me scrambling on the spot for an explanation. Or else she thought that I would notice and would have to concoct a story to explain the absence or else just sweat it out, hoping that Rebecca wouldn't notice. God, what a conniving little girl she was.

Ultimately, this turn of events made things easier on me. Whatever soft spot or shred of sympathy I may have held for Sheila was erased by her sad, childish excuse for a power move. It made it easier for me to exit the situation without holding on to any looming guilt. And it was necessary for me to move on from that dark stretch of my life and get back to doing what I do best.

I will admit, however begrudgingly, that Sheila's little ploy was effective. I concocted a whole explanation for the missing bookend, a story that was not only plausible but managed to cast me in a good light. To my surprise, I never had the chance to use it. Rebecca never inquired as to the fate of the ceramic lion, and so it became just one more thing that was never discussed. One more thing that sat, silently, untouched by two people living under a single roof. It loomed larger in my mind because of the omission, and I suppose this is where Sheila enjoyed a small victory.

But there was something I kept in mind during this time, a thought aimed squarely at this underhanded little girl who I let into my home and my bed. A thought that kept me warm at night, and it was this: *You want to play games with me? Well, you have no idea who my regular sparring partner is.*

It only takes that one slip. For everything to come toppling down.

seven

REBECCA

Before

AT FIRST IT was just sex.

Paul's marital situation wasn't conducive to more. We grabbed time when it worked for him. Fucked in nearly finished houses, in his car, in bathrooms. My life became about waiting. Waiting until the next time I heard from him. Waiting for him to sneak away for a few delicious hours. At best it happened once a week, at worst once a month. I became antsy when too much time passed and I didn't see him. Our phone calls between seeing each other became the only thing that mattered. The rest of my life melted away.

We didn't discuss the big relationship topics. At that point, I had no ideas about his views on children. We never spoke in terms of him leaving his wife or talked about what a possible future together would look like. There was an invisible fence around any topics that could lead to commitment, and I stayed outside of it.

My infatuation grew furiously. Being completely at the mercy of him and his life, I eventually reached a breaking point. I'd always prided myself on being the kind of woman who could be breezy, uncomplicated, and undemanding. But that was only because I'd never had a relationship quite like this one. It was bringing out a new needy side of me.

Paul was so good at keeping me on the hook, I never considered a pattern of behavior. I just believed our love was different and we'd figure it out as we went. I didn't focus on the red flags scattered about the perimeter of our situation. There was the obvious issue of his marriage, but there were other little things. I chose to ignore the way he looked at other attractive women we'd encounter, or his flirtatious way he called them all "sweetie." I didn't question him when I could tell that he was lying, when little details would change from one day to the next. He was hard to pin down and sometimes seemed to be somewhere else when we were together. There were a lot of little cuts that might have added up to a larger wound if I started focusing on them, so I didn't. I thought if I changed for him, he'd do the same. I became the model "other woman," the woman I believed Paul wanted me to be. I reasoned that it was his lie to tell, his marriage he was stepping out of. I was living my own life, the way I wanted to. So I subtly pumped him for clues about what he wasn't getting from his wife so I could give those things to him. But he said very little about that piece of his life, so eventually I stopped asking him about it. I contorted myself to his needs because I believed if I did, he would pick me. I figured, become a man's fantasy, and he will have no defense against it.

◆

THE CONVERSATION WAS eternally "next time." We went back and forth building each other up, turning up the pressure. What we were going to do to each other. How we would pleasure the other. That stopped turning me on after a while. I craved for him to tell me that he loved and only wanted me. I wanted substance and real intimacy. I wanted him to tell me about what he pictured for us long term, but he never spoke about anything other than the moment we were in.

One night, around the time I'd gotten my first prescription for anti-anxiety meds, I decided to push things. I took twice the dose the doctor had prescribed. I felt ballsy. I also felt desperate.

"Paul, I keep thinking about how much we don't know about each other."

"Okay, I'll bite. What have you been hiding from me?"

I was fed up, but I couldn't pinpoint about what exactly. He wasn't doing anything differently. It was me. I'd thought all of our sexual chemistry would evolve into a relationship. I never wanted to be someone's perfect mistress. I was tired of sharing him.

"I'm serious, Paul. You have done sexual things to me that there aren't even names for, but you don't really know anything about me." My voice was serious and steady thanks to the drugs.

His cadence shifted quickly to cautious; he was married, after all, and knew what a trap sounded like. "What don't I know about you, babe?"

"Like what my childhood was like. You don't know what I've been through."

I could hear the first trickles of exasperation in his exhale. "What is this really about?" His curt tone stung. We weren't fighters, so far, at least.

"It's about us acting like we are so close and crazy about each other, but I know nothing about who you really are. And I want to. I want more of you."

"What do you want to know about me, Madoo? I'll tell you anything. I have nothing to hide." I thought his wife might take issue with that statement.

I softened my approach. I didn't want to provoke a fight before I said what I needed to. "I'm sorry, honey. I just feel so close to you, but sometimes I feel like we could be closer. And I want you to know everything about me."

"Okay, babe. Well, we can talk about anything you want."

"I need to tell you about my parents, Paul."

He laughed. "Okay. Tell me, then. Were they religious? Hippies living on a commune? In a cult?"

I was silent while I weighed the possibility that he might pull away from me faster than I could say "I'm telling your wife." But I needed something to change with us and he was making no moves. I was going crazy.

"My parents are both dead. When I was eleven years old. My father murdered my mother and then he killed himself. And I was there." I wondered if there would ever be a day when I could tell him the whole truth of that night.

Paul was quiet for a long time. I imagined him grimacing, struggling to respond but not engage too much. He'd never talked in terms of feelings beyond the physical, and this was miles removed from that. He was silent long enough that I thought he flat-out hung up.

"Paul?" Regret surged. "Sorry. That was too much. I've never really told anyone about that. At least not anyone that wasn't being paid to listen." This was true.

He cleared his throat a few times. "My parents died in a car accident when I was ten. I was the only survivor."

I couldn't have guessed that we had this trauma in common, but once we found out, it just made sense. We recognized something very deeply in the other without knowing what exactly it was, and clicked.

"I don't really like to talk about the past." He was speaking much more softly and gently than I'd ever heard him. "But maybe I should, with you."

My heart swelled with the opportunity to connect with him.

Then it started being about love.

After

The pages are hot in my hands.

I never pegged him for the type, but there's no question that it's his. The familiar sweep of his hand on the page drives my desire when I know I should be hating him. Our love is tricky that way. Elegant and strong, his handwriting is a font all its own. It is way too beautiful for laundry lists but perfectly suited for love letters.

I can't stop thinking about you. You make me crazy. You preoccupy my thoughts when I should be thinking about a hundred other things.

I feel gravity changing beneath my feet.

I need to get out of this life. Everything has become stale and empty. I need to get rid of you so I can be with her. I need you gone.

I didn't think that the love and desire I felt all those years ago would ever be a feeling I would have again.

I've spent so many years not really saying what is in my head. There've been too many lies for too long. I want a new beginning. I need to change.

Paul's words are in his handwriting but not his voice. There is a different tenor to these pages. Something more realized and grown-up. He's opening parts of himself that I have never seen. He's reflecting on the man he's been and the man he wants to become.

I want to burn down this life that I'm stuck in and get away from the guilt. I can't keep doing this and acting like everything is okay.

I wipe away tears that come dangerously close to running the ink.

Catching my breath is a real struggle at the moment. It is clear that he's found someone else. Wow. And he didn't waste any time. And I'm standing in his way. His words are so hurtful I feel like I've been punched in the stomach. The pain overcoming my entire body feels so acute that I consider calling 911. My heart is slamming against my chest and I think lying down on the floor and just fucking dying makes the most sense.

That would work out perfectly for him. *I need you gone.* He'd be free to do whatever he wanted without the burden of me. Thankfully, the possibility of him thinking I'd died from a broken heart is enough to muscle through the panic and into deep breathing.

I slide against the counter and land on the cool floor. Duff bounds over and licks my face when I don't move to pet him. Eventually the salt on my cheeks and my apathy drive him to the water bowl.

I'm stunned. The dates of these entries are from the last couple of weeks. After the night in our bedroom. After her. But this isn't about her;

it can't be. I didn't know Paul had another round in him. After everything that has happened. I'm gobsmacked.

I could leave. Start over and hope for a second act. But that would be the solution of a different sort of woman. Someone who lacks imagination beyond movie montages and memoirs. I like to think I'm more unpredictable and creative than all that. There's a reason I wasn't able to leave yesterday, and now I see that it is because I'm not going to let him get away with this. Half of that money is mine, and I want it. Something is tearing open in me. I want to smash every breakable thing within reach. I want to scream. I want to kill.

I call Duff over and wrap my arms around his furry neck and squeeze tightly. His heart is beating as fast as mine. I start a mental list of everything that Paul loves the most in this world and think about how satisfying it's going to be to take those things away.

eight

Before

WHEN I STARTED fucking around on my first wife with Rebecca, it felt like the most natural thing in the world. It wasn't the first time I'd cheated. Hardly. But it was the first time it had felt like it was about more than just the sex. I had gotten married out of desperation, out of a need to have someone who wouldn't leave me, a fact that came uncomfortably into focus almost from the moment we exchanged vows. It was like that scene at the end of *The Graduate,* when Dustin Hoffman and Katharine Ross ride off on the bus and the terrible mistake they've made slowly dawns on them. I suppose I started looking for a way out before I had even settled in.

Rebecca was that way out. She understood the situation immediately. Our first meeting took me completely by surprise, eliminating any chance of tactfully shedding my wedding band. We locked eyes for a long moment, after which she immediately glanced at my ring finger. I can still remember the look on her face as she sized up the situation. The combination of terror and lust that I experienced in that moment is something that has stayed with me over the years.

We spent the next ten minutes walking around the yard, arm in arm, indulging each other in a conversation about one thing that was really about another and pretending that we weren't both acutely aware of what I was wearing on my left hand.

"So, what do you think? Are you in love?" I held her stare for a split second before I nodded in the direction of the house. She made a show of coughing as if she was caught off guard, but we both knew better. The air around us was electrified. As she mentioned the size of the house, and how ill suited it would be to a single owner, I slid my hand into my coat pocket and ditched the ring. When I pulled my hand back out, Rebecca didn't miss a beat.

"So, what about you? Are you in love?"

I stopped us and turned to her. "At first sight."

She looked to the house, then back to me. "Wow. A guy who knows how to make a house a home."

"If given the chance."

Her eyes narrowed slightly. "So, you're in the habit of taking chances?"

"Only when it would seem crazy not to."

I led her around to the far side of a tall rhododendron bush, where we kissed each other hard and deep, away from the prying eyes of the broker.

Nothing about my second marriage has been particularly traditional. When we met, we were a couple of kids who were just beginning to get our bearings in the world, and I suppose we enjoyed many of the romantic notions that go along with that. Rebecca even flirted with the idea of having kids, a sweet notion even if it *was* impulsive, impractical, and naive on her part. We were making plans to improve our financial picture, and it was certainly apparent that we were committed to the relationship. But, if I'm being honest, I don't know that either Rebecca or I are really the marrying kind. I'm sure that seems like a silly thing to say nearly two decades into a union, but I really believe that what's kept this boat afloat is how well we understand each other and how perfectly matched we are in the ways that really matter. I don't know that she or I would have enjoyed this kind of relationship success had we ended up with any other partner.

From the beginning, there was something different about Rebecca in the role of wife. She had never worn an engagement ring or wedding band before, and there was a certain charm in the way she would fiddle with them. At first, she seemed to have trepidations about having the rings on her finger. I felt self-conscious, as I hadn't had the means back then to swing the type of rock that a woman like her deserved. But I gradually realized that her discomfort had nothing to do with that. Whereas the ring that I wore during my first marriage began to feel like a vise from the moment it slid onto my finger, Rebecca regarded hers with a sense of wonderment. I think that it may have never occurred to her that she'd actually be in such a position, and I remember occasionally catching her—even years into our marriage— seeming to marvel at the idea as she studied the shimmering bands.

Even the most conventional aspects of our life together resulted from moments of spontaneity. The average couple puts together a careful game plan. We ended up with the dog and the white picket fence on a whim. Sure, we had our long-term prospects in place—the bank account, the Cold Spring Harbor property—but time and circumstance have had their way with those well-laid plans.

Expectation confounded can be a funny thing. When one is carrying on an affair, there are certain things that can be done to minimize the chances of getting caught. The first—probably the very cardinal fucking rule—is to not get involved with someone who has less to lose than you do. It would follow that the safe bet would be to take up with someone else already in a committed relationship. I spat in the face of this logic by starting something with Rebecca, yet at no point did I ever feel as if there was the danger of her meddling in my marriage. I could tell that she wasn't one to make a public scene, and it wouldn't have been her style to confront my wife or leverage the affair against me. I think we both sensed where our relationship was heading and were perfectly patient to let it evolve in the time it required. And by the end of our first serious conversation, we realized why we understood each other so reflexively. The bond became clear, and it was undeniable. It was love, and there was no turning back.

Sheila presented a different dynamic, which seemed ideal at the time. I met her as a married woman, and though the heat between us was palpable, she seemed at first to have a life that she was actively pursuing. Part of the initial excitement seemed to be the fact that we were acting out a forbidden fantasy—something unsustainable but nevertheless vital. Something each of us needed for our own reasons. But the dynamic gradually shifted, and our relationship became increasingly more erratic and tempestuous. Over time, it became clear we were people who should have never embarked on this sort of endeavor in the first place. And I couldn't help but think that my married mistress was becoming much more unpredictable than my single mistress had ever been. Funny, that.

My discovery of Sheila's little scheme with the bookend served as the moment of clarity that brought everything into sharp focus. I knew I had made the right decision in ending things with her, and I was optimistic about the prospect of a fresh start.

◆

AND THEN, one day, it happened.

The moment that a man in my position fears, and that we delude ourselves into believing will never occur. Because we're smarter than all of those other chumps who have the audacity to try to play up to our level.

It's the quiet lull after the holiday season. Storefronts in town are taking down Christmas lights, and there's a feeling of serenity in the wake of the bustle. The day is crisp but pleasant. Rebecca and I are walking down the street, hand in hand, when from a block away I see Sheila approaching. The ground underfoot shifts, my gut punches itself, my eyes sting, the inside of my skull feels as if it's suddenly upholstered with gauze, and time melts into itself.

Sheila walks toward us. Her eyes meet mine and then flick in the direction of Rebecca's. She smirks, before her mouth turns into something lascivious and vulgar.

Sheila walks toward us. Her eyes size up Rebecca before they sweep to mine, and she taunts me with her stare.

Sheila walks toward us. Her eyes dart away violently, defiantly.

Sheila walks toward us. She sees us, turns on her heels, and retreats.

Sheila walks toward us. As she passes us, she reaches into her handbag. She pulls out something that I don't recognize as ceramic until she's swinging it at my wife's head.

She reaches into her handbag. As she draws it out, I recognize the Chinese bookend. As she swings it at my wife's head, I grab her wrist and pry it from her hand.

As she draws it out, I don't recognize it until it's drawn behind her head. I watch as she buries it in the side of Rebecca's skull.

Sheila walks toward us. Her eyes briefly meet mine as she walks past.

Everything springs back into focus. I realize that I'm holding Rebecca's hand tighter than I was just a few moments ago. Our palms are damp. I haven't a clue whether I've clasped her hand tighter or she mine. I don't want to look at her, for fear of betraying this concern. Did she notice the exchange between Sheila and me, or are my nerves betraying me?

My brain summons the details of what has just transpired. *Where was Sheila's dog? It's not like her to be out for a walk without Molly. Seems like an odd—Wait. Wait. Where the fuck was her wedding ring?*

My mind zooms in on her left ring finger. I immediately think back to our first meeting—her trying to hide the ring—and am struck by the stark nakedness of that finger just moments ago. My stomach coils back into itself. I'm suddenly reeling, feeling more out of sorts than when she was in our presence, within striking distance. It's something akin to a deafening silence.

And as we now know, I was right. That missing ring was a harbinger.

nine

Before

OUR PAIN MATCHED.

Paul was the first person I'd met who knew how bad things could get. He understood how certain life events couldn't be unseen or erased, and how those things really fucked a person up, especially if they happened when that person was a kid. And when we told the other what we'd seen and I saw how he'd thrived in spite of it all, I was intrigued. Bordering on obsessed. I was as much in love with his sad story as I was with my own.

And while our sad stories were similar in many shades—orphans by the age of twelve, witnesses to the death of our own parents, foster care, shrinks, myriad questionable adults—the main difference was that Paul's life started out happy. He'd had a chance to be one of those few lucky kids with parents who were loving and attentive with him and each other. It was just bad luck that it was all taken away. The irony that, between the two of us, I was the one who wanted a family was not lost on me, but it stung nonetheless.

I wondered if he and I would have looked twice at each other if we didn't both see a similar pain in the other. Even if we didn't identify that the magnetism was about that from the start. We didn't talk about our sad stories more than once or twice, and certainly didn't dwell on the details. We didn't have to say much to understand how badly the other didn't want to remember.

I used to hide in the hallway closet when my parents would fight, cracked just enough to see into their bedroom. I guess part of me thought that I could intervene if things got too out of control. I often fell asleep in the small space with the winter coats brushing against my shoulders as I sat with my knees pulled in close. I'd pull on my down jacket with the hood strings pulled tight to block out the screaming.

When my parents were at their worst, I would think about how I never wanted to get married. How once I grew up I would avoid anyone who would make me so crazy. It seemed very simple; if someone made me mad enough to become that enraged, I would run the other way. Common sense.

I got older and turned it inward. If things didn't work out with people, I stopped seeing other people's bad behavior as the litmus, figuring it was just some deficit in me. Friendships and relationships didn't stick. I attracted people who didn't care about who I was, only how I made them feel when they were with me. Naturally, this was never sustainable.

Eventually, I concluded that no one would ever want to marry me. Something important was broken. Therapists had told me over the years that my sense of self-worth was barely intact because of the way I saw my parents treat each other, even before the night they died. While they were probably right, I stopped listening to how I might fix that fracture and accepted it as part of who I was.

The night they died, my parents were having the same fight they always did. It was about nothing and everything. They'd throw a lot of nasty words back and forth and then graduate to sharp objects. It was amazing we had anything breakable left in the apartment. And of course, things got much more dangerous. I could never speak about my part in that danger. Not to Paul, not to myself.

◆

AFTER WE COMPARED our sad stories, there was a seismic shift in how we saw each other. Paul approached our affair differently. He was gentle and protective. The sex was still a part of our connection, but it took a back seat to something deeper. I felt less like I was sharing him with someone else and more like he and I had always been bound for each other. His marriage was just another hurdle to traverse before we could finally be at home with each other. We talked about a future together. I traded out my skepticism for hope.

"I want to build the home that neither of us got to have. I want us to plan it from scratch and make it together." He wasn't a big feelings guy, so I knew the weight of his words.

"I want that too." I did.

We were sitting in his car on a back road in Cold Spring Harbor, one of the spots we escaped to when he'd been surveying potential properties. He was still married technically, but only technically.

"Give me your hand, Madoo."

I didn't expect it. Truly. I had hoped quietly, but that was it. And I'd certainly never asked for it.

The engagement ring was a small thing to him in the grand scheme of us. Paul knew it was important to me without my having to spell it out. That in and of itself was important. There were many things I wasn't able to say about what I wanted, and he intuited so much. Once he slid the ring onto my finger, I felt that I was deserving of getting whatever I wanted in this life, for the first time.

Somehow, this piece of jewelry on my hand was the antidote to all the fears I had about love. All my potential to be someone other than my sad story wrapped in gold and topped with a diamond. It was proof of my worth. He was utterly charmed by my infatuation with the ring and the gesture.

Once it was on my finger, I vowed never to take it off for longer than was necessary. I knew if I did, the spell would be broken.

After

I hear the house phone ringing, but I'm unable to move. I'm belly down on the couch; at least I've rolled off my shoulder in the night. It was dark when I closed my eyes, and now it is painfully bright. Dreams of unbreakable locks burn off as my eyes adjust. My hands look strange. They are mine, as much as they are attached to my wrists and arms, but something is off. It takes a minute to connect that my rings are missing. I have no memory of taking them off.

My bottle of Oxy is on its side. One pill remains just out of reach. My shoulder throbs at the sight of it. I could have sworn that I had at least five pills left when I last checked. I need to start keeping better track. I can see a slice of the kitchen. Fresh air from the open door moves through the house. I can't remember leaving the door open. A harpoon of pain shoots down my spine when I lift my head to see farther. I place my cheek back on the throw pillow.

"Duff? Come here, boy."

I wait for the click of his nails on tile. I need the sound for comfort as badly as I need water.

Silence. A terrible feeling takes root.

I get vertical quickly, grabbing the bottle along the way. I toss the pillows from the couch and find my phone nestled between the cushions.

Unbelievably, there is a group text from our spin instructor letting everyone know about a candlelight vigil ride tonight for Sasha and a reminder to join the "Find Sasha" FB group that has been started, seemingly overnight. Everyone is responding in a flurry for people to bring photos of Sasha to put on her bike, which will be left empty in her honor. I think about the only photo I have of Sasha. It is a candid shot taken at the Rep of the Year dinner ages ago. The four of us were sitting at a table together. Mark is looking off into the distance beyond the photographer. I am looking down at my hands, frowning, about what I can't remember, but it was probably that Paul had been ignoring me in favor of talking about high school memories with Sasha. And she is front and center, looking like she just stepped out of a magazine; Paul's eyes are deadlocked on her.

It is the last thing I want to do, but for many reasons, I need to show up. I reply.

I'll be there.

In the kitchen, everything appears to be in its place. I pull a bottle of seltzer from the fridge and chug the cold, fizzy liquid down fast. I look out the window and immediately avert my eyes. The morning sun hurts. A breeze flows through the open door and I pull the screen closed, leaving the glass open to inhale the fresh early spring air.

My phone vibrates on the counter. It is a blocked number so I reject the call. Almost immediately, the landline rings. I scoop the phone from the cradle and my hello is met with silence. This has been happening a lot lately. I start to call Paul but stop myself.

My naked ring finger motivates me to the sink to look in the soap dish, my go-to place, close by and in my line of vision. My wedding band sits alone. Visions of the diamond ring slipping down the kitchen sink and out to sea twist my heart into a knot. But the stopper is reassuringly where it was when I got home yesterday afternoon. The landline rings again and distracts me momentarily. I retrieve the cordless from its dock and hope for Paul's voice at the other end in a surprising moment of tenderness for him.

"Hello?"

Silence.

"Hello?"

I can't tell if the faint breathing on the other end is really there or if it is my own strangled breath that I'm hearing. I hang up and practically crack the hard plastic of the phone on the counter.

I slide the simple gold band onto my finger, which looks strange without its companion. I reach into a hiding place in the cupboard to pull out one of my pill bottles, but it isn't there any longer. I can't seem to keep tabs on anything lately. I scan through each room, looking, knowing, though, that I'm not going to find what I'm searching for. I'm not entirely sure which missing thing I am hoping to find. All of them. But mostly, the pills.

My phone vibrates to life.

Going through security at the airport. Is everything okay?

I'm about to respond when I see Duff's leash hanging on the coat rack next to the door. Without remembering anything specific, I know I've done something bad. I respond.

Everything is fine. Love you.

As calmly as my emerging panic will allow, I walk through the back door and tell myself I'm going to find Duff asleep under the willow tree in the shady section of our yard. Logic and routine dictate that I let him out last night into the safety of the enclosure. But the yard is still as empty as it was earlier. I try to convince myself that the wide-open gate before me is just an optical illusion. As I move closer, I can't deny it. The difference between slightly and completely open is not up for debate.

"Duff?!"

I feel tears coming and gulp them back. How did everything get so bad so quickly? I long for the life I had before. When I had a job and money and a husband I thought I knew. When I wasn't out of pills. When I had my ring. When I knew where my fucking dog was. Behind me, coming from the house, is the sound of the phone ringing again, but I continue in the opposite direction. A few feet away something in the grass sparkles as the sun emerges from behind a cloud. I'm momentarily bolstered by hope. I move toward the light-emanating beacon. I bend down and take hold of the object.

As I strain to make sense of the silver tag in the shape of a bone, now unattached from collar and dog, an unseasonably cold breeze blows through me. A few inches next to the tag is a prescription bottle. The one previously hidden in the cabinet. Now empty.

ten

Before

SOME PEOPLE JUST can't understand when things have run their course.

Rebecca and I had barely made it back to the car following our encounter with Sheila when my phone started buzzing off the hook. I hadn't had a chance to properly collect myself when the onslaught began. I somehow knew, as soon as my pocket began vibrating, exactly who was on the other end of those texts.

I had, of course, blocked Sheila's number on my call list, but here were a batch of messages coming in from an unknown number that could only belong to one person. Of that I was certain.

As he often had, Wes served as the perfect alibi. I was still shaky from the near run-in, and I was worried that I had somehow betrayed the situation to Rebecca. I could sense the change in myself following the incident, and I was afraid that my wife, as distracted as she'd seemed lately, had picked up on something. So when I drew the phone from my pocket and Rebecca asked if everything was okay, I at least had the presence of mind to blame Wes and the prospect of a new property on the market. The nature of the texts that were flooding my phone's display was, of course, of a much different stripe.

Great to see you today. You look well.

What a beautiful wife! What a beautiful couple!

Gosh, she looked so contented. Poor thing. She must have no idea who she's really married to.

You two really deserve one another.

◆

I'VE ALWAYS CONSIDERED myself a reasonably savvy bullshitter, but even I could feel the lies oozing out of me like toxins. After returning home that day, I spent the rest of the afternoon between the office and the back porch, in an attempt to convince my wife of a lie that I could barely get my head on straight enough to try to sell. I made a big show of taking my laptop out back as I called Wes to cross-reference figures and whatever other professional-sounding nonsense I could think of. Thankfully, it was one of those mild winter days, although the adrenaline coursing through my body was making me largely impervious to the weather. I remember the experience being akin to what one describes when recalling an out-of-body event. And as soon as I hung up the phone and folded the laptop closed, Rebecca was all over me.

"Quite an afternoon of wheeling and dealing, huh? Wes really has you all worked up."

"Yeah, he's really hot for this property. Talked my goddamn ear off all afternoon. Sorry, babe." I can't remember being more thirsty.

"Hmm." Her eyes seem to be staring through to the back of my skull.

"What's that?" *Calm the fuck down, man. Breathe.*

"Oh, nothing."

Something. Definitely a very big something. "You seem like you're think—"

"It just . . ." The pause stretches out for an unbearably long time. "Doesn't strike me as his style. Wes always seems so calm and collected."

75

Fuck. "I know, it's strange. He's not usually like this. But this property really seems unreal." I do my best to hold her stare, in spite of the fact that my eyes are burning terribly. I want nothing more than to blink. "But, you know, it's usually with the customers that he maintains his cool. He can get a little revved up behind closed doors." *You're overselling. Stop blathering, you fucking dummy. You're going to blow everything. Stop. Talking.* "Yeah."

"Huh." She seems to consider this. "I see."

As the afternoon faded into evening, I was finally able to get my head on straight enough to relax into what I felt to be some sense of normalcy, or at least the appearance of it. By this point, I had texted Wes to let him know that I needed a well-timed phone call during dinner prep. As I had volunteered to handle cooking duties that night, I figured that I could leave my phone on the counter while I had my hands full, allowing Rebecca to see Wes's name come up on the screen when the call came in. The timing worked out beautifully, and for a moment I thought I was in the clear.

Then the next wave of texts came in.

Paul, you really looked happy today. I'm happy for you. No hard feelings, okay?

I really do have fond memories of us. Let's just leave things where they are.

Let's let sleeping dogs lie, you lying dog. Enjoy your sleep, with your wife this time.

I didn't remember tasting a single bite of the food I'd prepared that evening. There was a rage seething behind my eyes that rendered all other senses moot. I did my best to entertain Rebecca's questions about the property that Wes had supposedly pitched me earlier in the day, but I was so distracted that the best I could do was to cobble together a template based on features from other houses I had sold. I was too deep inside my own head to notice if Rebecca actually bought into the yarn I was spinning.

The next thing I remember was the sex. There was a hunger to the fucking that I hadn't experienced with my wife in ages. Suddenly, I was present again. She bit my earlobe as she coaxed me out of my pants and began working me with her hand. What followed was a tidal pull of raw, animal passion. I remember unleashing on her ferociously, as if I could exorcise my mistress by conquering my wife. I remember being terrified at catching myself and realizing how thoroughly I had given over to reckless abandon. But the thing that I remember the clearest—the thing that terrified me most of all—was that look in Rebecca's eye; the look that encouraged me, that spurred me on, that delighted in the pain and the savagery and the madness of it all. I swear that in that moment I picked up on a flash of pure hatred lurking in her eyes, and I had no idea whom it was directed at.

That night, she slept like the dead.

When I was sure she was under, I swiped my phone from the night-stand and slunk out of our bedroom and into the hallway. I was ripe with the scent of sex, keyed up, and half-crazed. I should have left well enough alone, but I gave in.

Noticed you weren't wearing your ring earlier. He finally left your crazy ass, huh?

As soon as I hit SEND my adrenaline spiked. I felt nauseous and light-headed. I had to lean against the wall to balance myself. I waited for what felt like hours for her response.

Why are you so sure that HE left ME?

◆

THE NEXT MORNING, I was the first one up. I slipped out of bed and headed downstairs to put on a pot of coffee. I let Duff out and filled his food and water dishes. I found my phone and read the waiting text from Wes asking if things had shaken out okay the night before. After respond-ing, I plugged the phone into the adapter to charge the dwindling battery before I let Duff back in. He darted right for the bowl and I took that as my cue to get going on the pile of unwashed dishes from the night before.

As I scoured the pans and set them in the drying rack, my mind began to wander back to the events of the previous evening. Images fuzzed in and out of my head like a hastily edited highlight reel. Just as I was zoning out, the vibration of the phone against the countertop snapped me back into the room. I reached for it, anticipating a response from Wes. What I got instead jolted me completely out of the remnants of my daydream.

A slew of images came through from Sheila's new number. After a moment of hesitation, I opened the texts to find photos that she had taken when we were together. There were photos of me at the beach with the dogs, a shot of the dogs running around together in her yard, and a plausibly innocent selfie of her with me in the background.

The one that caught my attention, however, was a shot I hadn't realized she had taken. It was in her home, post-sex, and it was an image of me walking to the bathroom, naked. My face was obscured, thank fuck, but I certainly recognized my own build. As my eyes took in the photo, my breath caught in my throat. My gaze reflexively darted toward the staircase, to make sure that Rebecca hadn't come down the stairs at what would have been a very inopportune moment.

My brain began racing. *What does this crazy bitch want from me? Why the photos, why now? She's been sitting on them. He's out of the picture. Maybe seeing us sent her off the deep end. Christ, how far down the drain has she gone? And how much is she willing to pull down with her?*

As I was working through all of the permutations, my phone vibrated again. I opened a single text message from her, the last one I would receive, before she fell eerily silent.

You've made your bed.

◆

I'M A REASONABLE PERSON. I find that most people are. But want to make a reasonable person behave irrationally? Just impose irrationality upon them, and your work is done. Certain chains of events, once put into motion, are nearly impossible to stop. And there are boundaries that, once violated, serve to strip away any expectation of protection for the violator.

The way I see it, Rebecca never really had a choice.

eleven

Before

THE BEGINNING of us was one of the happiest times of my life. We belonged to each other.

For my first birthday that we were together, he'd brought me to a sweet little garden in Sagaponack for a picnic a few months into our affair. The garden was deserted, since it was the middle of the day during a workweek. On a blanket under the shady curtain of a massive willow, we sat close and watched the birds move to and fro on the grass as we sipped bourbon from a plaid thermos. We didn't talk and I leaned hard into him and let the silent heat between us build until we couldn't resist anymore. We made love, the smell of flowers and spring surrounding us. The feeling like we were the only two people in the world was intoxicating.

As we were leaving, I caught the name of the garden—Madoo—on a plaque near the entrance.

"Madoo—'my dove'—sweet."

"*You* are sweet." He pulled me up against him from behind and wrapped his arms around me.

"Did you know that doves mate for life?" I kept reading as he was breathing into my neck and every inch of my body awoke. "I always thought they were just better-looking pigeons."

"You are my beautiful dove. My Madoo."

I blushed. I was not used to him being so romantic. I liked it. He turned me around. All of my happiness was showing in his face like a mirror.

"I love you, Madoo." It was the first time he said it.

"I love you too. Always."

◆

SO MANY YEARS LATER, he still used the nickname, but it was out of habit, not affection. We'd experienced the natural ebbs and flows of a long-term relationship leading up to Paul's unemployment, but that occurrence had marked a major shift that didn't seem like something we could come back from. We didn't speak about the distance between us. We just lived with it, silently hoping it would leave as quietly as it had arrived. And it did, sort of.

After Paul went to work with Wes, and his fog of unhappiness began to recede, so did my resentment. The more he returned to a work schedule, the less hard on him I became. We both relaxed into the possibility of things returning to how we'd been before the economy tanked. With money starting to flow again from his side, his confidence and attention reemerged. One memorable night, he glided into the house after making his first six-figure commission as if he was on a parade float. "There's my dove." He smiled at me like I was something very delicious and forbidden he wanted to devour. I was still getting adjusted to this version of Paul, after having the depressed, unkempt edition around for so long, but I was open to him for the first time in the two years since his business had shuttered.

He sat on the couch and watched me as I moved around the kitchen, conscious of his staring. I wasn't minding it, just nervous from his focus. It was good to feel something other than distraction coming from his direction.

"Madoo." It was more command than statement. I shot him a look. "Come here." He patted the couch next to him.

I hesitated. I'd been turning away long enough that it had become reflexive. I went to him. I sat next to him for a moment before he pulled me closer.

"I miss you." He kissed me deeply. Funny how unfamiliar a kiss from your husband can feel after so many familiar ones.

"Where did you go?"

"I don't know. Not far, though." He paused. "You left too."

"I know."

"No more. Me and you."

"Always."

We fell into step together, and in love again. We started making love again at the pace of hormonal teenagers. I vowed to myself to stop taking so many pills, and eventually stop them altogether. I didn't want to be numb anymore. I wanted to be present and with him. I was able to act the part, but the chemicals interrupted my body's previous responses to his touch. My libido was undeniably affected by the opioids, but I didn't let on that anything was wrong. Our bed became a sanctuary. It felt so good to fall into each other that I willfully suppressed the irking feeling that something was still off beyond my own physical muteness. Looking back, we were seeking comfort in the other and masking a larger rift, but the immediate gratification of Paul wanting me again was all-consuming.

He became protective. His newfound attention to my well-being opened up a softer side. In the mornings he'd walk me to my car, open the door, and watch me drive away. He texted me throughout the day to see how I was doing. He sent romantic emails reminding me of how much he loved me. And if he beat me home in the evenings, he'd greet me at the door, looking happy and relieved, as if part of him expected that I might not return home that day. He began holding my hand when we were out.

I liked it. He pulled me into him for long hugs out of the blue, and held my face in his hands when he kissed me. I'd catch him looking at me pensively and then he'd deny he'd been doing it. There was a sea of unsaid things, but it added to the excitement. I liked being his mystery. He became mine too.

Now I realize that he was really just protecting himself.

◆

YOU WANT TO BELIEVE you had the intuition to see the unseen, that you saw the tide quietly recede before the wave swelled and crashed so powerfully, obliterating everything in its path.

With the return of our connection came a quiet psychic disconnect that I couldn't put my finger on. Even in bed, where our return felt the strongest, I sensed it. Burrowed down deep, a jagged glass pea poked at me.

There was a day, a few weeks after the return of the old Paul, before everything ripped apart so violently, when I woke up uneasy. Paul's snoring body was next to mine after a particularly athletic romp. I'd said to myself and then out loud, "The bed feels different." He'd murmured, "Love you too," and rolled over.

I suppose I knew. I just made the choice to ignore until the choice was made for me.

After

Without Duff or Paul, the walls around me feel like someone else's. To the extent that I'm not feeling like myself today, they might as well be. The anger about Paul's betrayals has started to wane, and a thick fog of depression has rolled in. I fight the call of our bed, the imagined relief of crawling under the blankets and giving up. It's not lost on me that this is how Paul must have felt when his business failed.

I sit at the kitchen table breathlessly staring at the open door, sweat rolling down the back of my tank top. The sound of the TV is playing low in the next room, but I can't recall turning it on. I've been running around the house for what feels like hours, although time has barely passed. Knowing that stopping too long will result in complete motivational atrophy, I stand up and start to pace. I blindly reach for my rings out of habit.

I try to replace worry about Duff with my will to punish Paul. Taking our dog from him was on my short list of ways to take his life apart when I was at my most irrational, piece by valuable piece, but having no recollection of what exactly I've done weighs heavily. I would never actually hurt Duff. But I'm stricken by uncertainty.

Now my imagination cycles through any number of terrible fates, and I suppress a cry from deep within. Worry is not an emotion I've given a lot of power to in my life, but I am overcome with anxiety about so many things now. I should be looking for our dog. I should be looking for my ring. I should be calling Paul. I can only focus on finding pills. For just a moment I consider how out of control my habit has gotten if this is how I really feel. I file the thought away to be dealt with later, after I'm chemically well stocked again and have the luxury of self-reflection.

It takes about eight hours for opiate withdrawal to kick in, and the countdown since my last dose is around six hours before things start to feel dicey. Paranoia, hallucinations, and disorientation already feel like they are rolling in. Things won't get debilitating until tomorrow, but the only other time I've undergone the painful process was like getting food poisoning in the midst of having the flu. And that was just the physical withdrawal.

After I've searched every one of my hiding places inside, I decide turning over the contents of my car is the most promising option and find not one errant pill on the floor or in the seats. This is getting desperate. I can't reach out to Mark. Not while Sasha is MIA.

I know what I need to do, as much as I don't want to face the outside world. I check to make sure my gym clothes and spin shoes are still in the back seat where I threw them two days ago. A lifetime ago.

I barely have the key in the ignition when I hear barking. In the rearview, I see Duff bounding toward our house. A flash of a figure disappears around the corner and out of sight before I can get a good look. I move closer to the street and fall to my knees on the grass as he leaps into my arms and knocks me over. I am panting as hard as Duff is, and I laugh and cry with relief into his fur, both of our hearts racing.

twelve

Before

AT SOME POINT, our pasts come looking for us.

I should have handled things differently. I can see that now. Then again, it's always hard to tell how a different handling of any one thing might affect the overall outcome. Nothing more than educated guesswork, really. Still, I could probably have done more to quell the fire. Or at least not actively fan the flames. I probably should have blocked Sheila's new number. But, if I'm being honest, it fed my ego and turned me on a little. I was intrigued by just how far she was willing to go. At least I was at first.

While the texts that I received just after the run-in were unnerving in the moment, I came to regard them differently as time passed. It was obvious that she was in a tough spot. She'd lost me, and who knew what the fuck had come of that marriage of hers. She lashed out immediately after what must have been a huge blow for her, seeing my wife and me hand in hand and contented. And I could understand how she felt. What she and I had was so visceral and raw that of course she would react strongly after she blew it up. So, by a week or so after that first round of texts, the whole thing had moved into the back of my mind.

Then she upped the ante.

I'll never forget the feeling of opening that photo on my phone. In the picture, Rebecca and I are sitting together at an outdoor table at the café where we would often laze over lunch on the weekends, drinking coffee and reading the paper together. We're holding hands across the table and laughing. That waitress with the phenomenal rack is waiting on the couple sitting next to us. Rebecca and I look as if we're having a genuinely nice moment in each other's company. But the context of the image gives it a sinister sheen. I realize immediately that the picture must have been taken months before the run-in, on account of the warm weather, which means that my shunned mistress, far from having accidently happened upon us in the street, had been surveilling us for who knows how long. My head was still wrapping itself around the implications of this when a text followed:

Want more?

The surge of adrenaline coupled with the feeling of violation at having this clearly unstable woman stalking my wife and me was enough to enrage me. I should have taken a breath and composed myself instead of firing off the text that I sent:

I will fucking end you.

I didn't hear anything back from Sheila after that. At first, I was keyed up with anticipation, waiting on her next move in whatever fucked-up chess game she thought we were playing. But the text never came. For days and days, nothing. I finally deluded myself into thinking that my message had terrified her into silence.

I should have come clean. I should have fessed up to my wife before things went where they went. But I was scared. The balance in our marriage was at an ideal point, and I didn't think I could risk upsetting that dynamic. I was concerned about her safety, of course, but that just pushed me to keep a more vigilant eye on her whenever I could be at home and present. The more of that I did, the closer we seemed to come together. And I started to fall hard for this new component of our relationship, which made the thought of ever coming clean to her nearly impossible.

And so it goes. Small things have a way of snowballing beyond reasonable measure, until the scale is so daunting as to render them no longer addressable. I could have put my wife's safety above my own pathological need to be the good guy. I could have admitted everything, told her how sorry I was, what a mistake the affair had been and how much it clarified for me the depth of my feelings for her. I could have tried to explain to her that my transgression had served to remind me of what was really important, and how I hoped she would realize how it had ultimately brought us closer together. I could have done any number of things differently. But things happen the way they happen. And in the end, it wasn't left up to me.

thirteen

REBECCA

Before

MY BIKE WAS always number six. Sasha's was number five. Always the front row.

When Paul got depressed, I started leaving the house earlier and earlier in the mornings, aimlessly driving around until my office opened. He didn't ask me where I was going, only brought up how much the charges on the gas card had increased. I didn't bother to lie about where I was spending my mornings because he didn't care, and I didn't have an imagined destination. Until I overheard Sasha telling one of the new pharma reps in the bathroom at our Rep of the Year dinner that she got all of her good pills at spin class. Suddenly I had a purpose on my restless mornings. And I was hell-bent on getting to know more about Paul's old girlfriend.

It was a place to click into the pedals and be restrained physically while becoming completely unrestrained emotionally. I started going every day, sometimes twice a day if I needed it. I spent thousands of hours and dollars whittling away the soft physical and emotional parts of me that I had always hated about myself.

It got to the point where I couldn't get through my day without wanting to murder someone if I didn't have that time to unleash. There was the bike high, which I came to need as much as the chemical high.

When I started spinning, I was only taking the pain pills that were prescribed to me—granted, sometimes from multiple doctors. And only Percocets. I had rules. Like me, Sasha liked to prescribe in her head which meds people could take to improve their flawed personalities. She knew me as Paul's wife but hadn't ever really paid me any mind. It took two months of going to the same classes as her religiously before she acknowledged that we knew each other. We were in the locker room and a particularly neurotic regular was having a meltdown waiting for the shower.

"I just don't understand how they could accept *that* child into a supposedly top-level private school when it is common knowledge what a little sociopath he is. And his *mother,* what a train wreck she is. The whole incident is making me rethink if I even want my Christina to be there. God, it is just *so* stressful, I cannot *even.*"

Sasha turned to me and whispered conspiratorially, "Someone could use some Xanax. Too bad I'm so attached to mine."

I'd been surprised that she'd spoken to me directly, and gone temporarily blank but recovered quickly. "Me too, although I think she'd need something far stronger than what you and I have."

She'd laughed and nodded. "You're Paul's wife, aren't you?" We'd sat at the same fucking table and she acted like it was the first time she was laying eyes on me.

"Yes. And I work with your husband." I was all smiles.

"How lucky for you." I couldn't tell if she was referring to my being Paul's wife or working for her husband. I was just glad she'd finally acknowledged me.

"You went to high school with Paul, didn't you?" I absolutely knew she had; Paul liked to drop it into conversation when the subject of Mark came up.

"That was *so* long ago. He had such puppy love for me." I'd heard Paul talk about Sasha as though they'd been on the verge of marrying out of high school if it hadn't been for some college guy swooping in and stealing her.

Each class after, she would return my greetings of "hello" and "how are you" until we got to the point of actual conversations. Usually they revolved around her while she was primping in the mirror for ladies' happy hour, which I never managed to get an invite to.

It was like high school all over again. I was used to being on the outside, something that had become hardwired in me from never really being a part of any of the families I lived with growing up, or never staying in schools long enough to grow any social roots. But that part of myself that was accustomed to being excluded, even subtly, never stopped me from wanting to be included. Even if it meant enduring Sasha's mean streak. She must have picked up on my sensitivity surrounding her and Paul's history, because it became a regular topic of mention in the locker room and endlessly amused her.

"Did you guys know that Rebecca's husband and I went to junior prom together? We were so nervous about losing our virginity. He cried. It was adorable."

"I'm so glad you and Paul found each other. I was worried he was never going to get over me, he was so destroyed when I broke up with him. The things he used to do to try and win me back."

"Does Paul still sing in the shower? He always thought he had such a good voice. He was always singing our song, 'Brown Eyed Girl,' though he was no Van Morrison, that is for sure."

I always laughed and played along, but Sasha knew it bothered me. I hated that she brought out a jealous side of me.

It was Sasha who introduced me to amphetamines. She fancied herself a kind of self-taught pharmaceutical savant but complained that Mark didn't give her whatever she wanted even though he had access. I had something she wanted. I had names of doctors I'd gotten to know through repping over the years who were liberal when it came to writing scrips for controlled substances. These were the old-timers, who'd come up on prescribing Valium like it was a cure for being a woman. I gave her referrals and she handed off some of her bounty when she felt like it. But we were hardly the only ones trading in mood enhancers.

The pill trades happened in the locker room. No one was obvious, but no one suspected well-heeled upper-class white women anyway. You had to know how to spot the like-minded women and strike up the right conversation.

"Oh my God, I am so distracted at work. Is it me or can you not get anything done?"

"I have to go to my mother-in-law's house this weekend and I could pull my face off. I'm fresh out of Xanax, can you believe it?!"

"I think I'm totally immune to coffee now; I'm still dragging. I swear I'm going to have to take up Ritalin!"

"My husband is cheating on me with the babysitter. The only thing that is keeping me from murdering them both is Ativan and chardonnay."

It was surprisingly easy to find empathetic traders. There was Adderall for Ativan. Oxy for Xanax. Percocet for fentanyl. Everyone had Ambien. Someone even still had fen-phen in the mix, for the hardcore who were more fearful of weight gain than heart failure.

I started to see what Paul found so fascinating about Sasha. She had an undeniable star quality that made everyone want to look at her. She'd walk into the studio and get as much attention as the instructors. She was easy to watch, not aware of the people around her and noticing little else outside herself in the mirrored walls opposite her bike. She was a spotlit blond bird of paradise, perched atop the bike, tapping back, tits and heart forward. Always in perfect time to the music, her arms and shoulders ropy and sharp. I hated her and yet I couldn't stop obsessing about her.

The whole time I was watching Sasha, I had no idea someone was doing the same to me.

After

When I enter the Lotus Pedal studio, one of the girls at the check-in desk hands me a votive candle with Sasha's name and bike number, 5, written on it in metallic Sharpie. She's wearing a shirt that I see on the wall with a "$47" sign next to it. The words "Missing You" are emblazoned on the front in silver script, and "Like Crazy" with the number 5 is on the back. Familiar women are milling around buying shirts and cradling votives, with somber but suppressed looks of excitement on their faces.

A remix of Everything but the Girl's "Missing" blares from the speakers as I work my way through a throng of frozen foreheads and strappy sports bras, swimming against the tide in the direction of the locker room as it empties out. Every color of hair is pulled into ponytails and buns—the few men included. I mutter to a straggler that I've got to pee as I head down the stairs to the lockers and bathrooms. I slide into the now empty hallway and do my best with the chintzy combination locks. I can only do one or two; otherwise, I'll look suspicious on the cameras. It takes mere minutes and I've got what I came for.

I'm the last one in except for the instructor, who is waiting to make her entrance. The studio is nearly full, with every bike occupied except for the bikes to the left and the right of mine. Sasha's bike is expectedly vacant. Someone has placed a lit votive on the seat, the small flame alive from the blast of AC above.

Madeline, Sasha's favorite teacher, sashays in, all hair and six-pack abs, and hops up to the stage, arms above her head, goading us to hoot and holler. The song ends, and a club version of Pink Floyd's "Wish You Were Here" blasts. People cheer.

Madeline lowers the lights, and the votives dot the floor of the studio all around us, like the night sky below. Sheila's empty bike is a surprise. I know she won't appear, but someone new had been riding on number seven since she stopped coming, and I'm surprised no one has claimed the prime spot.

I clip in. The absence of riders to my left and right leaves me feeling exposed. I sense eyes on me. The women behind me lean into each other on their bikes.

"Which is the missing one again?" a woman in a bike-riding Buddha tank top asks her friend. I don't tell them that technically, both women are missing. But only one seems to have left a hole.

"I think the skinny blond one with the Madonna arms." The cycling Buddha girl nods. As if her friend hasn't described nearly every woman in the front row, with the exception of me.

The music changes, signifying the start of class, and Madeline climbs atop the bike facing us and closes her eyes while the first few strains of Beck's "Missing" come on. She frowns at Sheila's empty bike and invites the woman behind it to move up front, anointing her. Her friend lets out a string of "Woo-hoos!" She clips in, tears in her eyes, and smiles hugely.

"All right, you beautiful soldiers of love and truth. Breathe. I want you to lead with your left foot and run this one with your eyes closed and your hearts open. Turn that resistance up high, because life ain't easy and change only happens if you ride through the hard parts as hard as you fucking can to get to the other side.

"Tonight we ride for one of our fellow warriors of light and beauty. She is missing in the great unknown and we need to call her back to the pack." I fight the urge to roll my eyes.

She turns the volume all the way up and the entire class falls into time together on a one-two beat, sixty pairs of eyes closed, heads swaying to the music, including Madeline's. I keep my eyes open and watch myself in the mirror. My face is without expression and my eyes look dead.

I should be feeling something about Sasha's disappearance. And I do, but not the right things. I'm glad she's gone. I'm glad Sheila's gone too. I realize I'm a little stoned from the Ativan I've stolen from locker number twelve when my legs slow down. Reflexively, I put my hand on the pocket of my Lycra hoodie and feel comforted by the weight of the Percocet bottle I lifted from locker eight.

How much can I really trust what Paul's told the police about his interactions with Sasha recently? Just about as much as I can trust anything he has said to me in the past. The repeated realization that I should have known better triggers a new level of outrage. My legs speed up again, propelled by the anger and the bass.

My anger is so big now I feel like I can't contain it. I shut my eyes tight and try to will the memories away, but they persist. So many images flood in, I pedal faster and harder to escape them but fail. The velocity pushes me headfirst into that night twenty-nine years ago.

I am pushing the closet door open after the yelling stopped and the sound of thunder gave way to silence. I'm standing over my mother's lifeless body and trying to make sense of what I'm seeing. The song changes and so do the images. A fractured image and the sound of my father calling to me and reaching out for help. A stream of blood running down the side of his face from the corner of his mouth. His strangled voice saying my name. Like always, I try to shut the memory down before I make that short walk to his outstretched hand. I try to make myself run away every time. The image changes from my parents' bedroom to ours. She is sitting on the chair watching us and waiting. My heart is beating so hard that I think I might be in cardiac arrest. I slow the bike and shakily unclip before I dismount, knocking over several candles on my way. I feel all of them watching me, their judgmental eyes following me as I bolt. The Percocet is in my mouth before the door shuts behind me.

I can't get her face out of my mind in the dark. I need to run from her.

Before

She came in the middle of the night. When I opened my eyes, she was watching us.

She was sitting in the nest chair under the window, slowly petting Duff. Her eyes wild and her body calm. She was unmoving, aside from the wave of motion running from her shoulder through her fingers. Duff was content, tongue hanging out. Evidently, they were old friends.

Part of me knew exactly who she was and why she'd come. And then I recognized her. Bike number seven. She was in our house, sitting in our room. I didn't understand why, but I knew enough to be afraid.

As my eyes adjusted to the half-light, Paul snored softly next to me, unmoved. He was deeply unconscious. My heart banged the walls of my chest so hard I hoped it might wake him. She hadn't said a word, but it was very clear to me from the look on her face that she intended to hurt us. The gun in her lap confirmed as much.

I moved my leg under the blankets across our enormous bed to try to nudge him awake, but the distance between us was too far. Even if I had been able to reach him, he'd taken a sleeping pill. I'd been keeping him up with my restlessness.

She remained completely still, aside from her petting hand. She looked completely at home in the plush chair, one leg pulled under her, as if she'd sat in it before. She'd lit a candle and the reflection of the flame danced across her face, giving the room the effect of a séance. As my eyes adjusted, her face became more visible. I'd never really looked at her that much in class, even though her reflection had been next to mine so many times.

She had a pretty mouth and eyes like saucers, even when narrowed. She was thin and polished like a shiny new toy. Her hair was impeccably blown out and I could make out a dark lipstick color that I recognized as one I regularly wore. She wore a sleeveless dress that seemed more costume than outfit. This was a special occasion.

She spoke softly and slowly. "Do. Not. Wake. Him."

I hadn't yet figured out who she'd come to shoot. I just nodded.

"He can't have everything."

I nodded again, put one hand out and the other on the bed to sit up. She didn't protest.

"I had so much. So much. And now I have nothing. I've lost everything.

First, my husband. Then my home and friends. Then Paul. And now Molly is gone."

She started to sob quietly. I couldn't even imagine who Molly was. The woman's instability was beyond anger; every tremble of her body indicated something deeply unhinged. A storm of frenzy.

"I'm done. I can't do this any longer. I can't keep feeling this way."

I'd hoped the raised volume and emotion in her voice would snap Paul out of sleep, but I also wanted to keep her calm as she agitatedly moved her free hand to the gun's grip.

"Your husband told me that he was going to end me."

I'd let my organic facial reaction speak for me. My shock seemed to empower her.

"He doesn't get to use me and just throw me away. He doesn't get to pretend that I never existed and threaten me when I remind him. He doesn't get to have everything and get away with it."

I was hit with a burst of angry heat from the inside out. I felt like murdering Paul too. For cheating, for lying, for cheating and lying with someone so clearly unstable. For putting me in danger.

She stopped talking and began tapping her foot rapidly. Duff matched her beat with his tail. Paul didn't stir. She was a ticking bomb in our bedroom that he'd activated, and he was unconscious.

I finally spoke, carefully. "I understand. He hurt me too. Let's do it together."

My voice was surprisingly calm considering my levels of fear and rage. I'd improvised with every inch of my life.

I didn't have to see her expression in the full light of day to know she was confounded by this response. I knew I didn't have much time or a real chance of her handing the gun over to me, but I was at a major disadvantage in the weapons department and I needed to think, not panic.

And then I remembered what I'd put under the bed when Paul had gone away on a trip some months before. I reached into the space between the headboard and the mattress and behind Paul's and my pillows.

The sound was louder than I remembered from childhood. The explosion of pain in my shoulder hit me moments before the hammer in my hand made contact with her skull.

◆

THE PRESSURE OF PAUL'S hand on the T-shirt wrapped around my shoulder registered before the sound of his voice. He was repeating my name with a tight grip on my shoulder, losing against the blooming bloodstain on his shirt. The pain was threatening to bring me to my knees, but I fought to stay upright.

She was crumpled facedown on the floor to the right of the chair. Next to her was the gun that looked suspiciously like Paul's. I couldn't stop staring at the blood splatter on the span of the floor between her and me. It was hard to tell whose blood it was, there was so much.

Duff was sniffing her hair and intermittently barking and yelping. The hammer I'd hidden in arm's reach for protection in case of an intruder when Paul was away was on the floor between us. Paul guided me to sit in the chair where she'd been only minutes or hours before. My grasp on time was shaky, at best. "You lost a lot of blood. You are in shock. Hold this tightly." He pushed my hand in place of his and I winced at the momentary release of pressure and the excruciating return of it. I nodded calmly but internally was violently cycling through shock and the smoldering fury at my husband.

"Wait here." He disappeared into the darkness of our bathroom, and the sound of him rooting around beneath the sink did little to distract me from the tangle of her hair splayed on the floor. I remember thinking she had pretty hair, and I'd never really noticed it, since I'd only seen her with it pulled up in a tight bun in class.

He quickly returned and carefully removed the blood-soaked shirt, replacing it with a large swath of gauze. The searing pain of the hydrogen peroxide in and around the wound brought on a nasty kick of nausea. Paul expertly cleaned the area, and once the blood had stopped enough for him to examine it, he nodded, relieved.

"It's not too bad. The bullet just grazed you. Just a flesh wound."

He placed a clean cotton rectangle over the point of impact and wrapped the gauze bandaging securely. The pain had moved from unbearable to excruciating.

"It's my bad shoulder."

"You should probably take a painkiller." I could see the reluctance in his face when he said it. I'd managed to taper my use down substantially since he'd gone back to work, and I hesitated. But I wanted one more than anything.

When I went to retrieve the hydrocodone in the medicine cabinet, I heard him repeat "Sheila" a few times, each time louder than the one before, as if lack of volume were the reason she wasn't moving. His voice saying her name made me shudder. I unscrewed the bottle and fished out two fat pills and swallowed them dry.

I returned, bottle in hand, and stood close to him. It wasn't either of our first times seeing a dead body, but he was acting like it was his.

After a moment of suspended animation, he knelt next to her, brushing her hair away from her shoulder. The gesture of sweet intimacy and my husband's hands on another woman caused a deep heart pang until he placed his fingers on her neck clinically and seriously, void of any tenderness. He pressed and waited, stone-faced. He moved his hand away and her hair cascaded down. He stood, pale and shaken.

"She's dead."

fourteen

PAUL

After

WHAT DID SHE do? What did we do?! Fuck! Fuck-fuck-fuck-fuck-fuck!

Route 25 was still pretty clear of traffic that morning, a fact I was very thankful for, under the circumstances. But the dawn light was peeking over the horizon, taunting me. Putting me on the clock. As I squinted hard in an attempt to focus, the image of Sheila's frozen gaze looking up at me—desperately, bewilderedly—from my bedroom floor flashed violently behind my lids.

She did what she had to. We were justified. I could still go to the police and explain all of this.

The sudden friction and whirring of the wheel on the rumble strip yanked my attention back to the road. I took a deep breath and exhaled. I wiped my palms one at a time on my jeans and realigned them on the wheel. I was aware for the first time of how cold and numb they were, but I needed to keep the windows open for the fresh air. I eased on the brakes to get myself back under the limit.

Should I just go to the police? It's not too late. Fuck. Of course it is. How are you going to explain moving the body?

"Open your eyes, shit-for-brains!" The exclamation from the irate driver of the Mazda in the lane to my right was underscored by a long lean on her horn. I watched as she recovered from her swerve and flicked a cigarette butt out the window in my direction.

I've got to do this. Everything looks so bad. Rebecca was right. There's no way they'd believe how it went down. Not now. Would they? Rebecca was right, wasn't she? Of course she was. She pled. She never pleads. Of course she was right. Of course she was. It was my gun. Sheila was holding it, but it was my gun.

The next thing I knew, lights were flashing in my rearview mirror. I experienced that terrible sense of doom in the hiccup between the lights and the sound of the siren. That moment when your stomach drops and the suspicion that you're fucked is utterly confirmed. I pulled over to the shoulder of the road. The police cruiser pulled in behind me.

As I came to a stop, I heard the thud of the rolled-up tarp hitting the toolbox behind my seat. The sound prompted an awful, hollow feeling inside my gut, and I tasted bile creeping up my throat.

"License and registration, please." He looked me up and down like he wasn't sure what to make of me.

"Morning, Officer." I produced both and handed them to him. My hands were curled as if still holding on to the wheel. I had to will them into relaxation.

"Mr. Campbell. Up and at 'em early today. You didn't slip a little something extra into your coffee this morning, did you?"

"No, sir. I apologize for the erratic driving."

"Everything okay with you, Mr. Campbell?" He gave the back of the Cherokee a visual once-over.

"Well, my wife's at home, not feeling all that hot. I'm working on a contracting job, and I'm trying to get these tools over to the site and get back to the missus." I nodded in the direction of the back seat.

"Wife's under the weather, eh?"

"Afraid so, yeah. She was up all night, tossing and turning."

"A real killer." He nodded to commiserate.

"I'm sorry?" I coughed.

"This flu. It's making the rounds at my house as well." He handed back the license and registration and patted me on the shoulder. "Good luck, my friend. And please slow down."

◈

I FIRST INVESTIGATED this plot of land near Smithtown Bay a few years back when we were looking at the possibility of parceling it into smaller lots and putting up condos. We got a team together to come out and test the soil, only to learn that the land was just a little too close to the water table to get zoning approval. The extra cash burning a hole in my pocket wasn't enough to persuade the surveyor to fudge some measurements, and so the land just sat here, undeveloped. In the blur of this morning, it was the first clear thing that came into my head.

I pulled the Jeep up, parked, and stepped out onto some very solid-feeling land. *Shit.* I opened the back door, hauled out a shovel, and gave the soil a tap. No give. I got a little height on the next go, and as I brought down the blade of the shovel with more force, it ricocheted off the frozen earth, driving the handle painfully into my numb palm. *Fuck.*

I sat back in the Cherokee, rubbing my hands together and blowing on them. I looked at the digital readout on the dashboard. The sun was starting to cast long shafts of light across the frozen ground, causing the tiny ice crystals to sparkle like gemstones. *This has to work. This'll work. It's practically swamp out here. Give it a few minutes. Just give it a few; it'll give.* I looked at the dashboard clock again, then shifted into reverse and backed up a car length.

I grabbed the shovel off the ground, stepped into the space in front of the Jeep, set the blade against the earth, and brought my boot down. The impact sent a jolt up my shin. *No. Please, no, no, no.* I heard a dog bark in the distance and dropped the shovel. My hands felt disembodied, and my stomach was hovering somewhere in my throat, choking me. I fell against the side of the truck and slid down onto the hard earth. *It's all over. It's all just fucking over. I can't get under the—Wait.*

I grabbed the lip of the back-door handle and pulled myself up. I had to lean against the door to think straight. *There has to be another way.* I ran through my options, as well as I could see them. I only had the one. The sun was not on my side. Nothing was on my side. This was my play. My only play.

I tossed the shovel in the back seat, hopped in the front, and pulled off. I retraced my way to the dirt road and followed that out to a network of back roads. I used trees that I passed on the way in to find the main road. Dogs bathed in the glow of front-porch lights barked in my direction as I passed. I became convinced that I was driving in circles. Finally, I noticed the tree lines receding as I approached the highway.

It was the last place I wanted to go, but it was the only thing I could think of. I pulled back onto 25, picked up speed, and headed to Cold Spring Harbor. It wouldn't be ideal, but it would do for now, until I could take care of the situation permanently.

fifteen

REBECCA
—————

After

THE LINGERING SMELL of carbonite in our bedroom was so evocative I was transported to my eleven-year-old self, standing between my parents' bodies, my father's most prized possession, an antique .44-caliber Smith & Wesson, lying next to him, blood pooling on the beige carpet beneath his shoulders and up around his head like a crimson halo. The blood from my mother's head appeared in red tributaries around my feet on the carpet between them. The gun had been in our family since the time of outlaws and cowboys, when my ancestors had to fight for their lives in the wilds of the West, or so my father had told me a dozen or so times while my mother rolled her eyes.

He'd let me hold the gun once until she had yanked the surprisingly heavy piece from my small hands and berated him. I'd stolen away to the safety of the closet and read by flashlight until the fighting stopped. There were so many more fights to come before their last one.

After I realized that my father was still breathing and he opened his eyes and saw me, after I moved toward him and he grabbed my arm and pulled hard, after he stopped breathing finally and I moved away from his lifeless body, I watched the gun on the floor as if it were a snake waiting to strike. I lay on the pillow I'd held close to me all night since slipping out of bed and hiding, and waited. I couldn't look at their bodies. Barely breathing, I kept watch on that gun. Knowing what it had taken from me.

◈

PAUL'S PISTOL LOOKED STRIKINGLY similar to my father's. An old barrel model with a smooth walnut grip. I'd never really looked at Paul's gun for more than a few seconds, but sitting cross-legged on the floor of our bedroom and very much in shock that night, I'd inspected it closely.

I didn't know Paul owned a gun until the day we moved out of the city. He was out getting coffee and bagels with Duff while I packed the last of our possessions and happened upon the red-bandanna-wrapped gun in one of the drawers under our bed. It was wedged behind some winter blankets on his side. I knew what it was before I uncloaked it just by the density of its weight in my hand. Before I had time to examine his secret for longer than a few minutes, I heard Paul's key in the lock as he returned with breakfast, so I hastily rewrapped it and returned it to the hiding place before he entered the apartment.

I wasn't a fan of guns and had vowed never to live in another house with one. But I kept silent about finding Paul's. I did have the fleeting thought that a guy with a temper like Paul's probably shouldn't own a gun, but I filed that thought away, never to be said out loud. We were so close to starting our life together with the move to Long Island I didn't want to make any waves. Up until that discovery, I hadn't really considered what Paul might be hiding from me.

On the floor of our room my legs had become numb from sleep. I didn't know how much time had passed before he returned with a rolled-up tarp; maybe minutes, maybe hours. The stillness of Sheila's body had frozen time. I didn't know if he had gone to get the police or just walked out and away from our life altogether. But when he returned with supplies, I quickly realized things weren't going to be as easy as that.

Duff had given up on his frenetic circling and barking, and curled up by my feet, his weight and warmth a simple but powerful comfort in the post-chaos haze. My gaze laser-focused on a section of the carpet free of weapon or body. The familiar tableau before me was too overwhelming. The body on the floor, the smell of the gunpowder, the bedroom carpet imprinted by the weight of a slight female body. Hair the color of my mother's. The throbbing in my shoulder.

After he'd placed the tarp on the floor and unfurled it, he rolled her over. He looked me in the eye and then at the gun in my lap. He leaned in and took it from me gently. He exited swiftly, to his office I assumed. When he returned his face was unreadable. Yet I'd understood what we needed to do.

"I need you to help me with this." He'd spoken carefully.

"Paul, please, let's call the police." Even as I said the words, I knew that it wasn't what I wanted to do.

"Madoo, if we call the police, they are going to arrest you."

"What about self-defense? She was watching us sleep, Paul! With a gun!"

"This isn't going to add up to self-defense. She had *my* gun." He was shaky as he riffled through her purse. I couldn't begin to imagine what he was looking for.

"She broke into our home! I was trying to protect us." It took every fiber not to point out that he'd slept through the whole horrifying scene.

Paul found what he was looking for and pulled out a familiar key chain—our spare key to the front door. I couldn't compute how this had gotten into her bag.

"It wasn't breaking and entering." His gaze went to the floor as he held up the key.

I finally understood the phrase "blind with rage." "Paul, how did this woman get your fucking gun?"

"Madoo—"

"And why does she have the keys to our house?!"

His expression was shame, followed by revelation. "She stole it from my desk." He said this to himself, and with a sense of disbelief that fueled my anger. "And she must have taken the key as well. I remember when she had the opportunity. I shouldn't have left her alone." I watched it dawn on him that his explanation was also a confession, and he flinched preemptively.

"You brought her into our house?" I fleetingly imagined picking up the hammer and crushing his skull too. But his look of desperation and hopelessness quelled the thought and transitioned into panic about the body on our floor.

"Honey, I'm so sorry. I ended things because she didn't mean anything to me at all. I never thought in a million years that something like this would happen. I never thought you would kill her!"

The wind was knocked out of me; his words were like another assault. There it was. Even though he'd brought this psychotic woman into our bedroom, this was my fault. I felt myself shutting down. I was speechless. Paul took this as a cue to take control.

"We need to move her."

Sheila lay faceup between us, eyes closed and mouth slack. I could see that her beauty was less about her natural features and more about strategic hair and makeup. But even with her well-appointed war paint, the true pallor of her skin was emerging, and the blue of her lips replaced the red of her lipstick. Her rapidly fading beauty fell short of making me feel better.

On my knees, I moved to the closest corner of the tarp and her feet. I held my breath as I straightened her legs side by side and slid my hand under the edge of the thick plastic, rolling her in tandem on Paul's command. The stiffness of her body was deeply disturbing.

We were rolling her forever. With every revolution of her body over another layer, we had to pull her toward us to make room for the remaining plastic to spread, and then repeat. Working together, we bound his lover away from us and then close, away and back. I winced with every movement, sickening pain shooting through my body emanating from my shoulder. When her body was completely encased in the thick tarpaulin, Paul motioned to lift the crisp scroll in unison. She felt much heavier than her 125 pounds of skin and bones suggested she'd be. The middle section of the plastic coil started to sag as we moved from the bedroom to the hallway, so Paul and I edged closer to the center with our grip. Duff followed alongside, panting happily at the prospect of going outside. It was the first thing we'd done together as a family in as long as I could remember.

I'd felt the weight of Paul's silence as we walked from our room and through the house. It was heavier than his dead lover's body between us. He left me with her in the entryway while he checked outside to see if any late dog walkers or teenagers were about. I watched him through the window as he opened the back door of the Cherokee.

As I stood in the darkness of the hallway, Sheila barely visible through the thick plastic wrapping, I'd imagined her shallowly breathing inside the tube, not quite dead. I could almost hear it. When Paul reentered the room I was midshudder, my hand on Duff for support. Fat, silent tears edged down my cheeks and onto my chest. He'd moved to me, wrapped his arms around me, careful not to put pressure on my wound, and squeezed hard.

"We can do this. We can get through this. Just keep it together." I knew he'd never allow the tears creeping from the corners of his eyes to fully fall in front of me.

"I didn't have a choice, Paul," I'd cried. I was still furious but also exhausted and in need of comfort.

"I know. I know. You did what you had to do." His mouth had felt warm through my hair, in my ear, his tone soft and soothing. My shoulder throbbed. The hallway clock warned us that time was slipping away.

"I need to get her out of here. I need you to keep it together and clean whatever you can. We'll burn the bloody clothes. Don't bother with the carpet; I'll need to rip it up when I get back. And don't take any more pills. I need you to stay sharp." His comment reignited a fresh wave of anger, but

I kept control. I was more concerned about taking a painkiller than I was about fighting him.

He propped the door open while I pulled Duff into the bathroom and closed him in. Paul gestured for me to grab the other side of Sheila. As we moved toward the Jeep, the air around us was crisp and fresh in the waning darkness.

Headfirst, she'd slid in easily.

"Where are you going to take her?" The shock was wearing off along with the last dose of opioids. I was desperate for Paul to get on the road, mostly so that I could take another Oxy. How quickly I was already sliding back into my old ways.

His face had drawn into seriousness. "The less you know, the better."

❖

WHEN I RETURNED to our bedroom I sat in silence and stillness for a long time. Eventually, I saw the bullet hole in the molding on the wall next to our bed. Beside it on the floor was his phone. It must have fallen out of his pocket when we were moving her.

Without hesitation I entered his passcode—the date of our anniversary, 0919—and opened his texts right away. With everything that had happened, it seemed silly to be looking for anything else. But I couldn't stop looking. I couldn't turn away. I wanted to understand. I longed for the beginning of the story.

It took me a while to find their exchanges. He'd stupidly held on to the texts instead of deleting them. He'd put her under "dog walker" instead of her name. It was easy to tell that it was Sheila, mostly from her naked selfies. My entire body was locked as I scrolled from the beginning of their flirting to just a few days ago. The full cycle, from seduction to sex to ending.

She'd refused to just go away.

sixteen

PAUL

After

I BIDED MY TIME. Each day, I woke from a restless sleep to an empty bed. Rebecca had been getting up and leaving the house early to hit spin class before work, and her absence first thing in the morning allowed for a small feeling of relief. I didn't want to involve her any further than was necessary, and I was afraid she'd sense my anxiety at the loose end dangling over our heads.

I got out of bed and checked the weather. The frost on the ground continued to taunt me. I made coffee and paced. The forecast each day was frustratingly consistent. Not a warm spell in sight. And winter wasn't exactly a hot time to show real estate, so I had nothing to take my mind off the problem.

Then one day, about two weeks after the incident, the weather broke. A warm front was scheduled to pass through the Northeast. This would give me the chance to take care of the situation before I drove myself completely nuts.

On that Tuesday, it warmed up as promised. I forced myself to be patient for the next couple of days, to let nature do its work. When I went to bed that Thursday night, I reviewed a mental checklist of the tools in the back of my Jeep. I didn't bother to offer Rebecca an explanation of where I'd be in the morning.

In the middle of the night, I slunk out of bed and out of the house. I made the drive out to Cold Spring Harbor, where I pulled onto our property. I parked the Cherokee so that the headlights were aimed toward the concrete staircase to the cellar. I left the engine idling, got out, and opened the hatchback. I approached the raw foundation of what I had promised my wife would one day be our home, and descended the stairs.

It was still cold in the basement, and the smell I'd prepared myself for didn't hit my nostrils as hard as I'd expected. I moved the bags of concrete mix to the side and rolled the tarp away from the wall. I crouched down and worked my arms underneath, reminding myself to lift with my legs. As I brought the tarp up off the ground, the feeling of taut, sinewy arm and leg muscle draped against my chest and forearms was sickeningly familiar. I got the tarp into the Jeep and headed back toward Smithtown Bay.

This time, I didn't have to race the sun. I got out to the clearing under full cover of darkness, killed the headlights, and let the engine idle for a good fifteen minutes. I pulled back a car length, cut the engine, and got out. I retrieved my tools from the back and got to work on the earth in front of the Cherokee.

The soil only gave so much against the blade of the shovel, so I switched over to the pickaxe. The ground began to break up nicely, and I got into a good groove. After a while, I felt the burn of taxed muscle in my arms and back, but I could tell that the adrenaline was helping to dull the pain. I had made about three feet of headway into the ground when a connected downswing caused a wave of pain to radiate from my wrists to my shoulders. I realized I'd hit frozen ground. I switched back over to the shovel to clear out the loose dirt and investigate the icy layer. I soon realized that my tools would help me no further. This was as good as things were going to get.

I attempted to lift the tarp out of the back of the Jeep, only to drop it immediately to the ground. My arms were fatigued to the point where I ended up having to roll the tarp around to the hole and kick it in. I filled the hole back in and smoothed it over with the flat side of the shovel head. I dropped the tools in the back of the Jeep and got inside. I flipped the headlights on as I keyed the engine, streaming light over what looked like untouched land in front of me. I let out a long exhale and dropped the transmission into drive.

I pulled off the lot and got back on the dirt road heading toward home, where I took a long, hot shower, desperate to wash all of this off of us.

seventeen

REBECCA

After

EVEN AFTER PAUL had taken her away, it felt like she was still in our house. The weeks passed slowly. I resumed my increased self-medicating. March approached April with the fog of what we'd done hanging low, but we made every effort to get back to normal. We returned to some semblance of our lives because there wasn't anything else to do. My shoulder continued to hurt to such a degree that my recreational pill supply depleted twice as quickly. I reached a point of desperation I hadn't yet experienced in myself and it started to worry me. I actually needed the painkillers for my shoulder but didn't dare go to a doctor for fear of exposing the bullet wound and drawing any probing questions or worse.

I kept going to Lotus Pedal before work to keep up my normal routine. Sheila's bike was now inhabited by some other nameless woman with taut arms and resting bitch face. The rides were getting harder the fewer pills I had.

Around the second week, I got desperate and borrowed some sample fentanyl patches from work, stored in a fairly easy to break into closet. The dosage of each patch is five times higher than the Oxys and Percocets I'd been self-prescribing, so I cut them into quarters to begin with. My tolerance was high and I graduated to halves after a couple of days. Pretty soon I was wearing an entire patch with only two left and no contingency plan to support my now fully cultivated dependency. But the patches had side effects that made it hard to discern what was actually happening and what was just chemical paranoia. My subconscious wouldn't let me forget what we had done. What he had done.

First it was just small things. A lot of stuff would go missing and inanimate objects appeared to have moved from one room to the next. I could easily write those off as being high and losing time. But then there were the hammers.

The first one was left on the hood of my car, leaned against the windshield. I told myself that someone had left it there accidentally. The second one turned up in the freezer between the Häagen-Dazs and the frozen burritos. The next turned up on Paul's side of the bed one of the nights he was out late. The last one I literally tripped on when I was walking in the backyard to add water to Duff's bowl in the shade. The handle edge of the hammer was sticking out of the soil and unidentifiable until I'd unearthed it.

I didn't tell Paul about any of the hammers, because I thought I was crazy. I asked him to leave the gun for me to have on hand when I was alone in the house. He'd become angry and yelled that he'd gotten rid of it for our safety.

We'd agreed to keep things as status quo as possible, and I didn't want to set him off or raise suspicion about my mental well-being or increasing pill use. In the weeks following Sheila, we mimed the gestures of an affectionate, happily married couple. But the quiet distrust sat deeply in me. I'd learned that Paul was capable of cheating on me, with an unstable woman in my immediate orbit no less, and I couldn't unlearn that fact. And he'd learned that I was capable of taking someone else's life. For as long a marriage as ours was, we were learning a lot of new things about each other. It never occurred to me at the time that he might be the one leaving the hammers.

Paul was cagey and on edge for weeks, until he came home from an early morning showing happier and more relaxed than I'd seen him in a long time. He climbed into bed with me after his shower and pulled at my nightgown frantically. We tried to assume the positions of a passionate, intimate couple. We held each other, made eye contact, said soothing, loving things. The harder we tried the less hard he became. He was frustrated and angry, and silently, I was as well. With a surrendering sigh we rolled away from each other and breathed in tandem. The silent questions hung in the air. Would we ever be able to get back to where we'd been before her? Would we get away with it?

Duff alerted us to their presence before the doorbell rang.

part two

eighteen

PAUL

Now

DUFF ALERTS US to their presence before the doorbell rings.

"Got someone to pinch-hit for me?" I ask Rebecca. I'm trying to keep things light in spite of our mutual frustration, but the joke falls flat.

She keeps her back to me but reaches behind to pat my thigh. "It's okay, babe."

I roll out of bed and pull on a pair of gym shorts and a T-shirt. As I head down the stairs, the aroma of the freshly brewed pot of coffee in the kitchen hits my nostrils. Duff stands guard by the doorway, barking. I approach the front door and scratch his ears as I open it.

"Mr. Campbell?" asks the taller and slimmer of a pair of men standing on my front porch. I immediately know they're cops, even before I notice the gray Crown Vic parked in my driveway. I do my best to maintain an air of nonchalance.

"Yes, Paul Campbell. May I help you gentlemen?"

"I'm Detective Wolcott." Tall-and-Slim wears a three-piece suit. The vest makes him look like an aspiring college professor. "This is my partner,

Detective Silvestri." Silvestri reminds me of a slightly better dressed and groomed Serpico. I can only imagine what sort of good cop, bad cop routine these guys roll out. "Mr. Campbell, is your wife at home?"

Shit. "Yes. Come in, come in. This is Duff. Don't mind him. Perfectly friendly." I step back through the doorway and stretch my arm toward the kitchen. The dog's tail smacks against the open door as he greets our guests. "I'm afraid she's just waking up. Can I offer you a cup of coffee while I roust her?"

"Is that a cop joke, Mr. Campbell?" Silvestri holds the stern expression for long enough that I can't tell if he's actually offended.

"Just brewed a fresh pot is all. Going to pour myself a cup as well."

"Just kidding, Mr. Campbell," says Silvestri as his mouth curls into a slim grin. "My partner here tells me that he can never tell when I'm kidding."

"Bone-dry sense of humor with this one," says Wolcott, nodding toward his partner as he pets Duff. "Also, a tea drinker. Myself, I'd love a coffee, black. And thank you."

"Of course." I lead them into the kitchen and approach the cabinet as Duff follows on Silvestri's heels. I retrieve three mugs from the shelf and begin to pour the coffee. My body is turned toward the island in such a way that neither of these fucks can see me gripping the edge of the countertop with my nonpouring hand. I manage to fill the mugs steadily and hand one to Wolcott.

"Thank you kindly."

"Of course. Now let me go grab my—"

"Good morning?" Rebecca walks into the kitchen dressed in her most modest nightgown and stops to assess our guests. I hand her one of the mugs. I pray she'll be able to hold it together for this. She's been shaky and erratic lately, pushing it a bit with the painkillers.

"Mrs. Campbell, I'm Detective Wolcott and this is my partner, Detective Silvestri."

"Ma'am." Silvestri nods.

"Ma'am? Goodness, you *have* caught me a bit early this morning. Or maybe you just need a cup of this. Paul, did you offer Detective—"

"He's a tea drinker, babe."

"Well, Detective, can we offer you a cup of tea, then?"

"No, thank you, ma— . . . Mrs. Campbell. I'm just fine."

"Well, what *can* we help you with this morning?"

"We understand that you work out at the Lotus Pedal studio in town?"

"I do, yes. Everything okay?"

Wolcott pulls a small photo from the breast pocket of his jacket. "One of the studio members seems to have gone missing, and we're just asking around to see if anyone might have noticed anything." He holds the photo out for Rebecca. "Does this woman look familiar?"

I watch as a look of alarm takes shape on my wife's face. "Babe." She looks at me, surprised. "It's Sasha."

I feel my shoulders drop. "Sasha?"

Wolcott looks from my wife to me. "You know Mrs. Anders as well?"

"I work for her husband," says Rebecca. "Mark and Sasha are, well, friends."

"That sounded more like a question than an answer," remarks Wolcott.

"Sasha and I went to high school together," I say. Out of the corner of my eye, I see Rebecca wince. "A million years ago."

"I see," says Silvestri, clocking her look. "Have either of you spoken with the husband?" He looks to Rebecca. "Outside of work, I mean."

"Just the usual. God, he hasn't really said anything lately."

"Lately?" asks Wolcott.

Rebecca looks to me, then back to Wolcott. She leans forward just a touch. "I don't mean to gossip, but there had been some strain in their relationship. He hadn't mentioned anything lately, but it was sort of an ongoing thing for a while. I'm pretty sure there was a short stretch there where she may have left to stay with family. But I only picked up on that because she had missed a bunch of classes. He was pretty mum about everything." She looks back to me. "Remember I mentioned something to you?"

"Yeah, babe. That sounds about right."

Wolcott turns to me. "And what was your relationship with Mrs. Anders?"

"We dated briefly, when we were in school together," I say. I hear Rebecca exhale.

"A million years ago," quips Silvestri. "How about more recently?"

"She'll show up to one of my open houses on occasion."

"I see," says Wolcott. "You're in real estate, then?"

"I am, yes." This answer still leaves a bitter taste as I say it.

"Had you noticed anything out of the ordinary with her lately, at one of these open house events?"

"Well." I look to Rebecca.

"Tell them, babe."

Silvestri perks up. "What's that?"

"The last time she showed up, she seemed a bit tipsy."

"I see," said Wolcott. "Was she acting inappropriately?"

"How so?" I ask.

"When people are intoxicated . . . Was she, and forgive me for the indelicacy, being forward or anything of the sort?"

"Oh," I respond. "Like, hitting on me? No, nothing like that. That's all completely behind us. She just seemed a bit, I don't know, sad."

"I see." Wolcott pulls out a pen and a small Moleskine pad from his trouser pocket and jots down a few notes. "Would I be correct, then, in saying that it sounds like there was some distance between Mr. and Mrs. Anders as of late?"

Rebecca looks to me, then back to the detectives. "I'd say so, yes. Just out of curiosity, was Mark the one who contacted you?"

"Just following up on an anonymous tip we received," explains Wolcott. "To that end, I'd like to ask you if *this* woman looks familiar." He pulls out another small photo and hands it to my wife.

I watch closely as Rebecca studies the photo. She looks at it a little too long, and her eyes narrow just slightly. She looks to Wolcott, then to me. "Paul, it's her." She hands me the photo.

I spit the coffee I'm sipping into the mug as Sheila stares back at me. My insides roil. I'm relieved to have the coughing fit to buy myself a few moments to figure out what the hell my wife is thinking.

"Mr. Campbell?" asks Silvestri.

"Sorry," I sputter. "Wrong pipe." I watch as the partners eye each other. I look toward mine.

"Honey, it's okay. You can tell them." Rebecca looks at me with an expression of resigned understanding.

"Baby?" I ask.

"Something we should know?" asks Wolcott.

"That woman is in my spin class, yes," volunteers Rebecca. "But we also have a history outside of that. You see, she developed a rather unhealthy interest in my husband that we were forced to nip in the bud."

Wolcott looks at me, inquisitively. "Mr. Campbell?"

I look to Rebecca for a cue.

"It's fine, Paul. It won't hurt my feelings." She nods and lowers her eyes.

As she looks at the ground, the thread becomes clear to me and I see exactly how it needs to unspool. "Detectives, there was a stretch a while back when I was out of work and pretty down. My wife was working, and I was sulking around the house here, having a tough time of it. During this stretch, I got into the routine of walking Duff to try and get out of my funk. I met this woman, Sheila, one day as she was walking her dog. We began to run into one another—or so I thought at the time—on a regular basis."

Wolcott is busy jotting things down in his notebook when Silvestri chimes in. "Or so you thought at the time?"

"Yes, well, we would run into one another around the same time each day, so I just assumed we were on the same schedule. As we got to know each other more, she began to open up to me about her domestic situation."

Wolcott picks up the baton. "And what was that, exactly?"

"She had a husband who sounded like not the greatest guy in the world. She mentioned ongoing infidelity with a work colleague, and what sounded like pretty bad emotional abuse."

Silvestri again. "Sounds like very intimate conversation with a dog-walking acquaintance."

I look toward the floor, as if ashamed. "That's where I made the mistake, and where I hurt my marriage. I was in a very vulnerable place, and I opened up to this woman more than I should have. I felt a certain kinship with her, I guess. I shared some intimate details of our marriage, betraying my wife's trust in the process." I look toward Rebecca, who is eyeing me attentively. "I fell into what a therapist might term an 'emotional affair' and I ended up encouraging this woman inappropriately."

"And this affair," asks Wolcott, "was purely emotional?"

"It was, yes," I respond. "Though that doesn't make it any less wrong, or make the damage easier to deal with."

"We're still dealing with it day by day," adds Rebecca. "And we're getting there."

"Sounds like some very enlightened marital rebuilding between the two of you," says Wolcott. "May I ask how the situation was resolved?"

"Paul came to me feeling very guilty when he realized how much he had encouraged this woman. It had become clear to him that she was delusional. And manipulative. She admitted that she had not simply run into him on those walks early on but had been eyeing him and synching her schedule as an excuse to chat him up. She also came to think that they were in an actual, intimate relationship. He realized that he needed to end things entirely."

Silvestri looks at me. "And how did that turn out, Mr. Campbell?"

"It was messy," I respond. "The husband ended up leaving her, and she convinced herself that we were meant to be together. I had to cut her out entirely, and she took it pretty hard."

"I see," nods Wolcott. "And that was how far back?"

"God"—I look to Rebecca—"a couple months?"

"Yeah," she responds. "That sounds about right."

"And no word since then?" asks Silvestri.

"No, she seems to have fallen off the map."

"Any idea where she might have ended up? Where she was from? Where the husband was from?" asks Wolcott, his notepad at the ready.

"Hmm." I pretend to think. "Never really got her background, as far as any of that goes. Sorry."

"Not at all," says Wolcott. He looks at his partner, who nods. "Well, you folks have been very helpful." He reaches into a trouser pocket and hands Rebecca his card. "Here's my number, if either of you think of anything else."

Rebecca weighs the card in her palm. "Of course, Detectives. We certainly will."

They thank us for the coffee and for our time as we usher them out the front door and onto the porch. We watch from the window as they return to the Crown Vic and pull out of the driveway.

Rebecca looks at me. "You okay?"

"What the fuck was that?!" I bellow.

Her expression twists. "I had to, Paul."

"Oh yeah? Getting off on that, were you?"

She looks at me like I've just socked her. "They're investigating her disappearance. Sooner or later, they're going to find the texts."

Now it's my turn to feel like the wind's been knocked out of me. My voice comes out much quieter. "You know about the texts?"

"Jesus, Paul. I'm not stupid. Yes, I know about the texts." Her eyes drop to the floor and then reconnect with mine. There's purpose in her gaze. "But that's all over now, right?"

"What do you mean? Sheila's—"

She puts a finger to my lips. "Not her. That's not what I'm talking about. I'm talking about you, my love. That part of *you* is all over, right? No more. Not again."

The tenderness in her tone cuts my anger short and my eyes well up. I feel as close to her as I ever have. I look her in the eye and no longer feel as if we're looking through each other. I take a deep breath. "Yes, Madoo. That's all over. I promise." I believe the words as I speak them.

"Okay." She nods and pulls me close. We stay like that for a long moment, both of us clutching each other and sobbing with a shared sense of relief.

I finally pull out of her embrace and touch her cheek. As I marvel at my wife, I feel myself smile. "I gotta say, you really sold the hell out of that story."

She lets out a relieved laugh. "Well, babe, I'm a hell of a saleswoman."

nineteen

WOLCOTT

"I'VE GOT ONE for you guys."

My partner is holding court again. Half of our department is gathered around his desk as he regales us with tales from his NYPD days, from which he's only a few months removed.

"Early on, new to the job. Still in uniform. Very green. I'm working out of Midtown South. Dead in the middle of summer, hot as shit," he continues. "You guys familiar with Ricky's?" The room offers a collective shake of the head. "It's a costume and cosmetics store. Bunch of 'em in Manhattan. Big around Halloween. So, we're on foot patrol one day, my partner and I, and we're walking down the block that one of the stores is on. Apparently, some skell who's high on PCP is inside trying to shoplift a bunch of shit for his boyfriend. While he's in there, the store has their millionth customer. This woman steps up to the register, and suddenly sirens and strobe lights start going off and balloons are falling from the ceiling and all that shit. So, this mope who's in there robbing the place flips out, thinking that he's set off an alarm. He books out of the place, but runs straight into a security guard as he's leaving. The two of them go down to the concrete immediately, and of course the dusted guy is freaking. Now, I don't know if you guys have ever had to deal with someone on PCP, but it's like some Incredible Hulk–type shit. Took my partner and me *and* the security guard just to keep this guy pinned on the sidewalk while we called for backup. Squirming around like an eel the whole fucking time. No joke."

The room is howling. Guy's been here a couple of months, and he's got them enthralled. I've got to admit, my partner is a natural-born storyteller. And he seems to thrive on the rush. At first, I worried that the lack of action on Long Island would slowly bore him to death. Then I realized why he ended up out here, and why they saw fit to partner us together.

"Ladies." Captain Evans enters the squad room, unamused. "Whenever you'd like to wrap up the tea circle, maybe we could get some police work done today." He passes through without a direct glance at anyone.

The detectives scatter to their respective desks, leaving Silvestri and me at ours. I let him bask in the satisfaction of his well-received tale for a long moment.

"So," I begin, finally. "This joint disappearance is probably the most action you've had on the job out here so far, eh?"

"Huh?" It takes him a second to come back. "Yeah, I was starting to get a little antsy."

"Well, time to break you in. Any ideas on this thing so far?"

"Been thinking on that. You know, the husband seems like a real prince."

"Mark Anders?" I say, flinching at the memory of the cigar stench during our interview with him. "Not the most attentive, so far as spouses go. Although that makes me less suspicious of him."

"How so?" asks Silvestri.

"When we questioned him, he seemed genuinely surprised to hear that his wife had been reported missing. And he mentioned that she took off on a regular basis. Gave us the number for the sister and the mother. I thought he came off as detached more than anything else. A guy like that, jealousy is long gone from the equation, if it was ever there in the first place. Doesn't seem like much of a candidate for a crime of passion. He seemed mildly annoyed about the fact that she might be spending his money, but his tone was more resigned than angry."

"Yeah," my partner says. "Now that you mention it, he did only seem to show any sort of alarm when we told him that her cards hadn't been used in weeks. Unless, of course, he's just full of shit."

"Oh, I suspect that he is. But that weak show of remorse that he offered up? That sounded more phoned in than anything else, like he was trying to tell us what he thought he should be feeling, but without enough emotion behind the words to really sell it."

"Maybe," says Silvestri, "he's just a bad actor."

"Could be. But he just didn't seem to care enough one way or the other."

"Plus," my partner reminds me, "his financials are in order. Guy's Big Pharma, after all. He can afford to lose whatever his wife's squandering at the Givenchy store to stick it to him."

"Look at you, with the name brands."

"I had a little culture under my belt before I moved out to the sticks."

"Uh-huh. Anyone else looking good for this, you think?"

Silvestri ponders the question. "I think it's a hell of a coincidence that Paul and Rebecca Campbell had connections to both of the disappeared women."

Rebecca hasn't been taking up much space in my head, but her husband's starting to give me the itch. I decide to see where a round of devil's advocate might get us. "This is a small town. People overlap in all sorts of ways. Same is true for any other member of that studio."

"But the fact that she worked for the husband doesn't bother you at all?" he asks.

"She just seemed pretty matter-of-fact when we spoke with her. Appropriately concerned, but not selling anything too hard. I *did* notice that Paul's relationship with the wife from high school was chafing her, though."

"You think the wick on that flame hasn't burned all the way down?" he asks.

"Wouldn't be surprised if his eyes had a habit of roving, at the very least."

"You might be giving the guy way too much credit," my partner muses. "He reminds me of a guy I knew once."

"Who's that?" I ask.

"An old stepdad of mine," he responds. "Real slick fuck."

"I'm going to wager that that ended poorly?" I ask.

"Ended great," he retorts. "Guy ran off with a coworker. My mom and I never had to deal with him again.

"How about Paul and Rebecca's story?" he asks. "You think it sounded rehearsed?"

"No, thought that whole thing came off pretty naturally. It was just the way he spoke about the other woman and the fallout from that."

"Yeah, the wife seemed more remorseful than he did," says Silvestri. "Jesus, we're just surrounded by fucking Prince Charmings around here, aren't we? And yet I can't manage to wrangle a decent woman."

"Maybe 'wrangling' is the wrong approach, cowboy." I like giving this guy the business.

"Pardon me, Soft Glove. Perhaps you can teach me the ways of women." He laughs. "Then again, you do have an old lady at home."

I nod in his direction and catch a forlorn look in his eye. Underneath the bluster, there's something else there. I feel for the guy. Just as quickly, he clears his throat and straightens up, and I see a look of curiosity take shape. Something is nagging at him.

"What's on your mind, Silvestri?"

"I keep coming back to Sheila Maxwell."

"How so?" I ask.

"Well, she seems like an afterthought in this whole situation. Aside from the anonymous tip we got, which led with the news of Sasha Anders, there's barely been any mention of her. Paul Campbell seems to be about the only connection to her. Even the other women at the spin studio that we spoke to hardly remember who she was. It's like she was barely on any-one's radar."

"Bit of a loner," I suggest. "You find anything on the husband yet?"

"Looking into that right now, and waiting on her phone records. Let's see what we can turn up on this chick. I'm intrigued."

"Go get 'em." I laugh. "Going to stretch my legs."

◆

I SIT ON THE BENCH out front of the station house, breathing in the crisp air. Spring is starting to rear its head. My favorite time of year, and my favorite time on a case. I watch the cars pass by on the main road and listen to the whistle of the cardinals. As I zone out, the pieces of the puzzle begin to take shape in my head.

I certainly take no pleasure in the fact that two women have gone miss-ing, but getting to the root of the mystery is where I feel most at home and useful. It gives me purpose. And it's been a slow winter. I've had a lot of time lately to ponder what it would have been like to do this on the federal level. To have been able to make this kind of action my day-to-day. But life unfolds in its own way.

The itch starts to take shape, as it always does. It hasn't arrived fully formed this time, but the feeling is there, and I need to sit with it and give my brain a chance to blow the dust off and get a clearer look at the picture. I can't quite see how I'm going to get there yet, but my instinct is leaning heavily toward a particular suspect: Paul Campbell.

◆

I RETURN TO THE DESK, coffee and tea in hand, and set the latter down on the coaster next to Silvestri's desktop. He's studying the screen intently and only notices me as I draw my hand away.

"Wolcott, there you are."

"Miss me?"

"Cute," he says. "Was about to call your cell."

"What's up?"

"Sheila Maxwell's phone records just came in."

"Yeah?"

"Yeah," he says, with a glint in his eye. "You're going to want to see this."

twenty

REBECCA

IT'S LATE IN the afternoon on Sunday. Paul has been in Miami for thirty-six hours.

He sent a few texts confirming that he and Wes landed and checked into their hotel on schedule. When I call his phone, it goes straight to voicemail. At a loss for what to say, I text back, asking him how the weather is. Nothing.

I take Duff out into the safety of the backyard on his leash. Even with the gate closed and locked, I feel like he could disappear if I let him off the lead. He looks at me holding the leash and then around the yard, confused. Eventually he lifts a leg and relieves himself and I lead him back to the house, closing the sliding doors and locking us in.

Chemically, I'm secure for the short term. I stocked up on enough stolen medication at Lotus Pedal to float me through the next handful of days (if I'm able to exhibit some self-control in rationing). I turn music on and start to clean the already immaculate kitchen. I aim to clear my head by keeping my body in motion, but the walls around me move as fluidly as

I do. I turn the music off, sit as still as possible in the quiet, and try to focus on one thought. I've let myself go off the rails for long enough. His letter and journal entries are cycling through my brain on full swing.

I go to the cupboard with the thought of making an entire pot of coffee and caffeinating for the next ten hours, or until I figure out what he's done with the money. The beans are absent from their usual spot and I remember Paul's Post-it note reminding us that we are fresh out, stuck next to the detective's business card on the fridge. I curse the Post-it and pull the plain white card with small black lettering from the magnetic clip. I run my jittery fingers over the embossed police shield and the letters forming "Wolcott." He was the taller of the two? Or maybe not. I can't remember. I say his name out loud before I put the card in one of the credit card slots of my wallet/phone holder for safekeeping.

I'm in no shape to drive so a coffee run is out of the question. My brain gets fuzzy again and I take a seat to regain composure. I remember the hidden Adderall in my rolling suitcase, taken from work just in case I needed help with motivation and focus. I've gotten good at not overdoing it on the Oxys and Xanax in general, but there have been one or three mornings where I'd swallowed one too many the night before and needed a boost to get through the workday.

Duff follows me to the walk-in closet in our bedroom and I extract the pill bottle from a makeup case that I've left in the front zipper pocket. Location number seventy-five that dear husband wouldn't think to look.

The bottle holds ten opaque rust-colored gel capsules. I shake one into my palm and hold it vertically as I pull one half away from the other, careful to not lose any of the tiny white orbs within. Carefully I pour a portion of the chemical granules under my tongue. I reconnect the capsule and save the other half for later.

As I sit on the bed my focus automatically goes to the spot near the lower corner of the frame where Paul spackled, painted, and scuffed a few subtle marks with his work boots to camouflage the glaringly pristine spot. The replacement carpet looks identical to its predecessor. While the dopamine boost begins, I try to push away the hurricane of thoughts about what they did in our bed. What else had he done in our house and with who else? I've been checking his pockets and bag when he comes home from work and is in the shower, trying to find clues to anything that might help.

Every day that I'm home, I dig up a little more about my husband. I've taken to routinely riffling through his drawers, feeling in his coat pockets, and going through old papers. This practice doesn't yield any earth-shattering revelations, but in the searches for comandeered painkillers or evidence of his other life, I've come across some interesting findings. For example, I notice that his sock drawer can't be closed when I try to push it flush with the rest of his drawers. When I pull the drawer all the way out and place it on the bed, I see what is disrupting the drawer's track. I extract the object from the recesses of the dresser and it regains its natural shape when I spread it out on the bed. It is a La Perla bra, size 32B; the cups are blue and green lace and metallic threading, making up the feathers of a peacock. The expensive and memorable item is not mine. And it looks exactly like one I've seen Sasha wearing in the locker room. When I make the connection, I practically throw Paul's drawer at the vanity, but my fury is diverted by the landline ringing. The outdated portable phone sitting in its cradle is like a sad plastic movie prop that only receives action from telemarketers these days. The incoming number is blocked on the ancient caller ID screen. I clumsily grab the receiver before it rings a third time, to spare my nerves, and hit the answer button accidentally. A female voice speaks before I can disconnect.

"Is this Mr. Paul Campbell or Mrs. Rebecca Campbell?"

I clear my throat. I don't think I have the wherewithal to interact with the outside world. But the official-sounding outsider saying both of our names, combined with the effects of the drugs, snaps me to attention.

"This is Rebecca Campbell. Who is this?" I don't bother hiding the disdain in my voice.

"My name is Melanie Wilkes and I'm calling from the fraud department of American Express to confirm that some recent charges made on your card are legitimate."

It takes me a minute to even place the card she's referring to. I pull open the drawer where the emergency Amex usually lives. It is missing, like so many other things around here. Paul must have taken it with him and the out-of-state charges have triggered a red flag. *Not so smart, are you, Paul?*

Well, this could be interesting. A little insight into what he has been up to in Florida may be exactly what I need to start connecting some dots.

I'm surprised he's using this credit card. I'd guess that he's charging things he doesn't want me to know about. He probably assumed that I'd completely forgotten about the card, and he was right. Though he clearly didn't count on bureaucratic intervention.

"What charges?"

"I'll need you to confirm some information before we go any further."

As I give her my social security number, mother's maiden name, and four-digit access code, my pulse begins to race. My brain is exploding with a hundred ideas. Thoughts while on Adderall practically take physical shape and push themselves through my brain on legs of their own.

"Now that I've confirmed your identity, Mrs. Campbell, I need to tell you that this call may be recorded. I'm calling on behalf of the American Express fraud department because there's been suspicious activity on your card ending in zero-zero-zero-eight."

Suspicious activity pertaining to Paul is the understatement of the fucking year.

I try to calm the growing excited curiosity in my voice and my increasingly speedy heart with a hand over my chest.

"What suspicious activity has been happening exactly?"

"Well, there hadn't been any activity on the card in nine months, and when a card has been dormant for that length of time, we like to follow up when activity starts up again to make sure it hasn't been stolen. Especially for purchases of this amount and frequency."

"Frequency?"

"Yes, ma'am, there have been ten charges in very quick succession made in five hours, totaling fifteen thousand dollars. We've actually been calling since yesterday when they were occurring but weren't able to reach anyone."

I see the red light on the answering machine blinking and realize that I've stopped paying attention to it altogether. Who knows what information has been blinking in front of me all along.

"We've placed a temporary freeze on the card until we could get a cardholder to confirm the activity." Her voice is almost robotic.

"I'm just curious, Melanie, have you been able to contact my husband yet?"

"No, ma'am, this is the only number we have for both of you—"

"That's fine. I was just wondering." I'm relieved. I realize the card is old enough that it probably predated our cell phones, and neither of us is very good at remembering to update that kind of information. It is good that Paul doesn't know they are trying to reach him.

"I'm going to go over the last couple of charges on your card, and I'll need you to confirm or deny if they are fraudulent or not."

"Okay. I'm ready."

"There was a charge for five thousand dollars at a vendor called Illusions made yesterday afternoon."

Sounds like a strip club. This makes my stomach hurt but could be worse. Wes and Paul didn't waste any time after landing, it seems. And five thousand dollars? That is a hell of a lot of lap dances.

"That could have been my husband." I force a boys-will-be-boys-tinged laugh and walk to the couch, where the laptop is.

"And there was a charge made at the Royal Palm steak house for five hundred dollars early this morning."

Spray-tanned skanks followed by a steak dinner with all the trimmings? Paul's dutiful-husband profile continues its descent at a swift clip. He is making it easier and easier to hate him today.

"It sounds like my husband had quite the night out."

I open my laptop and see that the battery is drained. I connect it to the charger. I'll need to use the Internet on my phone.

"What other charges are there, Melanie? I'm not entirely sure about these; they probably are Paul's, but he's not here right now. I've just texted him to find out."

I pull my phone from the charging station and enter "Illusions Miami" into Google. A one-star Yelp review pops up for a Spanish restaurant, but when I click through, it shows that the business closed in 2015.

"Um, let's see here. There was a purchase at a store called Wined-Down for two hundred dollars, and a five-hundred-dollar purchase at the Synchronicity day spa." I'm thrilled to hear that while I'm home sick with worry about the myriad disasters exploding around us, Paul is pampering himself. I need to get off this call and start some digging.

"Melanie, I can confirm that these are Paul's charges. He just texted me as much."

"Thank you, Mrs. Campbell. So I can lift the hold on the card?"

"Yes, that would be great." I don't want Paul to be alerted by a declined card and go into defense mode. If he hasn't already.

"Well, I'm sorry for any inconvenience we may have caused."

"Inconvenience?"

"We did have one attempted charge early this morning that came in after we'd suspended usage."

"Oh? What was that one?" I could only imagine. Was it middle-of-the-night karaoke or bottle service at some cheesy Miami dance club? Everything about this spending spree has Wes written all over it.

"It was for the Harbor Rose bed-and-breakfast this morning for four hundred and seventy-two dollars."

My blood runs cold. "Uh. No problem. He made other arrangements." I hang up.

Paul is not in Miami. Illusions is a jewelry store in Cold Spring Harbor. No need to Google search that one. I know it well.

My heart thrums at warp speed. I type in "Royal Palm, Long Island" and 1,023 images register. I click on one of the many endless photos of a gorgeous four-star restaurant on the sound, "a perfect place for a romantic celebration." It is half a mile from Illusions and within walking distance of the Harbor Rose.

The Harbor Rose. The bed-and-breakfast we stayed in the second night we were married and for anniversaries for years after. Until Paul's business went under.

Paul seems to be having quite the romantic weekend without me.

I step outside in the hope that the fresh air will quell the emerging headache blossoming behind my eyes. The sky is a beautiful painting of pink and blue and fading yellow in the waning afternoon. He's practically been in the backyard this whole time.

My phone shudders in my hands. I see my knuckles are white from gripping it so hard. His name surfaces.

Hey baby.

The weather is great.

I hate being this far away.

I'm watching a gorgeous sunset and wishing you were here.

twenty-one

SILVESTRI

I CAN'T NOT fuck with him.

As I look up to see Wolcott walking into the squad room in yet another three-piece ensemble, I give him an exaggerated roll of the eyes. "Again with the fucking vests. You look like Balki."

"What's that saying?" he responds. "'Dress for the job you want, not the job you have.'"

"Well, if you're looking to become a goat herder on the island of Mypos, you're on the right track."

"Just looking for a job that will let me upgrade partners."

"Aw, but without me, you'd miss out on all the witty banter," I say.

"And when exactly does that start?" he quips.

"Right," I say. I point at the cardboard cup on his desk. "Coffee's still hot."

"Appreciated. We've got Campbell coming in this morning, fresh off of his Florida trip, right?" As he checks his watch, I'm reminded that he's the only guy I know south of forty who still wears one. Though I guess we're both just south of forty these days.

"Yeah, he should be in shortly. You ready to work your magic?" I ask.

He shrugs. "Why not. Let me get a few sips of this down," he says, picking up the cup. "Then we'll have a little fun with the guy."

◆

I'VE BEEN LOOKING forward to this all morning.

I'm set up in the interrogation room when my partner walks Campbell in. I'm practically licking my chops with anticipation. It's been a long time since I've had the chance to really go in on a suspect, and I've never had a partner with the kind of interrogation savvy that Wolcott reportedly brings to the table. My idea of a good time.

My partner goes through the formalities of introducing us again and shows Paul Campbell to a seat across the table from me. Campbell is dressed in a pair of dirty Carhartt carpenter jeans and a thin thermal long-sleeve. Wolcott lays a comforting hand on our suspect's shoulder before rounding the table, unbuttoning his jacket, and taking a seat next to me. There's a dash of performance to the proceedings. I'm starting to understand the vests.

"Mr. Campbell," begins my partner. "Thank you for making the time to come in this morning. How was your trip to Florida?"

"Oh, great. Great." Paul seems distracted.

"You were down there for a real estate convention, no?" I ask. "Where do they put you up for something like that?"

"Umm . . ." He hesitates for a moment, then looks at us. "I need to confess something, Detectives."

"We've been known to dip into the confession business," I reassure him. "Have at it."

"I wasn't actually in Miami this weekend. I had a construction project in town that I needed to attend to, but I didn't want Rebecca to find out."

"I'm confused," I interject. "I thought you were in real estate."

"Oh," he explains. "Before I sold houses, I built them. Had a contracting company for many years. Got hit hard in '08 with the crash and had to pivot a bit."

"Hmm," says Wolcott. "So, you still do contracting as a sideline?"

"Occasionally, yes," Paul explains. "This is a little side project I'm working on at the moment. But I'm keeping Rebecca in the dark about it for now. Kind of a surprise for down the road."

"Interesting. It's around here?" I ask.

"A little west of here. A plot of land that I've had for a few years. Sort of a retirement plan, if you will."

"Makes sense," says Wolcott. "Catch the market on the upswing, build, flip it, and turn a profit."

"Yeah," says Paul. "That's the plan."

"An enterprising man," I add.

Our suspect offers a faint smile and looks between my partner and me. We let the silence hang in the air for a moment too long. Campbell shifts in his seat.

"Mr. Campbell," says Wolcott. "We asked you here today because we hoped you might be able to shed some light on what is shaping up to be a rather baffling case."

"Sure," volunteers Paul. "How can I help?"

"Well," says Wolcott, "we're hoping you can give us any kind of perspective on this Sheila Maxwell woman. She doesn't seem to enjoy a big presence around town and is virtually unknown even at the studio where she worked out with your wife. She was a reclusive woman, maybe?"

Campbell takes a moment to consider his answer. "I really only knew her in a limited capacity. We really didn't have any sort of social relationship, so it's hard for me to say."

I lean forward, which catches his attention. "You did use the term 'kinship,' I believe. And you mentioned that she had opened up to you about her husband's infidelity? I ask because these are all details that might help to paint a larger picture. Right now we don't have much to go on, I'm afraid. Can you maybe remember any specifics about the husband?"

His eyes move up and to his left. "I know he traveled for work a bunch. I guess he was having the affair with a work colleague. Sounded like kind of an asshole, the way she told it."

Wolcott jumps in. "'The way she told it.' That's an interesting choice of words, Mr. Campbell. Did you have reason to believe that she wasn't being truthful with you at any point?"

The idea that someone would lie to him appears to throw Campbell for a loop. "I mean, the whole thing struck me as a little weird, with the husband always being away, but I *assumed* she was telling the truth. Why else vent all of that stuff to me, right? What's going on here?"

"Exactly what we're trying to determine," explains my partner as he lays the scanned copy of the front-page newspaper story on the table between us.

I study Paul closely as he reads the clipping, unconsciously mouthing the words as he goes. When he gets to the part that should be a surprise, he freezes. His eyes widen; then his brow furrows. His eyes dart from the body of the text to the date on the header, then up to us. He looks utterly bewildered. "But, she . . ."

"*Was* married, to a Daniel Graves," says Wolcott.

"Kind of a morbid coincidence on the name." I can't help myself.

"She kept hers," Wolcott continues. "Daniel and Sheila were living in San Francisco until a few years ago, when Daniel died in a scuba-diving accident."

"On their honeymoon," I add.

"I realize this must be a shock to you, Paul. I know that you're principally concerned with your family's safety, and so we really need you to take us through everything, okay?"

He nods silently, dumbfounded.

"Paul?" Wolcott asks. "I'm going to run you through a string of text exchanges between the two of you from a couple of months back. I just need you to answer me honestly. If this woman is still out there, we don't want her putting you or your wife or dog in any danger."

He looks at my partner as if the dog angle hadn't occurred to him. "Duff?"

"Just trying to be thorough in our considerations," I add. "She was familiar with your dog, after all. And there's the suggestion that she may be an unstable person."

"Okay." Paul nods absently. "Sure."

Wolcott pulls the stack of printouts from under the table and sets them down. He begins to flip through them, making brief notations as he goes. A few pages in, he pauses. "Now, here's where we could use some clarification, Paul." He taps his finger on a text near the middle of the page. "There's a flirtatious tone that begins around here." He scans through to the bottom of the page. "Oh, and here it is. You invite her over to your house, and there's some suggestive language involved."

Campbell shifts in his seat and begins scratching his chin. "Okay, guys. I'm going to come clean with you."

"That's for the best," I say.

"There may have been a little more to the relationship than strictly emotional," he admits.

My partner and I nod understandingly. "We get it," I say. "You were dealing with some heavy stuff at the time."

"But I'm not proud of it," he clarifies.

"She was a good-looking woman," I say. "They both were."

He looks confused.

"Sorry," I clarify. "Sasha Anders." His body uncoils slightly when I mention the name. "You see, my partner and I are dealing with two missing women, so we sometimes think in pairs."

"Yeah," Campbell says. "Sasha was attractive. But it's not like that between us. At least it hasn't been for a long time. Not really my type these days."

"Oh no?" asks Wolcott. "Weren't they about the same type? Physically, I mean."

"I guess they were," says Paul. "I just meant that Sasha is kind of, I don't know, boring."

"Got it," says Wolcott, as he continues to sift through the text print-outs. "Okay, some photos of you two lovebirds. I'll just assume these are you," he continues, referring to the crotch shots and the photo of a nude male's back. He stops, suddenly, and looks Campbell in the eye. "Now, here's where my curiosity gets the better of me." He pulls the page from the top of the stack and places it in front of our suspect. "Could you read that for me?"

Campbell looks at the page and hesitates. He looks up at my partner first, and then at me, and finally reads out loud the highlighted words. "'I will fucking end you.'"

Wolcott enjoys a long, deliberate inhale and squares his shoulders. "Now, do you see where that might beg some questions, Paul?"

I can see the gears spinning behind our suspect's eyes.

"Detectives, I understand how that might look. You have to remember, I was really at the end of my rope. This woman had been stalking my wife and me around town, as you can see from those earlier photos. She was clearly unstable, and I didn't know what else to do. She wasn't responding to reason or logic, and the only thing I thought might work would be a show of force. In my desperation, I made a bad decision. I never would have followed through on it, but I responded in the heat of the moment, in a final attempt to get her out of our lives."

"You use the word 'final,'" Wolcott points out. "But you couldn't have known at the time that it would be your final interaction with this woman, could you?" I feel like I'm watching a surgeon operate.

I'm impressed by how quickly Campbell recovers. "I just meant, in hindsight, you know. It just felt at the time like she was on the brink. I was scared for myself and my wife. It was really jarring."

"I can imagine," says Wolcott. "And just to clarify, that text exchange was, in fact, the last contact you had with Ms. Maxwell, correct?"

I watch Campbell's eyes shift up and to his right before returning to meet my partner's. The liar's tell. "Yes, that was the last time I had anything to do with her, yes."

Wolcott props his right elbow on the table and begins to stroke his chin, all the while looking at Campbell across the table from him. I watch Campbell do his damnedest not to blink while my partner considers him. I wish I'd brought popcorn for this.

"Okay, then, Mr. Campbell," says my partner, in a tone that dispels the tension immediately. He places his palms on the edge of the table and stands up. I follow, as does our suspect. Wolcott rebuttons his suit jacket and rounds the table, where he takes Campbell by the shoulder and gently guides him in the direction of the door. "Thank you so much for coming in today. We'll be in touch with any developments on our end, and please do the same if you hear or see anything." He holds the door for Campbell, who can't leave fast enough.

"Will do, Detectives," says Campbell, out of the side of his mouth. "Thank you." He doesn't make eye contact with either of us on his way out of the interrogation room.

We step out into the hallway as we watch Paul Campbell hurry off and disappear around the corner. My partner lets the door close behind us and turns to me. A sly, satisfied smile takes over his face. He nods.

"He's going down," I say.

"Yes, he is."

twenty-two

PAUL
___

Suspicion Surrounds Honeymoon
Drowning of Seasoned Diver

THE HEADLINE FLASHES in my head like a blinker. God, I fucking knew it. She was lying to me all that time. And she was even crazier than I thought. She made that poor son of a bitch drown. Then lied about him. For years. Jesus. *Why didn't I listen to myself? I could sense it all along. What a fool.*

The spring sunlight is glaringly bright as I exit the station house and cross the lot. I squint as I head for the Jeep. I make it to the driver's-side door before I'm caught by a wave of nausea that churns my insides. *She wasn't just there to scare us. She was there to* kill *us. She'd done it before. And she was determined to do it again.*

I force myself to open the door, get inside, and start the engine. I'm sweating profusely and can barely grip the wheel, but I need to get the fuck out of this parking lot and away from this place. Who knows if those two dipshit cops are watching me from a window. *Take it slow. Breathe. Breathe.*

I pull out onto the highway and make it half a mile down the road before I'm forced to pull over onto the shoulder. I leave the Cherokee running as I race up to a line of trees and lose my stomach on the edge of the wooded patch. The coffee is bitter on the way back up, and the aftertaste of bile stings my throat and nostrils.

I look at a patch of discolored grass in the clearing before the trees, and suddenly I'm digging again, muscles burning. Dragging the horribly limp body to its shallow grave. As I move to kick the tarp into the hole, it unfurls. Sheila wriggles out and stares back at me. "It should have been you," she whispers.

The sound of a tractor-trailer horn whips me back into the moment. My hands are on my knees, and I'm panting. *Get your shit together.* I walk slowly back to the Jeep and take a seat. My head is throbbing, and there's a hole burning through the center of my stomach. I turn the engine off, as I don't trust myself to drive right now.

I can't breathe. I throw the door open and hop out of the seat, nearly falling over in the process. I make my way around to the front of the Cherokee and lean on the hood. The warm steel feels reassuring under my palms. I drop my head in the direction of the ground and let out a lung-shredding scream.

◆

THE LAST TWO NIGHTS were both the same. I stole away in the dead hours and drove out to Smithtown Bay. I needed to dig up the body, as I'd made a terrible mistake. I pulled up to the spot, parked, and grabbed my tools. The ground gave easily, so the shovel sufficed. I dug and dug, but it felt like an eternity before I'd made any headway. I fought through the exhaustion until I finally saw the tarp. I cleared the rest of the dirt away and dragged the body out of the hole. When I unwrapped the tarp, I saw Rebecca's lifeless eyes staring back at me.

Each night, I bolted up in a cold sweat, relieved that my wife wasn't

*sleeping next to me. My dear wife, who thought I was in Miami, even as I
slept in a motel room just a few towns away from her.*

◆

MY LUNGS BURN. I'm hoarse from screaming and my head is pounding.
I need to get back out to Cold Spring Harbor to check on the crew. I peel my
sweat-soaked hands off the hood and walk around to the driver's-side door.
I exhale deeply and key the engine.

As I pull back onto the highway, a Crown Vic sails by. I pick up speed
and catch up with the car. I pull past it and check out of the corner of my
eye. Not Wolcott and Silvestri. Those clowns are starting to irritate me.
I'm annoyed that I'm paying them this much mind, but they've got fuck all
on me. There's nothing on record to connect me to the lot in Smithtown
Bay, and thanks to Javier and his crew, there's now enough DNA in the
Cold Spring Harbor basement to turn a forensics lab inside out.

◆

"INS. FREEZE!"

"*¡Cabrón!*" The guys' heads whip toward me. "*¡Chinga tu madre!*"

"Just fucking with you guys." I laugh. "Javier, take lunch whenever you
want."

"Thanks, *pendejo.*"

As he rounds up the crew, I take a look at the skeleton of the home
we're building. The joists are laid in cleanly, and I've got the cherry already
picked out for the floors. The boys are making good time this morning.
I'm relieved I was able to get these guys lined up for the stretch. Detail-
oriented workers make all the difference. Plus, they're willing to bust their
asses on the weekends, and their immigration status leaves me with some
room to negotiate.

I close my eyes and let the structure take shape. I see the pine beams

147

and the cathedral ceilings. I see the fireplace and smell the wood. I feel the granite against my fingertips. I see the walls and smell the fresh coats of paint. This is going to be a beautiful home. Not the one that Rebecca and I envisioned when we started discussing our dream home all those years ago, but a grander, more sophisticated place. The commission from the Southampton sale is making all of this possible. For this is now going to be a different home, for different people. Change of plans. New beginnings. And my wife is none the wiser.

"Javier, I've got an open house in a bit. You guys okay for the rest of the afternoon?"

"Yes, is good. You happy with this?"

"Looking great, my man. Keep up the good work. I'll be back in the morning in time for the delivery."

"What's coming in?"

"Pine beams."

"Okay, boss."

I head for the gym so I can take a shower and get ready for the open house. As I open my locker, the odor sets off my still-delicate stomach, and I just manage to keep myself from throwing up again. A weekend's worth of work clothes gets ripe pretty quickly, it seems. Fuck. I'll need to run home one day this week and sneak in a load of laundry when Rebecca's at work. I can't let her figure out what I've been up to.

twenty-three

REBECCA

PAUL IS BACK from his trip but texted me that he needed to go straight to work from the airport. This was a relief, as it's the first Monday in twenty years that I don't have a job to go to. I haven't been able to come clean, because there's a sense of safety and balance in having my own arsenal of secrets. I open my phone and click on the photos of his journal pages for the umpteenth time in the last seventy-two hours.

The tracks get deeper the more I try to conceal them. I keep having the nightmare—I'm walking in a snowstorm barefoot, trying to catch up with my parents, and someone is following me. I am constantly turning around to cover my tracks, but the more I push the snow over my footprints, the deeper they get. The faster I walk, the farther away my parents get. And whatever is following me gets closer.

I'm surprised to see that he's written about his parents. He hasn't spoken about them except for casual mentions in a very long time. When we used to talk. I see his car pulling into the driveway. It is five thirty P.M. and earlier than either of us has been home together in a long time. I close out my phone and head to the kitchen, where my staging of a postwork routine of the past awaits.

Chet Baker is streaming from the Bose dock. On the counter, a Stephen King doorstop lies open next to half a glass of merlot with my lipstick imprint on the rim. I pull an Oxy from the Altoids box in my purse and pop it into my mouth. I check my recently applied makeup and blownout hair in the reflection of the sliding doors while I smooth my favorite Alexander Wang work dress, but not too much, so it looks worn from the day.

When he walks into the house, my heart responds separately from my brain. He looks rugged and tired, and handsome as ever. I don't know if it is the drugs, my nerves, or the reflex of hardwired excitement in seeing him, but the palpitation is strong. Once upon a time, this was my favorite part of the day. The days when we'd run home, so eager to see each other. The memory of that feeling now is jarring and so out of place.

A familiar look in his eyes registers as he passes over the threshold with a smile. I've mistaken this look before but now I know better. It is infatuation. It is consumption. It is insatiability. I know it well from our beginnings and retroactively from when he was fucking Sheila. The look stings me deeply, but there is some triumph knowing that I'm not three paces behind this time.

Paul is such a good actor, the emotion in his face is nearly convincing. I feel a peculiar nostalgia for when I didn't know better. It was a nicer place to live. Duff runs to him, frantic in his excitement. I rally my own enthusiasm. This is easier than I expected because part of me feels happy to see him. I chalk it up to having barely left the house for almost three days and being lonely for human contact.

"Hi, beauty. I am so glad to be home. I missed you." He's holding his computer bag and a bouquet of flowers. The tulips make me question every bunch he's ever brought me. How many of those were flower-shaped apologies because he wasn't man enough to actually make them with words?

He's wearing a suit I've never seen and is noticeably without a tan. I stop myself from pointing out either of these facts. I move toward him because just standing there feels like a tell. He hands me the flowers and I force a smile. "They're lovely." I want to grind them into the carpet.

"Hi." I let him pull me in close. "How was the trip?" I can't tell if his squeezing me is to conceal his own body tensing at my question. He slides his hand down my back and leaves it to rest there as he guides me to the couch. I try not to think about where else his hands have been recently. He sits next to me, smiles, and rubs his eyes.

"Hard day?" I lay my hand on his suit leg. "You look nice. Did you dress up for the flight attendants?" I pepper every word with playfulness.

"I had a suit hanging at the office, just in case. Wes received a text after we landed. Someone wants to preempt a major property that Wes hooked last week." He's not looking at me because he's making eyes at Duff, whose head has landed firmly on his other leg. An easy way to avoid looking at me while he's lying. He puts one hand on Duff's head and starts scratching him behind the ears, and his other on my thigh, where he also lightly scratches as though he can't move one without the other.

"What's the property?" It occurs to me that he may be driving this conversation in a direction opposite from his trip.

"A beach view in South Sag, on Crestview. Forty-four million asking. The buyer went straight to fifty without even seeing it himself. The owner is an old high school friend of Wes's." His eyes return to mine. If he's lying, he's doing so beautifully.

"Wow. That is a big fish. You don't seem very excited."

Paul not only got a job and dug himself out of his midlife crisis; he got one he was good at. With a commission level like that, I am totally dumbfounded. How much does he need? A shade of wifely worry for him blossoms. Paul owing someone large hadn't occurred to me. Surprising, for the daughter of someone who was perpetually in debt to someone and constantly hiding from those someones out of fear. It dawns on me that maybe the missing money is unrelated to the new bitch in his life. But I suppose they aren't mutually exclusive lies.

The tracks get deeper the more I try to conceal them.

"The commission is massive, but the house will take at least a year or two to close on. The guy who owned it is a trust-fund kid turned drug dealer who used the inherited house as a storage spot for moving mass amounts of drugs through. He was literally hiding the shit in the walls. Pharmaceuticals mostly. He didn't even need the money, was just doing it because he watched too many *Breaking Bad* episodes, I bet. The DEA ripped the place apart. Walls, floor, you name it. Until he is tried and his assets aren't frozen, that house isn't getting cleaned, inspected, or sold."

I try not to get too distracted by the idea of what pills lay in those walls and how much was seized. Wasted. I don't press him on the "cleaning" either. I'd rather not know.

"It was all over the *Post* last month." He says this as though he's speaking to a functional human being who is on dry enough land in her own life to take an interest in the misdeeds of others. Every fiber of me is alive with endorphins. I move closer to him and lean against his chest. Like a puzzle piece sliding into its rightful spot.

His hand feels good on my leg and then on my face and around the back of my neck. Goose bumps spread from head to toe. The Oxy has fully blossomed and I'm melting into his hands and the couch. I want him to put his other hand on me. Slide it up my body and around the front of my neck. Would I even fight him if he squeezed? I feel multiple selves inhabiting me. I try to fuse the disparate emotions into one coherent being.

"Who is the bidder?"

"No idea. They sent a lawyer. The guy was shady as fuck too. It was bizarre; he barely spoke. Took a lot of pictures on his phone and left without telling us. Then he texted us an hour later with the offer. The house hasn't even been listed yet and Wes still hasn't gotten a straight answer about who pointed the buyer in our direction."

"Huh." I'm losing the verbal muscles to keep having this conversation. Duff moves his head from Paul's leg to the small piece of couch between us. We both put our hands on his head and ears, our fingers grazing each other's as we do. Paul's quiet.

"Did you hear anything else from the detectives?" I'm careful with my words, not quite sure if we are even safe to talk about them, but I know their visit and new presence in our lives is one of the herd of elephants taking up space in our beige living room.

"I'm handling it. Don't worry. They won't be a problem. Just keep doing everything you normally do. Go to work, go to spin class, walk the dog. If we don't do anything out of the ordinary, there's no reason for them to keep on us." His tone is clipped, and luckily he's too distracted to take notice when I tense up at the mention of work. I'll need to keep a semblance of routine and normalcy, not just for the cops but for him as well.

As an afterthought he adds, "Take it easy with the pain meds, Madoo. I need you sharp right now."

I try not to show my hurt. He rarely acknowledges my pill use, but when he does it reminds me that maybe I'm not as successful at hiding my secrets as I think I am. I fight not to point out that neither is he.

"Anything else happen today?" The words float out of my mouth separate from the rest of me, who is watching us sitting on our couch, with our dog and our lies resting comfortably between us. He looks at me strangely and I straighten. Fuck, I need to act normal.

"You okay, Madoo? How was your day? Work good?"

"Aw, I'm fine. Work was the same old. I'm just tired." I pick up the unintentional thread. "Actually, I think I'm coming down with something. I may stay home from work if I feel this way tomorrow."

"Oh, babe. You should have said so. Get into bed. I'll whip something up for you. Tomato soup and grilled cheese?" His routine sweetness puts me on alert, which is silly since he's taken care of me the same wonderful way when I've been sick hundreds of times before. He's just being himself. Or he's been acting this whole time. I feel so twisted in my doubt.

"I'm really okay. Actually, I'd love to get some delivery, curl up on the couch, and watch a movie."

"Sounds perfect." I see a microhesitation pass through him. "Though, I need a shower. It has been a long day and I'm ripe."

I study his face and see that he's got a tiny bit of shaving cream and a fresh nick just south of his earlobe. His hair is damp and he smells like the body wash he uses at his gym. His suit looks fresh off the hanger. I move to the kitchen so that I can watch him from afar. *I see you, Paul.*

I return and hand him a glass of wine to justify my move from the couch, which he takes appreciatively.

"Go take a shower and relax. I'll order some food. It's your turn to pick something to watch."

"Are you sure you're okay? You seem, I don't know, a little off? I know the last couple of days have been stressful. But we'll get through it. We always do." I see how carefully he's saying this, hoping against hope that I don't want to have a big conversation right now.

"I'm fine. I'm exhausted too; work was a slog today." How easily we both lie. I hear the confident words coming out of my mouth so convincingly that I almost believe them myself. He smiles and nods and runs his hands through his hair. He reaches into his inside jacket pocket for his phone and looks at it. His brow furrows and something dark crosses his face. He recovers when he sees me watching him.

"Everything okay?"

"Yeah. Totally. Just Wes." He's distracted as he looks back down at the screen and swipes. In a flash his back is to me as he heads toward the bedroom.

As soon as he gets into the shower, I look through his bag for clues about his weekend away. Everything looks standard, down to the bathing suit and sunblock. Everything except for the red bandanna, which I quickly untie to confirm what I already suspected. The gun that Paul claimed he'd gotten rid of is heavy in my hand. I wonder why Paul needs to bring a handgun on a weekend trip, especially one that involved airport security. I put the gun back in his luggage and head to the bedroom, hoping I still have time to get into his phone.

His phone isn't in his suit jacket hanging on the back of the door. And it is not in any of the other usual places. I feel anxious about time. I get on hands and knees to see if it has fallen under the bed, when it occurs to me that he's taken it into the bathroom with him.

The bathroom door is open a crack and I hear him singing behind the curtain. I push the door open farther and through the steam can see it sitting on the counter. Before I can grab it he peeks out from behind the curtain and sees me in the mirror watching from the doorway. He grins. "Naughty girl."

Be playful. He doesn't know anything. I fuck him with my eyes for a few seconds and flash him before I pivot and beeline for the living room. I pull the MacBook from his laptop bag and open it quickly. In the search history, the last opened page is an article from the *San Francisco Chronicle* about a scuba-diving accident in Jamaica. I copy the link, email it to myself from Paul's account, and then delete the email from his sent and trash folders. I scan his emails but don't see anything out of the ordinary. I click on his IP address and jot the info I need into my phone.

"Madoo?" My heart is in my throat as I power down his computer and shove it back into his bag. "Can you please come here for a minute? I need to talk to you." He's out of the shower. I hear the tone in his voice and know it well. It is the sound of him wanting me naked and facedown. It has been a long time since I've heard this particular voice, and I'm surprised. I dread what he might do to me but am too scared to refuse. I unzip my dress on the walk to our room.

His phone is on his bedside table in my sightline. As his warm hands grip my hips tightly, he controls the rhythm. I look at him over my shoulder so he doesn't think I'm distracted, but his eyes are closed. He is too consumed in his own imagination to even notice that I'm barely there as well. I can't look away from the screen of his phone exploding with text messages, too far out of range to see who they are from or what they say, but close enough that I can see them flooding in one after another.

◈

I WAKE, feeling like my head is full of seawater and sand. I kept falling asleep during the movie from the pills. I overdid it, and I can't slip up like this again. I was so amped up from his phone blowing up with texts, I crushed a hydrocodone into powder and snorted it while Paul paid the delivery guy. I can't remember what the movie was, just that it was a really old one that he remembered watching with his dad when he was alive. He is clearly thinking about his parents lately.

"You really must be feeling sick, honey. You can barely keep your eyes open and you're all clammy. You barely ate," he'd whispered to me as he carried me to bed. My arms were around his neck. His lifting and cradling me almost made me forget everything. Now awake, I remember immediately and feel sick. But I have important things to accomplish.

Duff and Paul are snoring beside me. I've already kicked off the sheets and blankets because of the collective human and canine body heat, so I'm able to roll out of bed without disrupting the tide of sheets and pillows too much. I move across the carpet soundlessly and slide his phone from his bedside into my hand. In the living room I lean against the mantel, the lone lion bookend cold against my shoulder. I put my own phone on the mantel and dig into his first.

I'm a little surprised and relieved that he hasn't changed his password. He must be confident of my ignorance. I look at his most recent text and it is indeed from Wes, but it is from this morning. I quickly scroll through all of his texts, unsure of what I'll be able to access retroactively once the app is in place. I'll be able to read his texts, emails, location, and search history from the safety of my own phone for just two hundred dollars a month. Nothing current stands out as suspicious and I have a momentary pang of doubt. Maybe I'm letting my imagination get the best of me. But the empty bank account and Paul's increasing laundry list of lies have piled up too much to ignore his secret-keeping.

I enter "MindsEye" into the app store and it comes up immediately. I download and activate it with the log-in I created earlier. The eye icon appears on his main screen. I quickly go into the settings and click on "Hide Icon." When I get back to his home screen the eye has disappeared.

I spook at the sight of my uplit face in the mirror. The screen in my hand is casting a severely ghostly pallor. I wait as my phone leeches all the secrets from his. This is no longer accidental and out of my control.

The eye icon on my phone shows a check mark, and barely a breath after, the phones vibrate in unison. I go directly into Paul's text messages to suss out who was texting him during our rare instance of lovemaking earlier but find nothing except for texts from myself and Wes and no one else in the past three hours. He must have deleted them. I feel discouraged.

Just as I'm about to give up, an alert message indicating that Paul has a new email crops up. The name in the preview box is Dana. I search my brain for a "Dana" who either of us knows. I open the message on my phone, leaving his untouched. I don't know which is more overpowering, the ire or the validation of my suspicions.

Paul,

    It's late, but I've been thinking about you a lot. So wonderful to see you again. I'm so glad we've reconnected. I've thought of you often.

    I look forward to seeing a lot more of you very soon.

    —D

twenty-four

PAUL

You've been on my mind.
Amazing seeing you after all these years.
Looking forward to seeing more of you too.

Standing in the deli line, I press SEND and am hit with that glorious, hollow tingle in the pit of my stomach. Dana Atwell. Since I tracked her down a couple of weeks back, our conversations have left me with a sense of certainty. I don't want to count the years that have passed since I last saw her, but the feeling is undoubtedly still there. The sensation is different, though. She's still one hell of a good-looking woman, but there's more to it than that. The old tingle has morphed into something different, something deeper and more grounded.

I feel safe with her in a way that I haven't with anyone for longer than I can remember. I feel calm. And exhilarated. And centered. I know that seeing her will be what it will take to get my head on straight and put this unpleasantness with Rebecca behind me. This will be the fresh start I know we both need.

I keep thinking back to our last afternoon at her place. I'm lying there staring at the ceiling, describing the dreams that have been plaguing me. Dreams about the car accident. Dreams about snowstorms. Dreams about burying bodies and digging them back up. These last dreams aren't really dreams at all, but I've framed them as such, omitting names and details. Fearing that I'll lose my mind if I can't tell another human being. And she listens intently. I feel she's the only one I can tell. The only one I can trust. The only one who won't judge me.

"Order eighty-four? Are you here?!"

The tone in the counterman's voice suggests that he's called my number more than once. I've been daydreaming. *Back to planet Earth, Paul.*

"That's me. Sorry, sorry."

"Here you go." He hands me the bags in a way that tells me he wouldn't mind if I went and fucked myself, and moves on to the next customer.

I pay the cashier and head for the parking lot.

I've just set the bags down in the passenger's seat of the Jeep when my pocket vibrates. I withdraw the phone and find myself disappointed that the text is from Wes.

You sneaking around behind your old lady's back again?

He needs something from me.

What's it to you, muchacho?

His response bubbles back almost immediately.

Got a last-minute call for a showing. I need you in an hour and a half. You in, dirtbag?

Not ideal. Hmm.

Where is it?

He's back to me within seconds.

Harbor Beach Road, out in Miller Place. Practically your backyard.

Except I'm not at home. I can just make this work. Just.

Text me the street address. I'll be there.

This is going to take some doing. But I have to jump on every property I can right now. Once Javier's crew has the place framed, I'm going to need to be a lot more hands-on with the construction and coordinating the crews, and I may miss out on some sales. Get it while the getting's good. Plus, a waterfront in Miller Place would be a big, fat commission. A nice cushion to help start over with. And after everything that's happened, I desperately need this fresh start. Without it, I'm afraid I'll lose the thread altogether.

I'm on the road to Cold Spring Harbor. I can drop these guys their lunch, be in and out in five, and head back home to grab a fresh suit out of the . . . *Fuck!* I find my phone in the center console and manage to type a message with one eye on the road.

Madoo, just checking in to see if you made it to work today. Hope you're all better. Love you.

My phone has buzzed twice by the time I pull into the driveway. I hear the thwack of the nail guns as I check my texts. The first is from Wes, with the street address of the house. The second, from my wife.

Babe, still pretty out of it. Called in sick, and lying in bed with Duff. Thanks for checking in. Love you more.

Shit. Okay, okay.

Sorry to hear that. I'll swing by and check on you in an hour.

I slip my phone into my pocket. I pull a cup of soup from one of the bags and place it in the cup holder in the center console. I grab the bags from the deli and head for the construction site. The guys are ahead of schedule. Christ, I wish I had this caliber of workers when I was still building full-time.

"Boss, the beams came. We should have everything ready for putting in tomorrow, okay?"

"That's great, Javier." I lean in closer. "By the way, you said you could talk to your guy about the copper piping?"

"No problem, boss."

"Great," I say. "Tell him I can do cash, if he can still give me that price he quoted."

"Okay," he answers. "You going to make a lots of money flipping this house."

"You know it." I offer Javier a wink. "I need to run to a showing. You guys good if I leave you for the rest of the day?"

"Is good."

"Great. I'll be back first thing tomorrow to help lay in the pine."

"Okay, boss. Is no problem."

I walk to the Cherokee and get in. As I key the engine, my phone vibrates.

Paul, don't worry about checking on me. I'm fine. Just need to sleep, I think. Thank you, though.

That's not going to work for me.

Need to swing by the house anyway. I'll bring you some lunch.

Time is of the essence. I get back on the road and head for home.

❖

UPON ENTERING THE HOUSE, I'm able to quell Duff's barking quickly. I expect Rebecca to call out to me, but the sound of her voice never comes. I head for the kitchen, where I set the container of soup in the microwave to reheat. It's been an hour since I got it from the deli. I retrieve a soup bowl from the cabinet and set it on a wooden tray. I'm careful to stop the timer on the microwave before it beeps and leave the soup inside to maintain heat. If I can sneak a quick rinse-off in the downstairs shower and throw on my spare suit, I can get up to Rebecca and feed her before she's any the—

"Hey, babe."

I wheel around too quickly, to see my wife eyeing me. "You startled me."

"Sorry. Didn't mean to." She's wearing the frumpy robe, and her face looks drawn.

"It's okay. Was trying to be quiet, in case you were sleeping. Was going to leave some soup for you for when you were up again and hungry." I make a show of sweeping my arm in the direction of the microwave, as if I'm Bob fucking Barker displaying a fortune in fabulous prizes that might be hers.

"Thanks, honey. I'm sure you didn't need to warm it up."

161

"The guys at the deli didn't have it as warm as usual. And I didn't know how long you might be sleeping." *Shut up, nitwit.*

"You're sweet." She looks at me, as if reconsidering. "Everything okay?"

"Fine. Why?"

She eyeballs me. "I thought Wes had you set up with an early showing today."

"Yeah, the early one got bumped, which worked out fine, because I needed to take the Cherokee in for an oil change and tune-up. Wes sprang one on me in twenty minutes, though. I actually need to grab a quick shower and throw on a suit."

"Okay. I'm heading to the doctor in a bit. They had a cancellation, and there's strep throat going around. I want to get tested."

"Good thinking." On the way to the bathroom, I give her a quick squeeze and a kiss on the forehead. I'm surprised at how cool she is to the touch. "I'm meeting up with Wes after this showing to go check out a property, then grabbing dinner. He's in the doghouse again."

"God. Those two."

"I know. Text me after the doctor, and I'll be home later to look after my gorgeous patient."

"Thanks, hon. Go sell a house." As I turn from her, she smacks my ass. There's a glint in her eye.

"Feeling better, are we?"

"Getting there."

◆

I SHOWER, dress, and am out the door with just enough time to spare. With any luck, I'll get some action on this property and be able to report back to my trusting wife with news of a good feeling, a possible sale on the horizon. News that will reassure her that her dutiful husband is going about his business and not engaging in some real estate shell game that has her looking at one house while he's busy plotting the fate of another.

twenty-five

SILVESTRI

"The plot."

My phone displays 2:37 A.M. The light sears my heavily lidded eyeballs. "The fuck you going on about, Wolcott?"

"When we interviewed Paul Campbell, he mentioned that he had a construction project under way on a plot of land he had owned for a few years." My partner's voice is far too clear and energetic for this time of night. It's pissing me off.

"Where are you?"

"Down at the station house."

"What the fuck are you doing there? It's the middle of the night."

"Couldn't sleep. Something was bothering me, and I couldn't put my finger on it. Then it came to me. Two women go missing, and suddenly one of our suspects is building on a property he's been sitting on *for years*?"

I'm suddenly awake. "What'd you find out?"

"Looked up property deeds. Paul Campbell owns a parcel of land out in Cold Spring Harbor that he bought nearly two decades ago."

"Son of a bitch."

"Seems awfully coincidental, no?"

"I'll get dressed. You want to pick me up and we can go put eyes on the place?"

My partner chuckles. "Get some sleep. I'm going to do the same. But meet me here bright and early. We'll go poke around a bit and see if we can't figure out what this character's been up to."

"See you then, bloodhound." I hang up the phone, knowing that I'll get no more rest tonight.

◆

WE'RE SITTING IN THE CRUISER just down the block from Paul Campbell's Cold Spring Harbor property. Wolcott watches keenly as Campbell and his crew lay beams into the framed structure.

"So, you thinking foundation?" I ask.

"Maybe he's seen too many mob movies. I'll tell you, it would sure work with our timeline."

"You got that straight," I respond. A sickening thought occurs to me. "Jesus, you don't think he's got a two-for-one going in there, do you?"

Wolcott's stare breaks from the crew for the first time since we took position. He turns to me as a look of disgust spreads across his face. "Hadn't thought of that," he sighs.

"I just mean, if you're going to go to the trouble . . ."

He shakes his head. "I suppose we can't put it past him." He mulls this over for a moment. "But how would he get two bodies out here, with a crew to deal with, on a fairly visible stretch of . . ."

"What're you thinking?" I ask.

He opens the driver's-side door. "Let's make a house call."

◆

"MAY I HELP YOU, young men?"

We're standing on the front porch of the house next to Campbell's lot, where an elderly woman has answered the door.

"Good morning, ma'am," says Wolcott. "Sorry to bother you. My name is Detective Wolcott, and this is my partner, Detective Silvestri. May we have a moment of your time?"

She eyes us suspiciously. "I haven't done anything wrong, have I?"

Wolcott flashes his pearly whites. "Oh, heavens no, ma'am. Just a few questions about your new neighbors." He nods in the direction of the construction site.

"Oh, I see. Just finished watching my stories and was going to make lunch. Would you boys like to join me for a cup of tea?"

"We'd love nothing more," I say as she ushers us inside.

Audio from a soap opera blares as we cross the living room and enter the kitchen. I almost break my neck tripping over a cat that darts across my path and underneath the sofa. The old broad doesn't miss a beat. "That's Hannah. And Harold is around here somewhere."

Our hostess lights the burner underneath the kettle.

"Ma'am, I wonder if we might—"

"Call me Louise."

"Louise, my partner and I are following up on some noise complaints filed against the construction site next door. Could you tell me how long construction has been going on over there?"

Louise fishes three tea bags out of a porcelain cookie jar as she considers the question. "Well, let's see, now. My son comes over on Saturdays to bring me groceries. It was this past Saturday that they started working."

"Saturday?" I ask. "That's unusual in construction."

"Yes, yes," Louise insists. "It was definitely Saturday. I noticed it when I let my son in with the groceries. I had to turn the sound on the television way up to drown out the hammering."

"A real racket, I'm sure," says Wolcott. He produces the notebook from his pocket and begins consulting blank pages. "Now, Louise. Have you heard or seen anything past normal work hours? Any comings or goings late at night, say?"

"Hmm. I'm usually no good after I take my hearing aids out." She thinks for a moment. "I could have sworn I heard some commotion about a week ago, in the middle of the night, but by the time I got to the window, there was nothing there. But it might have just been the deer." She pulls three mugs from the drying rack and sets them on the counter. "Those deer are a real nuisance around here."

"Tell me about it. They wreak havoc on my wife's vegetable garden." My partner offers Louise a commiserative look, then goes back to consulting the nonexistent notes. "Now, before they started *building* the house, do you remember anything from when they were pouring the foundation?"

Louise pauses. She looks at me and then at Wolcott. "You mean the concrete part?"

"Yes, dear," I chime in. "The concrete part."

"Well, that was already there."

"I'm sorry?" says Wolcott.

"Oh yes. The concrete part was put in years ago. I always thought it was funny that it was just sitting there all that time, without any house around it."

"Louise, you're sure about that?" I ask.

"Oh, why yes. Herman—my husband—was still alive back then, so it must have been nearly ten years ago. He would always say it was just the queerest thing to have a basement with no house on top. Now, do you boys take milk and sugar with your tea?"

❖

"MAKES SENSE, with the crash."

"How's that?" I ask.

We're back in the car, watching the crew work away. "Campbell said he took a hit when the housing market crashed. He must have had the foundation poured already when the money dried up."

"Strange that he's just picking construction back up now."

"Well, maybe he got a commission off of a sale and finally has some money to move around."

"You don't think he's got them buried on the property, do you?"

Wolcott ponders my question for a moment. "Even he's not that arrogant. Plus, it doesn't make sense. If you can't bury them under the house, what's the point?"

"I'm with you on that," I say.

"You're right, though. Odd timing."

"Yup. Oh, and I've got a tip for you, with the deer."

"What's that?" he asks.

"Get yourself a spray bottle. Fill it with water, then add a tablespoon of vegetable oil, for viscosity, and a few tablespoons of cayenne powder. Give it a good shake, and spray it all over the vegetables. The deer hate that shit."

Wolcott laughs. "And here I thought you were going to tell me to shoot 'em."

"What am I, an animal?" I protest.

My partner's phone rings. "Wolcott . . . Yes . . . Is that right? Okay, thanks for the call." He turns to me. "The hits just keep on coming."

"How's that?"

"You know Gino's, that Italian joint just outside of town?"

"Been past it."

"The manager noticed a car sitting in the back lot for an unusually long stretch. Figured it was abandoned, phoned it in."

"Uh-huh."

"Car's registered to Sheila Maxwell."

"No shit?"

An approaching voice draws our attention back to the construction site. We watch Campbell bark at his crew as he crosses the lot. With his back to them, the workers give Campbell the finger and simulate humping.

"Look at this dickhead." I laugh. Wolcott shakes his head.

Campbell climbs into the Cherokee, backs out of the driveway, and turns onto the street.

"Shall we?" I ask.

"Let's."

We follow Campbell, from a distance, to a house out in Smithtown. He slows down and pulls into the driveway, next to a Honda SUV. We park down the block, where we're able to get a good vantage point as he approaches the front door. It's a two-story, probably three-bedroom, two-bathroom house, of a size to be well suited for a small family. I wonder what the hell he's doing there.

My partner gets on the radio. "This is Detective Wolcott. Badge number five-three-one-two."

"*Go, Detective.*"

"I need a ten twenty-seven on a white Honda Pilot. New York State license plate Alpha-Mike-Delta, one-one-zero-seven."

"*Copy.*"

We wait for the dispatcher's response, as a tall, attractive, thirtyish brunette opens the door and greets Campbell. They hug briefly, and he's inside the house.

The radio hisses. "*Vehicle is registered to a Dana Atwell. Eighty-two Cherry Lane, Smithtown, New York.*"

"Ten-four. Over and out."

The address matches the house we're sitting on. Wolcott jots down the name Dana Atwell in his notebook, then looks back toward the house. I can see the gears turning in his head.

"This guy sure works fast," I say.

Wolcott scratches his chin. "What is this son of a bitch up to?"

twenty-six

REBECCA

IT ISN'T DIFFICULT to convince Paul that I'm feeling unwell. After accessing his phone and reading the email from whoever the fuck Dana is, I haven't slept a wink and I look every inch of it. When he tries to rouse me with warm hands up my shirt, I fight him off and tell him I'm going to sleep for a few more hours and go into the office late. I'll need to venture out at some point, and work is as good a cover as any.

I burrow into the bed and remain without signs of life while he gets himself going for his day ahead. He's chipper and whistling his way in and out of the shower, enraging me with his blatant happiness. He has no idea that I've been up all night with a thousand thoughts of betrayal and disappointment ping-ponging around in my head.

I listen to the sounds of his morning routine with my breath held and teeth gritted. Before he leaves, he kisses my cheek and I stir just enough to force a smile and whimper before I roll beneath the blanket. I can feel the lingering weight of him on the mattress looking at me. I wonder if he wishes it were me he rolled in that plastic and discarded. My tears are absorbed quickly into the pillow. When I hear the click of the front door behind him, I exhale and succumb to a wall of sleep.

When I wake a few hours later, Duff has climbed into bed with me for a midmorning nap and I have to reach under his giant body to retrieve my phone. I click on the eye-shaped icon and open the mirror of Paul's phone. Looks like he couldn't even wait until he was out of the house this morning to respond to her emails. It's too hard to read those, so I look elsewhere.

There are also a few messages from Wes. The most recent one being a nearby listing address. I read from the bottom up their back-and-forth, which is innocuous, but come to one that is a gut punch. I smart at the realization that Paul's best friend and business partner is also hiding his secrets. But I don't know why I'm surprised.

You sneaking around behind your old lady's back again?

I turn the heat down on my anger toward Wes for his complicity and focus on Paul. The blue dot on the GPS tracker shows that he is in Cold Spring Harbor. The coordinates don't get more detailed than that, frustratingly, so I'm not able to zoom in on a specific address. This development of Paul's whereabouts presents a problem; Cold Spring Harbor is exactly where I'd planned to go today. I have questions that I believe only the proprietors of a certain jewelry store and the Harbor Rose can answer. I'm not sure I can risk running into him.

Instead of getting out of bed, I take a Xanax from my nightstand stash and settle into my email. There is an email from the HR director at Launaria asking me to review the attached materials and sign them. They "will conclude the process of my resignation." She's requesting that I sign and scan the papers and email them in response as soon as possible. Her unsubtle urging that I never set foot in that office again only makes me want to do just that. They want to be done with me too. I seem to have become deadwood to everyone in my life.

I don't open the attachment. I delete the email. An idea about work and Mark takes seed in an interior part of my brain for later. I know I'll need to lean on Mark in the near future for a number of things.

I open the article link from Paul's search history that I sent to myself last night, but before I can dip in, a text from him comes in. He's acting the good husband by checking on me, although I'm well aware of how unconcerned he actually is. I feel as though he's caught me in the act of spying, but the rational sliver left in me tells me otherwise. I take a deep breath and decide to hold off before replying since the only responses available to me at the moment verge on hysterical.

I let him know that I've decided to stay home from work. He responds quickly to say he's going to come home to check on me. Fuck. I hadn't counted on this and it makes me punch the pillow, disrupting Duff's nap momentarily before he lays his head back down and resumes sleeping. It looks like for the time being I'm stuck at home and in bed. I'll do what I can from here. The article sits behind the text, waiting for me when I swipe Paul away.

Suspicion Surrounds Honeymoon Drowning of Seasoned Diver

I don't need to read a word beyond the headline to fill in the blanks when I see who the woman in the photo is. She's standing next to a handsome ginger-haired guy cheerily posed in a wedding photo. The picture bears a quote below: "The couple during happier times." Her hair is a different color in the photo than it was on our bedroom floor, but of course I recognize her right away.

Before I can read further, I get a notification that Paul has received an email and I switch over. Dana has responded to his response from this morning. My stomach drops a few hundred feet. He's returned her sentiment of being in each other's thoughts. Her reply is shameless.

Maybe when you come see me tomorrow we can do some role-playing?

He takes no time to reply.

> I'd like that. It would be good to release some of this tension.
> I'm a little worried Rebecca knows something is up with me.
> And she's home sick, so I feel like I'm sneaking around even
> more than usual.

My guts coil into a painful knot. My phone shivers with a nearly immediate response from her.

> Is she asking questions? Do you think she has any idea?
> There's nothing to be ashamed of. You need to find your own
> happiness.

I'm confused by the tone and her words. This feels like a different kind of flirtation.

As I'm watching their intimacy blossoming in real time in front of me, I start to feel a strange sensation of dead calmness. It is a stillness beyond the antianxiety meds. It reminds me of being deep underwater. I can't look away.

> Rebecca will understand when I can finally tell her
> everything. It's still scary. But I know how much you can help
> me with that.

I have to sprint out of bed to make it to the bathroom in time. When I recover, I stand too quickly and get dizzy and sick all over again. After a few minutes with my burning cheek on the cool tile, I manage to right myself and splash my face with cold water. I hate that she knows my name. I despise that they are using me as foreplay. I'm fighting the urge to throw something at the mirror and watch it shatter. I stare at myself, in a standoff with the part of me who is on the verge of becoming homicidal and the part of me who is trying with every fiber to keep things under control. It is hard to tell who is winning.

I am taken aback by how awful I look. I have aged ten years in less than a week it seems. My skin is sallow, my hair is limp, and I've lost weight. I've bypassed svelte and gone straight to gaunt. Ironic how I've worked relentlessly for the last three-quarters of my life to get to a certain thinness, and all it took was for the bottom of my life to drop away to reach it, and then some. Trauma trim. If only I could bottle it. The money Paul stole would be pennies compared to what I'd make.

I consider taking a shower and washing some of the gloom off me. If I want to blend in with the outside world, I'll need to clean myself up. But I can't very well throw on makeup at this point, with Paul on his way home, and continue playing the sick card. I'm tired again and flip a mental coin to crawl back into bed or take some Adderall to perk my brain up. The bed wins. When I settle in to resume the article, a migraine has taken root in the back of my eyes so I close them and drift.

Less than an hour has passed when I hear the sounds of Paul arriving home. I stumble toward the back of the closet for my robe, the ratty one with loose Percocets in the pockets—one of my more ingenious hiding spots for quick-and-easy grabbing. I slide my arms through and help myself to a pill. Then I steel myself for another performance.

At least I know that I look the part.

◆

BY THE TIME I've eaten the chicken soup he's brought me and set up camp on the couch, I'm satisfied I've convinced him of an illness worthy of at least a week's stay at home. I tell him I'm going to the doctor for a late-afternoon appointment. This comes to me in a moment of clarity when I realize my doctor's office is midway between our house and Cold Spring Harbor, making my claim reasonable that I would be in that area, should by some comedy of errors I get spotted by someone we know or, unlikely but possible, I run into him.

If he's telling the truth, there's no reason to worry. As he's walking out the door he informs me that he is going to check out a potential sale property in the neighborhood and then have dinner with Wes at a bar close by because he's on the outs with his wife again. If ever a couple were divorce soul mates, it's those two. Any of these claims could be lies, but I'll have the GPS to keep an eye on him. And I figure I have a good four or five hours before he's back home.

As soon as he pulls away from the house, I jump into the shower and dress hurriedly in the smallest jeans and shirt I can find, since everything else I put on hangs off of me. I apply light makeup and pull my hair back into a tight ponytail, which helps temporarily smooth the creases on my forehead. I swipe on some lip gloss and decide a piece of jewelry for my errand would provide a good entree to my intended questions. I root through my jewelry box for the necklace Paul got me during our wedding weekend: two layered rose gold chains with doves on each chain, wings spread, giving the appearance of two birds flying nearly side by side. I'm not finding it among the usual tangle of necklaces. I suddenly remember that I was wearing it the day the detectives showed up, but can't recall where I've left it. Untangling the knot in my hand and finding a different necklace will take a good amount of time and patience, both of which I'm short on. I look at my phone and realize I only have an hour and a half before the store closes.

I go without.

◆

TRAFFIC IS WORSE than I expect and the drive takes nearly twice as long as usual. I find a parking spot with little time to spare before closing. It is still light out and there are enough people on the street to conjure the first warm feelings of imminent summer.

When I walk inside, the store is eerily empty. I hear activity beyond the half-open doorway leading to the back of the store. I walk up to the glass cases and peer in at the delicate necklaces of labradorite, moonstone, and opals encircled by delicate gold piping, each piece artfully draped over chunks of driftwood. I look around the store and get the feeling it hasn't changed much in the last twenty years. Although I'd only really seen it at night from the sidewalk looking in. Even though I've walked by the store many times since our wedding weekend, this is the first time I've ever stepped foot inside.

It was probably the best weekend of my life, if I had to pick one. The night we stumbled upon Illusions, it was very late and we were hand in hand, walking and talking for hours. It always felt like there wasn't possibly enough time to fit in everything we wanted to tell each other. I was euphoric over Paul finally leaving his wife and showing up at my door, insisting that we get married as soon as possible. We'd had to wait four months for the divorce to be finalized to get married, but Paul moved in with me immediately. We looked for our first apartment together and it felt like we were starting our relationship over again, the right way.

After city hall, we'd gotten into Paul's car and camped on our plot of land, where we planned the house we were going to build there. But despite the body heat and the September humidity, we were ready for a hot shower and warm bed. The next morning, we stumbled upon the charming bed-and-breakfast nearby with a deluxe room available and a generous proprietress who gave us a reduced rate in honor of our local "honeymoon." Fate seemed to continue in our favor at every turn.

We didn't emerge from the room until late that evening, starved from long intervals of naked entwinement and sleep. Everything was closed down except for a 7-Eleven, so we strolled around town with armfuls of sweet and salty snacks, munching and talking and walking in circles until finding a bench in front of the store that I'm standing in now.

When we'd eaten ourselves full of Cheetos and Devil Dogs and washed it all down with Budweiser tall boys, I'd stood watch for Paul as he went between two shops to relieve himself, both of us giddy and laughing. I'd been distracted by something shiny in the window and crept closer, wobbly from the beer and sugar, leaving Paul exposed. The dove necklace was hanging from delicate branches and backlit in the otherwise dark store window. Paul had come up behind me, his arms around my waist, head on my shoulder, investigating what had caught my eye. We stayed like that for a long time, not saying much and feeling a shared sense of "finally."

When I woke the next morning, the bed was empty. Before I could spiral into the familiar fear that Paul had chosen his wife over me, he burst through the door with coffee, flowers, and a wax paper bag hanging from his mouth dotted with butter stains from the warm croissants within. We ate in bed surrounded by flakes of buttery pastry. Satisfied more than I can ever remember feeling, I leaned back into Paul and closed my eyes. I wanted to lock all of these moments into a mold. I felt his hands putting the necklace around my neck and closing the clasp easily. When I opened my eyes and looked in a mirror by the bed, the two gold birds were perched on my clavicle.

Now, in the same store, I reach for my bare neck, punctuating the memory.

"Oh dear! I didn't realize anybody was in here! I thought I'd locked the door."

The woman peering out from behind a stack of cardboard boxes has a shock of purplish-tinged hair and a look of exaggerated surprise behind her oversize glasses. She looks to be about ninety years old.

"I'm so sorry if I startled you. I thought you were still open."

She parks the tower of cardboard down on the counter between us.

"I was just getting ready to close, but if you promise not to tell anyone, I can let you look around while I finish tidying up." She looks like what I'd always imagined a grandmother should. I never knew either of mine.

"Thank you so much. I really appreciate it. I came in because my husband was in here recently and I wanted to check if he'd bought anything." I realize how off-putting this admission might sound and wish I'd come up with a better story. But she smiles and shoots me a knowing look. "Sorry, that probably sounds a little sneaky of me."

"Not at all, honey. You wouldn't believe how many women come in to see if their boyfriends or husbands have bought them something special. Mostly rings." Her laugh is so much younger than her face.

"Actually, it's our twentieth wedding anniversary coming up, and I've been at a loss for what to get my husband. You see, he tends to always outdo me with the extravagance of his gifts and I thought he might come here since he knows I love your pieces. I figured I might be able to get a sense of how much he'd spent."

The lies tumble out so easily. She smiles even bigger and nods. "Aw, I see. That's smart. Well, you know, honey, the twentieth-anniversary gift is traditionally china, and we don't sell any of that."

"My husband would never get me china. He's definitely not traditional." I laugh lightly. "I saw him come in here the last time we were in town when I was getting us ice cream across the street. He didn't think I was watching."

She looks to the left and right of us as though we are about to hand off drugs. "Well, I'm really not supposed to do this, but if you tell me your last name and when your husband came in, I suppose I could take a peek at the invoices from that day and see if anything matches."

"That would be wonderful."

She pivots 180 degrees to face the computer and clicks into a screen with her back to me. The text is so big I can read everything clearly.

"My bad eyes." She chuckles, reading my mind. "My grandson makes fun of how big I have to make everything. My phone is even worse! You could see my texts from two states over! What was the name, love?"

"Our last name is Campbell. He would have been by in the last two weeks."

I feel my phone vibrate through my purse but don't make a move for it. My palms are sweaty and I rub them on my jeans. I'm tensing up as the dull pain in my shoulder begins to throb. I wish I could take an Oxy, but I know better with the nighttime drive ahead of me.

"Aw. Lookie here. You were right!" I can see Paul's name as clear as day from where I'm standing.

"I see that there's a credit card on file for a special order with your last name. What would the first name on the card be, and the last five digits?"

"Paul. Zero-zero-zero-zero-eight."

Her voice goes up an octave as she turns toward me.

"You are going to be pleased, I think. He's gotten a *very* beautiful piece for you. And he's spent a nice amount on it too. But I won't spoil the surprise. I'll just say we've had to special order it and it's being delivered straight to you on Tuesday. Oh! And you've got the same name as my daughter! What a wonderful coincidence. Now I don't feel so guilty bending the rules." She winks at me conspiratorially.

Maybe Paul really did buy something for me. I hadn't considered that my goose chase could lead me to myself. Another husbandly gesture to keep me in the dark and content in my sheltered world of us against everyone else? But I need to see it to believe it.

She turns her back to the screen, obscuring my view of the information below his name on the digital receipt. I lean forward, intentionally pushing the boxes over the edge with my elbow. They topple to the floor on her side of the counter in a small avalanche of string and cardboard.

"Oh my! I'm *so* sorry. I'm so clumsy!" I crane my neck to see the screen before she's even bent down completely to gather up the mess.

"Not to worry, honey." There is a tinge of exasperation as she starts to stack the boxes, and I see the address under my husband's name. The numbers and street name float around as my brain tries to process. It isn't our address.

As she's stacking the boxes on the counter, I move to help her and she softens. I steady my voice. "I'm curious, how did you know my name? You said it was the same as your daughter's?"

"Oh, the piece is personalized. I saw the inscription on the work order. I just love the name Dana!"

twenty-seven

PAUL

THIS LAST MONTH with Dana has given me more clarity than I ever knew I could experience.

I hadn't realized how much I'd closed myself off from my life and the people in it. How much I'd penned myself in with the walls I've built and the tales I've told. But all of that is changing now. I feel as if I've finally gotten in touch with a part of myself that was there all along but that I never recognized. Until now. And I have Dana to thank for all of it.

The kind of intimacy that I've experienced during our time together has allowed me to finally feel safe enough to let go of the delusions and bullshit I've been hanging on to for all these years. I can feel the artifice peeling away. I feel lighter. I feel like I can breathe more freely. I feel like I want to face myself, head-on. I can sense the weight of the deceptive behavior I've engaged in and am desperate to shake free of. And with one exception, I'm almost there.

Rebecca can't know. Not yet. Not until the time is exactly right. I just need to tie everything up and get my situation fully figured out, and then I can let her in on what's been happening. I'll explain my relationship with

Dana and how she's helped me to truly open my eyes. I know that Rebecca will understand.

◆

THE NIGHTMARES HAVE been arriving fewer and farther between. No longer am I driving nightly under cover of darkness to dig up the body that turns out to be my wife's. And the last time I dreamt of the snowstorm, it was hardly the nightmare I'd gotten used to.

I was trudging through the snow, in winter boots this time. I sensed something on my tail, but as I turned around, I saw that the snow was filling in my tracks. I spotted a line of trees just off to the side of the open field and cut sharply toward it. I hid behind the thick trunk of a snow-dappled oak and watched as the two detectives passed by, oblivious to my position.

I woke up next to Rebecca for the first time since she'd gotten over her illness. With a sense of relief, I rolled over and wrapped my arms around her. "I love you, Madoo."

She groaned and swatted me away, in the adorable way that she does. I rolled back onto my other side and slept straight through until morning.

◆

AS FAR AS I CAN TELL, Wolcott and Silvestri have grown bored of sniffing around. I thought I'd caught sight of them a couple weeks back as I was returning home from Smithtown, but I've become increasingly convinced that it was just a case of my nerves going haywire. They haven't been poking around the house, and Rebecca hasn't mentioned anything since she's been back to the office. I'm more than happy to be rid of those pests.

Javier and the boys are just about wrapped up with the framing. They've hustled their asses off thus far, and it looks like they've got room in their schedules to stay on with me to help with the roofing, siding, and flooring. These guys really seem to take pride in their work. Also, the fact that I can afford to pay them time and a half on the weekends doesn't hurt. At this rate, as long as the plumber, electrician, and painting crew can keep this thing from looking like a monkey fucking a football, we should be able to finish up construction just in time.

twenty-eight

WOLCOTT

"How long can we sit on this asshole?"

My partner and I are perched inside the cruiser in the dwindling light of dusk.

"Getting antsy, Silvestri?"

"No, I'm actually asking. How long will the department let us keep tabs on Campbell?"

"Well, luckily for us, Suffolk is a pretty sleepy county most of the time."

"Yeah, lucky us."

We've been following Paul Campbell to this house in Smithtown regularly. "Patience, my friend."

"Two weeks, Wolcott. Two fucking weeks. And so far, we've got Campbell screwing around on his wife. Little mystery there, considering who we're dealing with. Wouldn't take Sherlock Holmes to piece it together."

"Yeah, I suppose *Larry* Holmes could probably handle this one."

Silvestri chuckles. "You follow the pugilists?"

"It's the gentleman's sport, after all."

"Right. You mind if I eat dinner? I'm getting the growls."

"Have at it."

Silvestri reaches underneath the seat and produces the sack. He removes a jar and unscrews the lid, unleashing a wave of stench.

"Jesus, man. What went bad?"

"The cabbage." He takes a bite and chews it slowly.

"I worry about you sometimes."

"Don't worry about me. I'm taking care of myself, brother. Want a bite?"

I recoil. "Good God, man. No."

"It's just kimchi. It's fermented."

"I know what kimchi is. You're a fan, huh?"

"Fuck no. It's terrible. But it's great for your gut. Probiotics."

"You go in for that?"

"Swear by it. Science, man. Prebiotics and probiotics. Sets you up right."

"Wait, what are *pre*biotics?"

"Helps you digest the probiotics. Gets your stomach set up in a kind of a loop. The asparagus and garlic I was eating before? Good prebiotics."

"Hmm. How'd you learn all of that?"

"Read up on it, around the time I was really learning to cook. Had some time on my hands."

"When was that?"

"When the old lady left."

"She handled the cooking, huh?"

"No, I used to get down in the kitchen. But after she left, I figured out how to look after myself a little better."

"Hmm."

He's silent for a long moment. "I used to have a bit of a fucking issue with the sauce. After she took off, I took stock of some things. Changed up some habits. It's all part and parcel, living healthy."

"I hear you." I turn to look at my partner. "You still good on that?"

"The bottle? Yeah, all good there."

"Glad to hear it."

"Oh, here we go."

I follow his eyes to the front porch of the house, where a light has gone on over the doorway. After a moment, the door opens. Paul Campbell walks out, followed by a woman looking to be in her late fifties.

"What's this now?" asks my partner.

Campbell hooks arms with the woman as they walk down the path and toward the driveway.

"Interesting," I conclude.

As they approach Campbell's Jeep, the woman leans in for a long hug. They exchange words for a few moments, then trade a kiss on the cheek before Campbell gets in and starts the engine.

"Very cozy, these two," says Silvestri. He turns to me with eyes wide. "He seems to have charmed the hell out of the mother."

"Really embracing the 'family man' role. This guy is just brimming with surprises."

The woman waves warmly at Paul Campbell as he backs out of the driveway and turns onto the street.

I key the engine. "Let's see where this animal takes us."

◆

WE'RE HALFWAY BACK to Stony Brook when Silvestri's cell phone rings.

"Detective Silvestri . . . Yes, yes . . . You don't say? . . . Okay, great . . . Yeah, give it to me." He reaches into the glove compartment, takes out a pen and a deli napkin, and starts jotting. "Terrific . . . I could kiss you . . . Thanks a million." He hangs up the phone, a grin plastered on his face.

"What's up?" I ask.

"Well, this is one of those good news, bad news scenarios."

"I'll bite. Bad news first."

"Now, are you *generally* a bad-news-first sort of guy, or is it just—"

"I'm on the edge of my seat, Silvestri."

"You're going to have to turn around."

"Where are we going?"

"Huntington. We just got a hit on Sasha Anders's credit card."

◆

THE MOTEL IS A MODEST AFFAIR. Cozy, but wholesome-looking. We approach the front desk and are greeted cheerily by a young woman barely out of her teens.

"Welcome to the Huntington Inn. Will you gentlemen be checking in together or separately this evening?"

My partner nods in my direction and offers the young woman an exaggerated look of arrogant confidence. "He wishes."

I interpret her giggle as an opening and take a split second to consult the name badge on her polo shirt. "Good evening, Gina. My name is Detective Wolcott, and this is my partner, Detective Silvestri."

"How can I help you, Detectives?" The look of concern—and lack of suspicion—on Gina's face confirms that this is exactly the sort of establishment I suspected it was.

"Gina," I continue. "We're investigating a missing person, and it appears that their credit card was used here earlier today. Would you be able to look up that information for us?"

"Why of course, Detectives. What was the name of the guest?"

"Sasha Anders. A-N-D-E-R-S."

Gina taps away at the keyboard. "Oh, okay, yes. Here we are. Sasha Anders. Checked in for two nights. Put the room charges on the card and left just before checkout time this morning."

"And that's eleven A.M.?" chimes in Silvestri.

"It sure is." Gina's brow furrows as she studies the computer screen. "Oh, right."

"Everything okay?" I ask.

"It's just, well . . . this was weird."

"What was weird, dear?" asks my partner.

"I remember her when she checked in. So pretty. Looked really nice. Blond. Had this really gorgeous red Fendi bag with her too. Actually matched the convertible Jag she was driving. She was wearing a cap from Lotus Pedal, where I take spin. I was surprised I hadn't noticed her in class or anything."

"Okay."

"So, she checks in alone, goes up to her room for a while, then leaves for the afternoon. Says goodbye on the way out. Like, supernice. She comes in and out a few times over the couple of days that she's staying with us. I'm working most of that time, because Shannon, the other girl that works here, has been out with some kind of, like, stomach bug or something. Anyway, I only ever see Mrs. Anders coming in or out alone."

"Right."

"She checks out alone this morning. But then when housekeeping goes up to the room after she's left, the place looks like a tornado hit it."

"Is that so?" I ask.

"But, like, really bad." Gina leans in closer, and her cheeks flush. "I mean, lots of sex stuff and all that."

"Hmm," I ponder. "Not to make you uncomfortable, but what sort of stuff?"

She lowers her voice to a whisper, even though we're the only three people in the lobby. "Maria from housekeeping said there were condom wrappers, and lube, and the sheets were kind of all over the room and on the furniture and stuff. There were some pills lying around. Oh, and one of the lamps was broken. We were trying to reach her by phone earlier to let her know that we would be charging the damage to her card."

"You have a phone number on file?" asks Silvestri.

"Yeah, she gave us one when she checked in, but when we tried it, it was disconnected."

I take out my notebook and pen. "Gina, would you mind reading me back that number?"

She does, and I jot it down. "Great." I nod in the direction of the security camera pointed down at us. "Do you happen to have a camera on the floor where Mrs. Anders was staying? Maybe we can get a look at her companion."

"We do, but our whole system went down. The technician is scheduled to come in tomorrow and fix it. Sorry."

"Not a problem. Is there a chance that any of the debris you found in the room is still on premises?"

"We saved the lamp. I think they were going to try and get it replaced or something."

"How about any of the trash from the room?"

"No, housekeeping took care of that before the new guests checked in."

Silvestri leans in closer to the desk. "Any possibility that trash is still in a dumpster on the premises?"

"No," she says. "The trash gets picked up around two o'clock on Fridays. It's long gone by . . ." Suddenly, her eyes brighten. "Wait a minute," she whispers. "Are you guys looking for DNA or something?"

"You got us," answers Silvestri.

"This is so cool." She beams.

"Gina, are you happy here at the inn?" I ask. "Because we can always use young talent like yours at the academy."

She blushes again. "Oh, you guys."

I lean in slightly. "Before we take off, is there anything else you can remember?"

She thinks for a moment. "I mean, not really. Like I said, besides trashing the room, she was supernice." Slowly, a look of concern takes shape on her face. "Wait, she's not dangerous or anything, is she?"

I hold up an open palm. "Oh, we're fairly certain that she poses no public threat." I reach into my jacket pocket with the other hand and produce a business card. "Just the same, would you please give us a call if you see her again, or if you think of anything else that might be useful?" I hand her the card.

"Sure thing, Detectives."

Silvestri pats the desk. "Gina, you've been a big help. Thank you so much. Hope the rest of your shift goes quickly."

"Thanks, guys. You too. And stay safe out there."

twenty-nine

REBECCA

IT HAS BEEN two weeks since the trip to the jewelry store. Two weeks of waking up with the alarm and either getting dressed for work as usual or for a prework Lotus Pedal class. I've packed lunches as usual, pretended to read emails over coffee in the morning, and fabricated marathon meeting days. I keep waiting for the shoe to drop and for Paul to catch me in my lie, but he's too absorbed in his own to notice. Every day is a struggle to appear as though we are completely and totally back to normal. Paul is busy and preoccupied, but he's also lighter and happy. I am the opposite.

Our house isn't safe anymore. Most nights, I lie next to him unable to sleep, thinking I hear Sheila pulling herself along the carpet toward me. If I do fall asleep, I wake up every night around three A.M. The feeling that someone is in the house draws me out of bed every time. I walk through each room quietly, pulling back the shower curtain, checking behind the living room drapes, ferreting out any intruders in closets and under the bed. The only presence I find is myself becoming a little more unhinged with each passing night.

To gauge my sanity, or sanity lacking, I've been taking photos on my phone of each room before I get into bed and comparing them to what's there when the sun is up. I am not crazy. Closet doors and drawers that were shut are ajar by the light of day. Faucets are running that I didn't turn on, and windows that I have closed and locked mysteriously open in the night. A few times I've heard sounds throughout the house like someone is moving slowly and carefully around each room but I haven't wanted to wake Paul, since I haven't been entirely sure if the sounds were outside my head. One morning I swiped through the images from the night before and caught a flash of something in the foreground of the living room behind the curtain. A shadow about the size and shape of a person. I zoom in and it is hard to tell from the photo if what I'm seeing is anything more than a shadow of something inanimate. But the more I examine it, the more it looks like an outline of someone around my height.

I fight the urge to confide in Paul. He's good at shutting down and blocking out the thoughts that don't serve him. Sheila, the detectives, the truth about how he spends his day are all off-limits topics. I learned my lesson after a few nights of sleep deprivation, a healthy pour of wine, and one too many Percocets. He was falling asleep with my head on his chest. I was listening to the sound of his heartbeat and feeling warmer toward him than my usual furious state.

"Paul?"

"Mmmm?"

"Do you believe in ghosts?"

"Madoo, come on."

"What? Do you believe in life after death?"

"No."

"Not at all?"

"Not even a little bit. I don't believe in wasting time talking about ghosts, let alone believing in them."

"We never talk about this stuff."

"Come on, babe. This conversation is childish."

"But what about if someone dies violently and gets stuck in between the living and moving on to wherever the afterlife is? What about—?"

"By that logic you and I would have seen half a dozen ghosts between us."

"Maybe I have, Paul."

"Madoo. I'm not going to have this conversation."

"Well, technically you are having it."

"This is silly. Whatever you think you've seen is in your head."

I don't bring it up with him again. But I can't ignore that strange things have been happening in the last month. Small items continue to go missing, and missing things return. Last week, my engagement ring was sitting on the soap dish as though it had been there all along. This morning, my dove necklace was back in my jewelry box untangled and sitting pretty on top of the rest of my pieces.

It took a couple of weeks before I considered Paul might be gaslighting me. If he's capable of all the lies and secrets of the last year, who's to say he wouldn't have a little fun with my sanity before pulling the plug on our marriage? Revenge for killing his girlfriend? For standing in the way of his new love? The more I get to know about his new life, the more I think about how much satisfaction hurting him would bring me. Why wouldn't the same be true for him?

The only good thing about being haunted is the motivation to leave the house every day. Every night of half sleep and waking worry, I watch the sun come up, waiting for the time when I can escape from the encroaching danger in our home to the safety of watching hers.

◆

THE FIRST NIGHT I came to her house I was careless. I entered her address into my GPS, not even thinking that Paul might see it if he took my car. It was nearly eight P.M. by the time I ran out of the jewelry store, and without recalling the drive at all, I pulled up to the outdated Colonial in need of a fresh coat of paint and parked across the street. I wasn't more than five miles from my own house. The lights were on and I could see occasional flashes of movement inside. Paul's car wasn't there, but I could feel that this place was important to him. As I sat there in the dark, I got a burst of creativity. I felt energized with purpose.

The next morning I got up and ready for work as usual. When Paul left, I took an Uber to the Avis two towns over. I booked the most inconspicuous car they had with my specifications, dark in color with tinted windows. I got a nondescript black car to blend in with the fleet of others on the road. There were so many drivers on the road now, idling in front of businesses and houses waiting for passengers, I figured I could easily blend in. I even bought an Uber decal off eBay and had it overnighted. It's amazing how easy it is to pretend to be someone else.

I drove the town car to her house first thing and sat and watched for a full day. I tracked Paul's movements and texts on his phone and saw nothing suspicious. By four thirty P.M., I realized I'd been sitting there for nearly six hours without anything to eat or going to the bathroom. I'd taken very small amounts of Xanax throughout the stakeout but had been holding out on any painkillers, knowing better than to get high and risk falling asleep or getting pulled over on the drive home. I was disappointed as I drove the rental to the shopping center parking lot, and questioned whether I was actually losing my grip in the Uber on the way home. But I felt the lift of possibility when Paul emailed Dana that he was looking forward to seeing her the next day.

I parked farther away from her house than I had the night before and held my breath when I saw his Cherokee approaching her house from the opposite direction. He got out of his car and brushed his hands through his hair as he walked toward a side door off the garage. There was a noticeable excitement in his gait, like he couldn't get up the driveway quickly enough. I waited for a woman to emerge and jump into his arms. Nothing so dramatic played out, but without hesitation he turned the doorknob and let himself in. This simple, subtle, everyday move tore my heart right out of my chest.

I took a minute to collect my breath and stop shaking enough to start the car and pull away. I pictured Paul's new mistress looking through the window and commenting on the car that had been parked in front of her house for two days in a row, prompting him to confront and expose me. The scene played out vividly in my mind and made me tremble with humiliation. I vowed never to return as I accelerated away from the house.

I nearly stomped the brakes when I saw the familiar faces parked a few houses down from hers. The detectives were doing the same thing I had been moments earlier. I hadn't noticed them because I was so fixated on Paul. I flinched, thinking they would see me, but their focus was solely in the direction over my shoulder.

Seeing them affirmed my being there. Paul was their suspect as much as he was mine.

◆

I'M PARKED IN front of her house again. In days of watching and waiting, I still haven't seen her. Catching a glimpse of her is a more powerful craving than my pills these days. Despite my promises to stop coming here, I find myself pulling into view of her front door. I've watched him pull into her driveway, saunter up the walk unabashedly, and let himself in the side door so many times now. Like he fucking lives there.

I haven't been brave enough to stay until he leaves yet. Today I will. And today I will wait as long as it takes to see her. I've pulled my hair up into a blond wig from a few Halloweens back. I've got the darkest sunglasses I can find and have the synthetic hair tucked into a NY Yankees hat that I've pulled as far down over my face as I can without obstructing my view. I'm vaguely aware of how far I've let this go and how unhinged it all is. The lying about going to work every day, the tracking and watching, now the disguises. I keep waiting until it goes so far that even I can't rationalize this behavior. What started as my obsession has become my routine. I don't recognize myself anymore, even without the wig and glasses.

I watch the road for the detectives, but I haven't seen them since the first time I spotted them. I wonder if they are still watching him and what they think he's been up to. Do they also know about his double life? Being a lying snake isn't illegal, but it doesn't exactly paint Paul as a man of his word either. I catch him in lies daily now. About where he's going and where he's been. I've thought about following him to Cold Spring Harbor, where he's been going just about every day, but I haven't worked up the nerve. The drive is far and I don't trust myself not to get caught.

I watch the papers for any new stories about Sheila or Sasha, but the coverage of their disappearances has been eclipsed by the spate of overdoses across the island in the last two weeks. The pharmaceutical well has run dry, and desperate times are driving people to address their cravings by any means necessary. There is so much bad news every day now, two missing women is already old.

It is noon, which is earlier than Paul ever shows up. He's pretty consistent and I've learned his patterns. With all my new-found time, I've become an expert in patiently watching. There are many things I'm learning about myself since my forced retirement, and my failure to stop and look at my life when I was working all the time is a big one. Silver linings.

I enjoy being the observer more than I would have expected. I prepare myself for a couple of hours of waiting time and scroll through my new laptop for something to listen to. I think about listening to an audiobook about self-improvement, or a podcast that will motivate me into a different mind-set. I settle on a crime series about cold cases. Listening to lives worse than mine has become a source of comfort.

"Typically, men murder their wives with practical motives in mind: to escape their marriages, often because of affairs, or money and drugs and alcohol are often big factors. Women who murder their spouses are far more likely to do so out of passion. In the case of Stryker's, the husband, Roy, had motivations that were all the above."

I'm ten minutes into a host setting the scene when I see Paul's Cherokee making its way up the street in the rearview. He's driving in from the opposite direction than usual, and I slink down in my seat as he glides past me and pulls right up to the garage.

He steps out looking sunny as he walks around to the rear. I am on tenterhooks as he pulls a familiar shape from the back of the Jeep and leans it up against the garage door, face out. It is a "For Sale" sign, with his name, number, and face splashed across the white background. For a fleeting moment I relax with the notion that all along, Paul has been coming to this house for his job. Of course. He's selling the house and meeting with the owner regularly. I choose not to think too much about the engraved jewelry that has brought me here.

Garden spade in hand, he digs two narrow divots expertly. He looks content as he positions the sign and uses a mallet to hammer both sides of it into the grass at the foot of the property. As he replaces the displaced dirt and grass, a car that I've seen a few times parked in the driveway pulls up into the spot that he usually inhabits. He stands and waves.

I see his smile as he moves toward the car and offers a hand to the woman, whom I can only assume is Dana, exiting the driver's side. She's taller than he is and strikingly pretty. They don't kiss, but Paul places his hand on her arm in a gesture of familiarity so subtle it makes me flinch. I watch as he goes around to the back of the car and starts to unload grocery bags and walks them up the drive to the main entrance of the house. The woman has moved to the back seat and I see her leaning in for something. The afternoon sun is casting a glare on the windshield.

I watch Paul move to the front door and disappear inside. The woman is still leaning into the car and I can see that she is very thin. She's wearing stylish jeans and heeled booties. When she backs out of the car and stands, my breath hitches and my heart stops.

She has a little boy in her arms. He is probably around three or four, with one hand in his mouth and the other in the thick curly black hair around her shoulders. The little boy looks a lot like her, but with hair a few shades lighter. Hair closer to the color of Paul's. I try to chase away the thought.

Paul exits the house and makes his way down the drive toward them. The woman smiles while the boy claps happily in Paul's direction. She puts him down and he darts toward something colorful in the grass. A Nerf football. Paul and the woman stand shoulder to shoulder talking and watching the boy. He runs around them in circles like a herding dog edging them in closer with each lap. Paul says something and she laughs with her whole body. She is at least ten years younger than me and doesn't look like she's ever carried or birthed a baby. I'm feeling a rapid drop in blood pressure as a sickening pall ripples through my body inside and out.

The boy runs straight for Paul's legs, unable to stop the momentum of his motion when he reaches his destination full force. Paul bends over and lifts him up over his head, much to the surprise and delight of the toddler. The woman watches and laughs again, and steals looks at her phone as Paul and the boy chase each other around the front lawn and start tossing the football between them. The space around me closes in.

Seeing Paul's ease and happiness with the toddler slays me. I'm so overcome I fear I'll vomit in my closed surroundings, so I crack the window for some air. I lie across the seat and breathe deeply until the wave passes. When it does, I wipe the cold sweat from my face and resume my upright position.

Dana walks over to Paul and hands him the phone she's been looking at. She moves to the boy and picks him up, and Paul holds up the phone to take a picture. He lowers the camera and she walks over to him and puts her hand on his arm as he shows her the photo. My head starts to pound hard.

Paul gestures to the sign he's just planted. Emotion crosses her face. There is surprise maybe, but also apparent relief and happiness. She moves toward Paul and hugs him. The little boy watches his mother and encircles both pairs of legs as they hug in an embrace of his own. They are all laughing now. They look happy. They look like a family. A family that I'm standing in the way of being together.

I don't need to hear what they are saying to know what I'm seeing. The answers to all of my questions are as apparent as the "For Sale" sign in front of me. I have to say it out loud to hear the words.

"Paul has another family." This echoes inside my head as a looping scream. My knuckles are white around the steering wheel and I am shaking so hard on my seat with anger, my teeth are chattering. The woman and her son wave Paul to follow them into the house. He closes the front door behind him.

I see clearly that Paul does want me gone, and why. I am not paranoid. I am in danger. For all of the years I've stayed with him and put my dreams of a family aside, he's been making that life with someone else. And I'm in his way.

I am going to kill my husband.

thirty

PAUL

TODAY, I ALMOST died.

I was up on the roof with Javier, laying in shingles, when I lost my footing. If he hadn't caught my wrist, I would have gone over the side and into a rock pile below. It's my own fault, really. Between getting this house built, helping Dana out with her sale, and trying to be present at home, I'm fucking zonked. Dana's got me in a great headspace, but there's only so much I can do to stave off the physical exhaustion that's setting in. Lately, I've experienced moments of delirium. And it seems I'm not the only one.

The other week, Rebecca woke me up with some nonsense about ghosts. My formerly rational wife seems to be going off the deep end. I know she's been stressed at work with that asshole boss of hers, but I'm more worried about her behavior. The reinjury of her shoulder has caused her to up the dosage on her pain meds, and I've lately discovered her trembling and jittery. I'm also afraid she hasn't been able to put the incident behind her and wonder if her mind is dredging up those memories from childhood. She's been ill and acting erratically, and she looks drawn and gaunt. I'm afraid that confronting her will just push her to a place where

I'll no longer be able to reach her. I'm finding myself feeling increasingly anxious to get out of that house and escape this life.

With the exception of my nearly plummeting to an early death, construction is going smoothly, thank God. Summer weather has gotten a jump on us, and the mid-May heat is dogging the crew. We should have the roof wrapped within the week, mercifully. It'll be good to get inside and out of the sun.

The real estate market has all but come to a halt in anticipation of the summer season, which is a relief. Things are quieting down. My biggest issue is going to be coming up with excuses to be out of the house for the next few months while we finish the property. But if I can hold it together a little longer, I just might be able to keep all these balls in the air.

thirty-one

SILVESTRI

"YOU AND THE MISSUS got anything planned for Memorial Day, Wolcott?" The AC in the cruiser is the only thing allowing me to discuss the beginning of the summer season without becoming enraged.

"We'll probably hit the beach. My lady loves the beach."

"You're shitting me."

"What?"

"I can't exactly picture you out there sunbathing."

"Am I an albino?"

"I'm just envisioning Mr. Rogers, with the fucking cardigans."

"I need to get my vitamin D somehow. Being cooped up in here with you certainly isn't doing the trick."

"I've been told I'm a regular ray of sunshine."

"Yeah. Keep believing that."

The radio hisses. "*Ten-fifteen in progress at McNamara's Pharmacy.*"

"Again?! Shit. Step on it."

◆

"DETECTIVES, HOW NICE of you to show up." Our favorite pharmacist is standing in the parking lot as we pull in. He's not happy to see us. The feeling's mutual.

Wolcott throws the cruiser into park, and we step out onto the seething concrete. "Got here as soon as we could. They're gone, Leonard?"

"She sure is. But not without a couple of medicine cabinets full of pills." He turns and walks us in the direction of the pharmacy.

"She?" I ask. "That's a new one, at least. What'd she get?"

"The usual," he laments. "Oxys, Percocets, a few boxes of Demerol."

"Par for the course," says Wolcott. He jots the drug names in his notebook as we enter the shop.

"Fucking insurance companies are killing me. They don't want to pony up to cover the expensive stuff, so now I've got every soccer mom this side of Ridgewood coming in here and playing dumb with their opioid refills, not to mention some yo boy waving a gun in my face anytime I look up."

"We're dealing with it too." My partner flips to a fresh page. "Now, what did this woman look like?"

"Hard to say. She had a bandanna covering her face and another covering her hair. Maybe midthirties, from what I could tell. In pretty good shape. In fact, she was dressed like she was coming from an exercise class."

"And she was armed?" I ask.

"Yeah, she was waving around a gun that was too big for her. She was so manic I was afraid it was going to go off accidentally. Christ."

My partner closes his notebook and looks at the pharmacist. "We're glad you're okay, Leonard."

"Yeah, this time. I'm thinking about getting a gun of my own for the store. For protection."

"Get that idea out of your head," I say. "All that's going to do is turn a robbery situation into a homicide. Just let them go. You're insured."

"Yeah, a lot of fucking good that's been doing me," he fumes.

"I don't imagine you've gotten your security camera fixed?" I ask.

He's silent for a moment as he glares at me. "I've been a little busy making sure that I actually have prescriptions in stock for paying customers."

My partner interjects. "We hear you, pal."

Leonard looks dejected as he surveys his kingdom. "You guys looking for any help down at the morgue? I'm starting to feel like I'd much prefer to deal with the nonliving."

Wolcott pats him on the shoulder. "We'd be happy to put in a good word for you."

"I'd appreciate that." He offers us a pensive look. "Hate to say it, but I'd probably just end up dealing with these same folks on the other end of things."

◆

WE'RE IN THE PARKING lot returning to the cruiser when my partner's phone rings.

"Detective Wolcott . . . Yes . . . How long ago? . . . We're headed out there right now." He hangs up and looks at me. "We gotta go."

"What's up?"

There's the faintest hint of a grin on his mug. "They just called in a body."

thirty-two

REBECCA

My body is paralyzed.

"Stop fighting."

The dirt rains down on me in a cascade. I struggle to keep my head above the quickly rising soil.

The voice speaks again from the darkness.

"Let go."

I want to. I can't fight any longer. The exhaustion and defeat have become too much. I surrender and lay my head back on the ground rising around me. I'm so tired.

"I'm sorry." I can barely get the words out. All the air in my lungs is being compressed by the unmovable weight crushing my ribs.

As I begin to breathe in the dirt, I see Paul standing above me, the trowel in one hand and a "For Sale" sign in the other. He smiles at me as he kicks a large swath of dirt into the hole.

"You brought this on yourself."

Everything goes black.

thirty-three

WOLCOTT

THE ENERGY IS CRACKLING in the cruiser as we roll up to the lot on Smithtown Bay. Silvestri and I don't say anything, but we both know whose body this is.

As we exit the vehicle, we're met by an eager young fellow with a soaking-wet pair of ears. "Detectives, I'm Officer Litman. First on the scene." The kid has a firm handshake.

"Officer, I'm Detective Wolcott. This is Detective Silvestri." We walk him over to the body. "What are we seeing here?"

"Jogger stopped to retie her shoe on a run this morning and saw something poking out of the ground. Called it in. Ended up being a hand."

"That'll throw a wrench in your workout routine," I say. "How's the body looking?"

"It's a real mess. Female. With this level of decomp, hard to get a bead on her age. As you can see, she was wrapped in a tarp and buried in a shallow grave. If I had to guess, I'd say she's been in the ground six, eight weeks."

I look to my partner and exchange a quick nod.

"You guys got an idea on this?" asks Litman.

"Fits the timeline on a possible missing persons case we're looking at. Has the coroner been called?"

"On their way," offers Litman.

"Good," I say. "And let's try and keep the press out of this until we can get an ID on the body, yes?"

"On it," responds Litman.

"Good man." I pat the officer on the shoulder, and he walks back to his cruiser. Silvestri and I lean in and peel the tarp away from the face.

"Glad I skipped breakfast this morning," my partner says. "Jesus."

"You thinking what I'm thinking?"

"Depends. Are you thinking that Paul Campbell's about to make our list of things to do this week?"

"You're a regular mind reader, my friend."

thirty-four

REBECCA

I KNOW EXACTLY what needs to be done. It came to me this morning. I'd put on my daily costume: my work clothes, a full face of makeup, and straightened hair, looking the part of a well-dressed pharma professional, as I'd been doing every day since I'd been fired. Paul had just gotten out of the shower and winced as he dried himself.

"Paul, what's wrong?"

"My shoulder and back are acting up. Must be the weather. Would you mind grabbing my heat wraps from my bag, babe?"

Keeping with the dutiful, loving wife act, I smiled and made my way to his bag. I found the wraps easily. As I took stock of the contents, I didn't see the red bandanna containing the gun anywhere, which made me uneasy. The discomfort gave way to a perfect idea. It was so simple I couldn't believe that I hadn't thought of it earlier. But getting the materials needed could be challenging. I'd need to get into Mark's house when he wasn't there.

◆

"You don't have to be a psychic to know that a lot more people are going to die around here."

I can't see anything and I'm unable to open my eyes. I feel myself belted in tightly. There are men in the car with me. I should panic but my body feels so damn good right now.

"Drug-related deaths in this community are seven times what they were last year. And that isn't just overdoses. The homicide rate has doubled in Nassau and Suffolk Counties in that time too. Things are officially dire."

I pry my eyes open with my fingers and the daylight stings. I face myself in the rearview and wipe away the drool from my cheek. The seat belt has left an indentation in the left side of my face. I'm alone. And high as fuck.

"There are literally thousands of heavily addicted folks in our region searching for the best and most cost-effective solutions they can find, and the stakes continually get higher."

I turn the radio down so that the voices are a comforting, faint murmur. Everything feels soft and slow. Recognition releases another wave of cool happiness into my bloodstream. I am parked a few houses down from Mark and Sasha's house. His car was parked in the driveway instead of at work, where I'd expect it to be, so I figured I'd wait him out. He was bound to leave at some point, but there were no signs of that and I'd fallen hopelessly asleep. The ongoing deprivation isn't helping my ability to stay awake during the day, pills or not.

I can't believe it is five thirty P.M. I have missed my window of opportunity to sneak in today and still get home at a reasonable hour. I am furious with myself for not having my shit together.

I check his GPS location and see that Paul is in the general area. Texts with Wes update me that they don't have any showings today and Wes is getting an early start on the weekend in Montauk. I'm struggling to keep my attention focused on the phone screen for very long. Carefree times of beach bonfires and night swimming play like someone else's happy memories in my head. I think about how good swimming would feel right now and remember that Mark and Sasha have a much-boasted-about pool. Maybe I'll take a dip, but the thought melts away. The scene on Dana's lawn comes to mind, and a shock wave of anger rolls through the euphoria. I remember what has brought me here.

Thanks to Sasha lamenting her terrible memory in the locker room, she's already given me the key. I regularly made a point of having my locker near enough to hers so that I could learn her code. She always used her birthday. And she couldn't keep herself from bragging to one of her syco-phants at Lotus Pedal about how her husband had put the entire home security system on a password, using the one combination of numbers she could actually remember, after she'd forgotten the access code enough times that Mark got sick of the security company sending patrol cars to their house.

I'll come back tomorrow to pay Mark a friendly visit, and hopefully he won't be home.

thirty-five

SILVESTRI

"BUT WHO ELSE could it possibly have been?" I ask my partner.

"I don't know. Did you see anyone else going in or coming out of there this morning?" asks Wolcott.

"Yeah, but come on. It's gotta be Greene. It's as obvious as the crumbs on his chin. Fucking hump never met a snack he didn't like."

The loaf of banana bread that Wolcott's wife, Abby, baked for the station house has gone missing from the break room. My partner is incensed. "Did no one ever explain to that guy that consideration makes the world go around?"

"Take it easy. We'll siphon the gas out of his cruiser later. Would that make you feel better, big guy?"

His phone rings. "Wolcott." He shoots me a look as he straightens up in his seat. "Okay." He silently mouths the word "coroner" in my direction as he listens intently. I lean in. Suddenly the eager expression on his face is replaced by a decidedly perplexed look. "Is that right?" He looks at me and shakes his head. "Okay, thanks for the quick turnaround. Really appreciate it." He hangs up.

"What is it?" I ask.

He looks at me with disbelief. "I'm glad you're already sitting down for this."

thirty-six

PAUL

"I CAN'T BELIEVE it," I say as I inspect the finished roof. "We're really knocking this thing out."

"Yes, boss," Javier answers absently. He and the guys are glued to a portable radio set up on a sawhorse. Their breakfast sandwiches sit neglected as they hang on the reporter's every word.

I don't understand enough Spanish to get the gist of what's happening, but their intent focus is intriguing me. "What's going on?" I ask.

Javier keeps one ear on the proceedings as he turns slightly to me. "They found the woman out by the bay. Is dead."

No. Please, God, no. The pit of my stomach knots up. My hands go numb as they tremble wildly. The smell of the breakfast sausage causes bile to run up my throat. My insides burn as my extremities lose all feeling. My heart seems poised to bust through my rib cage.

"Boss, you okay?" Javier is now focusing all of his attention my way.

"Yeah, sorry. Forgot something back in the truck. Give me a minute."

I have to make a concerted effort to keep myself upright as I beeline for the Jeep. As soon as I'm close enough I fall toward the hood, barely catching myself as I do. I key into my breathing to keep myself from passing out. *Fuck-fuck-fuck-fuck-fuck. This can't be happening.*

I manage to get myself around to the driver's-side door and into the seat. I check my phone. Nothing from Rebecca. She must be blissfully unaware that our universe is about to come crumbling down around us.

I pull up the newsfeed on the phone. I'm both desperate to see what's happening and terrified to know the extent to which we're completely fucked. There's no way this development ends in anything but disaster.

Here it is. The top story on every news source on my feed. I scroll down, then back to the top, and click on the first link. It's a city paper.

Body of Long Island Woman Found in Shallow Grave

I look at the accompanying photo. I look back at the headline, then back at the photo. My brain feels as if it's just been rolled by a wave. It's finally happening. I'm losing my fucking mind.

I force my eyelids closed and squint hard. I open them to find myself looking at the same impossibility. This is not in my head. This is absolutely real. Even though it can't be.

Under the headline is a full-color photo of the victim, in happier times. The woman the cops dug up from a lot out near Smithtown Bay. A woman I know. Or, rather, knew.

Sasha Anders.

part three

part three

thirty-seven

REBECCA

I'M IN A DEAD sleep when Paul bursts into the bedroom waving a folded newspaper. Something terrible has happened.

"Rebecca! Where have you been? I've been trying to call you for an hour." His voice is shaky and hoarse.

It takes everything to pry myself out of the hole I've sunk so deeply into. Sleep after fentanyl is like falling into a coma. I've been dreaming about Sasha and Sheila and stewing in my anger. Now that I'm awake I struggle to assume my wifely mask. He is here now and I have to remind myself that as far as he's concerned, I'm still his loving, supportive wife.

The curtains are closed, making it impossible to determine the time. I'm not clear what day it is or how long I've been in bed.

The only certain thing is Paul's agitation.

"Sorry. I had a migraine. I turned my ringer off. Sorry, honey." I haven't the foggiest idea where my phone is.

He sits on the edge of the bed and puts a firm hand on my leg and speaks to the floor. I've seen this stance before and get a pang of fear for whatever he's about to say. Through my grogginess, I pull myself into focus as quickly as the building cortisol will take me.

"They found a body," he says.

My stomach starts to hurt. "Fuck."

"Right where I put her . . . there was a jogger who found it . . . but . . ."

He's got his head in his hands and is kind of rocking back and forth. The gravity of what he isn't able to say is dawning on me. I hear Sheila whispering that we are going to get caught.

"Okay. Let's talk this through. We knew this might be a possibility. We just have to figure out what to do next." I'm impressed by my own cool-headedness despite the panic exploding in me.

"Rebecca. They found a body where I put Sheila, but it isn't *her*!" Paul erupts. His temper causes me to withdraw. I feel like a little girl again being yelled at by my father.

"That doesn't make any sense. There must be a mistake."

"The police don't make mistakes like that. Come on, use your head. All of those pills are making you stupid." His whole energy right now is scaring me. He looks like he'd love to take a swing at me.

I speak to him like he's a feral animal and try to calm him as much as possible. Hard to do when I can't begin to calm myself. "How can you know for sure?"

"Besides, this body wasn't hit in the head. It was *shot*." His knuckles are white from clutching the paper so tightly. His face is twisted into something very dark.

I try to move away from him without being too obvious. "Whose body is it, Paul?!"

Dramatically, he puts a copy of *The Independent Press* on the bed. Sasha's photo is splashed in vivid color above the fold.

Local Resident Shot to Death
and Left in a Shallow Grave

The paper and Sasha's image seem to take up the whole room. *Sasha.* Shot. What the fuck did Paul do? Sasha's dead. Sasha's fucking dead. My mind reels in too many directions, to the point of dizziness. I feel sick and relieved. I never have to see her again or feel small in her shadow. There is no repressing this horrible part of me that is emerging. I'm glad she's dead. I lie back against the headboard. Paul barely registers my preoccupation. I wonder if he'll notice if I excuse myself to snort some Adderall off the sink.

"It's Sasha's body. Same timeline as Sheila." He looks up at my face and I see the fear in his. "Babe, it doesn't make any sense. I put Sheila in that ground. How the fuck did Sasha end up there?" He is nearly pleading. But a tinge of me feels like he is overdoing it.

I swallow hard. My mouth is a desert from the drugs, and pain rips through my throat. I lean back farther and close my eyes. In my dream, Sheila kept saying that Paul had done bad things. Believing a dead woman in my dreams feels more reliable than anything Paul has said or done in the last month.

We sit on the bed looking at each other closely, searching. The sum of his features makes up his face, but something crucial is absent. He looks different, not in any one specific way. Just off. Like someone who could murder too. He mistakes my scrutiny of his face for concern and takes my hands urgently in his. I fight the urge to recoil.

The slow spokes of my frontal lobe move through a few revolutions before I can get the burning question out from behind my lips. I'm careful to keep my words from sounding accusatory, afraid of what he's capable of.

"Paul, if they just dug up Sasha, then where the fuck is Sheila's body?"

thirty-eight

SHEILA

THE BEST THING about being dead is that nobody suspects you when bodies start turning up.

◆

THE NIGHT IN PAUL and Rebecca's bedroom wasn't the first time I died.

When I was five years old, my mother found me on the kitchen floor sitting next to an open bottle of insecticide. Always bordering on hysterical, she dissolved into a full-blown panic attack instead of calling for help. I lay next to her with my little hand on her shoulder, knowing something was very wrong but unsure of what to do.

I actually hadn't ingested any poison and was perfectly fine until she fell apart before my eyes. I internalized her stress and my body seized up with each jagged breath she could muster until I was paralyzed. As hard as I tried to move my arms and legs to help her, my limbs had turned into wood. We were side by side, frozen in our shared panic. Some minutes or hours later, my father arrived home and called 911.

By the time the paramedics arrived I was completely rigid, with a pulse so shallow it took two EMTs to locate it. As far as my father knew, I was nearly dead from poison and it was my mother's fault. Motherhood had been too much for her already fragile emotional constitution, and no doubt it wasn't helped by a husband who avoided being at home and who was a tyrant when he was.

The debut of my unknown nervous condition combined with an injection of atropine in the ambulance to counteract the insecticide slowed my already weak heart rate to undetectable. The ER doctor on the eleventh hour of his first shift declared me DOA. I don't know how my stoic father reacted when they told him the news. I've wondered if he was a little relieved. Even at my young age I could sense that he didn't like me. My mother was heavily sedated in another section of the hospital.

I woke up under a sheet, completely unaware of my surroundings. I could see shadows of light and dark cycling above me. The sounds of wheels squeaking on the floor stirred my second feelings of dread and awareness that day that something was terribly wrong. I flexed and wiggled my fingers and toes in a fleeting moment of relief to have some movement back but quickly began to thrash and scream under my shroud. I still wonder if the orderly wheeling me from the ER ever recovered from the five-year-old-girl who came back to life en route to the morgue.

Specialists were called. A research doctor from the university consulted on my case and was visibly excited by the rarity of my condition. Seeing my mother's reaction triggered a rare anxiety disorder called catalepsy, a name that sounded imagined by a child. When an attack comes on, the rare sufferer goes rigid and their pulse and breathing become barely detectable. It also decreases sensitivity to pain, something that contributed heavily to my survival that night at Paul and Rebecca's. And the freezing weather helped too, but I'll get to that later.

By the time I was reunited with my father, he'd gone through such an array of extreme emotions, there wasn't much life left in him. He seemed not moved, but rather inconvenienced at my resurrection. He stayed around long enough to pick my mother up from the hospital and drop us both at home. He left the engine running and didn't look back as he drove away that day. I wish I could say things got better after that. They didn't.

I've been left by men three times and died twice. What kills me only makes me stronger.

thirty-nine

WOLCOTT

"HAVE WE BEEN FISHING in the wrong lake this whole time?" As I steer the cruiser onto the highway, I look to Silvestri for reassurance that we haven't been completely off the mark. The possibility is jarring.

"Fuck if I can tell you," he says, shaking his head.

"Well, let's go see if we can figure out who's been impersonating a dead woman. That should get us started."

"Right," my partner answers distractedly.

Because of the advanced decomp, we weren't able to get a clean DNA pull off Sasha Anders's body. Sheila Maxwell's abandoned car didn't produce any leads either, and the theories we're considering seem like a tangle. I feel like I'm trudging through fog. Instead of finding answers, the more we investigate, the less sense it all makes. "I could have sworn I knew who was buried in that grave. And it's not who they dug up."

"You and me both," offers my partner. "But we were also assuming that Sasha Anders was off spending her husband's money somewhere."

"Right. That added up. This . . . I don't know."

"Okay, let's chop it up. We've got to consider Mark Anders."

"We do. You think money was a bigger issue than we figured?"

"Often is. Pressures of the job? Or maybe an affair?"

"Could be." I sit with the possibility. "Him or her?"

"Hmm. Think he's fucking one of his employees? That has a way of throwing things in a special direction. Or else she's getting in some extra-curriculars. Bored wife, not getting any attention at home."

"Or the two of them are keeping themselves amused."

"Right." Silvestri mulls the idea over. "Okay, I gotta take it back here for a second. Any chance Campbell's in the mix?"

"I mean, the guy seems good for this sort of thing. We just thought it was with a different woman."

"Right. But why are we assuming that this mope didn't do 'em both? Seems like the women around here who take a shine to Paul Campbell turn up in the ground, or not at all."

I give this some consideration. "Love triangle?"

"There we go. Wait—fuck—what if Sheila Maxwell was the doer? Found out about an affair between Campbell and Sasha Anders and lost it."

"Hadn't thought of that possibility."

"I mean, she's got the suspicious past, with the husband. Finding out about Paul Campbell with another woman could have sent her over the edge."

"Right. But didn't her case seem more like a disappearance? The abandoned car, the suspended credit card use, the unpaid utility bills."

"Unless she had to get out of town in a hurry."

"Okay. She could have left the car behind to stage a disappearance. Throw us off the scent."

"Unless Campbell *was* mixed up with both of them, and things got out of hand."

"Right. So the million-dollar question is: Did Sheila Maxwell skip town, or should we be looking for another body?"

"Jesus. This is a wreck."

A silence falls between us as we sink into our respective thoughts. I've never had the rug of presumption so thoroughly yanked out from under me during an investigation, and it's needling me more than it should.

When I finally address my partner, I'm surprised at the tentative quality of my tone, as if I'm overhearing my own voice. "I keep getting hung up on this one thing."

"What's that?"

"When we interrogated Campbell, he seemed genuinely disinterested in Sasha Anders. It struck me as one of the more truthful aspects of the conversation. I just didn't think that he was mixed up with her."

"He's a seasoned liar. Who knows? He might be pathological. Shit, maybe he wasn't quite as over Sasha as he'd have us believe. "

As I turn the thought over, my phone rings. I fumble for it before I pick up. "Detective Wolcott." The voice on the other end is the one we've been hoping to hear from. "We were just on our way to pay you a visit." I nod toward my partner as the air in the cruiser seems to lighten and lift. "We'll be there in no time."

◆

"Welcome to the Huntingt—Detectives!" Gina catches herself and looks around the lobby to make sure there isn't anyone else in the vicinity.

"Good morning, Gina. Can't tell you how happy we were to hear from you." We approach the front desk, offering her warm smiles on the way.

Our new friend is vibrating with energy. "Guys, I just read about the body in the paper, and I had to call you!"

"We figured our favorite bloodhound might be onto the scent," says Silvestri. "What can you tell us?"

"So, I see the headline, and the picture of that pretty woman on the front page, and I start reading, but then I get to her name, and it doesn't add up."

"What part doesn't add up, Gina?" I ask.

"Well, so I recognize the name from your investigation, but it's not the right person."

I look to my partner, then back to Gina. "How's that?"

"Well, obviously the picture in the paper is Sasha Anders. But that woman who checked into the hotel isn't the woman in the paper."

"Got it. I know you already gave us a description of the woman who checked in here under that name, but is there anything else you might remember now? Any little details that stick out?"

"Let's see. Blond hair, brown eyes. I told you guys about the hat, right?"

"You did."

Her eyes settle on the top of the desk for a long moment. They narrow as she concentrates. "I mean, she looked a lot like the woman in the paper, but not quite." She frowns. "A lot of these women look really similar, quite honestly. I hate to say it, but they're sort of, like, interchangeable."

I smirk at my partner. "We've noticed."

Suddenly, Gina's eyes widen. "Wait, did I tell you guys about the fumigation?"

"You did not," says Silvestri, perking up.

"Hmm. Must have been after your last visit. They had to call a guy in to have the room fumigated. The cigar smoke in there was disgusting."

I eye my partner before turning back to Gina. "Well, you've certainly got a talent for recall. It's been very helpful to us."

"Thanks, Detectives. Hey, do you still think I'd make a good cadet?"

"We'd be happy to put in a word for you," my partner says.

"You guys rule."

◆

IN SPITE OF THE WAVES of heat rising from the asphalt in the parking lot, Silvestri and I are tripping over ourselves to get back to the cruiser.

"Shall we go look in on our favorite cigar aficionado?" I ask.

Silvestri shakes his head in disbelief. "Anders actually has the stones to run around with some girlfriend impersonating his wife while she's in the ground?"

"Let's find out."

forty

SHEILA

THERE WAS A TIME when I would have said that I'd die for Paul. But we often say ridiculous things when love has taken the wheel from common sense. I admit, I tend to get a little wrapped up in my relationships, but Paul was different. He was the real thing. Certain events just got in our way before he was able to fully realize how he felt about me. And if I was willing to die for him, since I did die for him, isn't it only fair that he do the same? But I'm getting ahead of things.

I definitely didn't picture my birthday unfolding the way it did. Namely, I didn't imagine that it would end with me wrapped in plastic, thrown away like a piece of garbage. I suppose there is something poetic about being murdered by my boyfriend's wife on my thirty-fifth. All of those self-help books I'd tried to comfort and coach myself with over the years always promised that the most profound beginnings come from the most traumatic endings. But these were not the thoughts that were going through my throbbing head when I came to in the dark, swaddled in cold plastic. The thing in the forefront of my mind was how I was going to get free of the tight coil I was trapped in before I froze or suffocated.

Luckily they'd rolled me in such a way that my head was bent upward, and while highly uncomfortable on my neck, the angle allowed for a small range of mobility and limited airflow. My breathing is more shallow than most to begin with, and my cataleptic response to the scene in Paul's bedroom benefited me once unconscious and with limited air. As did the temperature. Ironically, Paul extended my chances of survival that night considerably. When a person's heart stops, or at least slows so much it appears to have stopped, keeping their body cold renders the cells in their body less in need of oxygen, therefore slowing down death. Leaving me in the nearly freezing basement probably saved my life.

Thanking him wasn't exactly on my mind in that moment.

I'd initially panicked when I regained consciousness, and started to hyperventilate. I was able to calm myself quickly enough, though. When you have an aversion to mood stabilizers and a condition that is triggered by high levels of stress, you have to learn alternate methods of control or else spend your life in a rigid state of panic. I took as deep a breath as I could and counted to five and then exhaled for ten. With each inhale, the casing around me constricted like a corset. With each exhale, I felt my heart rate slow by a beat or two.

I was still too disoriented to piece together the recent events of the evening up to that point. The last thing I remembered clearly was making the decision to take a cab to Paul's house after polishing off a bottle of pricey red in place of my uneaten birthday dinner. I'm sure I was a sad sight sitting alone at my favorite restaurant, where I'd first seen Paul, all dressed up, tears falling into my barely touched risotto.

In that moment, I'd told myself that confronting him and exposing our relationship to his wife was the only thing left to do if we were going to have any chance of being together. Any doubt or rational thought was replaced by the merlot-tinged adrenaline coursing through my bloodstream as I put the stolen key into his lock. Duff rushing to greet me and happily lick my familiar hand confirmed that I was meant to be there. At least that is what I told myself as I pulled Paul's pistol from my purse and made my way upstairs. I felt powerful holding it. I didn't know exactly what I was going to do when I reached their room, but I knew whatever it was, Paul wouldn't be able to ignore me any longer.

On the hard ground, I'd started rocking slightly side to side, and then more animatedly, to see how much breadth I had to work with. There seemed to be a good amount of space on either side of me, which was a relief. I wasn't completely sealed shut in my swaddle either, which was a very good thing. When I moved to the right, I could sense the flat edge of the seam where the plastic ended. I could also feel a sledgehammer of pain radiating from my head down into the rest of my body. My back felt broken on the hard, flat surface beneath me. Although it felt like concrete, which was more hopeful than a number of alternatives. Newly dug compact soil on all sides of me, for example.

I've always been naturally flexible and am pretty strong for my small size. That night, I was never so grateful for all of the core strengthening I'd conditioned working out nearly every day. Though little did I know I'd been working toward saving my own life. I used the strength in my abs and ass to start rocking more aggressively and was able to push myself and land facedown a half turn to my right. Still unable to see anything, I could feel the gravity of my new position as the blood ran from the back of my head to the front in an explosion of pain. Without access to my hands, I hadn't yet surveyed the extent of my head injury, but I could feel it from the inside out.

As long as there weren't any obstacles for a number of feet in the same direction, I stood a decent chance of rolling myself free. But I had no way of knowing if I was careening toward death. I could be forty feet up in a building yet to be finished and pitch myself over the edge unwittingly. I craned my neck as much as possible in the direction of the opening and waited for my eyes to adjust to the pitch black. Nothing changed or came into focus. It was a terrifying feeling to have so many of my senses disabled. Smell and sound seemed moot in the situation. But no sooner did the thought dissipate than I registered the absence of outdoor sounds. So if I was stashed in a construction site high above the ground, I most likely would have been able to hear wind or maybe even the ocean, depending on where Paul had thrown me away.

The instinctual will to survive over the intellectual is a powerful thing. Whatever reason and fear I had about going over an edge was eclipsed by my body's sideways momentum. Each exhausting revolution struck pain through every possible part of my body, but the hope keeping me in motion blossomed stronger with each plastic layer shed like a snake's skin behind me. When the roll was down to one layer separating my weak body from the world around me, I was able to shimmy my arms up and break through the final fold.

I cried with relief and self-pity for where I'd ended up. For what they'd done to me. And relief gave way to fury. I used that feeling to keep going.

Once I'd rolled away from my restraint, I sat upright slowly. A burst of blinding pain flashed a deceptive moment of light but then left me in the unrelenting darkness once again. No matter how long I remained in the gloom, my eyes could not adjust to make any sense of the space I was in. I was on solid ground, and the cold concrete was hard and unforgiving under my sore body. I moved my hands up to my head, and where my smooth hairline was supposed to be was a lump the size of an orange, screaming at my touch. A flash of the object in Rebecca's hand, a hammer, hadn't registered in the moment earlier in the evening but was certain in my mind now. I was grateful she'd hit me in the place that she did and not in one of the more vulnerable spots, like the back of my skull.

The euphoria of freeing myself was fleeting and was rapidly replaced by panic and pain. I knew I was at the very least concussed. My whole scalp was dry to the touch and there was no stickiness to indicate bleeding, which in the moment seemed like a good thing. But I'd absorbed enough about NFL head injuries to know that often the worst trauma didn't bleed on the outside. I rolled to my side and pulled my legs up into myself in a child's pose to will away the persistent image of blood hemorrhaging across a CAT scan.

When I felt around in the dark to assess the rest of my body's injuries, I was surprised to find that my purse was still slung across my body. I pulled my phone out of the small satchel and was encouraged to see that it still had some battery power remaining. I had to squint to lessen the impact of the light from the screen. There were no bars for service. I was seeing double and starting to have waves of nausea as I swept the flashlight from the phone across the terrain and saw that I was in a basement, surrounded by lumber and landscaping materials. I pulled a burlap tarp from the pile of materials and draped it over my body for warmth as I dragged myself toward the stairway a short distance from where I was sitting.

And then I began the slow and agonizing climb from the bottom up. To new beginnings.

forty-one

PAUL

"THEY'RE LYING, MADOO."

I stare at my wife, coiled up in the sheets next to me. The alarm clock on the side table reads 4:42. I haven't slept since we got into bed.

I know Rebecca is awake. Her brow furrows in a certain way when she's trying to will herself to sleep but can't quite reach it. It's another short moment before her eyes pop open and find mine.

"Who's lying, Paul?"

"Those dipshit cops."

She slides herself up toward the headboard, propping her shoulders atop the pillows. She seems wired physically, but there's a dull glaze behind her eyes. "What are you talking about?"

"Babe, I've been up all night trying to make sense of this. It's been driving me nearly crazy. But I've gone through every permutation, and I keep coming back to the only possible answer. They're lying about the ID."

Her eyes narrow as she appears to weigh the words coming out of my mouth. She takes a deep breath, presses her eyelids together, and meets my stare. "Tell me what you're thinking."

"Sheila's body was in the ground for weeks, rotting away."

"You mean Sasha's body." There's a tinge of panic underneath the resigned exasperation in her voice.

"No, babe. I mean Sheila's."

"But you said yourself that the police don't make those kinds of mistakes."

"I know. But this isn't a mistake. Just hear me out, okay?"

She sighs. "Go on."

"Unless we've both completely lost our shit, it was Sheila who was in our bedroom that night, correct?"

Her eyes dart to the side, then back to mine. She lets a nervous laugh sneak out. "I could have sworn it was."

"Right. I left here that night and stashed her body myself."

Rebecca bolts upright. "Wait, *stashed* her body?"

"The ground was frozen when I tried to bury her. I had to stash the body and wait until it thawed before I could put her in the ground."

My wife has crossed over into full-on panic mode. "Paul, you left her fucking body out for—"

"Madoo, I had no—"

"Don't you 'Madoo' me! You left the body of a woman that we . . . Oh God." She folds forward and dry heaves.

I take her by the elbows and prop her back up. "Rebecca, look at me." She eyes me defiantly, her stare boring a hole into mine. "Baby, breathe." She takes a deep breath. Then another. "You okay?" She narrows her eyes, then nods. "Okay, listen to me. I was very careful. I put her where no one would find her, then went back as soon as I could and buried her." I catch my tone and realize I'm talking to her as if she were a small child.

Her eyes narrow again, but this time her tone is much calmer. "Paul, I'd feel much better about the situation if she were still buried."

It's my turn to feel like the stupid kid, but I power through it. "I know. But here's where we're in good shape." She looks at me, daring me to make that last sentence make sense. I desperately hope I'm about to. "That body was rotting away in the ground for long enough that they couldn't tell who they dug up, so when they couldn't get an ID, they realized that they'd hit a dead end. They had two missing women, the story was all over the news, so they had to make it look as if they'd solved the case. They must have figured they had stronger motive and a weaker alibi with Mark, so they ran in that direction."

"But you said there was a gunshot wound?"

"They're fabricating details, to make the story more dramatic."

Rebecca looks away, and I can see her adding things up in her head. Her body seems to relax. "Okay."

"Think about it; when the cops spoke with us, we both painted a picture of a fraught marriage between Mark and Sasha, with money issues and all. They kept asking us questions and digging around deeper. But when they brought me in for questioning, they referred to Sheila as kind of a loner and someone who went unnoticed. The kind of person without roots, with a suspicious past, who might just up and skip town."

My wife has shifted her body toward mine. She listens intently. "Yeah, okay."

"So, you see, you and I both know that I buried *one* woman, but the police managed to dig up *another*. Because *Sasha* is a much more likely— and compelling—story. There's money, there's motive, there's a villain. I mean, babe. With all these stories in the news about prescription abuse and ODs and junkie crime, who better to pin things on than a Big Pharma bigwig? Think of all the papers that *that* version will sell."

Rebecca looks at me, and I'm brought back to that morning in bed, just before those idiot detectives showed up. The last moment we felt safe. She has a look in her eyes that tells me she's back to believing that we're going to get away with this. She grabs the back of my head, kisses me hard, and rolls over. Her shoulders relax, and I think she might be able to find her way back to sleep again.

As I lie in bed, a profound sense of relief takes over my body and I find myself regretting that I can't share this part of my life with Dana. I've opened up to her so fully, bared the contents of my being so completely, been so utterly naked and vulnerable around her, that it seems a shame that I have to disguise this aspect of my life. But, of course, this is how it has to be, for both our sakes.

I roll onto my back and close my eyes. The image of the house in Cold Spring Harbor appears before me. I can see the rest of it taking shape, and the end product looks exactly as I've been envisioning it. The details pop. I can see two pairs of slippers sitting on the cherry floors, next to the fireplace. I can feel the crisp autumn breeze as it blows through the open window, rustling the curtains. I can smell the scent of geraniums riding in on the breeze. It's perfect. And it will soon be ours.

forty-two

REBECCA

THE FACT THAT MARK has stopped leaving his house altogether has posed a major problem with getting inside. After driving by his house every day for a week and seeing no signs of his car moving from its spot in the driveway, I've become desperate. I've decided to try a different approach and pay him a condolence visit.

He looks like death when he opens the door. "Rebecca?" My name falls out of his slack mouth as part question, part plea. I can see that he's in terrible shape on every level. His sour alcohol breath smacks me hard. He's got a full beard and a life's worth of bad news hanging in his eyes.

"Mark. How are you?" I try not to overdo it with my forced concern. I feel awkward and weak standing at his doorway with the increasingly heavy condolence basket in my arms. I regret opting for the substantially heavier wine-and-bourbon variety over fruit and flowers.

"Come . . ." He doesn't finish his thought before turning inside, leaving the door ajar and the terry-cloth belt on his ratty robe sadly trailing behind him as he disappears somewhere into the dark house. Like him, the robe has seen better days. This may be easier than I thought.

I've always wondered what the enormous Federal held within. My invitations to Sasha's annual pool party had apparently gotten lost in the mail over the years, and even when we'd started communicating at the studio, there were no mentions.

The grand foyer is so extremely on brand with Mark and Sasha's unabashed wealth, I have to staunch a gasp and the urge to snap a picture. The marble floor, twenty-foot-high ceilings, and gold-accented double staircase feel more like the mouth of an opera house than a residence. I place the basket next to a sad pile of wilted flower arrangements and restaurant takeaway bags, no doubt containing hot meals in various stages of spoilage.

I venture into the house in the direction of Mark's path, guided by the sounds of televised debate. He barely looks up when I enter the living room, which is roughly the size of our entire house. He is sitting on one end of a white horseshoe-shaped couch that could comfortably seat twenty. He shakes the ice-filled glass in his hand in a gesture that I can't determine is an offer or a request. I take the tumbler and tip a generous pour of Lagavulin single malt from the drink cart immediately next to him. I don't make myself one, knowing clarity is more vital than self-medication right now, no matter how rough the edges feel. I am three hours into withdrawal and declining rapidly. Sitting on the couch next to Mark with mixed motives is officially my new bottom, but my depleted store had made my choice for me.

"Rebecca. How have you been?" The absurd nicety hangs between us. I'm obviously not going to share that I've been cycling at a regular rate from strung-out to homicidal. I can't possibly admit that I'm so deep into my drug dependency that I've quite literally lost track of time, space, and supply. That when I went to bed last night, I had half a bottle of Percocets—a miraculous find in one of my hiding places that I swore was pill-less in a tweaked-out search—that was completely empty this morning. I can't even level how "I've been" with myself.

Instead I put my hand on top of his free one and pat it. He doesn't move or appear to register the contact. The feel of his hand under mine draws a surprising wave of tenderness toward him. The feeling is fleeting and my contempt for him returns squarely to the front of the line.

"Mark, I'm so, so sorry about Sasha. I wanted to come over sooner, but I . . . I don't know why I didn't. I guess I didn't know what to say. I guess I just can't quite believe she's dead." This last bit is the only truthful crumb in the lot.

He doesn't say anything, and the talking heads on Fox News fill the silence with unbelievable news that feels so far outside of the life I've found myself in, I don't even register the words. Mark takes a long draw from the crystal tumbler and clears his throat.

"She's been dead for a long time, you know. But they won't let me bury her yet. Not until they get everything they need for the investigation. I never knew how long autopsies actually take. You never see that on TV."

He appears to be on substances other than scotch.

"I didn't realize how much I depended on her, Rebecca. I didn't really know how much she did for me until she was gone. I know I wasn't a perfect husband, but I did love her. I needed her."

"I know you loved her very much. She was a special woman." My lies continue.

He snorts and sits back, regarding me with a head-to-toe once-over, his gaze lingering on my breasts. "Please, Rebecca. You are so full of shit your eyes are brown. Sasha was a raging bitch who thought you were a wannabe, if she thought about you at all."

His sharp words come out in an impact-softening slur, and I can tell that he doesn't really expect a response. He's looking out the window now. I see an enormous in-ground pool and a fire pit and what looks to be a crematorium before I realize it is a grill. He appears to be engrossed in the beautiful spread before him, but I suspect he's folded himself deep into his own head, far away from where we are sitting.

I scan the room around me for any signs of the information and/or substances I'm after. The surroundings are free of pill bottles or photographic evidence of Sasha's exhumed body. The latter I know is illogical, but I expected the former to be as present and likely as the bottles of booze within arm's reach.

My surveying stops short when I see a gun sitting on top of a pile of unopened mail like a deadly paperweight. Mark owning a gun doesn't shock or surprise me, but leaving it out so casually and carelessly makes me worry about his mental state.

I look from the Glock to Mark and back to the dark metal and feel a pulse of genuine concern for the guy. I picture him sitting in the dark in his misery and filth, with the constant stream of badness in the world playing on a loop in surround sound, with a drink cart, a loaded gun, and a dead wife. There is no doubt in my mind that this is very much a man whose wife is dead.

"Mark, are you doing okay? Do you have anyone looking in on you? Do you need anything?"

He raises his eyebrows and moves his gaze to my breasts again, and then down my body approvingly.

"Unemployment suits you, Rebecca." Before I can fully reconcile how much I'm willing to degrade myself for what I need, his eyes move back in the direction of Hannity and a bleached-blond pundit in a low-cut crimson dress and matching Restylane lips. He speaks without returning his gaze to me.

"You know, Rebecca, when the news about Sasha came out, not one of those ass-kissing bitches she kept on retainer reached out. Neither did their boring husbands who I pretended to like and shared my good scotch and my eighty-two-incher with."

It takes me a second to realize he's referring to his flat-screen.

"Her family is barely speaking to me. And everyone at work has been radio silent. I've gotten a whole lot of flower arrangements and lasagnas, but not much in the way of actual human outreach. So, to answer your question, aside from our housekeeper, and the two jerk-off detectives investigating Sasha's murder, you are the only one 'looking in on me.' Funny that."

The iciness of his monotone is deeply unsettling. Mark has never been the warm-and-fuzzy kind, but all evidence of the playfulness and teasing that kept his sarcasm from being outright meanness is absent.

"Mark . . . I'm really sorry. I should have come over sooner. Or at least called."

"You were one of the last people I expected to hear from. I wouldn't have blamed you either. I fired your ass, or made you quit, I guess. I figured you hated me. To be honest, Rebecca, I didn't give a shit if I ever saw you again. You always caused more problems than profit.

"But the funny part of it is, the thing I need the most right now is something you can actually give me.

"The cops think that Sasha was murdered on Thursday, March fifteenth. They haven't made it public, but they are pretty confident about that date. The night in question is one that I was alone. If it had been a few nights earlier or later, I would have had some alibis that wouldn't have won me any husband-of-the-year awards but would have provided one or two female companions who could have put me somewhere other than alone in my house, unknowing that someone was snatching my wife between spin class and happy hour and shooting her. I happened to look back at my texts from that evening to confirm, and wouldn't you know it, you reached out that evening for a bit of the good stuff. I'm willing to bet that you were alone and in the neighborhood that night. I didn't respond to your text because I was having a solo party that evening and wasn't feeling that generous or in need of company."

I try to compute the developing leverage ahead of what I know he's going to ask. The raging itch for a hit of something doesn't help matters, or any confidence in negotiation power I might otherwise have. A cold sweat breaks and I feel the prevomit bile hit the back of my throat. I see Mark looking at my shaking hands. I clasp them to regain steadiness.

"Mark, can I use the bathroom? I'm not feeling so well."

"Careful, Rebecca. Your habit is showing." A smug, pursed smile settles on his lips. He gestures toward a door in the opposite direction from where I entered and resumes his drink and glazed news viewing without missing a beat.

I take off in the direction of the bathroom and barely make it in the doorway before I lose my stomach's contents into the bidet, a space of inches closer to the door than the toilet opposite it. When I compose myself and rinse with a swig of Listerine from under the sink, I let the faucet run on full blast to mask any sounds of the medicine cabinet reconnaissance I've been planning since I discovered my empty stash this morning.

There's nothing stronger than Advil, and I shut the cabinet, frustrated and nauseous again. I take a deep breath and smooth my shirt, procrastinating about what I know I need to agree to.

Mark is standing in the hallway inches away from me when I unlock and open the bathroom door. He's got a familiar orange bottle in hand and he shakes it like a rattle. My saliva glands flood and my heart races.

"Looking for these?" He looks haughty in his grimy pajama pants and stretched undershirt and robe.

My arm is outstretched before the thought to reach fully processes.

"Not so fast, honey." He takes my hand in his, not gently either.

"Okay, Mark."

"Okay, Mark, what?"

"Okay, I'll be your alibi. I'll tell the detectives we had to work late. I'll tell them I came over to go over a marketing presentation and ended up drinking too much and needed to sleep on your couch. Paul was working late that night, I'm sure. I'll think of something to tell him if I need to." As I say this, I can't remember if he was, but I pray. "I'll show them the text I sent you asking if you were home." I don't have to search my texts to know I absolutely hit him up that night.

He doesn't break eye contact as he uncaps the bottle and pours five hydrocodones into my hand. They are the good kind, the 750-milligram dosage. Before I can protest that the drugs in my hand are nowhere near fair compensation for a fabricated alibi, he places the index finger of his free hand on my lips.

"These will get you back to functioning enough to convince Columbo and Kojak that you were with me the night Sasha was killed. Once you do that, I'll set you up to cure what ails you for a good long while."

He knows the checkmate is his. I don't fight the defeat. My mind is on one thing and one sweet thing only. I'm nodding as I take one of the pills in my sweating hand and swallow it dry. I put the balance of the meds in a Kleenex and wrap them tight before pushing them into the pocket of my jeans.

I don't say anything to Mark as I brush past him and toward the grand foyer and out the front door. I also don't realize until I'm a few paces from my car that Mark hasn't once said that he didn't actually kill Sasha.

forty-three

SHEILA

SOMETIMES THE PEOPLE who become most important in our lives
show up in the least significant ways. Paul came into my life by way of an
overheard conversation while I was on line for the shower, sweaty and half-
naked.

The postclass Lotus Pedal locker room was teeming with red-faced
women in various states of undress. Rebecca was two people ahead of me.
Of course, at the time, I didn't know her as Rebecca; I knew her as the
hard face and body who spun next to me in the dark countless times and
never returned my smile or acknowledgment. Just another rich bitch.

She was talking quietly to a woman with frizzy carrot-colored hair who
I'd seen around the studio a couple of times. I didn't think they were even
friends, mostly because Rebecca didn't give the impression that she was a
woman who had female friends. The two spoke to each other in the way
that people who feel obligated to talk to each other do. Overly friendly to
conceal a general lack of enthusiasm over the interaction.

"Rebecca! I forgot you came to this studio! It is really too far from my
house, but when I heard that Chad B. was teaching, I had to book!" And

conspiratorially: "And my derm is here and is *so* worth the drive for his magical syringe."

The redhead was shrill in her too-small towel, her breast implants disproportionate to her otherwise petite build.

Rebecca looked trapped. She kissed her on the cheek quickly. "Erin, so nice to see you. How's the new house? How's Wes?"

"I mean, when he told me that he wanted to do real estate out here and leave the city permanently, I was like, ugh, I'd rather die. What the hell am I even going to do all day? But it has been so great not having to work and really focus on all of the self-care I wasn't able to do in the craziness of Manhattan, you know? And of course it is great for the kids."

Rebecca nodded wordlessly. I didn't have to see the contempt living behind her niceness to sense that it was there. I already hated this woman too.

"And obviously I want Wes to be doing this well, but I never get to see him!" She leaned in. "I mean, I would like for him to help me spend some of this money he is making!"

I tried not to roll my eyes. Rebecca looked like she might be trying to do the same. "I'm glad to hear things are going so well," she replied evenly.

"How *is* Paul doing?" Red delivered in a tone that suggested something bad had befallen whoever Paul was. "How has he been? I mean, his business failed *so* badly. How do you come back from that?"

Rebecca's face darkened a shade. "Paul's fine. He's great. He is figuring out what's next," she responded acidly.

Erin smiled wanly and nodded in a robotic way that indicated to me that she really couldn't care less. "This must be hard on your marriage. Are you guys still thinking about having kids?"

Rebecca's face contorts. "We are happily and decidedly child free. Always have been."

"Oh, I must have mixed you up with someone else. Good for you." I couldn't believe how rude this woman was.

"No problem." Rebecca's pursed lips told otherwise.

"I'm sure something will come up for Paul; he's a smart guy."

"I'm just glad he's getting out of the house semi-regularly to walk Duff." Rebecca warmed slightly.

"Oh, right! You guys have that enormous dog!"

"Sometimes I think Paul loves him more than me." Her laugh undeniably was forced.

"Well, maybe he can start a dog-walking business or something. Or a business building doghouses?!" Erin was amused with herself. Rebecca was not.

Clearly sensing Rebecca's irritation, Erin reached into her gym bag for her iPhone. "Sorry, it's my nanny."

"Of course. Do what you need to do."

Without looking up: "We should have you guys over for dinner sometime soon. I've totally gotten into feng shui! Maybe I could do it for your house? Free up some energy, spruce up Paul's career corner?!"

"Sounds great." Rebecca moved up to the shower as another woman stepped out. She hung her towel before sliding into the stall, her immodesty revealing small breasts and a painfully thin frame. As she leaned in to adjust the water temp, I tried not to stare at the delicate dove tattoo on her hip. She hadn't struck me as the type to have one.

◆

THE CONVERSATION STUCK with me all day and into the evening. I can't explain why I cared about a man I'd never even met. But my curiosity was piqued and I obsessed for the next few days. After a week or so passed, the encounter and my interest in Paul were replaced by other thoughts, and I'd almost forgotten about him completely. That is, until the universe sent me a sign as clear as Paul himself standing in front of me.

◆

AFTER I REACHED the top of the dark stairway on my thirty-fifth year into the unknown, it was many hours past my actual birthday. I was able to get my bearings enough to see that I was standing on a spacious concrete slab. It took me a few moments of walking around on the surface and peering over the edges to realize I'd been tossed in a basement below a house foundation, sans house. The property was surrounded by a dense landscape of trees. As my eyes adjusted, I took in the expansive surface and imagined the size of the house that would sit atop the footprint one day. I lay out on the cold concrete and watched the plumes of cloud traveling over the surface of the full moon above. I didn't feel rushed to do anything other than let the evening's events take root in me. I wasn't surprised exactly—my life had taken terrible, unbelievable turns before—but I couldn't quite get a foothold on what to make of my current situation.

The scant battery power remaining on my phone allowed me to use the GPS and determine that I was twenty-one miles from home. I vacillated between the urge to call 911 and the desire to call Paul. I couldn't yet accept his part in all of this. He hadn't been the one to drop the blow to my head. He'd been sleeping, blissfully unaware of what was transpiring in his own bedroom. I imagined him waking and seeing my body splayed out. Unable to contain his shock and devastation at what his bitch of a wife had done to me. Had he cried? Pounded the floor?

Looking up at the constellations above, I silently asked for a sign. Logic told me that Paul was absolutely the one who'd brought me here. But I couldn't be angry at him. I was having sporadic recollections of coming into hazy consciousness completely encased, disoriented and catatonic, but able to hear the sounds of an engine running and Paul's frustrated grunts with each loud sound that followed, a dull thud of something very heavy being dropped over and over.

I rationalized that he'd had no choice but to get rid of my body because she'd made him. Maybe he couldn't put me in the ground because it was frozen, but he could have weighed me down and thrown me into the ocean. He wasn't ready to let go of me any more than I was of him. He'd changed his mind and put me somewhere safe. I couldn't forgive him completely for throwing me into a dark basement. But as far as he knew, I was beyond saving. All kinds of possibilities were coming to me through the excruciating throbbing in my head.

I had an opportunity that most people wish for. I could be a ghost in the world of the living. I could move among all of it without being seen. I could watch them. I could see how the person I knew in his heart really loved me survived after I was gone. Would he fall apart? Would his marriage implode under the guilt of my death? I could measure how much he really cared for me by how he suffered. I could watch her and figure out the best way to ruin her life as she'd ruined mine. And I could have some fun watching them both suffer along the way.

And I could come back when he needed me the most.

There was so much to do. But most pressingly, Paul would be coming back for my body and I needed to make sure there was one in my place when he returned.

forty-four

SILVESTRI

THE RECEPTIONIST OFFERS us an incredulous look. "Um, Rebecca Campbell hasn't been with us for quite some time."

"Is that right?" Wolcott tries not to betray surprise. "Can I ask the reason for her departure?"

We're standing in the lobby of Launaria Pharmaceuticals, and we're oh-for-two on persons of interest being on premises. Having been told that Mark Anders is out for the day, we figured we'd check in with Rebecca to see if she might be helpful. But it appears she hasn't exactly been level with us either.

Our charm seems to have already worn thin with the receptionist. She's toggling between distracted and mildly annoyed. "You'll have to consult HR," she says as she points us in the direction of the floors above.

I give it a go. "I'm afraid that time is of the essence here. It would really be helpful if you could—"

"I'm not at liberty to divulge that information," she answers.

My partner tags back in. "You wouldn't happen to have a date for her—"

The finger pops up for an encore. "HR." She says it as if talking to a set of toddlers.

"Well," I say, "you've been an enormous help. Have a wonderful day." She waves us off wordlessly as she answers the phone.

◆

"HOW CAN I help you, honey?"

Wolcott and I are sitting across the desk from Cecilia, in Human Resources. She seems to be more of a people person than her colleague downstairs.

My partner holds his hands in his lap as he offers her an easy smile. "Cecilia, we just need a bit of information on one of your former employees, Rebecca Campbell."

Her eyes go wide, and she curls her lips inward to stop herself from talking. She looks toward the door, then back to us. "What would you like to know?"

"We understand that Mrs. Campbell recently left her position with you after a long tenure, is that correct?" he asks.

"That is correct, yes." Cecilia leans toward us. "It was a shake-up, for certain. I don't want to call it a *scandal,* exactly, but . . ."

It would appear she's a bit of a Chatty Cathy, and it seems time to pull the string. "Sounds intriguing, Cecilia." I rest my elbow on the desk and my chin in my hand. "Do tell."

"Well," she says. "Rebecca was recently let go due to some questionable handling of prescription samples in our stockroom." Her voice drops a decibel. "Also, we received an anonymous tip that there had been some inappropriate goings-on between she and Mr. Anders." She raises her eyebrows to send this last part home.

Wolcott nods conspiratorially. "Quite the soap opera around here."

"Can you believe it?" she says with a gasp. Then, catching herself, she clears her throat and tugs on the neckline of her blouse. "But you didn't hear it from me."

◆

WE'RE BACK IN THE CRUISER, and my partner's got the phone to his ear. He mouths the word "voicemail" to me silently before laying on the casual tone. "Mrs. Campbell, this is Detective Wolcott. I'm sure you've been following the tragic events in the news as of late. We're reinterviewing a number of people from your spin studio to see if there's anything we may have missed the first time around, and we'd like to have you come in when your schedule allows. If you could please give me a call on my cell, I'd appreciate it. Thank you." He hangs up the phone and turns to me. "To the McMansion?"

I nod, and we drive off.

◆

THE GATED COMMUNITY we're driving through strikes me as paradoxical. Each house is different, yet they all retain a cookie-cutter quality. And although every resident is clearly trying to one-up their neighbors, all of the homes manage to underwhelm in their own gaudily unique way. Ah, the absurdities of wealth.

We're heading over to the Anders estate, to check in on our favorite delinquent pharma boss. Wolcott is drumming his thumb against his knee as he stares out the window. He turns to me. "Well, this is an interesting development."

"Certainly is," I say.

We round the corner onto the Anderses' block and park along the street, at a comfortable distance from the house but with clear sightlines to the front door. I'm relieved to immediately register the lack of news vans lining the street. The reporters haven't descended upon the home, which is promising. Best to catch everyone without their guard fully up.

Wolcott checks his phone, then nods at me. We each move to open our doors when my partner suddenly freezes, his eyes glued in the direction of Mark Anders's house. "Well, well. What do we have here?"

I turn to see Rebecca Campbell walking out onto the front step. She appears disheveled and out of sorts. Her face looks pale and drawn, and her shoulders are rolled in on themselves. Anders stands inside the doorway wearing a ratty bathrobe and looking just as stale as his companion. As she turns to him, he leans through the doorframe and hastily plants a kiss on her. She partially deflects the kiss, turns, and heads for the street. He calls after her, but she simply waves a hand as she continues toward her SUV. There's a sense of desperation in the way she lunges away from the house with each step.

"Looks like we may have been eyeing the wrong lovebirds all this time." I'm genuinely surprised at this new turn of events. Then again, this is a case that's become genuinely surprising lately.

"I'll be damned," says Wolcott. "Did not see that one coming." He resumes tapping his thumb, then stops and looks over at me. "Let's call an audible, now that we've got eyes on Rebecca Campbell. I'm dying to see what a lady of leisure does with her idle time."

I wait for Campbell to start her engine before I key the cruiser, but she sits in the SUV for a long while, appearing to stare at the floor. She shakes her head a few times, then tosses it back and stares at the ceiling.

"Poor thing," my partner says. "Must be grappling with a heavy burden there."

"Looks that way."

"It helps to talk, Rebecca. And we're here to help."

"We can help lift that off your shoulders," I say, eyes glued to the figure in the driver's seat. "It's what we do."

"Just missed the priesthood, Silvestri."

"By inches."

Rebecca leans toward the passenger seat, then straightens up. She raises a hand to her ear. As she does, Wolcott's screen lights up. He looks at it, then at me.

"Well, speak of the devil."

forty-five

REBECCA

"Mrs. Campbell. So nice to finally have you over to our place." Wolcott pulls out the metal chair for me and gestures with a sweep of his hand. My eyes go to the metal pipe bolted to the center of the table. The lighting in the room is awful. I've applied a generous amount of makeup to conceal my lack of sleep but didn't factor in the fluorescents.

"I apologize for the lack of ambiance in here. We've been meaning to spruce up the joint," Silvestri deadpans.

"Please, call me Rebecca. Mrs. Campbell makes me feel so old." I laugh lightly.

Silvestri hovers a few feet away from the table. He doesn't appear to be in a hurry to sit down. My eyes rest on the handcuffs hanging off his belt.

"Don't worry, we aren't going to add any bracelets to your outfit today," Wolcott quips as he takes his seat. I laugh again, this time too loudly.

I feel the sweat running down my back and am grateful I wore a dark shirt. I need to remember that I'm here because I chose to be.

"It was a rather serendipitous turn of events that finally brought us together today, wasn't it? You calling us at almost exactly the same time we were calling you?" Silvestri is so at ease in his stance, he looks like he should be holding a cocktail.

"I guess it was meant to be." I decide to play along with them.

Wolcott smiles warmly. "We had some follow-up questions for you after our last conversation." He takes a beat. "As you probably well know by now, Sasha Anders is dead."

"Yes. It is so awful." I wring my hands. "Do you know what happened to her yet?"

"Well, that is what we are trying to get to the bottom of. We know that she was murdered, but I'm afraid I can't say more than that at the moment."

"Sure, I understand. I just can't believe she's dead." I put my hands on the table. "You're sure it's her?" If they find my question odd, they don't let on.

"We're certain."

"Do you have any suspects?" They both seem amused at my brashness.

"We have a few persons of interest," Wolcott replies. "We're still in the eliminating phase. It's not as quick of a process as seen on TV."

"It's always the husband, isn't it?" My joke falls flat, and I immediately regret it.

"Yes, sadly it often is. The husband, or the boyfriend." Wolcott searches my face.

"Rebecca, why don't you tell us to what we owe the pleasure of your visit today?" Silvestri isn't much for foreplay.

I take a deep, serious breath for effect. "I wanted to tell you that I was with Mark the night that Sasha disappeared." Silvestri and Wolcott both raise their eyebrows.

"You were with Mr. Anders?"

"That's right."

"And how did you happen to hear about the date she disappeared? I don't remember that detail being in the news coverage," says Wolcott.

"From Mark."

"So you've been in touch with him recently? Tell us about that." Wolcott's pen is poised on the small pad he's retrieved from his shirt pocket.

"Yes. Well, we work together." Wolcott looks at Silvestri. My temples start throbbing. I fidget.

"Rebecca, you seem a little agitated. Is everything okay? There's nothing to worry about." Wolcott is being a real Boy Scout, but Silvestri seems unmoved by my discomfort. He's looking at me squarely in the eyes now. I do my best to stand my ground and hold eye contact.

"I'm fine. I guess I *am* nervous. This is all so crazy and terrible. I spoke to Mark yesterday because he hasn't been at the office, and he told me the date Sasha disappeared. I called as soon as I realized that he and I were together that night."

Silvestri finally takes a seat. He taps his fingers on the table, making me wonder if they are communicating through code. "Rebecca, when you say you were with Mark that night, can you be more specific?"

"We were working. I went to his house after hours because I needed to go over a presentation with him. I reached out to see if he was still at the office after I took a class, and he told me he'd already gone home but that I should come over."

"Let's start with the time frame," Wolcott encourages me.

"It was after the six P.M. spin class."

Silvestri probes. "Was Sasha in class?"

"Yes." I'm fairly certain they already knew the answer to that. Wolcott makes a note. Silvestri nods at me to continue.

"So, it was around seven thirtyish that I texted Mark and then went to his house shortly after that." I pull out my phone and have the text ready to show them.

"So, there was no response text from Mark telling you to come over, just you asking him if he was home?" Silvestri asks.

"I was already in the neighborhood and took the liberty of stopping by shortly after I sent the text." I'd been anticipating that one of them might ask this.

"Got it. Please, go on." He nods.

"We worked until about midnight, and, well, we'd had a couple of drinks too many so I ended up sleeping on Mark's couch for a few hours and drove home around five A.M."

Wolcott reads the text and jots something down on the page before handing it to Silvestri, who doesn't look at it but places my phone in front of him instead of handing it back. "And as far as you knew, where was Sasha all that time?"

I'm trying not to let the fact that my unlocked phone is now sitting in front of Silvestri distract me. "Sasha always went to happy hour at Le Vin with her friends after class. So I assumed that's where she was that night."

Wolcott makes another note. "Did you hear her say happy hour that evening was her plan? Or did Mark?"

"No. I didn't ask."

"Were either of you concerned that she might come home and be unhappy playing three's company with an attractive coworker of her husband's sleeping on her couch?"

"We were working in the guesthouse. I don't think she ever goes out there. And I'd just assumed that she came home sometime late after I'd passed out."

"And was Mr. Anders with you the whole time?"

"Yes."

"He didn't leave the guesthouse?" I shake my head. "How about when you were sleeping?"

"Definitely not."

"How can you be sure?"

I smile bashfully and hesitate. "We were both sleeping on the couch. I'm a light sleeper. I would have known if he got up."

Wolcott and Silvestri look at each other and back at me. Whether they are judging me, I can't tell.

"And did you happen to notice if Sasha's car was in the driveway?" Silvestri's question feels like a trick.

"I didn't think to look for it."

"And where did your husband think you were that evening?"

"He was working late himself. I didn't tell him that I was staying over because he ended up crashing at his business partner's house. They had a pretty heavy dinner with clients and he didn't want to get behind the wheel. He does that occasionally."

"You have a very trusting relationship, don't you?" Silvestri's tone is without sarcasm.

"Yes. We do." I feel claustrophobic in the windowless room. The space between the wall behind me and my chair seems to have narrowed. The table between us is too large for the space and I want to move it away from me to feel less boxed in, but the legs are bolted to the floor. "Would it be possible to open the door?"

"It does get a bit stuffy in here, doesn't it?" Wolcott passes behind me and cracks the door. "Apologies. We wanted privacy. If we were out in the bullpen, it would be like trying to have a civilized conversation during feeding time at the zoo."

Silvestri chuckles. "I personally don't mind spaces without walls. Funny how people are complaining about most companies switching to open plan these days. The tech people made it cool, but we've been doing it all along."

Wolcott nods in agreement. "It's a good way to really get to know people intimately. Wouldn't you say, Rebecca?" I can smell the bait, but I'm not sure what they are fishing for.

"Isn't your current office open plan?" Silvestri leans forward slightly.

"Yes, it is. All open cubicles. Except for the bosses; they have offices."

"So, Mark Anders has an office. Is that right?"

"Yes, that's right." They've pivoted the conversation again.

"And just so I have the hierarchy correctly, he's your boss?" I take in Wolcott. He is handsome in a wholesome, boyish kind of way. I subtly glance at his left hand and spot a weathered wedding ring. He looks like a one-woman kind of man, but I suppose I'm hardly a good judge of that.

"Yes. Mark is my boss." The fact that he is asking a question that he already knows the answer to irritates me. I feel like I'm being led in circles.

"Mrs. Campbell. Sorry to nitpick, but don't you mean Mark *was* your boss?" Silvestri doesn't even look up as he asks this. He is flicking the tea bag string hanging from his mug to and fro like a cat.

I don't respond. I assume they are deciding which one of them is going to spike the ball. Wolcott jumps at it.

"Look, Rebecca. This is only going to work if you are honest with us." Wolcott is pleased with himself. "We all keep secrets. And we usually keep them from our spouses when we are trying to protect them from something. But keeping secrets from detectives during a murder investigation is not protecting anyone, least of all you."

The way he's speaking to me reminds me more of the shrinks from my childhood than the detectives. I don't like it. "I'm not keeping secrets." This comes out with more edge than I intend. Men generally don't appreciate aggression in women, especially men with guns.

"Let's try this again," Silvestri says gently. "Would it be accurate to say that you haven't been completely honest with your husband as it pertains to your current employment status?"

"Yes. No. I mean, yes, it would be accurate."

"And just now, you weren't being honest with us?"

"Correct. I wasn't being honest with you."

Wolcott is watching me closely while his partner continues. "Mrs. Campbell, what you do or don't tell your husband is not really our concern. We just need a clear picture to work with. We recently spent some time in your former office, and frankly, I'm surprised you didn't walk out of the place sooner. But just for clarity's sake, when exactly did you leave?"

"April first." They don't pause or look at each other, but I imagine dots are quickly connecting.

"Interesting. So, you tendered your immediate resignation on the same day that we paid a visit to you and your husband about Sasha and Sheila. April first was an eventful day for you." I look for a lead in his expression but Silvestri is inscrutable.

"One had nothing to do with the other. I'd been unhappy at work and was planning to quit long before you showed up at our house."

It is becoming impossible to sit still. I don't know if it is the drugs waning or the increasing temperature in the room, but I feel the pressure building to an unbearable level.

"So, you've maintained regular contact with Mark?" Silvestri has taken the wheel. I can't say I prefer him. He's also handsome, but darker and brooding and harsher in his delivery. The kind of man I would be attracted to as a partner, but not so much as an interrogator.

"Not regular contact, just occasional. I've been checking in with him since Sasha's disappearance," I reply.

"And what exactly is the nature of your relationship with Mark Anders?" Silvestri follows up.

"We're colleagues." I correct myself before they can. "*Were* colleagues. And friends. I've been trying to be supportive to him during this time."

"So why is it that you've kept your early retirement from Paul?"

"I didn't . . . I don't want to worry him."

"It would worry him that you left a job that you've been unhappy at? That seems like the kind of thing you'd want to discuss or even celebrate with your husband." Silvestri looks like he has more to say but holds back.

"We respect each other's decisions and we don't ask permission when it comes to personal decisions." Keeping the defensiveness out of my voice is proving to be increasingly difficult.

"And you aren't concerned that Paul is going to notice the precipitous loss in your income?" Wolcott jumps in.

"Paul and I don't get hung up on money. We have separate checking accounts. We aren't keeping track or tabs on who is bringing in what. Besides, we are fine financially. I'm just taking some time to figure out what I want to do next." Deep inside, I am cringing.

Both detectives look satisfied with this answer, or bored. Silvestri looks at his partner and leans forward. I sense the tide shift again before the next question is out of his mouth.

"Would you categorize your friendship with Mark as very close?" The way Silvestri's watching my body language more than my face is making me extremely uneasy.

"Not *very* close."

Wolcott sips his coffee and smiles gently. "But close enough to have a sleepover. I get being close to your co-workers, but I hear Silvestri snores, and I don't plan to ever find out firsthand." Silvestri chuckles and my blood starts to boil.

"I told you, I had too much to drink and I fell asleep. Mark must have fallen asleep too."

Silvestri looks thoughtful. "Do you and your husband often drink to the point of being unable to make it home?"

"No. Not at all. It was a stressful patch."

He seems satisfied with my answer and shifts gears again. "Why do you think that Mr. Anders didn't tell us that he was with you the night of Sasha's disappearance? He originally told us that he was home alone working," Silvestri says.

I sigh to buy myself a few extra seconds. This is the question I've been anticipating.

"Because he was protecting me."

Something dawns on Silvestri, but he remains silent. Wolcott does not.

"He must be extremely protective of you if he was willing to perjure himself."

I try to conceal the growing alarm backing up in my body. My face is on fire. I remind myself again that I chose to come here, but it's getting harder and harder to keep a grasp on why.

"Well, he was my boss and he didn't want to be cast in a certain way. It was my fault. I had fallen behind on my projects and I needed help. I asked him not to say anything about our late-night work sessions. I didn't want anyone at the office to think I was getting special treatment." They aren't buying any of it.

Silvestri considers this before forging ahead. "So, you asked Mark not to tell us that you were together that night?"

"No. Before I knew anything about Sasha. The handful of times that Mark and I worked late together. I asked him not to tell anyone. With the world as it is now with harassment in the workplace, I didn't want any trouble for Mark or for me. Obviously this all changed when Sasha was found and Mark had to account for that night. But he was falling on the sword for me." I'm talking myself into a corner. They aren't giving me anything but a length of rope now. I inhale dramatically and look up as I try to think of an effective pivot myself. Both men sit expectantly.

"As you can imagine, I was very upset to find out that my husband had been having an emotional affair with some random woman in the neighborhood—"

Silvestri cuts in. "Random? Didn't you and Sheila work out at Lotus Pedal together?"

"Yes—"

"You were side by side on bikes, weren't you?"

"Yes, but we didn't—"

He keeps steamrolling over my attempt at getting back on script. "And, in fact, Sasha Anders's bike was on the other side of you. Isn't that right? Pretty close quarters for randomness."

I'm not sure which of his rapid-fire questions to answer. "Sheila worked out at the same studio, but we didn't actually know each other. I didn't even make the connection until after she was out of the picture." The detectives seem unfazed by my poor choice of words.

"I was really upset when I found out about Sheila. I had no idea she was the woman I'd been spinning next to; we'd never even spoken in class. I knew nothing about her."

"So then, tell us how your husband's relationship with Sheila and your unhappiness about it connects to you being Mark's alibi on the night in question." I'm appreciative of Silvestri's help getting back to dry land. I take a sip of water and try to quiet my nervous system.

"After I found out about Sheila, I avoided being home. I put in a lot of extra time at the office. I was working on a multimillion-dollar drug launch with Mark. We spent a lot of late nights preparing for the presentation and recruiting the sales and marketing teams. He was there for me during a difficult time."

"Just the two of you? Or was there anyone else in your office?"

"Just the two of us."

"Was Paul aware that you were spending so much time after hours with your boss?"

"He knew I was working a lot. He didn't ask who with or what I was working on. He was ashamed about Sheila, so he wasn't prying too much into how I was spending my time. He was working just as much as me at the time, if not more."

"Rebecca, are you and Mark Anders having a sexual relationship?" Silvestri's good cop seems to have left the room.

"Not anymore."

I'm trying to remember how I ended up in this room, having this conversation. How my lying to the police about sleeping with my former boss is possibly going to make things better. And then there's the absurdity of worrying that any of this will get back to Paul. I can't imagine he'd give two shits about Mark anyway, but I'd rather not unpack this particular lie with him. "Rebecca?"

I have to stay focused on the current shit storm in this room and not get distracted by the one outside of it.

"Look, things went a little too far. Paul doesn't know anything, and it is over. Mark didn't want to tell you that I was at his house because he knew Paul might get the wrong idea and become upset."

Wolcott interjects gently. "Rebecca, does your husband have a temper?"

"Not any more than anyone else. He gets mad and then he gets over it.

But Paul would never hurt me. He'd never hurt anyone." I squeeze the webbing between my thumb and pointer finger to try to find the calming pressure point.

"And what is the right idea, Mrs. Campbell?" Silvestri asks pointedly.

"Pardon?"

"You said your husband might get the wrong idea. What is the right idea?"

I'm on the verge of screaming. My heart is beating so fast that I can barely speak.

I stammer. "We slept together a couple of times. It was just sex. Paul had his thing, and I had mine." My raised voice startles me but releases some of the built-up tension and I'm able to take a breath. The detectives remain as calm as ever.

"And where was Sasha Anders in this scenario?" Every time I get my footing, Silvestri purposely throws me off.

"What do you mean?"

They are batting me back and forth like a toy.

Wolcott scratches his head. "Do you think she had any idea that your relationship with her husband had become sexual?"

"I doubt it. She wasn't very interested in anything other than herself. And they had problems."

"Was she also going outside of their marriage?"

"I have no idea. Like I've told you before, she and I weren't friends."

"Did you ever suspect that she and Paul might be rekindling old fires?" Silvestri says this casually. My patience with him has all but faded.

"No. Paul tolerated Sasha. They were ancient history." I cross and uncross my arms quickly. Wolcott makes a note.

"So, Mark never said anything to you about Sasha being unfaithful?"

"No, we weren't close like that. We didn't talk about his marriage. What happened between us wasn't anything serious."

"It seems pretty serious if you were with Mr. Anders the night his wife went missing and he failed to peg you as part of his alibi when we first questioned him. Don't you think?" I can't tell if Silvestri is enjoying this, but he seems like he might be. I've completely lost control of the conversation. I feel like a suspect.

Wolcott jumps in. "Mrs. Campbell, Mark Anders was your boss. It sounds to me like this dynamic was a major abuse of power, especially if you felt like you had to quit in the end. Did you feel pressured by him? Did you ever speak with anyone in your company's HR department about any of this?"

"No, it wasn't anything like that." I feel like I've just run a marathon and am moments away from collapsing. I take the water bottle from the table and gulp it down until it is empty.

Silvestri appears to read my mind. "Why don't we take a break? Maybe you'd like to use the ladies' room?"

◆

WHEN I RETURN, they are both seated quietly. The room feels less like a furnace. I'm slightly calmer after splashing some cold water on my face and dissolving an Ativan under my tongue. I take my seat and flinch when I realize that my phone is still sitting in front of Silvestri.

"Mrs. Campbell, just a couple more questions and then we'll get you out of here."

"Sure." I realize I've completely lost track of time without my phone. I have no idea how long I've been here. It feels like hours.

"Rebecca. Something's not sitting right with me." Fuck.

"What's that?"

"You said that you didn't make the connection between Sheila as the woman you were spinning next to until way after the fact?"

I don't understand why they are bringing Sheila up again. "That's right."

"And did you ever see your husband and Sheila together?"

"No, I did not." My jaw tenses.

"Then how is it that you recognized her in the picture that morning in the kitchen when we visited?" Silvestri looks confident that he's got me. But I'm ready for it.

I let the tears I've been holding back fall freely. "Paul's phone. I saw pictures of her. Mostly of her naked body, but a few of her face." I don't have to force the disgust in my face recalling the pictures. "That is how I found out about their affair. By the time I found the pictures and put two and two together, she never came back to the studio."

"But Paul said in the kitchen that their relationship never went too far—"

"She sent my husband pictures of herself, and he sent a few of himself, but he told me that was the extent of it. I believed him. I didn't dig too deeply."

Both men look uncomfortable with my light sobbing as our soundtrack and I finally see a light at the end of the tunnel. Wolcott leaves the room, presumably to get some Kleenex.

"I'm sorry. I'm such a mess. This has all been incredibly painful to re-hash and I'm not sure I can keep doing it."

Silvestri nods. "Of course. Apologies for being too hard on you."

"Detective, are you married?"

"I was. I'm not anymore." This answer is not without pain.

"Then you can probably understand that this whole business with Sheila is something that Paul and I just want to put behind us. And I hope I don't ever have to tell Paul about Mark. We've done a lot of work on our marriage and we are finally in a place of healing."

"Of course." He softens slightly. "I can understand that. But we may need to speak to you again."

"I just wanted to do the right thing, Detective. That's why I came in."

"Well, we certainly appreciate that you did," Wolcott says from behind me as he places a box of government-grade tissues on the table. I pull one from the box and thank him with a look. It is hard on my face as I blot my cheeks.

I make a move for my jacket, and my phone vibrates on the table. I can't read it upside down. Silvestri slides it across the table. "We'll let you get on your way, then."

I scoop the phone up and exit as quickly as I can without appearing like I'm going to make a run for it. I blanch when I look down and see Mark's name and three texts in quick succession.

What is taking so long?

Is it done?

We had a deal.

I hold my breath as I wait for one or both of the detectives to read me my rights and cuff me to the table. But Wolcott just smiles and sees me out the door.

forty-six

SHEILA

I DIDN'T SEE the end coming until it was too late. In retrospect, I regret letting myself into his house uninvited and sneaking into his office, the one room we had yet to fuck in.

Paul seemed to be cooling on me a little bit and I wanted to heat things up. I picked a time for my surprise when I knew his wife would be gone. I'd imagined a sexy-secretary scene and let myself in through the back door, which I'd noticed never seemed to be locked.

He was in the shower upstairs when I entered, so I made my way to his office, changed into my costume, and positioned myself behind the desk in a come-hither posture. I couldn't wait to see his face when he discovered me in stilettos, legs up on his desk, and nothing else except for one of his ties. I'd nabbed it a few weeks earlier.

He was taking a long time to finish his shower and come downstairs, and I got curious. I wanted to know everything about Paul, and he was not very open with details. I didn't think snooping around a little would hurt anyone. I only got as far as the top drawer, when I saw the bandanna-wrapped gun, before he caught me. He was not as happy as I'd hoped he'd be; in fact his face was so full of rage that I worried he might scream at me. But luckily my outfit diverted his anger into desire. He bent me over his desk and enjoyed the act thoroughly, but as soon as we finished I could sense that something was wrong.

"Sheila, we can't do this anymore." His voice was without emotion. I was naked except for his tie.

"Paul, I'm really sorry I snuck in. I won't do it again. I thought you'd like it."

"This isn't because of today. I think *this* has run its course."

"I thought we were getting closer. I think we have something really good here, Paul." I was struggling to keep the panic out of my voice.

He reached his arms out to me in what I thought was a gesture of affection until he loosened the knot on his tie and slid it over my head. "My wife gave this to me."

I deflated. I'd gone too far. "I'm sorry."

"Let's part ways before things get too complicated."

I was stunned and didn't protest. I held back the tears and conjured a brave face, but on the inside, I was dying.

When he walked out of the office to let me get dressed, I helped myself to the key labeled "front door" in his desk. I would add it to my collection of Paul artifacts, knowing it would give me unrestricted access.

I was destroyed in the days following our break-up. I was manic without him and was still infatuated beyond function. Every day that he didn't call or text, I became less grounded. I walked Molly for hours, waiting to run into Paul and Duff. I believed if he saw me, he would change his mind about us. I pedaled daily and furiously next to Rebecca, who seemed to be in a perpetual trance. The sight of her, and knowing she was going home to Paul, ripped my heart out day after day.

I watched them. I saw him pretending to be in love with her. They were everywhere. Talking, laughing, holding hands. I knew he was looking at her and seeing me. This was a game he was playing and I wanted to play something else. I was losing the grip on where I had fit in his life. I needed to know he had been real and I hadn't made it all up.

I still loved him so much. I sent him reminders that I still existed from a new phone when he blocked the old one. I would be unrelentingly persistent until he came around. I couldn't let him forget me and that I had been his and he'd loved me.

Molly left me too. She ran away one day when she was untethered at the beach. I didn't have the energy to run after her. I didn't expect she'd return. I was well versed in being abandoned.

I walked into the ocean up to my waist, pulled off my engagement and wedding rings, and threw them into the surf. The farther I tried to walk out, the more the tide pushed me back to shore. The ocean didn't even want me. It had already taken Daniel.

I let myself into their house after I watched them drive away together one day, her head resting on his shoulder as he passed me, clueless that I was there.

In their house, I looked for the most meaningful thing of his I could take. I had his key, a set of cuff links, a childhood photo of him taken off a pegboard. I needed something more substantial. Something that would send a message about how I was feeling.

I knew what I wanted. In his desk I found the gun right where I'd seen it the first time. I didn't know exactly what I wanted to do with Paul's gun, but his text had pushed me about as far as I could stand. I put it in my purse and immediately felt better.

forty-seven

PAUL

I WALK THROUGH the door.

It's a rush to see the place in the stage where one can start to envision it as an inhabitable house. The plumbing is coming along, and the electrician is lined up to be on hand as soon as the pipes are all laid in. I'll assist Javier and his crew with the drywall and flooring, and we've got an ace painting team ready to go.

I've long been able to see the final product in my head, but my other senses are kicking in. Standing within these walls, I can smell the floor wax and feel the warmth from logs burning in the fireplace. I can hear a bath being drawn upstairs as I taste the tomatoes that we'll grow in the garden outside. She's going to love it.

I'm feeling butterflies in my gut, and I'm finding it to be a truly invigorating experience. I can't remember the last time I had a case of nerves with regard to a property, but this isn't just any property. This is a burial of the past and an eye toward a beautiful future with the woman I've come back to after all these years.

Not that there aren't a few chainsaws to juggle. Wes is nipping at my heels about gearing up for the fall real estate season, and he'll only become more persistent in the coming weeks. But the plumber being on-site gives me some leeway, and I'll have another pocket of time with the electrician, then again with the painting crew.

My explanation of the Keystone Cops' ineptitude seems to have calmed Rebecca down for the moment. She hasn't appeared as nervous or distracted over the last couple of days, and I pray that she's finally getting some sort of handle on her meds. She needs to hold it together, for both of our sakes.

Dana has been a godsend. I really don't know how I could have made it through these last months without her. The universe seems to throw things our way when we most need them, and this has been a time of great need. And it looks like we might have some bites on her house in what is generally a slow season in the business. It's tempting to think that this all might work out in the end.

A quick spasm in my lower back shakes me out of my daydream. I reach behind and work my thumb in circles between two particularly tense strands of muscle. My body will thank me when this construction is wrapped up. It needs some downtime to recuperate. Dana has been all over me to go to a massage therapist, and it's getting harder to argue against it. The heat patches are doing as much as they can, but these old bones are really starting to howl.

As I knead the muscles in my back, I think of Rebecca. It's the night of the incident, and I'm tending to the flesh wound on her shoulder. A new wound atop an old wound. The pain of both, and the masking that's followed, the suffering that's still buried, the pills that have ravaged her body while managing her pain.

I'm a kid again, in the back seat of the car. My dad's driving, and my mom is turned to me. "Paul, honey. It's just for the weekend. Mom and Dad need to take care of some things. You'll have fun at Uncle Nick's."

"But I don't want to go there. I want to stay with you guys," I protest, tears welling. "Don't leave me there!"

"Oh, honey." My mom laughs. "We'd never *leave* you there. We'll come back for you, silly."

"You promise?" I plead.

I can hear the irritation in my dad's voice as he turns his head to look at me. "Paul, I need you to get it together. Okay, bud?"

I see the brake lights of the car ahead of us, but I can't speak. I watch as we careen toward them. I can't say a word. I can only watch.

A shot of pain runs up my side, pulling me back to the moment. My shirt is drenched in sweat, and there are tears burning my eyes. *I can't do this anymore. It can't fucking go on. This needs to end.* I ball up the fabric around the neck of my shirt, stuff it in my mouth, and let out a scream. I breathe deeply and feel a semblance of calm come over me as my eyes scan the house. I take a moment to steady myself before stepping outside and heading in the direction of the Cherokee. It's about time to grab lunch, but first I'll need to apply another ThermaWrap patch, check my phone, and make sure there are no fires to attend to.

forty-eight

WOLCOTT

"What's burnin' your ass, pal?"

Silvestri has a look in his eye that's new to me. It appears to be a mix of determination, agitation, and sadistic delight. Plus, he's driving a bit too fast through suburbia.

"I don't like bullies," he answers.

"No one does. Something eating at you?"

"Mark Anders is a bully. I'm looking forward to getting in a room with that guy and taking him apart."

"Easy, tiger. We need to soft-glove him for the moment, until we can figure out how we're going to jam him up."

"Did you see what kind of shape Rebecca Campbell was in? Far as I can figure it, he's got her good and doped up, and he's either using the drugs or the affair as leverage to keep her doing his bidding. I mean, that alibi?"

"Okay, and which part of that are you going to prove at this moment?"

"The guy's arrogant, pushy, and not all that smart. We'll get him."

"Of course we will," I say. "Just be patient. Better to walk over the drawbridge than swim across the moat. Know what I'm saying?"

"Aristotle?" he cracks.

"Something like that. And slow down. You're scaring the squirrels."

◆

WE APPROACH ANDERS'S garish spectacle of a home. My partner slows down to a crawl, then pulls into the driveway.

"Couldn't help yourself, eh?"

He winks and offers me a self-satisfied grin. "It's the little things, Wolcott."

We get out of the cruiser and approach the house. Before we're close enough to knock, Mark Anders has swung the door open. He stands in the doorway, looking half-crazed. The stench of sour booze wafts off him, and the mangy bathrobe he's got on looks as if it could stand up on its own and take a few laps around the place.

"Top of the day to you," offers Silvestri. "How goes it, Mr. Anders?"

"Well, my wife's dead, and now I've got you two characters standing at my door. So, you know. How goes it with you?"

"Busy investigating your wife's case, in fact." My partner holds Anders's stare. "We have a few follow-up questions. Hoping to hammer out our timeline once and for all. May we speak with you inside?"

Anders shrugs. "I don't see why not." He lazily waves us in.

The living room resembles a bomb shelter. It's a grim scene in there. Anders sees us eyeing the place.

"I gave the cleaning lady the week off," he says. His tone sounds matter-of-fact.

There's a tower of pizza boxes that looks poised to topple at any second and a collection of empty booze bottles strewn about the room. The blinds are all drawn, and the low hum of the air conditioner drones on in the background. The house gives off all the charm and ambiance of a dank cave.

"Gun!" Silvestri announces.

My hand instinctively goes to my holster. I follow my partner's eyes to the coffee table. In the low light, it takes me a moment to make out the pistol sitting on the stack of magazines. My eyes dart to Mark Anders, who stands still, seemingly untroubled by this new development.

I draw a handkerchief from my vest pocket and use it to retrieve the gun from the table. "Mr. Anders," I say. "Why do you have a Glock 19?"

"Um, some asshole murdered my wife," he shoots back.

"Well, well. A matching set," says Silvestri, indicating our department-issued weapons. "Got a permit for that, Mark?"

Anders looks at my partner coldly. "I don't need a permit, genius. It's in my home."

Silvestri doesn't hide his grin. He snaps the cuffs off his belt as he approaches Anders. "Mark Anders, you're under arrest for unlicensed possession of a firearm." He cuffs our irate friend, who attempts to slither out of the bracelets.

"What the fuck are you idiots doing? I'm going to sue you for false arrest."

"You may want to brush up on your legal statutes, Mark." Silvestri is enjoying this.

We walk Anders out of the house, kicking and screaming the whole way. He hits us with a flurry of angry insults and empty threats as we steer him toward the cruiser. Various neighbors who are out in yards and jogging through the development stop and stare at the free entertainment. He eyes them defiantly as we pack him into the back seat and drive off.

◆

I'M AT MY DESK when Silvestri approaches. He sits himself down on the edge and nods at me.

"Yes?"

"Wolcott, you ever use Venmo?"

"The payment app? Can't say that I have."

"There's an interesting feature with Venmo that people aren't necessarily aware of. Unless you change your setting to private, it displays your transaction history for anyone to see."

"This is fascinating trivia, partner." I can see in his eyes that he's warming up to something.

"You remember that twerp out in the Hamptons who got busted a little while back? Morgan Kaufman. The 'Trust Fund Dealer,' the papers called him?"

"Oh yeah. They ripped the house apart. Found all kinds of shit in the walls."

"Bingo," he says. He pulls his phone out of his pocket, taps the screen, and hands it to me. I'm looking at the Venmo page with Mark Anders's transaction history. "Now, here's the question of the day: What's a known drug dealer doing sending payments to the head of a pharmaceutical company?"

"No shit?" I say. "Anders was supplying this kid?!"

"Looks like it. Guess Mark wasn't happy with his day job. Needed a little sideline hustle to really get the blood flowing."

"Son of a bitch," I say. "Silvestri, you beautiful beast. Let's get a warrant for Anders's place."

My partner offers a satisfied nod. "Already on the way."

forty-nine

SHEILA

I HAD TWENTY-ONE miles to decide who to murder first.

I'd been dead for thirty-six hours as far as Paul and Rebecca were concerned. I'd come to in the early hours of the morning after my birthday, long enough to ascend the stairs and look at the sky before losing consciousness for most of the day on the ground floor of the unbuilt house. I was lucky they'd thought enough to throw my coat into the plastic coil, or else I might have fought my way out and up, only to succumb to exposure. The lot was remote enough that I went undiscovered as I drifted in and out of concussed sleep throughout the day. By nightfall, I felt stable enough to start my trip home.

My options homeward were extremely limited if I truly wanted to remain missing and dead. I knew that as soon as I used my phone to call for a ride, a traceable timeline would begin. I needed Paul and Rebecca to believe that they'd rid themselves of me for good, and for the police to believe that I had vanished. I used the last remaining juice in my phone to map out my trek before I shut it off and threw it into the thick wooded area on my way out of the property. I was grateful that I opted for leather riding boots over heels on my birthday night; the seven-and-a-half-hour walk from Cold Spring Harbor to Stony Brook would have been impossible otherwise.

Initially, I thought murdering Rebecca and putting her body in place of mine offered a perfectly symmetrical ending to this ordeal. The image of Paul hauling the plastic tube to a grave he'd painstakingly dug, thinking it was me, and then discovering Rebecca's corpse was delicious in theory. But, it was doubtful he'd take the time to unwrap the plastic sarcophagus. However, imagining him realize he'd almost buried his own wife got me through a handful of lonely and disorienting miles of back roads in the dark.

I needed someone who I wouldn't mind killing, maybe even enjoy. Someone who was roughly my same height and weight. And who had money. I would need a lot of that. Sasha popped into my head almost immediately. And her murder would have the added bonus of ruining Mark's life. He'd long been on my list. After that decision, everything just came together.

By mile thirteen, I could feel the bleeding blisters and my concussed head screaming in blinding unison. As the sun was beginning to creep up into the nightscape, I realized the sight of a woman matching my description walking along the Jericho Turnpike in the early morning was way more likely to draw suspicion than a truck driver blowing through town giving a lift to some sad girl doing the walk of shame at dawn. I found a ride easily at the first gas station I came to, careful to avoid video cameras, and evaded conversation by pretending to sob into my hands. Few men want to engage with a woman who's crying.

I got dropped a few blocks away from my house and hobbled to my back door, where I retrieved my emergency key from under a planter. Happily, none of my neighbors were about and I was able to slip undetected into my house for some much-needed sleep and provisions for my new life. I didn't expect that anyone would be looking for me until I tipped off the authorities. I had that going for me.

I'd forgotten how easy it was to slide out of my existing life without anyone noticing, like a snake shedding its skin and slithering away silently. I'd made it back to my bed from the dead. When I woke I would start over. It wasn't the first time I'd walked away from my life with barely a glance backward. I was getting pretty good at it.

◆

I APPROACHED SASHA'S murder in the same way I would an elaborate surprise party. I made mental lists of what I needed to do, and the more I planned, the more I realized how perfect a target she was. Sasha had all of the things I needed rolled into one tight body. I plotted multiple options to land on the best element of surprise and leave the least amount of evidence. I knew Sasha's schedule better than her husband did, which was hardly at all. I knew she always traveled with a lot of cash and credit cards her husband didn't even know she had, because of her humblebragging in class. I knew she proudly carried a concealed handgun on her, in spite of New York State's laws to the contrary. And I knew her husband, Mark, who'd been the deciding factor in my choosing her ultimately, would be easy to frame. I could depend on him not noticing her absence immediately and I had plenty of sordid things on him that I could lead the authorities to when the time was right.

I had to kill her as soon as possible. If she was going to be a convincing body double, she needed to disappear around the same general time that I had. I envisioned a few choose-your-own-adventure outcome possibilities and was more excited than nervous to see how things unfolded, or in the case of Paul, Rebecca, and Mark, how it all unraveled.

It wasn't hard to get Sasha alone after class. Her car was unmistakable, rich and flashy, like her. She always parked in the same place and was consistently the last one of her happy hour posse to leave the studio on account of her taking twice as long as everyone else to do her makeup and perfect her blowout. She liked to make an entrance. I'd already surveilled the parking lot for CCTV cameras and the only ones I could find in shooting distance were pointed in the direction of the adjacent Best Buy.

I waited for her to walk to her car and paced behind on the passenger side. I adjusted the wig I was wearing, the same exact blond shade as her hair, which was lighter than mine, and smoothed the outfit I knew she'd wear, a tight black top, skinny jeans, and suede booties. She unlocked her car remotely and dropped her bag in the back seat. I sped up and slid into the passenger seat just as she was getting in on the driver's side.

I felt the heaviness of the club hammer from my neighbor's garage in the small Sephora shopping bag on my lap. Its short handle made it perfectly and conspicuously portable.

Her enormous brown eyes were almost black in the dark car. She was startled and then irritated.

"Um, excuse me? Who the fuck are you?"

I calibrated my voice a few octaves higher than normal, not that she'd live to recount any details of what I was about to do.

"Oh my God!" I laughed. "I totally thought this was my husband's car. He was supposed to pick me up and you have the same exact model. Isn't that hilarious?"

Her smug smile didn't have more than a moment to change into a perfect O before I withdrew my weapon with gloved hands and brought it squarely down on her skull.

She rocked forward and landed on my shoulder. If anyone had walked by, we would have looked like old friends embracing.

The blow to her head didn't kill her, so she and I had that in common. And it wasn't my intention that it would. The cause of death would be a gunshot wound, inflicted by her own gun, which was registered to Mark. Once suicide had been ruled out, which would be immediate, Mark would be suspect numero uno. I just needed her unconscious long enough to get her to Cold Spring Harbor.

Luckily, on the drive there, Sasha never came to, but I rode with her loaded gun in my lap just in case. It was remarkable how easy it was to get firearms from my neighbors. She provided the weapon of her destruction, the handgun she proudly kept in the front pocket of her fire-engine-red concealed-carry gun purse. It was custom-made in the style of a three-thousand-dollar Fendi bag she'd wanted, retrofitted with the side-zip front gun pocket. She boldly defied the concept of concealed when she did show-and-tell with it after class one day, not even caring who overheard her.

She was much heavier than she looked, and it took more time and strength than I'd anticipated to pull her out of her car. I figured it was less messy to shoot her outside, and laid the plastic tarp I'd been wrapped in along the ground nearby and rolled her on top of it. It was my first time firing a gun outside of a firing range, something I'd done on an early date with Daniel and been surprisingly excited by, and the unmonitored, open-air target practice on Sasha was more exhilarating than I had imagined. And much louder.

After it was over and the barrel was cooled, I placed her gun in my own purse, just in case. I rolled her up in a fraction of the time it had taken me to free myself from the same tarp, and pulled her to the bulkhead doors leading to the basement under the foundation, around the side of the property. I opened them with a little bit of a struggle and pushed her below with a thud. It wasn't hard to drag the plastic coil to the back of the basement where I'd been stowed, and I was happy that I'd paid attention to my distance and placement when I was escaping. I felt confident that my changeling was exactly where she needed to be for when Paul returned. If my luck held, he wouldn't realize that one corpse had been replaced by another.

fifty

REBECCA

HE's GETTING READY to kill me. This morning when he was still asleep, my bottle of pills from Mark was missing. I knew Paul had confiscated them, and I was jonesing badly. I looked everywhere I could think of—in his gym bag, his pockets, and his desk—before it occurred to me to look in his car. I didn't find the pills, but there in his glove box was the red bandanna–wrapped gun. I left it where it was and tried to calm myself as the morning continued.

On his way out the door, he said, "Madoo, what do you say we go for a drive this weekend, like we used to? Saturday?" He stressed *Saturday* like it was especially important.

The words are glass in my mouth. "Sure, babe. That sounds great."

"It's a date then." He practically skipped out the door.

I'm officially afraid of my husband.

◆

I SIT IN MY CAR and process how bad things have become before I make the drive to Mark's. I take in our little house. I've never spent much time looking at it from this vantage point. From the outside it looks like a lovely cottage with all the possibilities of happiness dwelling inside. And it was that once, when the promise of something grander and more mature awaited us. I wonder how different my view would look right now if we'd succeeded with that dream. The devastating reality is that Paul has plans for a completely different dream with Dana.

I'm cycling through the present and the far past. Silvestri and Wolcott's circular questioning yesterday has gotten me thinking about the night my parents died. Sitting in a similarly claustrophobic room, but one with a worn, colorful rug and some kids' toys strewn around, a female social worker asked me questions as I tried to recall everything I had seen. A man sat with us but didn't speak. I'm just realizing now that he was a detective.

I was still wearing my pajamas, the ones with the moons and stars on them. Someone had put my shoes on and tied them for me.

"Rebecca, do you know what happened tonight?" The social worker's voice was sweet and she smiled warmly. The detective did not.

"My parents hurt each other."

"Yes, that's right. Do you know why they hurt each other?"

"My mom said something and my dad got very mad."

There was a carton of chocolate milk on the table in front of me that I kept my focus on. It was easier than meeting the eyes of the two adults. I knew by their expressions that I'd done something very bad and I was in terrible trouble.

"And then what happened?"

"I hid in the closet. They thought I was asleep in my room."

"And what could you see and hear from your hiding place?"

"I could hear things breaking. Dad opened the drawer in their room. Mom started yelling for help. There was a very loud noise and I couldn't see her until she lay down on the floor."

The detective was a large man, maybe twice the size of my dad. He was sitting in a chair that was too small for him. The image would have been comical under different circumstances. He wasn't talking, and when I looked up from the chocolate milk to his face, his eyes were red. He kept wrinkling his nose like he was about to sneeze.

"Rebecca, what happened after your mom lay down?"

"My dad went into my room."

"And what did he do when he didn't find you in there?"

"He called my name and started looking around the apartment. He came to the closet, but I'd buried myself all the way in the back behind the coats and covered myself."

"Why didn't you come out when he called?"

"I knew I was in trouble. So I stayed really quiet and small."

"And then what happened?"

"I closed my eyes. I pretended I was somewhere else. I think I fell asleep; I can't remember."

"And what woke you up?"

"I heard another loud noise. I didn't hear anything else for a while and went to see what happened. Dad was lying down near Mom. I think they were really tired from all of the fighting. I couldn't make them wake up. Then the police broke the door down."

"That must have been very scary."

"It was . . . I'm really sorry."

I began crying and the detective pushed the chocolate milk closer to me. I lifted the carton to my mouth and took a sip from the straw. The milk tasted salty.

"What are you sorry about, sweetie?" His voice was deep and soothing.

"I did something bad."

I had done something bad. And I wanted to tell the detective. But I couldn't.

"Sweetie, was your dad sleeping when you came out of the closet?"

I'd only nodded. I couldn't speak anymore, or I wouldn't be able to stop.

"How did you hurt your arm, honey? Who yanked on it?"

My memory is interrupted as my phone buzzes next to me on the seat.

Showing a house out in Bridgehampton and then out with Wes. Won't be home until later, go ahead and have dinner without me. Love you.

The tracker on his phone shows that he is at her house again. My anger renews a sense of motivation and replaces the exhaustion. I'm happy to be brought back to the present. I start the engine and head toward Mark's to get what he promised me in our deal, and then some.

◆

WHEN I NEAR HIS HOUSE, I'm jarred to see that Mark is being led out in handcuffs. He thrashes around in his robe, his hair and eyes are wild like a feral animal's. I can barely look away. I was assuming that he'd be home as usual and I would have to improvise in order to convince him, but now, I think luck might be in my favor today for once. Mark's, not so much.

I don't speed up or slow down as my car glides past. Luckily, none of the men are looking in my direction. In an incongruously tender gesture, Silvestri is guiding Mark into the back of their car with a hand on his head. I drive around the corner, park a few blocks away, and watch in my rearview for their car to pass before I retrace my steps back to his house on foot.

I figure I have a few hours at best to get what I need before the property is crawling with cops.

I make my way through a backyard one street away that I know shares a property line with Mark and Sasha's. There aren't any cars in the driveway, but I prepare a story of a runaway dog in case any of the inhabitants emerge and confront me.

When I reach his backyard, I cut over to the guesthouse. I hadn't thought about it when I came to visit Mark, but it is so obvious to me now that this is where he'd be keeping the drugs. I'd only ever been in the guesthouse twice, and only briefly, when I'd been desperate and picked up pills from Mark outside of office hours. Of course we'd never actually fucked in the guesthouse like I'd told Wolcott and Silvestri, or anywhere else for that matter. The thought made me sick to my stomach.

The sun is getting high in the sky and some gray clouds are gathering around it. I edge myself along the periphery of the yard, as close as I can get to a straight shot to the small house sitting back from the pool, in the shade of numerous trees. I am surprised at how lucid and energetic I feel, then realize that I haven't taken a pill yet today.

The lock isn't difficult to crack and I'm inside in less than two minutes. As expected, the guesthouse is on the same digital alarm system as the main house. The electronic keypad immediately inside the door chirps confirmation after I enter Sasha's birthday. There is enough daylight coming in from the windows that I don't have to turn the lights on. The interior is one large room with a loft above, accessible by a ladder. A couch, coffee table, and flat-screen take up the majority of the space, and a bar is set back from the sitting area. There is a small bathroom off to the side.

I move to the bar that Mark has modeled after some circa 1970s home-basement man cave, complete with a neon "Miller Time" sign against the backdrop and differently shaped glasses hung from above. I open some cabinets and drawers half-heartedly but know that he considers himself too clever not to have a dedicated hiding spot. I knock on the walls for any hollow sounds, toss the couch cushions, and lift the throw rug to reveal any floor safes. Nothing. I scan the walls for a safe-concealing piece of art, but the gray walls are naked of any photographs or paintings.

The sun has been overtaken by fast-moving dark clouds, and a gloomy light settles inside the guesthouse, making it feel much later than it actually is. I use the flashlight on my phone to guide me. The bathroom door is shut, and I'm floored by the smell of chlorine when I open the door. I can barely fit inside because the small space is nearly completely taken up by a large industrial pump, which I'm only able to identify because of Paul's building days and a few anxiety-ridden cases of flooded properties. It strikes me as an odd thing to be keeping in the bathroom instead of the garage, but a few cursory knocks on the metal body and I'm convinced it isn't housing any pharmaceuticals. I don't realize how powerful the smell of chlorine is until I step back out and have to sit down from the dizziness.

I venture up to the loft. The light casts a spooky glow as I move it around the room from above. The loft itself is really too small for much beyond a few boxes marked "Records," which I open to find a collection of vinyl as advertised. I'm getting frustrated now and feeling the effects of the lifting adrenaline giving way to craving.

I stand at the top of the ladder and examine the space below me for any signs of something being out of place or a container in disguise. Maybe Mark knew it was only a matter of time before people came looking, or got spooked when the cops started coming around and got rid of his bounty. He could have moved it, or maybe I'm wrong and his hiding place is in the main house or his garage. There is still a lot of potential square footage to search, and who knows when the police will be coming back. I'm starting to feel frantic.

The small window in the loft looks onto the pool and the main house. I accept that what I'm looking for isn't in here. I'll have to go in if I'm going to get what I need.

When I exit, the smell of chlorine seems to have followed me outside even after I've closed and locked the door. I walk around the path encircling the pool, imagining countless parties that have taken place here starring Sasha. I doubt there will be any more celebratory gatherings for a long time. As I make my way across the yard to the house, I notice that in spite of the warm weather, the pool cover is still squarely secured to the surface.

I walk about five more paces toward the house before I turn on my heels and decide to walk around the perimeter of the pool after all. I know it is risky to be so out in the open, but something is pulling me in the pool's direction.

I make it about halfway around before I see something. One of the metal hooks meant to secure the cover is undone. I crouch down to try to lift the taut material to shine my flashlight into the pool. It is too tight, so I unhook the next three fixtures, which make up the rounded corner of the cover. With the metal railings above and stairs into the pool below, I think I can leverage an entry point. It is a bit of a struggle to unmoor the hooks, and I hold on to one of the railings while I work to avoid inadvertently pitching myself into the tepid water I don't actually expect is waiting below.

With the fourth hook undone, I can peel back enough of the cover to shine light into the pool. The stairs and the space surrounding are completely dry. The pool has been drained. I step down into darkness in a crabwalk and have to crouch once I reach the bottom step because it is too shallow to stand where the cover is still firmly in place. I move to hands and knees and feel a momentary coziness in the dark enclosure. I move the light against the far end and see that as the pool deepens, the space is filled with a large mass. I'm too far to make out what exactly I'm moving toward, so I half crawl to the midpoint of the pool, where I'm able to stand without having to crouch too much. By the time I reach the six-foot mark, I identify two stacks of Rubbermaid tubs and I'm able to stand completely. My heart is racing so hard and my hands are shaking, the light bouncing around like a strobe. I steady it enough on the tub closest to where I'm standing to unlatch either side easily. When I lift the lid, I nearly swoon.

Stacked in beautiful piles before me are five-hundred-tablet bottles of every painkiller I could imagine, and some I didn't even know to imagine. I wish I'd brought a bigger purse as I jam as many of the giant bottles into my bag as possible and then crack one of the seals on another bottle and pour as many loose pills into my hands and fill one of my dress pockets. I open another tub and find box after box of liquid morphine and meperidine. The tub after that is a treasure chest of antianxiety-laden jewels. I have to get through two more tubs before I find what I'm looking for. I'm not surprised Mark has put this all the way in the back. Given the potency and body count from the trials, it's amazing that he's still holding on to the stuff. But I knew he would. He's probably banking on the fact that someone will eventually figure out how to dilute it enough to sell it without every dose being fatal. For my purposes, it is exactly the right strength and form.

I take one tube and wrap it in a piece of paper from my purse. I slide it carefully into the loose pocket of my dress as though it were a grenade. I won't need more than a fraction of that, and once I use it I will have to figure out how to dispose of the remaining cream in a way that no one could ever accidentally come upon it. I close the tubs and stack them the way I found them, although I wonder if Mark will ever be back to claim his buried treasure.

As I shimmy back into the shallow end and up the stairs, I hear cars approaching. I can't tell if they are aimed at the driveway or just passing, but I don't waste time trying to refasten the pool cover and instead run as fast as I can back in the direction of my car, weighed down by the many pounds of life and death in my pockets.

fifty-one

SILVESTRI

"You're killing me, guys." I'm giving a pep talk to the team of cops currently sledgehammering the walls of Mark Anders's pool house. "We're not in a museum. Put a little elbow grease into it. And remember, in addition to the drugs, we're looking for a .22-caliber firearm."

A uniform leans over the railing of the loft space above us. "Nothing up here, Detectives." We've been at it all morning, and the collective enthusiasm is ebbing. We're standing inside a pile of rubble with no more answers than we walked in with.

Wolcott has that faraway look in his eye. He visually scans the remnants of the walls, the ceiling, and the floors. He absently nudges the rolled-up carpet with his shoe as he takes the walkie-talkie from his belt and calls over to the main house. "Anything cooking in there?" The radio crackles back. "We got nothing." My partner's nostrils flare as he frowns at the floor.

◆

WOLCOTT AND I STAND on Anders's back deck. The satisfying sounds of destruction from inside the house have wrapped up, giving way to frustrated confusion. The uniforms are milling around aimlessly.

"At this point," says my partner, "I'd take the drug stash *or* the ballistics match on Sasha's murder weapon. Either one's a slam dunk."

"Well, we know Mark Anders has a Bersa .22 registered in his name. What are the odds it's *not* his gun that did her?"

"Circumstantial." He shrugs.

"This shit's gotta be right under our noses," I say. "This guy ain't that clever."

Wolcott wrinkles his nose and looks in the direction of the swimming pool. "Wait a second. Why is the pool cover on in the middle of summer? And if the pool's closed, why are there fresh chlorine burns on the grass?"

We exchange looks and cross the lawn.

As we near the pool, I notice that the hooks on one corner of the cover are undone. I crouch down and peel back the corner, revealing a drained enclosure. "Well, this is a waste of a recreational opportunity." I begin to unhook the rest of the cover running down the side of the pool as my partner attends to the hooks along the shallow end. He finishes with the hooks and descends the stairs. I chuckle as Wolcott's moving head causes the pool cover to ripple, as if a sea monster is lurking beneath. Halfway along the length of the pool, I watch his head stop in place, then double back. He ascends the stairs, walks over to me, and leans down. He places his hand on my shoulder and smiles heartily.

"You want some good news, partner?"

"What the fuck are you waiting for?" I ask.

"DEA gets to give us a hand with the paperwork now. This case is about to go federal."

fifty-two

SHEILA

WHEN YOU KNOW, you know.

Daniel was the love of my life. He was my person, my best friend, my missing piece. This I knew as soon as I met him. He was also a lying cheater and apparently a fucking sociopath. This I didn't find out until much later.

We were three weeks from our wedding. Everything was bought and paid for. Our registry had been pillaged; many pounds of fat and tears had been shed. We were absurdly close to being married. Nothing was going to get in the way of that.

I'd just gotten a makeup and hair trial for the big day and was walking to my car with a full face of eyeliner, mascara, and blush, and an armful of wedding dress, when the text came in from a college friend.

I thought you should see this. Sorry.

In my hand was a screenshot of my fiancé's Tinder profile, active within the last hour. There was no mistaking him. He had a very particular scar on his forehead from meeting the wrong end of a tree branch skiing as a teenager. Like most things in life, something that would have otherwise been disfiguring made him more attractive and desirable. He was a bastard like that.

I'm not entirely sure how long I stood in the middle of the intersection reading his profile, but it was long enough to miss my plastic-wrapped dress blowing in the street and the honking cars speeding around me when the light turned.

Headline: "Looking for adventurous sexy fun and zero crazy."

His likes: I was aware of all of them.

His dislikes: Even more aware.

Relationship preference: "Unethically Polyamorous." This was news.

The full face of makeup and coiffed hair are important because the woman who pulled me out of the intersection responded to my desperate plea of "What do I do?" with a compact mirror and a pack of Kleenex. "At least your hair looks good, honey." When I inspected myself, I saw a grotesque mess of black mascara streaks bleeding into crimson cheeks and seemingly bloody lips. I was the saddest, scariest bridal clown ever to cry over a man.

I gathered my dress from the asphalt, washed my three-hundred-dollar face, and didn't cancel the wedding.

◆

I WOULD DESCRIBE myself as passionate and focused. The medical professionals throughout my life would describe me as obsessive-impulsive. But I'm generally cautious of people who give advice for a living.

I was a widow at thirty. I inherited all of Daniel's money once his death was ruled an accident. Since we were only a week into our marriage when he drowned, his family and his friends were outraged. Daniel had never been forthcoming about how profitable his company really was, so that was never a motive for me, just an unexpected bonus. It was one of a number of major aspects of his life he hadn't been honest about.

I had the means to do basically whatever I wanted, but no idea what to do with myself. I'd joined Tinder leading up to our wedding to try to hook

Daniel and keep tabs on him. Funny, I checked all of his boxes in my fake profile, but we never matched. Instead of deleting my profile, I deleted him. After the honeymoon and the autopsy, I started swiping.

Enter Mark Anders.

He was on a business trip in Palm Springs and was looking for some company while he was in town. We had an amazing sex-fueled week together. He referred to me as his "dream woman" more than once. He boasted about his perfect house and utopian town on the East Coast.

We texted for a few weeks after he left and I was infatuated. I learned everything I could about lovely Stony Brook, Long Island, and rented myself a house by the beach without leaving my desk chair. I was going to surprise Mark with the gift of me.

When his wife opened the door, I only got to see the inside of his perfect house for a moment before I realized my mistake. His subsequent text was not open to interpretation.

Stay the fuck away from me, you crazy bitch.

◆

I HADN'T REALLY LOVED MARK, so the sting of that rejection didn't last long. But the first six months in Stony Brook were lonely. All I had was my daily routine, which I modeled after Sasha's. Since Mark didn't want me, I decided to observe how the only other person I knew in town was spending her time. Lotus Pedal, spa treatments, happy hours, shopping, repeat.

To blend in, I changed my look to be less West Coast and to mitigate the chances of Sasha recognizing me as the random woman who'd shown up on her doorstep months earlier. I liked being chameleonic and fully embraced my new style. I traded out my boho clothes and naturally wavy waist-length hair for athleisure wear and a sleek shoulder-length keratin-straightened cut. And then I met Paul.

Everything about my new life improved when I met him. I forced fate's hand a little on that one, but only after it brought us together in a restaurant the same week I'd heard Rebecca complaining about him. From my usual corner of the bar, I saw them sitting at a table, barely talking. There was something about him. I just knew he was the reason I'd moved east.

I went out and adopted a dog the next day and began a new daily routine.

◆

I DIDN'T INTENTIONALLY keep Daniel's death from Paul for as long as I did or purposely mislead him. I hadn't been able to take my wedding rings off yet. When we spoke for the first time, I sensed his relief in thinking I was married, so I didn't correct him.

I'd planned on telling him my story when the time was right. But the longer I'd gone acting like Daniel was alive, the harder it became to explain my behavior. I'd gone as far as to put some of his clothes in the closet and leave his watch and cuff links on the dresser, knowing Paul would see them when he came over. It was morbid, I guess. But I was committed to his comfort.

We had an amazing year together. My love for him was much deeper than what I had with Daniel. I felt him falling in love with me as much as I was with him. I could see that he was growing unhappier in his marriage and pensive about how to end things with Rebecca. I didn't push him to talk about his feelings and I waited to tell him my story. I figured the longer we were together, the more forgiving he'd become. I saw him whenever I could and pedaled beside her every day, hating her silently. I knew he needed to plan how he was going to get away from her, and I would be patient and not try to manipulate the situation.

Paul dumping me was a heartbreaking curveball, but I held out hope that he was just confused and would make the decision I knew he really wanted to make, eventually. I decided to be an adult and not act too hastily in doing something I might regret.

But then they killed me, and the fear of regret was replaced with the force of revenge.

fifty-three

PAUL

WITH THE HEAT of summer ebbing, Dana and I sit on her back porch enjoying the setting sun. She looks at me tenderly. "Paul, I really want to thank you."

"For what?"

"All of your help selling the house. It's a big part of a whole new start for us."

"It was nothing."

"I just really appreciate it." She cups her hands and shakes her head gently. "You're a good man, Paul Campbell."

"Dana, stop. I should be thanking you. I hope you know what these last months have meant to me. To have my life back again. I just . . ." I feel my throat catch.

"I know. I know."

"Thank you."

"You never have to thank me."

We sit in silence for a long while, looking out over the fence at the pastel-hued sky. I turn to her, and she returns my smile.

"So," she asks, "the house is almost ready?"

I can feel my cheeks burning. "Yeah, just putting the finishing touches on. Nearly there."

"Oh, Paul." She beams.

"It's amazing, just seeing this thing that I've built for us with my own two hands. Watching it come into being, day by day. I'm really thrilled."

"Well, I can't wait to see it."

"Yeah, it's going to be perfect."

"So, when are you going to tell Rebecca?"

I peer at the line of clouds lit underneath by the escaping sun. I inhale deeply and catch a whiff of burning charcoal from a neighboring grill mingling with the scents from the flower beds next to us. I smile at Dana. "Oh, don't worry," I assure her. "I've got that part all figured out."

"Oh, Paul! I almost forgot. Thank you so much for the beautiful necklace."

"I don't know what you're talking about," I tell her.

She smiles at me conspiratorially as she shakes her head. "Of course you don't."

fifty-four

WOLCOTT

I'M SITTING IN the deli parking lot lost in thought when Silvestri piles into the cruiser with a grocery bag packed to the gills. It looks to contain enough chow to feed a modestly sized island nation.

"Have you named him yet?" I ask.

"Who's that?"

"Your tapeworm."

"That's a hoot, pal. You been hitting the Tuesday night open mic at the coffee shop with that gold?"

"Seriously, are we getting lunch for the entire station house?"

My partner shakes his head and chuckles. "Fuckin' Sal, man. He made our sandwiches and then just kept stuffing extra shit in the bag. 'For you two heroes, on the house!' he says. Oh, and he wanted me to give you his best. We may not have gotten the collar, but it's starting to look like we'll never pay for lunch in this town again."

"Yeah, Abby told me she was down at McNamara's picking up a prescription from everyone's favorite pharmacist, and he was actually cordial. I was amazed."

"Hey, these guys have kids, and businesses," says Silvestri. "Getting a guy like Anders out of circulation helps make the town a safer place. And with the number of manslaughter and negligent homicide charges that the feds are gonna bang him with for the fentanyl, the guy'll never see the outside of a cell again. Doesn't even matter we haven't turned up the piece."

"Yeah, glad we nabbed him," I say. "But it's bigger than just Anders. They hit a stash house over in Riverhead the other day and grabbed up a boatload of the stuff."

"Flowing down-island, eh?"

"That's right. I'm afraid this shit is here to stay, partner."

"I hear you. But you've gotta start somewhere."

"I suppose you do," I say.

"Plus, it'll keep the two of us out of trouble. 'Idle hands' and all."

"Idle hands." I snicker.

We dig our sandwiches out from the bounty of chips and baked goods, place them in our laps, and begin unwrapping the deli paper. We eat lunch to the sounds of passing cars and the occasional crackle of the scanner.

fifty-five

SHEILA

WHEN SASHA TOOK my place in the plastic coil, I took her place outside of it.

Given the amount of cash on her, it seemed like she was planning to skip town at any moment. All signs indicated that she wanted out of her life with Mark as much as I had once wanted in. I'd done her a favor spiriting her away. But it wasn't her death I was really interested in. It was Paul's and Rebecca's.

Using cash and easily passable documents ordered online and shipped to a PO box, I rented a small apartment a few towns over under my new alias and found someone on Craigslist looking to unload a car, sans paperwork. I was tempted to cruise around in Sasha's Jag but thought better of it and stashed it in a parking lot at the mall under a cover. I knew they would find it eventually, but I also knew it would take a while.

I only allowed myself the basics to live on. It felt good to live unburdened by stuff. If I needed anything, I could take it from Sasha or Rebecca.

I knew I needed to be patient and wait long enough after my birthday to start haunting Paul and Rebecca. Let them ease into the comfort of thinking they'd gotten away with it and then start the show. At first it was devastating to watch them. My experiment didn't go exactly as I expected.

They got closer. They appeared to band together. She didn't punish him for cheating, and he didn't become cold and distant for what she'd done to me. Watching them support each other made me sick. But without the lows of seeing them reconnect, I wouldn't have had the highs of flipping the switch on them. And the thrill of reporting myself missing.

When everything was in place, I sent an anonymous email to the HR department of Launaria Pharmaceuticals expressing my concern for a certain employee. I made a call to the Stony Brook police about a missing friend. It was all so easy. Each pebble I skipped along the surface of their boring lives rippled into small chaos. It was the most exciting thing that had happened to their basic existence.

It was so easy taking things from Rebecca. First I took her job, then Duff, then the dove necklace she was wearing in every last photo of her and Paul that I could find on Facebook. Then her ring. I took them long enough to use them to be her, returning what I'd taken to put doubt and unease in her little by little. I took her sense of security at home by lurking in the shadows and shifting things around just slightly. Well, not *so* slightly. The hammers were a stroke of genius, and I had fun coming up with places to leave them. The bathtub with the blade was a favorite too; part of me thought maybe she'd off herself and cut my fun short, but she's too selfish for that. Most important, I took her drugs. Sometimes I replaced them. I needed a way to control her capacity to think clearly and her motivation to act dangerously, as needed.

The beautiful part was there were so many things happening outside of what I was doing that made the chaos even more so. Paul didn't waste any time finding a new sparkly someone. This I hadn't counted on. It enraged me for a short while, but the value of Rebecca's suspicion and subsequent fury was too delicious not to savor and use to fuel her borderline breakdown. Watching Rebecca obsessively track Paul provided some of the most rewarding moments. And I was able to stoke her suspicions so easily.

I had fun. I found that my new routines could be different every day while shadowing them. I discovered my criminal side and held up the pharmacy with Sasha's gun when I needed drugs to control Rebecca. I worked out some unresolved rage when I checked into the Huntington Inn as Sasha, gun tote and all, and threw a private sex party with Sasha's credit card. I had endless fun placing sex toys around the room and flipping the mattress while I puffed on Mark's favorite cigar, to make sure his disgusting, smelly calling card was left behind.

I used pieces of info Paul had inadvertently told me over our year together. When I wanted to go to another town to be outside with him and feel like a real couple, he listed all of the places that we couldn't go because they'd spent time there together or this place was significant to them because of whatever stupid sentimental reason. The little things all added up to a lot of important information. I took copious mental notes.

I loved every minute of leading her to the old spots of her and Paul's happy life. Assuming her identity. Booking their honeymoon suite. Picking out the necklace and having it sent to Dana's house. Leaving little bread crumbs of Paul's double life scattered around, not sure which ones she would pick up and delighting in how many she did. For someone who was so medicated, she was a worthy opponent and played along better than I thought she would.

I almost felt sorry for her when I called her that night, pretending that I was a customer service rep at the credit card company. Her voice sounded so small and defeated and inebriated. She was so clearly impaired and I did wonder if I was punching below my weight with her. But any momentary doubt about my actions was gone when I remembered her bringing the hammer down on my skull.

Paul was lying left and right to Rebecca. He amplified everything I was doing to another level without knowing he was helping me. I liked that we were in step together in some realm. He didn't see anything that was going on at home with his wife between visiting his new girlfriend and working on the house he'd tossed me into the basement of. It took me a little while to realize he was finishing the house as a kind of memorial to us. It was clear he was trying to reconcile his guilt about what Rebecca had done.

I had fun. I had purpose. I was getting back at all these people who had taken me for granted. As soon as I saw them sigh with any relief or find comfort in the other, I turned up the burner. And when Sasha's body was found, things got really good. I had no idea how it was all going to end, but I knew it was going to be good.

fifty-six

REBECCA

THE EUPHELLIS TUBE in my trunk is wrapped five times in tinfoil acquired at the 7-Eleven closest to Mark's house. Also purchased: three new boxes of Paul's preferred brand of heat wraps, a box of straight-edge razors, and superglue. Following that, I went to Home Depot and purchased three pairs of the strongest nitrile-coated gloves I could find, in small, medium, and large for layering. I'm ready.

After Mark's, I stashed my stolen bounty in my trunk overnight until I had the time to do what I needed to. I'll retrieve it all tonight when Paul's asleep. Knowing the Euphellis is so close brings up the darker days at work, the times I've conveniently pushed into the recesses with my increased pill intake.

Euphellis was a mouthful of a drug name when it came out, but it represented exactly what it promised: euphoria by way of skin. The idea behind the stuff started in the right place, providing a parenteral option for the dying in unimaginable phases of pain. Topical morphine, Dilaudid, and fentanyl being the most successful and effective drugs for people who aren't able to swallow or have painful skin wounds, in particular. Euphellis was a triad of all three. It worked so well it took away not only the pain of the most-suffering patients but also their caregivers.

Not a terrible way to go if you are ready for it, but 50 percent of the casualties were completely healthy people seemingly with their whole lives before them.

The engineers in Launaria's medical labs were either overly zealous because they'd inhaled or absorbed too much of their product, or grossly incompetent at their jobs for not fully testing all possible vulnerabilities of protective administering gear. The few survivors of Euphellis described it as being on Ecstasy while simultaneously orgasming in zero gravity. Not a bad sales handle. When it got out how powerful it was, trucks of the stuff started disappearing en route to medical facilities overnight.

It was an unmitigated disaster. A lot of people died, and quickly. It was a full rollout for the Euphellis trial, with the maximum number of trial patients and participating palliative and hospice care centers. Only a fraction of the recalled product ever made it back to Launaria.

What did make it back mysteriously disappeared from the recall warehouse before it was due to be investigated and ultimately destroyed. Mark saved the day by keeping the settlements down to a minimum, without the product to scrutinize. No doubt in my mind, he was able to come out the hero as a result of orchestrating the whole disappearing act. Launaria only had to pay out thirteen billion in settlements, versus the fifty-billion-dollar class-action payout speculated by NASDAQ and legal experts.

How he did it exactly, I don't really know. But I spent enough time watching him and working alongside him doing damage control, so I knew he'd found a way to help himself in the shit storm. Five of my territories were affected and twelve people died. I didn't know their names or whether they were ill or perfectly healthy. It was too hard to live in that part of my brain so I disengaged from the details. It was around that time that Paul lost his business and I started to self-medicate in earnest.

◆

WHEN I WALK IN, allegedly from another day at the office, Paul appears to be hypnotized by the absent space where the missing lion bookend used to live. I wonder if it had remained intact, we might have as well.

"Madoo?" The sound of his voice saying my nickname makes me shudder.

"Hi." I wait for the inevitable question about the ceramic lion's whereabouts. Our dog is curled up safe and sound at the foot of where Paul is standing, leading me to wonder how long he's been in that spot.

"Come here." He starts toward me with his arms open. Duff stirs, raises his head to investigate the disturbance, and retreats back to his sleeping posture. My heart starts to pound as I move to him. Every gesture he makes is a possible assault.

"I missed you. I feel like we haven't seen each other for days."

"I'm here." I tense in the hug. He shows no signs of releasing me.

"I'm sorry I've been so busy. Tomorrow I'll explain everything."

"Oh?" I try not to stomp on his feet and punch him hard. *I fucking know what you've been up to.*

"I have a surprise." He is tentative with the word "surprise." Like he is trying to make a horrible thing sound like something I want.

"Surprise? What for?"

"Tomorrow. All will be revealed." He finally pulls back and searches my face. His smile is borderline laughing. He's fucking with me.

"Tomorrow?" I pull away from him so that he doesn't feel me shaking.

He just shakes his head. "Babe, you and me. Twenty years tomorrow." His face is tired, but his eyes are excited and clear.

I'm in awe that he's using our anniversary as a ruse, but I don't know why I'm surprised. The degree of Paul's cruelty seems boundless. I pull myself to attention and turn on the good-wife act fast. I put my hand on my forehead. "Oh my God. Of course. Things have been so crazy for the past few weeks, I almost forgot it was tomorrow."

His face changes into something more serious. I worry I've upset him.

"Paul, what is it?"

"Nothing. I just really love you." His ability to be so convincing is terrifying. My husband, the sociopath. My husband, the murderer. I wonder if he told Sasha that he loved her too before he shot her.

"Me too," I force.

He sniffles back his feelings. "Listen, I need to go do some last-minute things for tomorrow. Are you going to be okay to do dinner without me?"

I try not to show the desperation of needing him to leave. There is a nagging faint voice between all of my hurt and anger that believes him. That he still loves me. But I know better. So much has happened that I can't ignore. Every moment that passes I realize how little time I have left to prepare. He's so confident now, he's smiling and laughing about whatever horrible, humiliating thing he's planned for tomorrow.

"Sure. Yes, absolutely. I have some planning of my own to do."

He moves toward me and I flinch. Luckily he doesn't notice and kisses me without question.

As he grabs his keys and heads for the door, I ask him without turning around, "Paul, do you know what happened to the other bookend?" Did somehow my shattering it cause all of this to happen?

"Honey. Confession time." He clears his throat nervously. "I wanted to get the lion with the chip on his tail fixed for you as part of your present. But it got broken on the way to the place. I dropped it in the parking lot and it was too many pieces to glue back together without you noticing. I've been trying to figure out how to tell you for a while. I feel awful. I'm so sorry."

I am furious. He lies so easily now, and I think about how good it would feel to throw the other lion at his head and worry about the consequences later. I stand my ground but swivel my head and smile at him warmly.

"Don't worry, baby. It's only a thing. A cheap knickknack. At least we still have the other one." My fists are clenched so hard I think I feel my fingernails breaking open the skin on my palms.

He looks relieved. I muster the calmest, most loving voice I can conjure amid my rage. "Paul?"

"Yes, love?"

"If you are heading to the store, don't worry about stocking up on any more heat wraps. I picked up a bunch for you on the way home. I saw that you were running low."

Instinctively he touches his arm. "You are the greatest."

His car is barely out of the driveway before the ceramic lion hits the back of the fireplace and breaks into a thousand pieces.

Any remaining doubts I had are gone. Every part of me tells me that tomorrow is the day.

◆

PAUL'S BEEN ASLEEP for hours. He got home at midnight and rolled into bed next to me and was snoring within minutes. I waited in the dark, obsessing about what was going to happen tomorrow and wondering why I hadn't just run away when I'd had the chance. But I never really had a chance. The money was gone. My addiction had gotten too unmanageable. I didn't have the strength to confront the mess my life has become. I keep coming back to the only thing left to do. Protect myself.

It is three A.M. and I've been in the downstairs bathroom wearing three layers of nitrile-dipped gloves and saturating the wraps. I have the window open and a fan running and a mask on my face. I'm surprised at how woozy I feel even with all the precautions, but I shouldn't be, given how lethally potent the cream is. I need to work quickly. I carefully tear open the plastic on the heat wrap, unfold, saturate, refold, place it back in the plastic, and Krazy-Glue the opening shut. I repeat this three times for each wrap and seal the top of the box that I've carefully sliced open with the letter opener. Once I've finished, I put the Euphellis tube, the gloves, mask, and glue in a plastic bag and wrap it many times over and put that in another bag. For the time being, I'll have to hide it. On my way to the closet, I deposit the letter opener and the box of wraps in my purse hanging on the back of the kitchen chair.

I push back to the deepest recesses of the closet, where the zipped wardrobe containing my winter coats is hanging. I unzip the plastic casing and place the paraphernalia in the sleeve of a down coat and zip the bag. I'm walloped with a wave of dizziness and sink to my knees in the dark closet between the snow boots and an upright vacuum. It is a tight space but there is enough that I can fit comfortably and rest my head against the wall. The bottoms of the coats are resting on my head. I am engulfed in a feeling of familiar safety becoming danger. I close my eyes and am transported.

I'm back in the closet hiding. I can hear him yelling. My mother is crying hard. Something hits the wall and shatters. A door is opened and slammed shut. The walls shake. My father growls. My mother yells louder, this time pleading, "No, no, no. How could you? What's wrong with you?!"

"You make me like this. This is your fault. You push me and push me and push me." I barely recognize his voice; he sounds like an animal.

She screams back, "I wish you would just go away and leave us alone. Rebecca is the only good thing you've ever done, and you can't even be a father to her. You are worthless." I've heard this fight a hundred times before. I prepare for a long night in the closet.

"You wish that I would go away? This is MY house, I just let you live here. You would have nothing if it wasn't for me!"

My mother starts laughing.

"Stop laughing at me, you bitch!"

She continues. I don't understand why she is laughing. Nothing is funny.

"Stop laughing!"

A click. A bang. A thud. This is different. I strain to hear my mother.

"You should have stopped laughing," he says.

I sit in the darkness of the closet as still and silently as possible while shaking violently. There are no other sounds from my parents' room for a very long time. I think I hear my father breathing, but I can't tell for sure over the sound of my own hyperventilating.

At some point I hear the creaking of the floorboards, the flick of a lighter, and the sound of glass coming into contact with a surface. My father calls to my mother once, then twice. She doesn't respond.

He lets out a sound that is part groan, part sigh. And a click followed by another explosion rips through the night.

I don't know how much time has passed when I emerge. My pillow is clutched to my chest. I creep into their bedroom and see my mother lying on the floor. Her eyes are closed and her mouth is open. When I put my hand on her arm, she doesn't move. I don't see the blood until I kneel beside her. And it soaks into my nightgown. I whisper in her ear, "Mom? Time to wake up, sleepyhead." She doesn't move at the sound of my voice. I push her again and nothing happens. I don't know what is wrong with her, but I know she's not sleeping.

I hear my father before I see him. He is trying to say my name but making gurgling sounds instead. Blood is coming out of the sides of his mouth and I start to cry because he looks so scary.

He reaches his arm in my direction. It is shaking hard, and drops of blood are falling onto the carpet below. My eyes go to his other hand, which is covering the side of his face, blood seeping out around his fingers. His eyes are wild and I'm scared to get any closer to him but can see his desperation for me to do so. He's opening and closing his outstretched hand, and I move in his direction, my pillow still safely covering my chest and throat. I put my hand in his. "Help," escapes his lips in a strangled whisper. "Phone."

I start to move to the phone on their dresser when I see the Smith & Wesson lying nearby. A moment of clarity dawns. He did this. I pivot from the direction of the dresser and back toward him, and his eyes widen and he shakes his head back in the direction I was headed.

I look at my mother's unmoving body and feel an emotion so new to me that it feels as if I am boiling from the inside out. The decision is made before I can fully understand what I'm going to do.

I put the pillow on his face and throw my body over it. He pulls me hard and sharply, and a blinding light of pain explodes in my shoulder. I lay my knee on his arm to keep it from pulling on me again. His grip weakly reaches for the pillow covering his face and I bear down. I shut my eyes tight until he stops moving beneath me. I stay that way for a very long time.

I don't move until I hear the sound of the police breaking down the door.

The sounds of knocking rouse me. I'm still in the front hallway closet and Duff is panting over me, his giant tail thumping against the door. I can see slivers of the morning sun coming in through the windows around Duff's body, which feels even more enormous than usual in the small space we are sharing. I'm no sooner out of the enclosure and on my feet than Paul bounds down the stairs, dressed and beaming. He wraps me in a big bear hug and lifts me off the ground. "Today's the day, Madoo!"

I don't think I've ever seen him so excited.

fifty-seven

PAUL and REBECCA

HE TIES THE blindfold tightly.

"Can you see anything?" he asks.

I look down and around. Only the smallest sliver of light shines through. "Nothing."

"Ready to go for a ride?" His hand protectively guiding my arm contradicts the subtly sinister tone in his voice. It has been a long time since he's put a blindfold on me, and it was under much different circumstances. I'm realizing how close fear and desire lie. But today, I am all fear.

I let him guide me into the passenger side of the car and close the door. Without sight, my hearing is the only guide to Paul's moves. I suppress a gasp when the familiar sound of the back door of the Jeep opening is followed by a loud thud. Warm breath and panting in my ear momentarily calm my fractured nerves. I'm surprised that Paul's decided to bring Duff along on this particular outing. Sensing my unease, Duff nuzzles my shoulder.

I reach into the bag on my lap, comforted that I've kept my weapons close. I wrap my hand around the Celtic letter opener I placed in it last night. The feel of the cool knotted handle comforts me slightly.

Paul gets into the Jeep and starts the engine with one hand on my thigh. He gives a firm squeeze.

"Ready?"

◆

SHE'S RIGHT WHERE I want her.

Duff settles into his spot in the back seat. Rebecca seems on edge with anticipation. I back out of the driveway and onto the street. Before we get going, I switch the stereo on. The playlist I've made for the occasion is cued up, and as we set off for our destination, the opening strains of Van Morrison's "Into the Mystic" spill from the speaker.

I feel my body vibrate with excitement. A dull throb takes hold of my bicep as the adrenaline kicks in. I let out a pained grunt.

"Paul, what's wrong?" she asks.

"Just a little sore, babe. It's nothing. Don't worry."

I recover, take Rebecca's hand in mine, and squeeze purposefully. I can feel the rush that she's experiencing as she squeezes back.

◆

MY HAND IS CLAMMY IN PAUL'S. He keeps squeezing, reminding me that there is no place for me to go. But now I see an opportunity.

"It doesn't sound like nothing. You're in pain. I have some of your wraps in my bag; you can put one on when we get to wherever you're taking me." If the drugs do their work in time, I may not need the letter opener after all.

The sounds of our early relationship are playing in the car and Paul is quiet beside me. Paul has strung together a soundtrack of our love through the years in a perfect slow knife twist.

"Where are we going, Paul?" I hear the nervousness in my voice.

"It wouldn't be a surprise if I told you that, Madoo."

Next to the dagger, I feel the more comforting smoothness of the pill bottle. Without sight, I can't know for sure if Paul is looking at me, but I take the chance when I hear him lower the window and start whistling to the croon of Elvis's "Can't Help Falling in Love." Our song. As I work the top of the bottle off with my fingers and slide an Oxy out, I think better of it. I want to have my wits about me. I let the song take me back and think about our slow dance in the footprint of our house-to-be. Something turns over in my heart. I never realized how much this song sounds like an ending.

"How much longer until we get there?"

"Not too long. Just sit back and relax."

Easy for him to say.

◆

AS WE SPEED ALONG the Northern State Parkway, my mind slips back in time. I remember this same drive, with the dawn light on my heels and another woman in the back seat. How much has happened, how far we've come. The mistakes we've made, separately and together.

My heart feels at once heavy and relieved. After tonight, everything will be right with the world, and I can enjoy the life I was meant to live. I can let go of the burdening weight that once threatened to drag me under.

Nearly there now. Nearly new again.

◆

PAUL TURNS DOWN the last strains of Dire Straits' "Romeo and Juliet" and the absence of the song gives way to the sound of wheels on gravel. I feel the car slowing and, in protest, my heart speeding up.

"Sit tight for a minute, babe. I'll be right back for you." The excitement in his voice is deeply unsettling.

His door closes and the back door opens, an excited Duff ambling out and landing heavily on the gravel below. Paul calls to him and the sound of leash connecting with collar clicks in the air. Paul's footsteps move away from the car, followed by the excited scramble of four legs behind him.

I'm alone in the silence. I open the glove box and feel the cold metal of the gun. Before I can slide it into my bag, I hear Paul's footsteps approaching. I slam the glove box shut, just as I hear the passenger door open. Paul reaches across me and I hold my breath as I hear him open and remove something from the glove box.

Whatever we've been building up to is finally here, for better or for worse.

◆

"MADOO. IT'S TIME."

I clasp her hand and help her out of the Cherokee. Her palm is slick with anticipation. I place my other hand on the small of her back and lead her along the gravel path. I feel her body tremble excitedly and feel a jolt of pain in my own.

"Babe, I'm going to take you up on your offer," I say, eyeing her bag.

"Of course," she counters, reaching for the box of wraps. She hands them to me, and I remove a packet, open it, roll up my sleeve, and apply the wrap.

Duff has bounded ahead of us, and he begins to whine impatiently. Rebecca tenses under my guiding touch. I lean close and whisper into her ear. "Almost there, my love. Just a few more feet."

◆

THE PATCH IS ON HIM. There's no turning back now.

His breath is warm on my neck as he unties the blindfold. I keep my eyes closed. I want to stay in the dark. He laughs.

"Madoo, open your eyes."

He wraps his strong arms around my waist, pulls my hair to one side, and kisses the exposed skin on my neck before resting his chin on my shoulder. The contact sends chills up and down my entire body.

"Happy anniversary, baby."

I open my eyes and the scene comes into static focus. Paul releases his hold and walks a few feet ahead. He watches my face intently as he ascends three wide steps leading to an enormous wooden door. My speechlessness pleases him. He reaches his hand out.

Instead, I back up a few paces, putting distance between us. The wind blowing through the pines takes my attention from the house to the crests lining the perimeter. The house isn't what is familiar; the trees are. We've been here before.

The disparate pieces before me are configuring themselves. Sky above, house in front, ground below. Paul, Duff, a threshold. Our missing life savings. And above the door, a wrought-iron bird hanging.

A dove.

◆

"MY DOVE."

My wife seems overwhelmed. She remains in a daze as I lead her inside our new home. The home that almost never was.

◆

I FOLLOW PAUL into the house and gasp when I see the entryway. The ceilings are so high it feels like they are in another time zone. I walk around the open space looking upward and around and down, because my surroundings are unbelievable and because looking at Paul feels too difficult.

The afternoon light is pouring in through the sunrise window above the doorway. Everything in sight seems to have been sprinkled with fairy dust, each angle and surface picking up a different cut of the light and projecting it in a prismatic sheen.

Paul sweeps his arms up and around. "*This* is what I've been doing."

I'm speechless.

"Are you okay, Madoo?"

"Yes. I'm just . . . just overwhelmed." I try to smile and fail while I search for words. "Can I have some water?"

He's overjoyed with my request, and I realize why when he takes me by the hand, pulling me into a breathtaking kitchen. It is nearly the size of our entire cottage and composed of every detail he and I ever discussed. The marble countertop runs the length of the space, with leather stools lining one side of the surface. A place to sit and talk while the other is making dinner, just as we always wanted.

I scan the room and see the brand-new chrome appliances and the glass-front cabinets along the top half of the wall behind Paul. He whistles while he gets me a glass from the stocked shelves and draws water from the refrigerator door. He hands me the glass of water. His face is expectant.

"Paul, you did all of this?"

"Well, I had a lot of help. But, yeah. I designed everything, picked out all of the appliances, fixtures, and materials. I kept all of the notes we've made over the years. Remember that pizza box we wrote on, on our wedding night?" I nod. A relic from a hundred lifetimes ago.

He points to the wall behind me. I see the cardboard that Paul crudely sketched our floor plan on, framed beautifully. Along one side, in my handwriting, a list of our house must-haves. I walk over to it and put my hand on the glass, not quite believing it is a thing I can touch. My tears are coming fast.

"Paul. I thought—"

"I know. I didn't think we'd ever do it either."

"No, but, I thought you'd been—"

"It's kind of amazing that you didn't guess it. Every day I kept waiting for you to confront me about the money in the shared account. Lucky for me, you've been so busy with work."

He spins me around and there is a mirror along the wall behind a breakfast nook.

"Look at us. Twenty years, honey. We made it. Better than ever."

Tears roll down my cheeks. I struggle to remember something, but the flood of information drowns whatever it is I can't recall. My face looks strange and distorted in the reflection.

"Paul, it is so much. How did you do it all? How did you keep it from me?"

"Honey, you haven't even seen the half of it." His face becomes deadly serious. "But before I give you the tour, there's something we need to talk about." My heart drops into my feet.

◆

I GUIDE REBECCA to the stuffed leather chair in the corner of the living room, next to the double-sided fireplace. I sit her down, then reach into my pocket, pull out the box I had stashed in the glove compartment, and get down on one knee.

"Madoo, this is the ring you've deserved all along. The one I couldn't afford to get you back then but have always wanted you to wear." She stares in disbelief as I slip the old ring off her finger and replace it with the new one. I'm taken aback by the horrified look on her face. "What's wrong?"

My wife is weeping. I kiss the palms of her hands, then move to stand up. My knees shake, and I feel a wave of dizziness and nausea roll through me. I sit down next to her and she stands and moves away from me.

"What about your other family?" she asks, with a mixture of fury and terror.

"Who are you talking about?"

"Who's Dana?"

"Dana? She's my therapist."

"Your therapist?!"

"From when I was a kid. 'Dr. A.' Her name is Dana Atwell. I told you about her. I've been going to her again . . . after what happened . . ."

"Paul, stop lying! She's younger than you are!"

"Huh?"

She's irate now. "I saw your *family*. The three of you . . . You were a perfect picture together in the yard. I saw you with her and the little boy—he looks just like you!"

"What are you . . ." It hits me. "Baby, that's Dana's daughter. And grandson. They're staying with . . ." I feel a rush of euphoria as the floor gives out.

◆

"I THOUGHT YOU were going to . . . Oh my God!"

He is on the ground before I can break his fall. The memory of what I've done and forgotten in the flurry of Paul's surprises rushes in as quickly and cripplingly as the drugs that have now overtaken his bloodstream. The extent of how wrong I've been is unimaginable.

"Paul, I'm so sorry. I'm so sorry. Oh my God, what have I done?"

"Madoo, what's happening?" His face is a mix of confusion and bliss.

I kneel and prop up his head with one hand. I frantically tear at the wrap on his biceps and pull it away from his skin. He looks at me for an explanation.

"Paul, I did something terrible."

"It's okay, baby, I know about the pills. We are going to get you help." His moans express his struggle to string words together.

I pull his head into my lap. "I found the letter, Paul. You wrote that you wanted to kill me! I had to defend myself." I can barely breathe through my tears.

"Kill you? Don't be silly, Madoo." His head is lolling from side to side. "I love you."

317

I'm trying to remember if my phone is in the car or in my purse in the entryway of this house. I can't tell how much of the Euphellis has permeated and if there's a chance I can undo what I've done.

"Madoo?" Paul's eyes are half-open.

"Paul, stay with me! I'm going to get help!"

"Yes, I'm going to get you help, Madoo. I've been so worried about you . . . I've been writing to your addiction." He has a goofy smile crossing his face; the drugs are overwhelming him now. "To try and separate you from it. That was the letter I wrote. I know this isn't who you are."

I'm surprised how carefree and wonderful I feel. I'm overtaken by chemical rapture, and surprised because I haven't taken a pill in hours. I look down at the wrap intertwined with my fingers and realize I'm not going anywhere. In my frenzy, I've been squeezing the Euphellis into my bare palm.

Instead of opening my hands to discard the heat wrap I squeeze them tighter to make sure every last drop of the Euphellis bleeds into me.

There is no help for us.

◆

"MADOO? WHY?" I can barely muster the air to push the words out.

"You were going to kill me. The gun. I saw the gun, and there were so many lies." Her words are coming out in whispers.

When I speak, my voice sounds like molasses oozing inside my skull. "The gun? Babe, you were scaring me, with the pills. I wasn't going to leave a loaded gun in the house."

Rebecca appears utterly defeated. "I'm so sorry. I thought you didn't want me anymore."

I stare at the love of my life as a fresh wave of euphoria soaks me from the inside out. Duff's wet snout nestles against my neck.

I feel a wave slowly pulling me into the floorboards.

◆

MY EYES SCAN THE ROOM and are drawn to the matching set on the mantel. They look almost identical to the shattered pair, now seemingly back together.

"What? I broke them. How?" I'm not sure what is real in this room anymore.

He can barely keep his eyes open now, but he knows what I'm referring to. "Twenty is the china year. It took me a while, but I found them. Happy anniversary, baby. Welcome home." Paul's body sighs and his face releases. Duff begins to whine and bark. Before I close my eyes, I get one last look at the house he built me and the guardian lions watching over us.

fifty-eight

SILVESTRI

DUFF KICKS UP waves of sand as he bounds after the tennis ball I've thrown him. Wolcott sits on the bench, consulting his notebook. The bay remains calm as the fall breeze picks up.

"Come here, fella."

Duff retrieves the ball and runs at me, nearly knocking me over. I scratch him behind the ears as he slobbers down my pant leg.

"We gotta get back," my partner calls out to me.

"Right on."

We approach Wolcott as he stands from the bench, looking amusedly at Duff and me. "Never would have pegged you for such a softie, Silvestri."

"What, was I gonna leave him in that house? Morbid fucking scene, brother. I've got a little more decency than that."

"So, just doing the right thing, eh?" He shakes his head.

"Something like that," I answer, stifling a grin.

"Speaking of which, I just got word that the murder house is on the market."

"Jesus. Who'd buy that thing up?" I shake my head. "If they had any idea what went down in that place."

"Buyer beware," he answers. I see that look of intent curiosity take shape behind his eyes.

"You'll be keeping an eye on the place, I imagine."

My partner grins at me. "Don't see as I'll much be able to help myself. Anyway, let's hit it."

◆

WE'RE ON OUR way back to the station house when Duff starts howling from the back of the cruiser. I look out the window in the direction of his protests and see a black Lab sitting on the front porch of a home, pawing at the screen door. "Wolcott, slow down."

"What is it?"

"Isn't that Sheila Maxwell's place?"

"I believe it is." He pulls the cruiser over to the side of the road.

I step out and open the back door. Duff shoots straight past me toward the Lab. The dogs meet in the middle of the lawn and proceed to roll around in a heap of fur. Wolcott steps out of the cruiser and walks around to my side. He nods in the direction of a neighbor who's watering flowers in a window box. We approach the house.

"Pardon me, ma'am?" he says.

The woman turns and smiles warmly at us. "Yes?"

"Sorry to bother you. I'm Detective Wolcott, and this is my partner, Detective Silvestri."

"Well, hello, Detectives. How are you today?"

"Fine, thank you. Beautiful petunias," I say.

"Well, aren't you just the sweetest! How can I help you?"

"We were wondering if you could tell us about any activity you may have noticed at that house," he says, pointing next door.

"Oh goodness," she responds. "There was a young woman living there who just up and disappeared some months back. I hadn't seen the dog for a while either. But she's been showing up again recently, looking for her owner. Poor thing. I was debating whether to call animal control."

"We'll take care of it. Thank you for your time."

"Of course. Find her a good home, okay?"

"We sure will, ma'am," I say.

We cross the lawn to corral the dogs. The Lab approaches me and begins licking my hands as my partner pets Duff. I reach down to get a look at her ID tag. Printed on one side is the address of the house we're standing in front of. I flip the tag over to read the name "Molly" etched into the metal. I pet her behind the ears as she pants happily. "Okay, sweetheart. Let's get you out of here."

epilogue

WES

OKAY, STAY COOL. You've got this.

As I turn in to the driveway, I see a charcoal-gray Audi parked just past the front door. The woman leans against the driver's-side door, taking in the expanse of yard. She's early—generally a good sign with a prospective buyer. And this prospective buyer is attractive. Hot, really. Not a bad perk. More important, she has an optimistic look to her: open face, relaxed body. This could go well.

I hear the muffled sound of the soft give of pebbles as I come to a stop and turn off the engine. I take a deep breath, collect myself, and step out of the BMW. The woman approaches and extends her hand warmly. I return the effort.

"Ms. Graves?"

"Please, call me Molly."

"Wes."

"Thanks for coming out, Wes."

"My pleasure."

She looks over my shoulder toward the BMW. "Bloodred. That's a bold choice, Wes. I respect that."

"Speaking of, that's quite a stone you've got on your finger."

"Thank you," she says. "It's something of a hand-me-down."

"Well, fortune favors the bold, as they say."

She smirks. "You're not going to charge me a fortune for this house, I hope."

I smile. "I'll be gentle with you."

"Chivalry is not dead." Her tone is decidedly flirty.

I key the lock to the front door, and we enter. I walk just a step ahead and study her eyes as they move from detail to well-executed detail: cherry floors, pine beams, stone fireplace, cathedral ceiling. The midday light spilling through the picture windows sets off every surface. I feel a pang of envy at the artistry on display in even the smallest flourish. She is calm. She takes her time, savoring the experience. When she finally turns to me, she speaks in a measured manner. "So, let's get down to it."

She's read up on the case and knows very well what transpired within these walls—or at least the way the papers reported it. Troubled marriage, adultery, double suicide. But the media never gets the full story. They can never know the victims the way those close to them did. The love and devotion that lived below all the drama and conflict on the surface.

I mention that the deceased were friends, a revelation that engenders her sympathy without putting a dent in her resolve. She's market savvy, and when I suggest what this house would fetch under normal circumstances, she doesn't hesitate to lowball me. We volley numbers. She's long on the charm, and before I know it, she's managed to get me to agree to go below my number.

We shake on the deal. She exudes warmth, even in the wake of her cold and clinical negotiation. I find myself captivated by the transaction. She clearly knows what she wants and just how to get it, as evidenced by the check for the deposit she produces and hands to me. I marvel at the number displayed on the check, a sum lower than I thought I'd ever agree to. There's something about this woman.

She turns away to take in the details of her new home. When she turns back to me, her other hand has moved to her face. She cups her cheek. I watch as her finger traces its way down her throat and out along the length of her collarbone. She smiles at me.

"Ever seen something for the first time and known it was what you'd always wanted?"

acknowledgements

While *The Woman Inside* was written in a little over a year, it has been in the making over the course of our twenty-three-year friendship.

It wouldn't have been possible without the love, support and encouragement from so many people. And while there is just one name on the book, and two writers, there is an army of people who've made this book a reality.

For the early reads and invaluable advice (and the best damn sourdough bread), a huge thanks to our incredible agent Christopher Schelling, and to Augusten Burroughs. We are grateful beyond words.

To our foreign rights and translation team; Chris Lotts, Nicola Barr, Lara Allen, Liberty Roach, thank you for all your work on our behalf to bring this book all over the world.

We were incredibly lucky to have the UK publishing dream team at Trapeze, to our editor Katie Brown, for believing in this book. Thanks to sales director, Jen Wilson and the rest of the sales team, much gratitude to designer Lucie Stericker, Jessica Tackie in marketing, Alex Layt in publicity, Ellie Kyrke-Smith and Rachael Hum in export sales, Paul Stark and Amber Bates in audio and Claire Keep in production. We are so appreciative of all your support.

To everyone at Dutton in the US. From the incredible editorial talent in the hands of John Parsley who believed in this book so enthusiastically from the beginning, and Maya Ziv's wise editorial guidance at every turn, and Cassidy Sachs ongoing support and help, we are so very grateful. So many thanks go to our powerhouse publicity and marketing crew made up of Kayleigh George, Amanda Walker, Jamie Knapp, Kathleen Carter and Jon Reyes. Special thanks to Christine Ball for her amazing support from first read, and to Madeline Mcintosh, Alison Dobson, and Lauren Monaco (and her amazing sales team) for their enthusiasm for our book. And to our brilliant book designer Christopher Lin, and everyone else who typeset, copyedited, designed, etc.

To our intrepid film agent Pouya Shabazian who saw the potential for our book to be adapted to TV early on and got into the hands of the awesome team at Blumhouse; Jason Blum, Marci Wiseman and Jeremy Gold, and everyone else there who is developing the series, and to JR McGinnis at Felker Toczek Suddleson Abramson LLP.

To our incredibly supportive families; Anne, Susan, Gordon, John, Eva, Rich, Veronica, Carole, Madeline, John, Charlie, Thomas, Jesy and Bernadette. To Lori and Lis, and especially Tom and Nina for the love of all things books, writing and storytelling.

To our writing groups through the years, with special thanks to Ruiyan Xui, Brian Selfon, Jason Boog, Joelle Renstrom, Sacha Wynne, Sarah Stodola, Erum Naqvi, Douglas Belford, Matthew Gilbert, David Litman, Matt Laird, Dave Hill, Sebastian Beacon, Jesse St. Louis, Michael Dowling, Eugene Cordero, Ron Petronicolos and Chris Swinko.

To Anna Dunne, whose enthusiasm, faith and love helped make this such an exciting journey.

To Trebor Evans, for all the shop talk over the years. You helped make Wolcott and Silvestri come off the page.

To Margery Masters, Maryellen LeClerc, Arthur Cardone, and

Anthony Mangano, Don Gilpin and Nancy Himsel for fostering a love of the written word at an early age.

To everyone at Macmillan, Bob Miller and Amy Einhorn and everyone at Flatiron Books and to Carisa Hays, who gave me my first job in publishing and has always encouraged me to reach for the stars. For early reads, advice, mentorship, and support, special thanks Don Weisberg, Andrew Weber, John Sargent, Fritz Foy,Pace Barnes and Thomas Harris.

Melissa Shabazian for her incredible championing and coaching. Brian Pedone for inspiration, motivation and pugilist life lessons. Leslie Padgett for cosmic and earthly advice and championing and support from the incredible writers and friends in our lives; Maris Kreizman, Holly Bishop, Elizabeth Stein, Daniel Mallory, Hank Cochrane, Rennie Dyball, Glennon Doyle, and Jenny Lawson.

To everyone from Screaming Muse Productions, and for lifetime friendships on-stage and off, with Maurice Smith, Jason Weiner, Daniela Tedesco, Mike Bromberger and Natasha Tsoutsouris.

A special thanks to JL Stermer whose friendship has been a lifeline and a source of strength, laughter, and motivation for both of us to keep telling stories together

And to the people who are no longer with us, but who've been so important in our lives, we thank and miss you; Richard Wands, Bill Rosen, Elizabeth Calhoun, Carey Longmire. Tom and Nora Keenan, Patricia and Gordon Sabine, and Paul Williams.

credits

Trapeze would like to thank everyone at Orion who worked on the publication of *The Woman Inside* in the UK.

Editorial
Katie Brown
Charlie Panayiotou
Jane Hughes
Alice Davis

Audio
Paul Stark
Amber Bates

Contracts
Anne Goddard
Paul Bulos
Ellen Harber

Design
Lucie Stericker
Joanna Ridley
Nick May
Clare Sivell
Helen Ewing

Finance
Naomi Mercer

Jasdip Nandra
Afeera Ahmed
Elizabeth Beaumont
Sue Baker
Victor Falola

Marketing
Jessica Tackie
Lynsey Sutherland

Production
Claire Keep
Fiona Macintosh

Publicity
Alex Layt

Sales
Jen Wilson
Esther Waters
Rachael Hum
Ellie Kyrke-Smith
Viki Cheung
Ben Goddard

Mark Stay
Georgina Cutler
Jo Carpenter
Tal Hart
Andrew Taylor
Barbara Ronan
Andrew Hally
Dominic Smith
Maggy Park
Elizabeth Bond

Rights
Susan Howe
Krystyna Kujawinska
Richard King
Jessica Purdue
Hannah Stokes

Operations
Jo Jacobs
Sharon Willis
Lucy Tucker
Lisa Pryde

about the authors

E. G. Scott is a pseudonym for two New York City–based writers. One, **Elizabeth Keenan**, is a writer and publishing consultant. She has worked in book publishing for eighteen years for imprints of Simon & Schuster, Penguin Random House, and Macmillan. And the other, **Greg Wands**, writes for the page and screen. An avid, lifelong reader, he grew up in Sag Harbor, New York, and now calls Manhattan home.